firefly

BIG DAMN HERO

firefly

BIG DAMN HERO

firefly

BY JAMES LOVEGROVE

ORIGINAL STORY CONCEPT BY NANCY HOLDER

TITAN BOOKS

Firefly: Big Damn Hero
Paperback edition ISBN: 9781785658280
E-book edition ISBN: 9781785658273

Published by Titan Books
A division of Titan Publishing Group Ltd
144 Southwark Street, London SE1 0UP

First paperback edition February 2020
10 9 8 7 6 5 4 3 2

A CIP catalogue record for this title is available from the British Library.

Printed and bound by CPI Group (UK) Ltd, Croydon, CR0 4YY

Did you enjoy this book?
We love to hear from our readers. Please email us at
readerfeedback@titanemail.com or write to us at
Reader Feedback at the above address.

To receive advance information, news, competitions, and exclusive offers
online, please sign up for the Titan newsletter on our website
TITANBOOKS.COM

This novel is respectfully dedicated to the supremely talented artists, technicians and craftspeople who created the 'verse, peopled it with such memorable characters, and left us wanting more

So here's how it is…

We've been flying for about a month on fumes and tears. Zoë and I are the ones hit hardest: we carried the coffin of Tracey Smith, our comrade-in-arms, out of Serenity *and into the snowfall, where his folks stood in silence. We did not tell them that Tracey had run afoul of a gang of organ smugglers and taken refuge with us. Or that he had lied to us and nearly killed Kaylee, and that Zoë and I had both shot him mortally. As he died in our arms, he remembered when we were soldiers. We had fought on the right side, even if it was the losing one, and risked our lives to make sure everyone came back. Now he's dead, and we told his folks that he was a war hero.*

War does a lot of mean, miserable things to people. Makes 'em nurse grudges. Makes 'em swear vengeance. Makes 'em tell stories about how the Browncoats went down in defeat.

And a lot gets lost in the translation.

The Unification War ended in 2511. It's 2517 now, and

my memories come in waves. Sometimes I'm back home on Shadow, signing up to join the Browncoats with my best friends Jamie Adare and Toby Finn. We were so young, just kids. We thought war meant freedom and glory. And sometimes I still dream about Jamie's sister Jinny, and when I wake up, my heart is as hollow as a drum.

That's all in the past, and I've got way more than enough present to deal with. Inara gets these faraway looks—don't know what it means, but I know not to ask. Still got the Tams on board, and Jayne hasn't tried to sell 'em out since we got those medical supplies on Osiris, so that's a plus. Shepherd's still reading his book of fairytales. Zoë's still my first officer, and I wouldn't have any other. Kaylee keeps us running, and Wash keeps us flying.

Is it a good life or a bad one? The answer doesn't matter. It's the only life we have.

Captain Malcolm Reynolds

Why can't things just go easy for once? Mal Reynolds wondered as he ended the communication with Guilder's Shipwrights. After a week in dry dock, their shuttle repairs were complete—just a couple-few things Kaylee could have fixed herself if they had had the right tools. But they couldn't afford them. And the repairs had cost more than the original estimate. Of course. Still, it would be nice to have it back. The loaner shuttle Guilder's had given them had a faulty injector regulator and guzzled fuel like a drunk guzzled beer.

Mal was standing in the cargo bay of *Serenity*, and after weeks of searching for a job, any job, he was having second thoughts about taking this one, despite the hefty repair bill that loomed on his horizon. Deafening alarm bells were going off in his head—about safety and about survival.

The roaring outside *Serenity*'s open cargo bay spiked to earsplitting as space transports and private craft simultaneously took off and landed on either side of them in Persephone's Eavesdown Docks. The violence of the comings and goings shook the ship's loading ramp and peppered the hull with a rain of dirt and small pebbles blasted into the air by thundering rocket exhausts.

There was only one way to describe the operation of the docks: organized chaos. Well, not so organized. Burned-out hulks of spacecraft lay in craters of their own making, scattered here and there along its sprawling length. It was a gorramn miracle there weren't more midair collisions.

You might think with all this dutiable trade, all these comings and goings and the excise levied on them, that Persephone would be a rich planet; but you would be wrong. The Alliance taxed businesses and citizens with a gleeful rapacity. And what did Persephonians do in response? Why, they celebrated the day they signed their lives away and joined the Alliance. The anniversary of which was today.

And how did Mal celebrate it? By taking another job from Badger.

The sleazy minor crime lord was willing to pay them a scant bit of coin for risking their lives with a dangerous load that had to be hauled halfway across the galaxy. Actually, that sounded somewhat like the last job they took from him—transporting a herd of cattle on behalf Sir Warwick Harrow. The cows were delivered fine on Jiangyin until the gunfire commenced, and then Shepherd Book was shot and nearly died from his wounds. This dangerous cargo was different from that load, because if something went wrong with it, all of them would die.

As a bonus, a small side-job had slid in alongside Badger's offer. Mal, Jayne and Zoë would deal with the secondary job planetside once Badger's cargo was loaded. Which meant Taggart's Bar on Alliance Day, just about the rowdiest drinking establishment on Persephone, on the rowdiest day of the year.

Talk about combustible.

About five feet away, Zoë was saying something to Mal, or trying to, murmuring to avoid being overheard. Zoë was the kind of woman who spoke softly and carried a big gun. Mal motioned for her to come closer. She walked over with her arms crossed, and leaned in, so close that her breath brushed against his ear.

"I don't like it, sir," she said, biting off the words.

"Duly noted," Mal said. He didn't like it much either, but when the choice was bad choice or no choice, you smiled wide and said thank you.

On the loading ramp behind the two Browncoat veterans, a forklift strained to carry its oversized burden up the slope and into the hold. The weight squashed the front tires nearly flat and made black smoke pour from the tailpipe. The metal crate was easily three times as big as the forklift and rested so heavy upon the forks that they wobbled like they were made of rubber, with the result that the load teetered precariously on its perch.

Grim-faced, Zoë and Mal backed well out of the way. Zoë wore her curly darkish auburn hair gathered in a ponytail, her signature leather cord necklace hanging over her leather vest. Mal had let his brown hair grow out a mite longer than military regulation, and wore his trousers with the stripe, his customary suspenders, and a tucked-in red flannel shirt. Both had looped their thumbs under their gun belts, observing closely as the last of the five steel containers was carried across the ship's deck by the woefully lurching forklift.

On the other side of the hold's entrance, a pair of Badger's men likewise kept a sharp eye on Mal and Zoë, hands hovering close to gun butts. Trusting your business partners was like trusting a rattlesnake not to bite you: noble but misguided.

Behind the wide-bodied goons stood the cocky Cockney racketeer. Badger was dressed in his own version of business casual—a black bowler, threadbare suit jacket and matching vest over a dingy white T-shirt, a jauntily arranged silk necktie, and a pin on his lapel shaped like a flamingo and made of fake gold encrusted with no-less-fake gemstones. In common with his namesake, Badger was cranky, stubborn, and tough, with something decidedly rodent-like about his face, but he was also irritatingly jovial at times. That trait seemed particularly in evidence today, which Mal couldn't help but find suspicious.

Though it appeared the crime boss was dutifully fulfilling his side of their bargain, Mal assumed Badger would try to cut corners somehow, in his own favor, of course. If everything was completely on the up and up, it wouldn't be commerce as usual.

"Pull 'er forward nice and slow, and set 'er down beside the last one," Badger told his forklift operator. Then he beamed at Mal, showing yellow, crooked teeth. "Just about done with the hard part."

"Remind me again," said Mal. "Is the hard part loading the cargo, or is it me gettin' over the fact that you still owe us for those cows we didn't get paid for transporting to Jiangyin?"

"Mal, Mal, Mal." The more genial Badger sounded, the

more it made Mal's toes curl and his trigger finger itch. "Oh mate, you still holding a grudge about that?"

"Kinda definitely."

"Okay, so the deal went down the khazi. Wasn't anybody's fault. These things happen. Business is business."

"Don't think my understandin' of that word is the same as your understandin'."

"What we 'ave 'ere," Badger said, waving an arm towards the crates, "is my way of making recompense. Your fee, in case you 'aven't noticed, Reynolds, is well over the odds for a straightforward planet-to-planet run like this. When it's done, you can consider the debt between us settled."

"Just sayin' I'd rather it'd been settled at the time."

"What can I say? I 'ad cash-flow problems."

"So did I, in as much as the cash wasn't flowing from you to me."

"But that's all in the past. We're chums again now, ain't we?"

Mal grunted. He was very picky about who he was "chums" with, and Badger would never qualify for that status.

"Sir," Zoë said, with urgency, into Mal's ear. "Don't want to come across like a worrywart…"

"Then don't, Zoë."

"But I'm going to say it again: this is a bad idea. This cargo is too volatile."

"I know, I know," Mal replied.

The crates weren't big, maybe five feet a side, but they were mighty—jam-packed with chemicals used for mining.

Explosives.

Highly specialized, highly explosive explosives.

The substance in the crates was, in fact, a crystalline compound known as HTX-20, an abbreviation that according to Badger stood for something long and complicatedly scientific with more syllables than you could count. When he heard the deal Badger was proposing, Shepherd Book had told Mal that he knew about HTX-20, and his grimace had said everything Mal needed to know about what the preacher thought of the stuff.

"Not for nothing is it nicknamed Satan's Snowflakes," Book had commented, and yet again, Mal had found himself wondering how in heck a man of God knew about such things.

Badger had assured Mal that as long as the HTX-20 stayed in the crates, snug and tight in its flame-retardant foam packaging, there was no danger of it blowing up before it was supposed to. Oh, and everything would also be fine as long as the HTX-20 didn't get wet. Or too hot. Or was jostled unduly. But apart from *that*, things were just dandy.

Mal figured Badger *would* be upfront about the perils of the job, since he was the one who stood to gain the most if the payload made it to its intended destination, a rhodium mining operation on Aberdeen. Still, it gave him pause to see the yellow-and-black hazard stripes on the outsides of the boxes, like a swarm of hornets, and the decals plastered every which way, saying things like:

In other words, treat these crates like newborn babies or life would no longer be interesting; it would be over. If there was one thing Mal hated, it was surprises, and an explosion counted as one of the worst kinds of surprise he could imagine. Surprise marriages being another.

But not to dwell on the negative. Mal watched Zoë flinch as the forklift operator almost took out their ball hoop. The vehicle's twin metal tines had held so far, but the crates were burdensome, that was obvious. He couldn't wait for this to be over.

Persephone, a middling-sized planet on the periphery of the White Sun system, served as *Serenity*'s primary stomping grounds when it came to the face-to-face details of life. This meant shaking hands and moving cargo, mostly, though sometimes it also included inadvertently trafficking in cryogenically frozen mad geniuses. Their resident, fully thawed mad genius was River Tam, who generally bounced off the bulkheads like a rubber ball. Her brother Simon was uncomfortable on this planet, to put it mildly, and was more than usually defensive about his sister. Even out in the Black he was quick to justify his sister's unpredictable outbursts of screams and destruction by reminding you that the Alliance had made her insane. As in, it was not her fault. Mal found this a rather odd strategy for ensuring her continued passage on his boat. He didn't much care why River was insane. He cared that she was insane at all.

Mal had warned Simon to keep River out of sight until Badger was gone, and Simon was happy to oblige. Alliance bulletins about two missing fugitive siblings on the run came out over the Cortex now and then, but so far Badger seemed unaware that he could make way more money turning the Tams over to the authorities than he could trafficking in cows and explosives.

Life sure had gotten complex. No doubt about it, Mal preferred staying in the sky. The silent void of the Black was ever so much more to his liking. But such was not always practical. He had to touch down from time to time, in order to take on supplies and get paying work.

Persephone had never been all that pleasant of a rock, even before the Alliance's victory over the Browncoats there. In the years since, it had become immeasurably worse. The slums had spread like rot in a ripe peach, the stink of ramshackle dilapidation festering wide. Power supplies to the blighted areas were cut off when the residents couldn't pay for the privilege. Folks began cooking on open fires and warming themselves at burn barrels. The haze of rank smoke permanently tinged the sky a pale yellow. To survive, most people had to steal what they couldn't barter. Decent citizens shuffled with downcast, fearful eyes, trudging sunken cheek-by-jowl beside unbearably smug rich folk in silks and satins who flaunted their wealth as it if were God-given—not that there was a God, not to Mal, not anymore.

And if there is, He ain't welcome on my boat, Mal thought.

Lawlessness on a planetary scale did have a plus side, though: it encouraged and facilitated the kind of work that came Mal's way—primarily smuggling items the Alliance forbade or taxed beyond reason, that sort of thing—and loose, corrupt enforcement allowed quick escapes in case a deal went sideways.

Beyond the open cargo-bay door, Eavesdown Docks

spread out in all its rusty, gritty glory. The yellow-tinged atmo stank so bad you could practically chew it—a chunky, inedible stew of rocket exhaust, carbonized garbage dump, spilled rocket fuel, unwashed humans and animals, and mountains of boiled protein blocks. As they set down and crawled back up into the Black, ships kicked up brittle tea-brown newspapers and foam plates slathered with plum sauce. On the verge of the field, brightly colored paper parasols twirled. Dogs of varied size and indefinable breed ran in packs through the potholed street. Horns honked rhythmically, or maybe it was someone's donkey braying? Here and there, ship's captains of ill repute casually bribed customs officials, and hordes of filthy folks crawled through and over the debris of civilization like ants—some looking for work, others looking for trouble. If he was being honest, Mal had to admit he currently had a foot in both camps.

Hoban Washburne, *Serenity*'s pilot and Zoë's husband, had landed them at the docks at crack of dawn shipboard time. But it was five-thirty in the evening here on Persephone. Daylight, sickly sad as it was, had already begun to ebb away and a bruise-colored dusk was setting in. Only three quarters of an hour had passed on-planet, but for Mal, each minute spent with Badger felt like an age. He didn't know which drove him the craziest about the man—his thuggish swagger, his blockheaded stupidity, or his chirpy attitude that masked a personality so crooked it made a zigzag look straight—but Mal could feel himself getting tetchier and tetchier. With an effort, he looked away from him.

"Sir," Zoë prodded. "All the 'danger' decals, sir."

"What danger decals? Don't see none."

"The ones you've been giving the evil eye since the moment the crates arrived."

"Oh, *those* danger decals. Well, folks sometimes exaggerate. On account of the legal liability. Coverin' their asses." Mal tried to sound credible, but even he wasn't buying it.

"Yes, sir," Zoë said. "But regarding liquids, sir. If the contents of the crates come in contact with water, they'll blow. Says so right there. And last week that toilet up by the rec area backed up…"

"Kaylee put it all to rights," he reminded her. "And nothing got as far as the cargo bay."

"That's true, but even so—"

"And the crates look solid and watertight," Mal cut in. Still not sounding entirely credible.

"Easy does it, now," Badger cautioned as the forklift crept across the deck with its suspension-crushing load.

Everything was going according to plan, then suddenly, not so much.

Whether the temper of the right-hand fork's steel had been damaged on a previous job or more recently compromised by the combined weight of the three other containers, it suddenly gave way, bending downward towards the deck with a hair-raising shriek. That end of the huge crate abruptly dropped, sliding off the edge of the intact fork. It smashed hard onto its nose, then toppled full length onto the hangar deck with a resounding crash that rattled Mal's bones. As the operator leapt from the vehicle in panic, Badger dropped into a crouch, squeezed his eyes shut, and clapped his hands over his ears.

"*Tā mā de!*" Mal bellowed.

Seconds passed.

Then a few more.

Nothing happened.

"Oops, sorry about that," Badger said breezily as he lowered his hands from his ears. "Why don't we leave it there, then? Meanwhile I'll just wait for my sphincter to unpucker." He nodded sharply at the forklift, and the driver climbed back in, hit reverse, and quickly backed away. From under his coat, Badger pulled out what appeared to be a manifest and began pawing through it.

Zoë sighed.

"The HTX-20 isn't supposed to explode unless it gets bumped around too much. Right, Badger?" Mal pressed.

"That's right. Or gets wet or hot or all that other gubbins. We went over it, didn't we? You need a refresher course?"

"No, it's just, that crate got bumped. How do we know things are still all right?"

Badger looked at him as if Mal was the stupid one. "We're not dead."

Hard to argue with that.

At that moment, as if Mal didn't have enough to contend with already, River Tam appeared on the catwalk overlooking the cargo bay.

"The box wants to dance," she announced as she trotted down the stairs. She was holding a bamboo flute and wearing her pink sweater, ruffled skirt, and calf-high boots.

"Best go back up," Mal said, careful not to address River by her given name in front of Badger and his employees. "Cargo bay's going to be off-limits for a spell. *Dǒng ma?*"

River thrust out her lower lip in a pout. Mal supposed life on a spaceship had its dull moments for a teenaged girl. Or dull days, or even duller weeks. Still, she wasn't just any teenaged girl. She was a kid who made her own fun, and her idea of fun wasn't necessarily the safe, happy kind. More usually it was the "What the hot holy hell just happened?" kind.

Mal darted a glance towards Badger, who was observing the exchange with bemusement as he cleaned under his fingernails with a corner of a document.

"'Ere, I thought the little tart 'ad an accent like mine," Badger said. "Bit of the old Dyton patois, know what I mean?"

"Oh, I does, guvnor, and no mistake," River replied, switching to the aforesaid accent. "I ain't seen you in ages, me old china. Mind the dirt," she added, gesturing to Badger's hand. "Don't want no contamination, do we now?"

"Oi, bint, none of your lip," Badger retorted, but truth was, he had a soft spot for River, cultivated last time they'd met, when he'd held the crew hostage. "I washed before I come 'ere today. Clean as a whistle."

"No, luv, what I'm saying is that's *your* DNA, innit?" River said. "If we're investigated, it's you what'll show up, not us."

"Well, that's right thoughtful of you to take into account," Badger said, with a chuckle. "But my side of this exchange is above board and legitimate."

Mal said to Badger, "You know the drill. Half now and half on delivery." He held out his hand. Badger plunked a leather bag full of jingling coin into his palm.

"Feels light," Mal said as he hefted it. It actually felt just about right. Tricky customers like Badger expected you to put up a fight even when there was no call for one.

"It's all there," Badger said, puffing himself up indignantly.

"Maybe I should count it all out, just to be sure," Mal said. "Anybody can make a mistake." He didn't dump out the coin. He just stared Badger straight in the eye. Although the crime boss didn't blink, after fifteen seconds or so a muscle in his left cheek started to twitch.

Satisfied that he'd made his point, Mal slipped the pouch in his pocket, money uncounted.

Badger grinned, displaying those rickety, off-color front teeth again. "So," he said, "if we're all done 'ere, I'll be 'eading back to town. Today being Alliance Day, I do a brisk trade in moonshine, float, angel tears and other such recreational substances. I gather you lot 'ave other things to attend to in town as well?"

"Where exactly did you gather that?" Mal said. He figured Badger was just fishing. No sense giving him information he didn't need.

"Well, I just assumed." Badger stuffed the manifest back in his pocket.

"Better see to your 'shine," Mal said. "And also to mindin' your own business."

Unruffled, Badger strolled to the edge of the loading ramp, waving for the forklift operator to accompany him. The forklift itself was *Serenity*'s own and remained on board. Then Badger and the other two minions descended. One of the goons got behind the wheel of a battered land speeder parked near the foot of the ramp. Badger climbed into the seat beside him, waving at Mal and Zoë like he was the crowned king of Londinium.

"Perhaps we'll run into each other in town," Badger said as the speeder's engine noisily started up. "Over a libation celebrating the end of a completely unnecessary and yet ultimately obscenely profitable war."

"I'm thinkin' probably not," Mal said.

"War's over, Captain," Badger reminded him. He grinned at Mal. "Officially, anyway."

Mal didn't respond. Lot of folks enjoyed reminding him of what he already knew.

Then Badger and his lackeys putt-putted off, the gray clouds of exhaust drifting up into the haze. Mal knew he had a tendency to underestimate Badger because the man seemed so gorramn stupid. But stupid and dangerous weren't mutually exclusive.

Look at Jayne.

"Well, that's over," Zoë said, the relief in her voice. "Time to chase up that other job."

"We're not gettin' investigated or arrested today," Mal told Zoë sternly. "Not calling attention of any sort to ourselves."

"Of course not, sir," Zoë said.

"Good," he said. "Now let's go into town and bust up a bar."

She gave him a look.

"Just kidding," he said. "Jayne, you coming?"

Jayne Cobb had just sauntered into the cargo bay. He tugged down the earflap chin ties of his yellow and orange woolen hat, seating the thing on his skull and centering the pom-pom atop it. His adoring, semiliterate mother had designed and knitted the fetching item of headgear, and it was one of Jayne's most prized non-lethal possessions. The sidearm strapped to his leg in a tactical black nylon holster fell into the other category. Jayne had pet names for all his weapons. There was his Callahan full-bore auto-lock rifle, of course, which he had christened Vera, and there was the massive .38-caliber Civil War-styled wheelgun he was toting now, known affectionately as Boo. Scooting around River, Jayne joined Zoë and Mal at the top of *Serenity*'s loading ramp.

"I don't know why you two hate Alliance Day so much," he said. "If it hadn't been for the war, we wouldn't be here."

Mal didn't say a word. Explaining irony to Jayne was like teaching a fish to bark.

"Make us proud, you guys!" a voice called down cheerily from the catwalk. It was Kaylee, *Serenity*'s resident ray of sunshine, as well as a prodigiously gifted engineer. Then her eyes got huge. "*Gŏu shĭ!* How many gorramn warning signs are there on those things?"

"The boxes are busy," River said in a matter-of-fact tone.

Kaylee cast a stricken look at Mal, then looked back at the crates. Then back at him. "Uh, Captain?" she said.

"We keep that powder cool and dry and it's all good, you hear?" he said.

Kaylee nodded and returned her gaze to the crates one more time. Mal had a feeling she was counting how many decals there were. And not liking the total.

As if to distract herself, she turned to River. "Hey, River, Shepherd and I are making casserole for dinner. Wanna help?"

"Okay," River said brightly, skipping up the stairs to

join her. "I'll do the chopping." She made a brisk slicing motion with the edge of her hand.

"Do *not* let her near anything with a blade," Mal cautioned. He beckoned to Jayne and Zoë. "You two, duty calls. Got less'n a half-hour to get to Taggart's Bar. Better hustle."

"Get there early, maybe we can have ourselves a little japery first," said Jayne.

Mal shook his head. "I know what your idea of japery is, Jayne, and it ain't gonna happen. We're there to work, not punch folk."

"Not even a little?"

"Nuh-uh."

"Awww." Jayne sounded as petulant as a child. "Remind me again why I come with you on these trips."

"'Cause you're so damn handsome."

Jayne frowned, puzzling it out. He decided his captain was being sincere, and grinned. "Yeah, I am at that, ain't I?"

"Gorramn Alliance Day," Zoë muttered.

Alliance Day was Persephone's own special holiday, like Unification Day, but local. It signified the signing of the treaty that welcome Persephone into the Alliance, and Mal nursed the hope that folks celebrated it with gusto only because it was a good excuse to take off the day and get drunk. But like Unification Day, Alliance Day didn't sit right with Mal either. Not right at all.

On lines strung across the streets, between the rooftops overhead, rows of gaudy Alliance flags—one half a blue field, one half red-and-white stripes, with a swirl of different-sized yellow stars overlaid on a red square—flapped like wagging tongues. They seemed to be taunting him: *you lost, you lost, you lost*… Bunting with the same pattern hung from balconies and utility poles, and yet more flags were plastered inside every dirty window frame that still held glass.

Mal, Zoë, and Jayne trudged down a winding alley, forced to jink every few steps to avoid head-on collisions with the people walking the opposite direction. A lot of them sported little plastic Alliance badges pinned to their ragged coats and hats, and more than a few had dressed for the occasion in their old Alliance uniforms, proudly displaying medals won for destroying Browncoat strongholds and slaughtering Browncoat troops.

Eyes narrowed to slits, jaw clenched tight, Mal kept pace with Zoë, who could do stoic better than anyone he had ever met, mostly by virtue of looking mildly pissed about everything all the time. Some folks said Mal was hard to figure out, but he knew he wasn't. There was a core of bitterness that ran the length of his soul and drilled down into his heart, and there seemed no way to get rid of it, ever. He supposed that was all right. It kept him going. Kept him flying.

Didn't necessarily keep him out of trouble, though.

Least of all on Alliance Day.

Three tipsy young women dressed in matching red satin, high-necked embroidered jackets and black trousers ran towards Mal and Zoë. Their hair was wound into round little topknots on either side of their heads. They were waving a couple of little Alliance pennants on sticks and giggling at each other.

"Happy Alliance Day!" one of them cried, and they all burst into shrieks of laughter.

Zoë uttered a caustic oath as she sidestepped and pushed past them, and that made Mal smile. Zoë losing her temper was just the funnest fun ever. And under normal circumstances it would bode well for their bar run. The prospect of cracking a bushel of Alliance-loving heads and breaking up some furniture would have raised Mal's sagging spirits. However, there was work to do, and that took precedence.

Stepping up beside Zoë, he played dumb. "What was that all about?" he asked.

"I hate stupid women, sir," she said.

"They are truly despicable," he agreed amiably.

"Hey, what's the rush?" Jayne called at them.

When Mal looked back, Jayne had his arms around two of the intoxicated young women, and the third was carefully threading the stick of her Alliance pennant through the stitches of his left earflap.

"I love your hat! You look so *cute*!" the pennant-threader squealed.

The blondest of the three reached overhead, jumping repeatedly as she tried to touch the orange pompom crest. Grinning from ear to ear, Jayne reveled in the attention. Mal and Zoë didn't comment, just kept on walking up the street.

"Hey, wait up," Jayne shouted at their backs. The girls detached themselves and reeled away, laughing.

Jayne closed the gap, still savoring his moment of adulation. He adjusted the fit of his hat and the angle of its newly acquired decoration. Unable to control himself, Mal snatched away the loathsome symbol, threw it to the pavement, and ground it under his boot heel.

Jayne didn't bend down to recover the pennant. Emotionally, it seemed he had already moved on. "After we get our business done, how's about we spend the night in port? There's so many parties…"

"And we have a cargo bay full of chemicals I don't particularly want to hang onto any longer than necessary," Mal said.

"Oh, right. On account of they might blow up on us." Jayne smiled unpleasantly, less of a smile and more of a scowl with bared teeth. "I swear, sometimes the jobs we take—"

Irked, Mal rounded on him. "Are what, Jayne? Dangerous? Foolhardy? Scrapin' the barrel so hard, we've dug right through the bottom?"

"Well, yeah. Why do we bother with 'em?"

"'Cause those are the only jobs we can get and stay under the radar. They're what keeps us flying and out of prison, or maybe getting our necks stretched."

Jayne waved him off. "Ease up, Mal. Don't take it out on me. I'm not the one who lost your war for you."

Zoë thrust herself between them, stepping toe to toe with Jayne. Chin raised, she bored her steely gaze into him. "I think you might want to shut your mouth, Jayne, before I shut it for you."

It was a serious threat and Jayne took it as such. "Didn't mean nothin' by it," he groused. His cheeks were red, this time from embarrassment. Jayne hated backing down. "You two are livin' in the past, is all. Like Badger said, war's over. Been over a long whiles. Might as well make the most of the peace."

Zoë opened her mouth to speak, then seemed to catch herself. She gave Jayne a long, measuring glance, like the slowest burn a Firefly-class transport vessel could achieve.

"What?" he protested indignantly. "It's just the plain truth. The war *is* over. And losing's not so bad. Ain't as if it's the end of the world. I've lost stuff lots of times. Poker games, loot from robberies, a horse, my virginity, and…" He glanced down at the pennant Mal had stomped into the dust. His eyes widened. "Oh, no!" he groaned, reaching down and grabbing up the torn pieces. He held them out to Mal accusingly. "She wrote her wave code on it. See? Now I can't read it. You scraped off half the writing."

"Losing ain't so bad," Mal echoed. "Besides, she weren't no good."

"How d'you figure that?" Jayne asked.

"She liked that hat of yours."

Jayne drew himself up to his full, considerable height. "My *mom* knitted this hat. You're just jealous."

"Keep telling yourself that," Mal retorted.

Muttering to himself, Jayne tried to piece the pennant back together. He gave up after a few seconds and in frustration threw the tatters into the air.

"All right, listen up now," Mal said as they drew near Taggart's Bar. "The meet with Hunter Covington is at six sharp. We establish whether he's above board, or elsewise. If he is, we receive whatever it is he wants us to carry, then we fetch Kaylee and have her verify our shuttle's all fixed. I'll pay the repair bill, we'll get rid of that loaner, and meantime Wash'll be prepping for dustoff."

"Did this Covington fella tell you what he's got for us to transport?" Jayne asked.

"Said he preferred to discuss it in person rather'n by wave," Mal said.

Hunter Covington was one of the things that Mal liked least, an unknown quantity. He had requested a quote for shipping "a small item" to a nearby location that would be disclosed when they met. Mal wasn't keen on the vagueness, nor on doing business with an out-and-out stranger, but had nonetheless arranged a meetup at Taggart's since they were on Persephone anyway. Only a rich man or a dolt turned down potential paid work, and Mal was certainly not the former and trusted he wasn't the latter.

"Crucial thing," he added, "we don't mention that we might get blown up before we deliver his goods. Got that?"

"That's smart," Jayne said earnestly.

They strolled past the store where Mal had bought Kaylee her pink, frilly layer-cake dress for that society ball a while back. Today the living mannequins were dressed in the colors of the Alliance, holding flags and waving at the window-shoppers. The folks in the street cheered and waved back at them.

At another store farther down the row, a scrap-merchant-cum-pawnbroker, Mal and Kaylee had haggled many times over parts for *Serenity*, while across the street was the grocery where the crew usually purchased protein blocks for the galley. Every gorramn shopfront had put up a flag to celebrate the day when Persephone had joined the Alliance. Or maybe it was just to avoid being blacklisted by Alliance loyalists. Maybe secretly they were as angry as Mal was. He could hope.

The trio cut down a narrow alley that was made even narrower by avalanches of bricks that had cascaded out of the walls of the three-story buildings on either side. High overhead, a transport barge rumbled and popped, belching a trail of smoke as it crawled up into the sky.

After a right turn into the next adjoining street, Mal, Zoë, and Jayne found themselves face to face with another gaggle of drunken girls, these wearing Alliance-flag capes and hats. After they'd filed past, one of girls called back to Mal, "Want my wave code, honey?"

Jayne let out a low growl.

From that, Mal reckoned he hadn't been forgiven yet. But Jayne was never one to hold a grudge for long. Not because of any charity on his part; he simply had a very short—and narrow—attention span.

As they progressed along the street, the stores got shabbier and shabbier and became interspersed with boarded-up, roofless commercial buildings inhabited by a few scattered squatters. The smoke was thicker here; it rasped the back of Mal's throat and it smelled like the inhabitants were burning dried dung. A beggar sat cross-legged on the sidewalk with a dirt-caked hand extended to passersby.

They kept going, to an even more desolate and sparsely inhabited part of town. Their destination was one of the few drinking establishments still open for business on this street. Above the entrance a hand-painted sign, hanging somewhat askew, read "Taggart's Bar and Lounge." It might as well have said, "Abandon hope all ye who enter here." This was the kind of place where Mal did the kind of deals he was forced to make these days.

The rumble of music and shouting from inside could be heard half a block away. The front wall of the squat, cinderblock structure had been whitewashed once upon a time, but now it was covered by a band of graffiti from the sidewalk to as far as a person could comfortably reach, layer upon layer covering all but a few specks of the white. The green metal double saloon doors were cracked and rusting.

The holographic front window hummed and shorted in an erratic, irritating rhythm. Under the window, a puddle of something on the pavement glistened purple and sticky in the dim light. Could've been blood.

Taggart's was deep in the seam of urban rot, the kind of dump the authorities wouldn't bother sticking their noses in unless someone set off a hand grenade, and maybe not even then. Exchanges of gunfire from within would be ignored: that just meant fewer lowlifes to arrest down the road. Should fisticuffs break out, the police could claim it was none of their business. The hand-to-hand battle could be prolonged and epic.

All the same, Zoë's dander was up. Mal could see it in the set of her jaw and the take-no-prisoners look in her eyes. Wouldn't take much to provoke her to violence. And Jayne? Well, Jayne was Jayne. Almost as volatile as HTX-20.

Persephone had been one of planets where the fighting for the Independents' cause in the Unification War had been the bitterest and most protracted. After Earth-That-Was got used up, the human race had flown out into space to make new earths—terraforming moons and planets, like Persephone. Hopeful, gullible settlers got dumped onto the worst pieces of land while the elites staked possession of the best. The fat cats also took control of planetary governments, enacting laws that favored themselves and ultimately joined together to form an over-arching, galactic authority they called the Alliance.

Every inhabited world had to become a member, the Alliance decreed. Ninety-nine percent of the populations of the outlying moons and planets never saw a scrap of the new technologies and other benefits an expanding civilization was wont to provide, like decent housing, steady food supplies, medical care, and schooling. What they got instead was exploited for cheap labor; the natural resources stripped, and the land left polluted for pennies on the dollar. The gap between haves and have-nots widened. The already fat grew morbidly obese. Most everyone else turned into walking skeletons. It was so obviously unjust that Mal was always amazed when he met someone who had fought on the side of the Alliance—or supported it. Inara, his own shipside Companion, was such a person.

She ain't mine, he reminded himself. *Inara belongs to no one but Inara.*

He had fought for justice and fairness and the freedom for every person to make his or her own way, but he had lost and been punished severely for it. Funny thing, if he had to do it over, he would've done it again—just with fewer stars in his eyes.

"Okay, we're here for business only," he reminded his two crewmates. "Not pleasure."

"Yes, sir," Zoë said, while Jayne blew the air out of cheeks in disgruntlement.

"Hope this Covington guy pays for our drinks," Jayne said.

"If he does," Mal said, "it's because the deal ain't fair to us and he's trying to butter us up."

"A free drink's a free drink," Jayne argued.

"Except when it's not."

It was clear that Jayne wasn't tracking. No matter. Mal took point, pushing both swinging doors inward. Zoë was close behind at his right shoulder. They burst into a maelstrom of stink and noise. The reek of spilled ale, food fried in rancid lard, and tobacco smoke hung in a fog over the heads of grubby drinkers, who huddled on bar stools and chairs, or leaned against walls to keep themselves upright. Fifteen-foot-diameter circular rings marred the bar-room floor. It looked like big vats had once stood there. Acid and vats. Mal's best guess: the place had been a tannery before it was converted to a bar, and the new owner's redecoration had been minimal verging on negligible.

A loud, rhythmic, grating noise blared from a pair of speakers at the edge of a low stage set in one of the rearmost arches. A lone performer sat on a chair playing a computer keyboard, with a microphone duct-taped against the side of his neck. The song had a jaunty, all-too-familiar refrain:

> From Core to Rim, from sun to moon,
> On this we all agree:
> Like oxen yoked up to a cart
> United we are free!

Mal bristled. The Alliance anthem. The bastard was singing the Alliance anthem, and not just singing it but *throat singing* it. And the gorramn drunks packed shoulder to shoulder in front of the stage were swaying their arms in the air and tunelessly bellowing along. Despite the synthetic organ, horn section, and string accompaniment, the whole thing was about as musical as *Serenity*'s struggling sump before Kaylee cleared the clog, and much less pleasant to listen to.

Tamping down his ire, Mal focused on the matter at hand. He scanned the packed room for Hunter Covington. He wasn't here yet.

Mal reached for the photo printout in his pocket, just to be sure. In the Black, out of the blue, Serenity had gotten a wave from someone—Hunter Covington—with a job offer. The money wasn't spectacular, but work was work. Mal had run some background checks, asked around among various associates about Covington, and learned nothing that filled him with an abiding sense of mistrust but nothing that much enthused him either. It seemed the man was a fixture around Eavesdown, with fingers in many a pie. In that respect, Mal had been somewhat surprised the name was unfamiliar to him, but then he couldn't be expected to know every trader, merchant, crook, stealer, dealer, and double-dealer in a city that had such a plenitude of them to choose from.

On the vid screen Covington had spoken in a rich, low purr, presenting a well-dressed, well-spoken figure, with a tidily knotted Ascot tie nestled above the button-down collar of a silk shirt, a tailored velvet jacket, and a shot-silk vest. His luxuriant beard merged with bushy sideburns.

"Looks like the cat that got the cream," Jayne said, glancing over Mal's shoulder at the photo, which had been screen-captured from Covington's wave.

"The cat that got the monopoly on the cream," Mal said, "and cornered the kibble market too."

"You sure about this, sir?" Zoë said. "Is it worth the risk?"

"Badger's mission is way riskier," Mal replied. "Hopefully this is something we can tack onto the job to make it more profitable without much additional effort or burned fuel."

"I don't see Covington around," Jayne said, squinting into the smoke.

"We'll just settle in and wait then," Mal said. "Free table over there."

The table was free because the four occupants had just fallen out of their chairs, dead drunk.

"Let's grab it quick," Zoë said.

They pushed forward before someone else could poach the table. All around them, plastered Alliance-loving patrons were busy outdoing each other with all manner of glass-raising, back-slapping, and top-volume-pontificating on the benefits that Alliance membership had brought to their dusty world. The continuing postwar enthusiasm for all things Alliance was a phenomenon Mal found simply baffling. It was like folks had been struck blind—or bag-of-rocks stupid. The recipients of the Alliance's "bounty" scrabbled desperately to eke out a living, accepting wages that were meager, and giving away most of what they made in taxes with nothing to show for it in return. The system had been designed to flow one way: up.

"Wonder if they've anything good to eat," Jayne said as they sat down. He picked up one of the half-emptied plates that had been left on the table and sniffed the congealed contents. The chef had made an attempt to disguise the taste of protein block chunks using a cacophony of spices and sauces. Jayne looked at it twice, hesitated, then put it back on the table. "This has gone bad. I'm starving." He looked around. "Maybe Covington'll buy us some grub when he gets here."

"I'm not sure that what they serve at this place is edible," Zoë said.

"Be nice if there was some passable quim here, too."

Zoë shot Jayne a look that could have carved a diamond in two.

"No disrespect," Jayne added hurriedly. "Passable unmarried quim, is what I meant."

"That's okay, then," Zoë drawled. "I'll take it as a compliment."

"You should."

"Well, since no one else is goin' to buy us a round," Mal said, "guess I'd better."

"Now you're talking," said Jayne.

Just as Mal bellied up to the bar, a man wearing a long, mustard-yellow duster and a dented ten-gallon hat laid a small piece of folded paper on the bar beside his elbow. Wasn't Covington. Might well be a messenger from Covington.

Mal palmed the piece of paper, and without a word the man in the mustard-yellow duster turned away and drifted off into the crowd. Mal placed their order, and while the bartender was filling it, he teased the paper open and glanced at the note like he was checking his hand at a poker table.

Outside. Alone.
— HC

To Mal's right, another deluded citizen of Persephone was hoisting his glass in honor of the Alliance, slopping brown ale all down his shirtsleeve, going on about "peace in our time."

Not to mention malnutrition and radiation poisoning, Mal thought.

With an effort, Mal let it slide. Business before pleasure. He paid the bartender, picked up the order, and headed back to their table.

"…only thing the Alliance coulda done a better job of is if it had killed off a few hundred thousand more Browncoats," the deluded citizen was saying, addressing the entire room in a slurred shout. "So-called Independents don't value human life like we do. Don't value it at all. Lying cowardly scum killed more civilians than soldiers, an' you *know* that's the truth! I wager every person in this room lost kith and kin on account of them savages."

"Yeah!" chorused the surrounding folk, angrily thrusting their glasses towards the towering ceiling.

Mal couldn't contain himself a moment longer.

"Hey, just hang on now…" he began, then buttoned his lip and carried on towards to the table. Nobody had noticed.

Zoë gave him a hard, searching look as he set the drinks down with hands that were a tad unsteadier than they might have been.

"Sir?" she said.

"Got slipped a note," he said just loud enough for Zoë and Jayne but no one else to hear. "Came from a fella in a ten-gallon hat and a duster the color of pus."

"I saw him. Hard to miss, with that coat. He went out the back way straight after. What's the note say?"

"Looks like it's from Covington, and he's waiting outside."

"Sounds kinda fishy, if you ask me," Jayne said.

Mal considered. "Yes and no. It's awful loud in here and awful busy. Maybe Covington just wants some quiet and privacy."

"Alone, though?" said Zoë, glancing at the note. "That's fishier."

"I agree. But I guess if I don't do as asked, could be the deal's off. The two of you stay here, hold the table. We've all got comm links. I'll keep a channel open. Anything sounds like trouble, come running."

"How about an emergency code word, sir?" Zoë suggested. "Just in case."

"Okay. I say 'strawberries,' that's your cue."

"Strawberries?"

"Strawberries."

"But what if the word crops up in conversation?" said Jayne. "You know, Covington asks what's your favorite fruit, and you just automatically say strawberries?"

Mal blinked. "We'll cross that bridge when we come to it. Comms check." He pressed the send button on his comm link. "Zoë?"

"Can't say I'm hearing you very well," she informed him, touching a finger to her earpiece. "Lot of interference."

"But you can hear me a little."

"A little," she confirmed.

"Jayne?"

"Reading you. Just barely."

"It'll have to do."

Mal added the purchase of new batteries for their comm links to his long list of supplies they could not currently afford.

"I'll be back shortly," he said. "Jayne, don't misbehave. Zoë, make sure Jayne doesn't misbehave."

Head lowered, jaw clenched, Mal turned for the exit.

3

Man, them two are sore losers, Jayne thought, downing the last of his beer. The brews at Taggart's were right tangy. *War's been over for years. What's their beef?* He thought about finishing off Mal's drink as well since it was sitting right there in front of him and Mal wasn't. He guessed Mal would be a mite sore if he came back and his glass was empty, so he let it be.

The singing and dancing showed no sign of abating. Jayne opened his mouth to join in, caught Zoë's glare, and thought the better of it.

"Browncoats bombed the hell outta my village rather'n let the Alliance save it!" a tall drunk yelled nearby.

Jayne could see how something like that would piss people off. Way he figured it, the rebels were lawless and disorganized; their only real purpose was to make a mess of things. The Alliance had overcompensated for that, sure, 'cause they had had the sticks up their behinds like they did now, but the Browncoats hadn't been no angels neither.

Leastwise, that's what he'd heard. He hadn't taken sides during the war. He'd basically robbed soldiers on both sides of it. Neutrality was profitable.

"Killed my cattle so's I wouldn't provision the Alliance!" the drunk bellowed.

To everyone else in the room, Zoë looked calm as a Buddha as she sipped at her drink and studied the crowd. But Jayne knew her pretty well. Well enough to recognize a slow burn when he saw it. She was getting mad.

He wondered whether things were going to get entertaining after all.

"I got these here missing fingers on account of Browncoats!" the offended citizen raved on, spraying his closest audience members with a mist of saliva on the final, sibilant "s." He held up a hand that was good for hitchhiking and picking his nose with but not a lot else. "They *said*"—more spray—"they was fighting for the common man but you know they was just a bunch of *gǒu shǐ*!" Yet more spray. "Tip over a rock and you'd find one of them with his hand out, threatening to kill your whole family if you didn't pay him off."

If Jayne had known the Browncoats were so enterprising, he might have joined them.

"Yeah," another man chimed in, "or they'd wipe out your whole family if you didn't agree to let 'em stash their weapons in your root cellar."

Zoë's lips were compressed so tight, the color had started to drain out of them. Jayne sat back and laced his fingers behind his head, watching her shift uncomfortably in her chair. Was she going to snap? No. Zoë wasn't like Mal.

She never started a fight. That wasn't to say she wasn't real good at ending them, though.

"All this anti-Independent talk gettin' to you, huh?" Jayne commented.

"Nope," Zoë said.

Jayne knew a lie when he heard one too. "Must sting like a sumbitch. Wouldn't be surprised if you lashed out."

"Unlike some of us, I have self-control."

"Sure, sure."

A guy in a patched Alliance jacket and an abnormally large forehead staggered towards their table. "Hey, you two, you hearing what they're saying about those murdering Browncoat bastards?" he demanded.

"Yeah, I'm hearing it," Jayne said amiably.

"Yeah, and listen to *this*…" Large Forehead began. He paused, swaying back and forth like a reed in a breeze, his eyes narrowing as he studied Jayne. "Hey, Earl," he shouted over his shoulder, "come over here and look at this clown hat!"

Jayne blinked. "Huh?" he said, fingers still supporting the back of his skull.

The guy called Earl staggered up to the table. "Well, I'll be…! You're right, Mitch. That is one ugly-ass chapeau." To Jayne he said, "Don't suppose you'd mind removing that abomination from your head, hoss? To avoid upsetting those of us with delicate stomachs."

Jayne's frozen grin rapidly melted away.

"I can't decide whether that contraption makes me want to laugh or throw up," said Large Forehead, a.k.a. Mitch.

Several people within earshot chortled merrily. "All this anti-hat talk gettin' to you, huh?" said Zoë.

"Yup," Jayne said.

"Stay cool. We're not here for this. Low profile."

Drunken louts at the surrounding tables rose awkwardly from their seats, pushing in closer to take a gander for themselves. Pointing at the hat which Jayne's dear mother had made him with her own two hands, they roared with laughter.

This was becoming too much for Jayne. He let his arms drop to his sides, uncoiling like a snake.

"Take it easy, Jayne," Zoë warned. "I mean it."

Unfortunately, Mitch overheard the caution. "His name's Jayne!" he hollered to the throng. "Can you believe it, this witless moron's name is Jayne! And li'l Jaynie is wearing a baby hat!"

The crowd of maybe a dozen bar patrons pressed in even tighter, with more moving in behind them, filling in the vacated space.

"She's probably wearing a baby diaper, too," Mitch cried in delight. Flattening both hands on their table, he leaned forward and slurred into Jayne's face, "Want us to change it for you, Li'l Jaynie?"

Jayne glowered at him. "No one mocks my mother," he snarled, and began to rise.

Zoë rolled her eyes. Matters were about to get out of hand, and there was nothing she or anyone could do to prevent it.

4

The hairs on the back of Mal's neck prickled as a man stepped from the shadows along the street outside Taggart's, about ten feet from the swinging doors.

The newcomer had three others with him. One was a lanky, sallow-skinned type who looked several meals short of a decent diet and had jet-black hair with a pronounced widow's peak. Another of them was tall and rangy, with a complexion as wrinkled and leathery as rawhide. The third had a droopy walrus-type mustache whose tips extended down past his jawline.

Now that the sun had gone down, just about the only light in the street came from the fritzing holographic bar window. Still, Mal could make out enough of the main man's sleek, smug face to recognize him from the wave pic.

"Hunter Covington," Mal said.

"None other," the fellow confirmed. Covington was somewhat bulkier than he had appeared on the vid screen. It was likely he used a real-time appearance tweaking program—software beloved of the vain and the ugly throughout the 'verse—to make himself look thinner than he really was in waves. He was just as nattily dressed, however, right down to the feather-sprouting homburg on his head, the spats on his patent leather shoes and the rosewood cane in his hand. The cane seemed less a walking aid than a fashion accessory, since he did not lean on it as he stood. Its silver knob was carved in the shape of a cobra's head.

As Covington and his cohorts approached, Covington himself made a straight course towards Mal, whereas the three underlings spread out in a way that Mal did not like, a way that made him more of a target, and them less. A couple of steps in either direction, and they'd be flanking him.

In response, Mal's hand dropped to the butt of his holstered Moses Brothers Self-Defense Engine Frontier Model B pistol, known affectionately to him as his Liberty Hammer, and rested there all casual like. He was making what he hoped was a subtle but clear statement: *Don't even think about it.*

"Pleasure to make your acquaintance in person, Mr. Covington," he said, "and that of your three very diverse pals. Mighty fine evening for a nice, professional, businesslike chat with no threat of violence whatsoever, wouldn't you say?"

Covington half-smiled. "As we discussed, Captain Reynolds…" he said.

"Call me Mal. Bein' as I'd like to keep this on a friendly basis."

"Very well. Mal." He spoke as smooth and slow as syrup. "As we discussed, Mal, I have an assignment for you. A small package to be delivered down Bellerophon way next time you happen to be in the vicinity. No rush at our end. There's a research scientist there, Professor Yakima Barnes, who wants to buy what we've got to offer. Thing is, he's under house arrest so there have to be a couple of middlemen involved in the transfer. You being ours, if you want the job."

I can walk away right now, Mal told himself as he eyed the quartet. *We already have the Badger assignment. We could make do with it in a pinch.*

But he was greedy. He knew it; accepted it. The more cargo he could pack in the hold, the more profitable the trip. Besides, Kaylee needed expensive replacement parts for the engine, including a new cross-braced adaptor port for the oxidizer preburner. Plus there was fuel and such. The crew had to eat. And bribes had to be paid. It all added up. And there was nothing awry with this situation that Mal could put his finger on just yet. It was just a feeling he had. And his feelings had often been wrong. Like when he'd been sure that Command would send air support to Serenity Valley and the Browncoats would win the war.

"And what is it we might be deliverin' for you, Hunter?" he asked. When Covington didn't reply, he prodded, "Is it poisonous? Bigger than a breadbox? Have claws and big scary teeth?"

"It's a rare type of metallic ore," Covington told him. "A small rock, like so." Tucking his cane under one arm, he estimated the size between his hands—about that of a cantaloupe melon. "Weighs around twenty, twenty-five pounds."

Mal nodded slowly, not particularly reassured. Something being small didn't mean it wasn't dangerous. Look at River Tam.

"Does this rock throw off toxic fumes?" he asked. "Radiation? Anything like that? I need to know for the safety of my ship and crew, and my other cargo."

Growing up on the Reynolds family ranch on Shadow, Mal had learned about horses, cows, and alfalfa. In the war, it had been all strategy, tactics and field dressings. But in his new line of work, there were too many things to learn and he had to play it by ear much of the time. That meant asking a lot of questions, covering your bases as best you could, and reading the reactions of those trying to buy your services.

"Comes in a lead-lined container," Covington replied, which was not exactly the answer Mal had been hoping for. "Perfectly safe," he added. "If you want, Mal, you can examine it before you take the job. We're keeping it just down the next alley." He jerked his cane in that direction. "We got a place we're staying at there."

Dark alley.

Strangers.

Four-to-one odds.

Inside his head, Mal heard warning bells.

He said, "Know what? No offense, you seem like a great buncha guys an' all, but I think I'm gonna pass."

"Money's good," Covington insisted. "Plenty of platinum in it for you."

"Yeah," Mal said, with a show of regret that wasn't entirely un-feigned. "Wouldn't be surprised if I'm walkin' away from the bargain of a lifetime, but still. Fine upstanding citizens like yourselves mightn't understand this, but sometimes a man in my line of work's just got to listen to his instincts, and mine are telling me it's time to fold my tent and move on."

"Captain Reynolds…" said Covington.

No more "Mal". And a distinct note of menace in the voice.

Tension crackled in the air. Mal's gaze flicked to the eyes of each of the four men one after another. Covington's three underlings were, in turn, darting quick glances towards their boss. Looking for instruction. Waiting to be given the go-ahead.

Covington's eyes narrowed. The eyes of the other three followed suit. So did Mal's.

Fingers twitched. Shoulders squared. Jaws clenched.

Any moment now, someone was going to make a move.

Then there was a fizzle and snap from the holographic front window of Taggart's Bar. The illusory glass dissolved and a man came flying through the opening, head first. A massed roar from inside the bar trailed him like rocket exhaust, blasting into the street as he skid-rolled across the sidewalk, ending up face down and unmoving in the gutter.

It was as if this was the cue the three goons had been waiting for. That, or they were so jumpy, so wired, that any sudden, unexpected movement would have provoked a reaction from them.

The one with the widow's peak sprang first.

Mal, just as startled as they were by sight of a man being hurled forcibly out of Taggart's, reacted a fraction of a second too slow. His hand snapped around the butt of his Liberty Hammer and he drew, but not fast enough. Widow's Peak managed to grab him by the wrist and pin the gun in its leg sheath. Mal let his right hip go soft, twisting in the direction of the incoming force, and used the extra momentum to supercharge a short left punch to the side of his attacker's head. It felt like he'd hit a brick. Widow's Peak groaned and tumbled forward past him, onto his hands and knees.

With three more attackers bearing down fast, Mal took advantage of the unguarded moment to snap kick Widow's Peak in the face, a blow that rolled the man moaning over onto his back, clutching his face in both hands.

Continuing the spin to his right, Mal cleared leather. As he swung around to confront his remaining opponents, he brought up his weapon. The quarters were so close, they were practically standing toe to toe. The other three had drawn their guns but for some reason didn't open fire.

Mal had no such qualms, but before he could touch off a shot, the man with the complexion like rawhide darted in, grabbed hold of his hand and the pistol and shoved the barrel towards the sky.

The gun went off with a sharp, ear-stabbing *crack!* that echoed off the ruined buildings and rolled away down the street.

Rawhide Complexion clutched the Liberty Hammer in a death grip. Mal had the choice of letting the gun go and taking his chances bare-knuckled, or fighting for it. No way was he going to give up the weapon. He kicked Rawhide Complexion in the kneecap, feeling something break loose under the sole of his boot. The man screamed and dropped to the pavement, releasing the gun to grab his leg.

In the same instant the pistol came free, Mal sensed a rush of movement behind him on the left. He fired wildly as he turned away from that threat, trying to hit the man on his right, the one with the walrus mustache. Bullets sparked and ricocheted off the building opposite.

"Zoë! Jayne!" he yelled into his comm link. "Help!" Remembering the code word, he added, "Strawberries! Strawberries!"

Hunter Covington loomed on his left. Mal glimpsed the cane in his hand. He thought he was about to be struck, but instead Covington thrust the silver cobra-head knob up close to Mal's face. The snake's jaws snapped wide open, much as though it was baring its fangs. Inside, a small tube was revealed, from which came the short hiss of gas being released under pressure.

Mal smelled an acrid odor that he didn't recognize. Something—some instinct—told him not to breathe, but by then it was already too late. Whatever the gaseous substance that had emerged from the cane was, Mal had inhaled some of it. Enough of it that his brain suddenly seemed to be whirling round and round within his skull like a child's spinning top, gathering speed; and just when he thought it couldn't turn any faster, not without gyrating clean out of his cranium, everything went black.

The man called Mitch couldn't have seen the punch coming. Jayne Cobb might be big but he was fast too, when he needed to be.

It was a solid sock to the jaw, and Mitch went flying backwards, arms windmilling. He was caught by a couple of members of the crowd, who thrust him back towards Jayne, encouraging him to retaliate. Unfortunately for Mitch, he was too dazed to muster any kind of response. Glassy-eyed, he swayed in front of Jayne, who polished him off with a tidy right hook that dropped him to the floor like a felled tree.

Mitch's buddy Earl now weighed in, swinging for Jayne. Jayne blocked the blow with a forearm and drove his fist into Earl's paunchy midriff. The air whooshed out of Earl. His eyes and cheeks bulged like something out of a cartoon. Jayne followed up the gut-punch with an uppercut which fair lifted Earl off his feet. Earl flew bodily onto a table where four men were playing Tall Card. The table collapsed, sending cards, coins and drinks hurtling in all directions.

The card players were not exactly best pleased about this. As one, they lunged for Jayne, on whose face was plastered a big, sloppy grin.

It was at this point, with Jayne considerably outnumbered, that Zoë felt obliged to join in. She would much rather have sat out the fight, and she'd have been happy to watch Jayne get the tar beaten out of him. It would have been something of a bonus, in fact.

However, he was, all said and done, her crewmate and he had come to her aid more than once when they'd gotten into a scrape. More importantly, she needed to end the fracas before it escalated further. Brawls in a bar like this had a tendency to spread fast. A room full of unruly, very drunk people was like tinder: it only took a small spark to set the whole place on fire.

She decked the first of the card players with a simple, straight-fingered jab to the windpipe. He went down choking and spluttering, out of action for the foreseeable future.

One of his fellow card players, seeing this, made a grab for Zoë. She batted his outstretched hands aside, then pivoted on one leg, shoving the man past her. His face collided with the edge of her and Jayne's table with a sickening crunch. Blood gushed from his nose, which was crushed flat by the impact. He slumped to the floor with a deep groan.

Jayne, meanwhile, grappled with his two opponents, who were raining punches on him. He managed to land a left-hand roundhouse on one of them but it was a flailing shot with little bodyweight behind it. The guy shrugged it off and walloped Jayne hard enough to make his eyes spin.

Zoë took the man out with a kick to the back of the knee

chased up with a downward elbow jab to the top of his skull. He fell into an ungainly sitting position, legs splayed out in front of him, before keeling over sideways, out cold.

Being freed from one of his attackers enabled Jayne to give the other his full attention. He seized the man by the shirtfront and wrenched him close, before delivering a ferocious head butt to his face. Stunned, the man drooped in Jayne's clutches.

"You look kinda peaky there, ol' buddy," Jayne remarked. "Maybe you need some air. Zoë? Wanna help?"

Zoë took one arm and leg, Jayne took the other, and together they swung the man back and forth, once, twice, before tossing him through the holographic window.

Zoë brushed her palms together. She assumed that was it. The fight was over and done with. Just a brief little taproom scuffle, no big deal.

One look around the bar told her she was sorely mistaken.

As she watched, someone in the drunken throng took umbrage because someone else had shoved in front of him to get a better view of the fight. The first guy—a farmer, to judge by his ruddy face and the smears of dried dung adhering to his clothes—picked up a near-full glass and broke it over the other guy's head. Beer and blood sprayed.

This offended greatly the person whose beer it had been. She, a big bruiser of a woman with a plethora of homespun tattoos, thumped the farmer square in the face, adding a knee in the groin for good measure. As the farmer went down, gasping and clutching his nethers, a woman next to him who was most likely his wife uttered a wail of outrage. She leapt at the big woman, grabbing a handful of her hair. The two of them wrestled, howling like banshees.

By accident one of them spilled a drink with a jostling elbow. The man whose drink had been spilled thought someone else was responsible and duly hit that person.

From there, the situation rapidly deteriorated. It was a swift chain reaction, insult leading to insult, punch leading to punch. It unfurled with the incendiary inevitability of a forest fire. Chairs crashed down on heads. Bottles and table legs were pressed into service as makeshift weapons.

Above it all, a lone voice appealed for calm, that of Taggart himself, the bar owner. From behind the counter he begged his patrons to stop fighting and behave themselves, while the other bartender, his employee, crouched down in an attempt to avoid getting embroiled in the chaos.

Taggart's efforts to restore order were curtailed as a bottle came flying his way, narrowly missing his head and shattering against the back wall behind him. At that, he vaulted over the counter and joined in the fray.

Zoë turned to Jayne. "We've got to get out of here."

"Aw man," said Jayne. "Really? Things were just gettin' good."

"We're supposed to be keeping tabs on the captain, listening in case he gets into difficulties. Not scrapping with the locals."

She was halfway to the exit when her eye fell on a kid— couldn't have been more than seventeen or eighteen—who was on the receiving end of a pummeling from two men much older and larger than he was. The boy was attempting to fight back but the men kept whaling on him viciously. He was screaming in defiance and pain, but this just seemed to incite his assailants to hit him harder.

Zoë's blood boiled.

Grown adults busting one another's heads was one thing. Ganging up on a kid half your age and gleefully beating him all to hell was completely another. She doubted the boy had done anything to deserve this punishment. He'd just been in the wrong place at the wrong time.

Barely even thinking about it, she charged at the men. If there was one thing Zoë Alleyne Washburne could not abide, it was bullying. What was the Alliance's behavior, after all, but bullying on a 'verse-wide scale?

She got one of the boy's assailants in a headlock from behind, pulling on his throat, choking him. He reeled backwards, slamming her against an I-beam support column hard enough to loosen her grip. At the same time he rammed his boot-heel into her shin. Agony flared up Zoë's leg. She bit back a cry, channeling her fury into a piledriver of a punch to the small of the man's back. She caught him above the kidney. As he crumpled she clutched his ears with both hands and wrenched him down, simultaneously bringing up her leg, and felt as much as heard the *crack!* of the back of his skull connecting with her knee. His body went lettuce-limp and she threw him aside.

The other bully was still pounding the kid, but Jayne, taking his example from Zoë, intervened.

"Pick on someone your own size," Jayne said to the man, who responded with a sneer. Jayne, though tall, was still several inches shorter than him and a whole heap less wide in the chest.

"That," the man said to Jayne, "is one sorry excuse for a hat, pal."

It was the last thing he would be saying for a long time.

"I am sick and tired," Jayne growled, spitting out each word, "of folks disrespectin' Mama Cobb's knitting."

Fifteen seconds later, the man was sprawled on the floor, unconscious and bleeding in several places.

Zoë went over to the kid, who was also bleeding profusely, and whimpering too. Her leg was throbbing agonizingly where the bully had kicked her, and she couldn't put her full weight on it. She had a feeling her shinbone might be busted.

"You okay?" she asked.

The boy tried to nod.

"Come with us. This ain't no place for the likes of you."

The kid was groggy and didn't look like he could set one foot in front of the other.

"Jayne," Zoë said, "help him."

Before Jayne could reply, there was a sudden burst of static on their comm links. In the midst of it they both heard Mal's voice, just audible above the surrounding mêlée.

"—berries! Str—"

The rest was lost amid sweeps of white noise.

"He say strawberries?" Jayne asked.

"Sounded like it."

"Mighta been 'breeze.'"

"Pretty sure it was strawberries."

"Only I wouldn't wanna rush outside, guns blazin', just to find he didn't say strawberries after all. It'd be kinda embarrassing."

"Jayne," Zoë sighed, "we're leaving. Come on."

"Okay, okay." Jayne got an arm around the boy and half-carried him.

They made for the door again, but were thwarted. There were just too many writhing, battling bodies blocking their path. They couldn't make any headway through the scrum.

"Window," said Zoë. They'd thrown the card player out through it. Why not follow him their own selves?

They struggled back towards the window. Zoë had to wrestle people aside and in one instance deal with a man who blundered dazedly into her and clung on for support. He refused to let go, so she broke a bottle over his head and he disengaged.

At the window, the boy managed to get one leg over the sill. With Jayne's assistance, he clambered outside. Jayne followed.

Zoë slid herself through the holographic glass, sensing a slight shiver of electrons around her as she went, like she was penetrating a meniscus of warm mist.

Outside, she scanned the street both ways, looking for Mal. She fully expected to see him, maybe tussling with Hunter Covington.

Not a sign of him.

She tried her comm link. "Mal? Sir? Do you read me?"

No reply.

She didn't allow herself to feel concern. Not yet. There was an alley close by. Could be Covington had invited Mal to join him down there in order to conduct their business out of sight of passersby. She limped over to its entrance to check, unholstering her Mare's Leg just in case. The cut-down Winchester Model 1892 carbine had a six-round tubular magazine, with one up the pipe, an oversized cocking loop, and no rear stock. It felt good and hefty in her hand.

The alley was empty. No Mal. No anybody. It was as if he had vanished into thin air.

"Where's Mal?" Jayne said.

"That," said Zoë grimly, "is the honking great question."

6

Zoë's comm link crackled.

"Sir?" she said, thinking—praying—it was Mal.

"Zoë?" Not Mal. Kaylee.

"What's up?"

"'Well, howdy there, Kaylee. Lovely to hear from you.'"

"No time for that," Zoë said tightly. "The captain's disappeared. Might be he's in trouble."

"*Shén me?*" Kaylee declared in shock. "What's happened?"

"Don't know yet."

Before Zoë could continue, the teenage kid she and Jayne had rescued let out a low moan. He sagged to the ground.

"Kaylee? I'm going to mute you for a second. Be right back."

Zoë hobbled over to the boy. He was in very bad shape indeed. His face was swelling all over and his eyes had a lost, unfocused look, the pupils severely dilated. He needed medical attention, she reckoned. He might have concussion, maybe even a brain injury.

"Kid?" she said. "Kid?"

"Allister," he mumbled.

"Allister? Is that your name?"

"Yeah."

"Listen to me, Allister. We need to get you to a hospital."

"No," said Allister. "No hospital. Can't afford. Mom… My mom. Nurse."

"Your mother is a nurse?"

"Used to be. Got sick. Got fired. No money now. But she can help me."

"Where does she live?"

"Our apartment. Over in the riverside district."

Zoë ground her teeth. The kid wasn't her and Jayne's responsibility. Sure, they'd saved him. That didn't mean they were stuck with him. She had more important things to worry about. Namely Mal. It was possible the captain was fine and well, just off somewhere with Hunter Covington thrashing out a deal. She didn't think so, though. He had almost certainly said "Strawberries" over the comm link, once if not twice. The fact that she couldn't raise him on the comms now was also worrisome. His link had already proved faulty but at least there had been some signal. Now there was none at all, implying it might have been switched off, or even smashed to bits.

"Okay," she said. "Listen, Allister, you think you can make it back home?"

The kid nodded weakly. "Figure I can." But when he tried to stand, he almost fainted.

"It's no good. Jayne, you're just going to have to take him."

"What?" said Jayne.

"Like it or not, Allister needs our help. We can't just leave him in the street. People are still fighting in there." Zoë gestured at Taggart's. The noise coming from within hadn't quieted. If anything, it was getting louder. Things were crashing and splintering. After the ruckus was over, there probably wouldn't be a stick of furniture in the bar left intact. "Only a matter of time before it spills outside, and Allister will get caught up in it all over again."

"But why do *I* have to take him home?" Jayne groused. "I ain't no crummy babysitter. Why don't you do it?"

"My leg is injured," Zoë said. "Might be broken, even. I can barely walk myself, let alone help someone else along. It has to be you."

"What about Mal? I'd say he was more important than some kid we only just met."

"Bad leg or not, I'm going to go look for him."

"Two of us could do that better'n one."

"Agreed. So as soon as you've gotten Allister to his house, contact me. With any luck I'll have found Mal by then, but if I haven't, you can join in the search."

"And if I can't get ahold of you?"

"Go to *Serenity*. I'll be back there at some point."

Jayne bellyached some more, but Zoë was adamant. In the end he relented.

"All right, all right. Gorramn it." He extended a hand to Allister and unceremoniously hauled the youngster to his feet. "Which way?"

Allister waved a vague hand in a westerly direction.

"Okay, get me there, kid. Zoë, the moment there's any word on Mal, you let me know."

"Will do."

Supporting Allister, Jayne headed off.

Zoë unmuted her comm link. "Kaylee? Me again. Kaylee? Do you copy?"

"Oh, good, hi," Kaylee said. "Sorry. I got, ah, distracted. Are you guys coming back anytime soon?"

"Distracted? What's going on there?"

"River says *Serenity* needs to take off. She keeps saying it over and over. She can't exactly explain why, but she's getting a little—well, a lot—jumpy."

"Jumpy? Jumpy how?"

Something clattered and then someone shrieked in the background at Kaylee's end of the transmission. Maybe it wasn't so much as shriek as a laugh? A wild, crazy laugh. Either way, Zoë was sure it had come out of River. Wearily, she touched her fingertips to her forehead and felt wetness. Blood. She didn't think it was her own.

"Jumpy how?" she repeated.

"Oh, like really scared," Kaylee said. "She made a fort."

"In her room?"

"No. The dining area. Table's all sideways. She's brought in her blankets and pillows for the walls."

"What about Simon? Can't he take care of her?"

"Well, he's doing his best," Kaylee said uneasily. "Inara too. We all are."

"Okay, Kaylee. Keep a lid on things there if you can. Also, tell Wash to try to raise the captain. Let me know if, when, he gets through."

"Aye-aye. What do you figure's happened to Mal?"

"I wish I gorramn knew."

Zoë set off down the street in the opposite direction from the one Jayne and Allister had taken. She estimated it had been five minutes since Mal's alarm call. He couldn't have gone far in five minutes.

However, Zoë couldn't walk anywhere near as fast as she would have liked. Each time she put weight on her injured leg, it was like a jolt of electricity was shooting up from shinbone to kneecap. She told herself to ignore the pain but the pain told her it wouldn't be ignored. Soon every step was eliciting a curse from her, while sweat broke out on her forehead and dampened her armpits. Maybe she should have listened to Jayne. Maybe they should just have ditched Allister. Mal was the priority. But then the kid was their responsibility, and even Mal, she thought, would have said she had made the right decision. The captain might be big on self-interest but he wasn't selfish.

She pushed on, but after a good quarter-hour exploring some of the city's grimiest, most deprived areas—neighborhoods that were run-down even by Eavesdown's admittedly low standards—she had to stop and rest. Murmuring "*Zǎo gāo*" to herself and panting hard, she leaned against a wall.

Just as she was preparing to renew the search, Kaylee buzzed her on the comms. "Zoë? Any luck finding Mal yet?"

"No. What's the situation like with you?"

"Not shiny." Kaylee sounded agitated, which, for someone as usually upbeat as her, was disquieting. "River's getting more'n a mite antsy now."

"What's bothering her so? Why's she so anxious *Serenity* should take off?"

"It's the boxes we took on board. You know, Badger's big metal crates. She's saying they're not safe and then all kinds of other stuff like there's going to be a surprise, a nasty one, and that's why she's made the fort. It's like the worries in her mind are suddenly too much for her."

"Put Simon on."

Moments later, Simon's well-educated voice came on the comms. "Hello, Zoë."

"Is there something you can do about River? She seems to have Kaylee spooked."

"I'm sure she's going to calm down soon." He didn't sound convinced.

"Could you perhaps tranquilize her?"

"Tranquilize her?" Simon echoed.

In the background, River cried, "No needles!"

"I don't think that'd be a good idea," Simon said. "As you can hear, she's not likely to be cooperative, and when River won't cooperate…"

"*Needles!*" River hollered.

Zoë knew that if Simon attempted to sedate River, she would fight back. Someone would get hurt, and it wasn't liable to be River.

"Okay, then can you just talk to her? Maybe settle her that way?"

"What do you think I've been doing?" Simon's well-to-do upbringing prevented him from giving vent to his true feelings, but Zoë could hear the exasperation underlying his words.

"River, no, sweetie, don't touch that," Kaylee said in the background.

Then came Inara's voice, also gentle and soothing.

"She's right, darling. Someone might get hurt."

There was more crashing.

"Fire the thrusters!" River cried.

"River, no!" said Simon. "Put the cleaver down. Don't wave it around like that." To Zoë he said, "I have to go. I think she might do something to Kaylee and Inara if I don't stop her."

"Okay."

"Oh, Shepherd Book's just walked in. Thank God."

Book's voice said, mock-sternly, "Taking the Lord's name in vain, son?"

"Sorry, preacher," said Simon. "Can you see to River? You're good with her."

"I am when my hair's tied back, at least. Who are you talking to on the comms? Is it Zoë?"

"Yes," said Simon.

"I'd like a word with her, if I may. Pass me the handset. Zoë?" Book's warm tones fell on Zoë's ears like honey. There was something about the preacher—an aura he had—that put you at ease. He managed to remain unruffled in even the most trying circumstances. He was a living, breathing argument in favor of the spiritual life. "I infer, from what I've overheard, that Mal has gone missing."

"That's right." Zoë said. "He went out of Taggart's to meet Hunter Covington alone. Now he's gone and I can't find hide nor hair of him."

"Then perhaps I can bring you some succor in that regard. I've just come from the bridge. Your husband reports that not five minutes ago Guilder's called. They want their loaner shuttle back. Our shuttle has been picked up."

"Huh," said Zoë.

"Is that not good news? The captain has collected the shuttle. He'll be here shortly, you and Jayne can join us, we can take off, River will quieten, all will be well."

"Yes, it's just… If Mal's taken the shuttle, why didn't he let me know? Sure, we're having comms difficulties, but it seems like at the very least he'd do is try to get in touch, especially since he could have used the shuttle's link, which has to be working better than his own. Also, he could have come back for me and Jayne at the bar after his meeting with Covington. Why go straight to Guilder's without us? It just isn't like him."

Not to mention the "Strawberries" distress signal, she thought.

"Anyway," she went on, "wasn't his plan for Kaylee to make sure the repairs were complete before we paid and turned the loaner in?"

"Now that you put it like that, it doesn't seem to add up, does it?" Book said.

"Listen, Shepherd, would you do me a favor and go to Guilder's? Check out if it really was Mal took the shuttle. Take along a picture of him and have them verify he was the one."

"I think I can manage that."

"Meantime, I'll keep looking for him around these parts. I'm thinking if I head back to Taggart's, there's a chance things will have cooled there. If Mal isn't aboard the shuttle and everything is in fact okay, it's a good bet he'll go back to try to find us the last place he saw us."

"Cooled?"

"Yeah, the situation got a little hairy. Bit of a dustup."

"What happened?"

"Jayne happened."

"Say no more. I'll contact you as soon as I have any further information, Zoë." Book cut the connection.

Zoë was clutching at straws, she knew it. Eavesdown Docks was a vast, sprawling place, crammed with people, many of them transients passing through. The odds of her finding Mal just by wandering around looking were close to nil. The odds of him returning to Taggart's were also pretty low. Her suspicion was that the meet with Hunter Covington had somehow gone badly wrong and that if Mal was aboard the shuttle that had taken off from Guilder's, he wasn't there willingly. In the absence of any other plan, though, Taggart's it was. You never know, she might get lucky.

Lucky? Zoë said to herself as her damaged leg sent up a fresh protest of pain. She and luck had been barely on nodding terms these past few years, not least since she'd thrown in her lot with Mal as his second-in-command. The one undeniably good thing to come out of her signing on with the crew of *Serenity* was meeting its pilot. Hoban Washburne was hardly the handsomest man in the galaxy, nor the best built, nor even the bravest. He suited her, though. He was funny and wise and loving. He respected her and deferred to her, but without being a pushover. She and Wash were a perfect fit.

As she neared Taggart's, Zoë saw that the fight had indeed run its course, as she'd hoped. A couple of hover ambulances had arrived and were taking on board the people most badly injured in the brawl. A paramedic was kneeling beside the man she and Jayne had tossed through the window, tending to him.

She was about to venture back into the bar when her gaze lit upon a familiar figure. It was the man in the ten-gallon hat and mustard-yellow duster, the one who had passed Mal the note to go outside. He was loitering on the sidewalk some distance from Taggart's, looking on with a bemused detachment. A matchstick was clenched between his teeth and he rolled it back and forth in contemplation.

Zoë approached him with as much casualness as her injured limb would allow. She had her Mare's Leg cocked and ready.

"Hey, pal," she said, lodging the barrel of the gun in the small of the man's back.

"Whoa there," Yellow Duster said, raising both hands and looking over his shoulder. "Take it easy." He squinted. "I know you?"

"Come with me."

"Well now. Beautiful lady like you, that's an invitation I'd gladly accept, whether or not you had a gun in my back. So what say you drop the firearm?"

"Not a chance." Zoë ground the Mare's Leg harder into his spine. "Please don't think I won't hesitate for one moment to fire."

"With all these folks around?"

"I wouldn't even bat an eyelid."

"I believe you," said Yellow Duster. "And in this part of town, chances are they wouldn't bat an eyelid either. All right, you got me. I'll come quietly."

She steered him towards the alley she had scoped out earlier when she'd first realized Mal was missing. Halfway along, beside some overflowing garbage bins, she halted. Scavenging animals—rats, dogs, raccoons—had been through the bins, and trash was strewn across the alley in reeking mounds.

"Turn round," she ordered.

Yellow Duster did as told. "What now?" he said, grinning around the matchstick. "I drop my pants?"

"You should be so lucky. All I want from you is talk."

"I can do much better things with my mouth, you give me the chance."

Zoë resisted the urge to clobber him. "You gave a note to someone tonight, in the bar," she said.

"Did I?"

"Don't even try to lie. I saw you. The man you gave it to is a friend of mine."

"So?"

"So what happened after?"

"What do you mean? All I did was drop off a note I never read. Something go sideways?"

She scrutinized him. Yellow Duster had clearly mastered the art of the poker face. She said, "My friend is missing."

"That's too bad. But I promise you, I had nothing to do with it. I was paid to take the note into Taggart's—half up front, half afterwards. I was given a description of the fellow I was supposed to hand it to. Your friend matched the description. I slipped him the note, and he didn't seem surprised to receive it, so I knew I musta had the right man. After that, I left."

"Who gave you the note in the first place?"

"Some guy."

Zoë leveled the Mare's Leg at Yellow Duster's crotch. "You can be more specific than that."

The man tried to maintain his cocksure air, but the matchstick drooped in the corner of his mouth, somewhat giving the game away. "Never knew his name. Never asked. Somebody offers me good coin for a simple job, I say 'yessir' and keep the questions to zero."

"What did he look like, the man who hired you?"

"Well heeled. Slick. Beard. Dressed like a gentleman."

Hunter Covington. Had to be. Not that Zoë had been in much doubt.

"He give you any clue what he intended to do with my friend?"

"None whatsoever, and I didn't inquire. I prefer to know as little as possible about the dealings of others. The kind of people who hire me like to keep their business private, too."

Zoë had few doubts on that front. Yellow Duster was a classic go-between, the type of guy you could rely on to be incurious about the whys and wherefores of a job so long as the money was right.

She pressed him for further information anyway. Maybe he knew something useful about Covington without knowing he knew it. "How did the man who employed you contact you? Are you part of an organization, or—"

"I'm on my own. Freelance. Sole trader. Got no organization to answer to."

"So how did he contact you?" she repeated.

"In person," Yellow Duster said.

"Not by wave?"

"No, ma'am. People who have a need for me can find me. They don't necessarily invite me out for dinner and a slow dance, although it's been known to happen. But we always meet in person. Every time you send a wave, see, it leaves a trail that can be followed. People I work for don't like trails. That's why they come to me in the first place. I'm known for doing odd jobs around the docks for people. I'm also known for having something of a reputation. I'm reliable. A straight shooter. You give me something to do, it gets done, no quibble, no mess. No trail."

"Anyone doing odd jobs in Eavesdown would need consent from the criminal operators who run the docks," Zoë said. "Such as Badger, for instance."

The mention of Badger's name earned a flicker of recognition from Yellow Duster, but then that was hardly surprising. You worked in the shadier edges of Eavesdown, you'd at least know *of* Badger, if not associate with him personally.

"Actually it's not as simple as that," he said, smirking. "Everything in this town—and on Persephone overall—is more like live and let live, up to a certain point. And 'by a certain point,' I mean the amount of platinum on the table. Folks who are careful can earn their daily scratch without answering to higher-ups, Badger or anyone else."

"So the man who paid you for handing over the note isn't a higher-up, then?"

"Could be. Sure looked like he was. Don't know his name, though. Not that I'd necessarily reveal it, even if I did. Another part of my reputation is my discretion. I'm famous for it."

"I already know his name," Zoë said.

"Well, bully for you! Then I reckon that makes you one up on me. Look, lady, are we finished here? I've told you all I can. Figure it's high time you lower that cannon of yours, an' maybe then you and I can go somewhere, have a drink, see what develops, you know what I'm sayin'?"

In case she might misinterpret his meaning, he gave her a slow, lascivious wink. It fair turned Zoë's stomach. She firmed her grip on her gun.

"I still have a couple more questions," she said.

"Fire away," said Yellow Duster, hastily adding, "Not literally."

"Your 'employer,' for want of a better word. Where did you and he meet?"

"Right here," he said, as if it should have been obvious. He nodded in the direction of Taggart's.

"How did he know to look for you in Taggart's?" she pressed, but Yellow Duster simply smiled. "Right, your lofty reputation preceded you."

"Lots of dealings go down in Taggart's," he said. "Reckon you already know that."

Zoë felt herself growing increasingly vexed. Time was slipping away, and the man was giving up what little useful intelligence he had in a very relaxed and roundabout fashion. Plus, nothing he'd said could be verified beyond doubt, so there was no reason to believe he was playing straight with her.

Inadvertently she shifted onto her bad leg. A spike of pain made her grimace.

"Hold your horses now," Yellow Duster said, misreading her expression and taking it for a precursor to homicide.

There was a first, faint hint of panic in his voice. "I've been accommodating so far, ain't I?"

"Not nearly enough."

"Well, I can be even more accommodating, if you'll just let me."

"Go on. As long as that's not innuendo."

"Not this time. When he hired me, the fella muttered something about this had been a long time coming. Said there'd been a betrayal. Said there was a price that was long overdue paying, and now was the reckoning." Yellow Duster looked at her expectantly, optimistically. "Didn't understand it myself. Guessed maybe your pal owed him money going way back. Is that what he meant?"

"It's possible," Zoë said. Mal doubtless had past financial debts he hadn't honored. "Anything else?"

"That's all, I swear." The man was emphatic. "Of course, the remark wasn't addressed direct to me, so I may have misheard."

"He was talking to somebody else? Who?"

"A woman," came the reply. "Real quiet type. Fidgety. She came into Taggart's with him. He said it to her."

Zoë seized on the new information. Covington had an accomplice. Maybe his wife? "What did she look like?"

"She was pretty. Light brown skin, black hair, all kind of curly and long. Not unlike you, though not as intimidating. She kept staring at me with these big greenish eyes, hard, like she was trying to tell me something. Ask me, I think she was frightened."

"Frightened of what?"

"Who she was with. Like she didn't want to be with him."

"Maybe she was trying to solicit help," Zoë bit off. "Hence the look. Sounds like she could have been a kidnap victim, or else a bondswoman. She was pleading with you to do something about her situation."

"Why would she do that?" Yellow Duster said.

"Because she mistook you for a decent human being?"

He cocked an eyebrow. "Now, now, darlin'. Don't get all high and mighty with me. You run your life and I'll run mine."

With effort, Zoë reined in her aggravation. "How long ago did this conversation happen? When were you hired to hand over the note?"

"Just a couple days ago. The guy came into Taggart's with his lady friend, asked for me by name, and I chanced to be in that day."

Zoë decided to take a risk and reveal her hand a little further. "The name Hunter Covington mean anything to you?"

Yellow Duster looked at her keenly. "Not a smidge. Should it?"

Zoë fancied he was mentally filing the name away for future reference, in case it proved useful income-wise. "Not necessarily," she said. "Where did you go after you gave the note to my friend?"

"To get the second half of my money."

"Where?"

"Some old flophouse, not ten minutes' walk from here."

The hairs rose on the back of Zoë's neck. Finally, something tangible to work with. Maybe it would connect the dots. The flophouse might even be where Mal was.

"Who did you meet there?" she asked. "Covington?"

"That the gent? No, not him. Some other guy. No one

76

special. Pale hair. Couple scars on his face. That's about as far as it goes for distinguishing features."

Scars were not rare in a postwar era; nor, for that matter, on a hardscrabble world like Persephone. "And do you think you can find your way back to this flophouse?"

"I look like I just stepped off the boat? Like I don't know my way around these here parts? Course I can."

Zoë pondered her options. Shepherd Book was heading to Guilder's. Jayne was taking the kid Allister home. Kaylee, Inara, Simon and Wash should stay on board *Serenity*, all hands being needed to deal with River. That left Zoë to follow this lead, her and no one else—and sore leg notwithstanding, that's what she was going to have to do.

"Then take me there," she said.

"Now, I'm not the sort who does anything as a favor," said Yellow Duster. "I think you've had enough out of me for free. How's about a little cash reward for my services?"

She gave him a look. "How's about I don't blow a hole in you?"

He pursed his lips speculatively. "Seems fair."

They stared at each other for a couple of seconds. Then Zoë waved the Mare's Leg meaningfully. "Flophouse. Let's go."

"Ladies first," Yellow Duster said with a mock-courteous ushering gesture.

"Couldn't agree more," Zoë said, stepping behind him and prodding him forward with the gun.

"But you're a… Ohhh, I get it," the man said. "Very funny."

"Yeah," she said. "Ain't I just a barrel of laughs?"

"You carrying?" Zoë said as they walked

"Now she asks," said Yellow Duster. "Yep. Six-gun. Shoulder holster."

"Maybe you should give it to me."

"You don't trust me?" he said, making out as if his feelings were hurt.

"Don't take it personally. I don't trust anyone."

The man reached under his coat for his weapon.

"Nice and slow," Zoë warned. "Use your fingertips and keep them well away from the trigger."

He passed the six-gun to her as instructed—a snub-nosed .38 caliber Baird and Chu Special. Zoë slotted it barrel first into her belt.

"You got a name?" she inquired.

"Call me Harlow. It's not actually my name, but I answer to it," he said. "What should I call you?"

"Hopalong."

"Really? On account of the leg, I suppose. Bet that

ain't actually your name either."

"Depends."

"What do your friends call you?"

"They call me Hopalong."

"I see," said Harlow. "This relationship of ours, y'know, it's seeming kinda one-sided to me."

"That's just how I like it."

They wended their way down back streets, passing under lines of washing that had been hung out to dry but were probably just getting dirtier in this polluted air. A mangy, one-eyed cat yowled at them from a doorway, then turned tail and fled. The route they were following was so labyrinthine, Zoë was having trouble mapping it in her head and wasn't certain she would be able to retrace her steps unaided. Her leg continued to voice its complaint. It wanted nothing more than for her to sit down and rest it. She wished she could but knew she couldn't.

All the while, she kept an ear out for Book or Jayne buzzing in, or possibly the captain himself. From now on, to avoid another *gǒu cào de* communications mess like this one, she was going to make sure they double- and triple-checked their comm links beforehand.

"Down here," Harlow said.

The alley he was indicating was no more than an arm-span wide. The roofs of the two-story buildings that bracketed it were perfect for a no-survivors ambush. To make matters worse, there wasn't a single streetlight in the vicinity, only the faint backwash gleam from a couple of nearby windows.

"Got a flashlight," Harlow said. "Okay if I take it out?

Don't want you getting all itchy-fingered on me."

"Go ahead, but do it slow, like with your gun," Zoë said, firming her hold on the sawn-off pistol grip of her holstered weapon. "Shine it in my eyes to try and blind me, and you are a dead man."

Harlow took out the flashlight. He aimed it down the alley and flicked it on, creating a bright corona of illumination directly ahead of them.

Maintaining a comfortable distance behind Harlow, Zoë kept a lookout on the edges of the rooflines and the upper-story windows. There was no sign of movement from above, and none in the alley ahead.

They continued on without speaking. The alley wound back and forth, taking a hard dogleg to the right, then the left. Between the roars of takeoffs and landings at Eavesdown Docks, Zoë could hear distant sounds of celebrations. Strings of fireworks or automatic gunfire. Yelling and cheering. The Alliance Day revels were still ongoing but it all sounded far away, as though they were taking place on another world.

After approximately three minutes at a steady pace, the buildings on the right gave way to a high wall topped with concertina wire. The wall was broken by a closed, heavy wooden gate ten feet high and wide enough for a land speeder to pass through. It and the walls on either side were decorated with a sprawl of colorful graffiti tags. Most were crude and obscene, but some were kind of arty. One was an interpretation of the Blue Sun logo, tweaked so that it read "Blue Scum," while on the gate itself was spray-painted DEATH TO ALL TRAITORS in tall, cringingly bright lettering. She thought back to the hatred the drunks in

Taggart's had shown for the Browncoats. Usually the worst that she heard was contempt for the losing side of the war. Folks around here sure had strong feelings on the matter.

Closer to, she saw that the DEATH TO ALL TRAITORS graffiti was fresher than any of the others.

"Any idea who these 'traitors' might be?" she asked Harlow, running a finger beneath the word as though underlining it.

"Beats me," Harlow replied indifferently. "Could describe any number of folks, I guess. But being as it's Alliance Day, and that looks to have been added sometime in the past week… Well, you do the math."

"Browncoats."

"Not just a pretty face."

"And when Covington mentioned betrayal in connection with Mal, do you think that's what he meant? That, rather than not paying money?"

"Lady, I try not to think too much about anything except keeping my head on my shoulders and platinum in my pocket." Harlow reached through a hole in the gate, pulled something to unlatch it, then swung it open a crack. It squealed, possibly alerting any confederates that he had arrived. He stood aside and gestured for Zoë to go first. She just stared at him, so he shrugged and did the honors.

The gate opened onto an even shabbier-looking street lit by Harlow's flashlight. Brick buildings gave way to teetering, derelict tenements made of wood and plaster. This older part of the city was deserted but for squatters who didn't mind the missing roofs and windows, the lack of power and running water, and the profusion of vermin. The street was empty. Even squatters were out celebrating the glorious anniversary.

Zoë closed the gate and followed Harlow across the road and up a creaking stoop to a scarred door whose knob and lock had been broken off. As he shoved it open and crossed the threshold, Zoë peered past him. His flashlight revealed a floor of planks and walls garlanded with cobwebs. There were footprints in the dust, lots of them, overlapping. Holes had been opened in the interior walls to access ducts and electric wiring which had then been looted. There were no furnishings. No signs of a struggle. No Mal. No evidence that he'd been there, no hint where he'd gone.

Disappointing, to say the least. Unnerving, to say something else.

"Nobody's home, looks like," Harlow said, sweeping the flashlight beam around the room.

He couldn't see it, but she was giving him the stink eye. This whole thing felt wrong.

"When you got paid, was my friend here?"

"Nope. Just the scarface guy."

"And how long did you stay?"

"Long enough to get the second half of my fee. No longer. Why hang around? Might have been more work waiting for me at Taggart's."

Zoë went to the door at the opposite end of the room and opened it, then shoved Harlow through. They stepped out onto a small wooden porch whose railings had rotted away. An empty field spread out in front of them, a square of flat, featureless dirt lit by the burnt-umber glow of the night sky. Beyond, at the edge of the flashlight's range, were more skeletal tenements. Firecrackers *rat-a-tat-tatted* in the distance.

She descended the shaky back staircase with him in tow. Harlow swept the flashlight beam in front of her. That was when she saw the comm link, or rather the wrecked remains of a comm link, lying in the dirt.

"Hold the beam still," she told Harlow.

She walked over to the spot. She couldn't be certain but the comm link sure as hell looked like the one Mal had been carrying. Someone had stamped on it, leaving it in smithereens.

Well, if he wasn't incommunicado before, he certainly is now.

Nearby she spied twin furrows in the soft dirt, roughly shoulder width apart. Furrows made by boot toes. Fresh. Other bootprints accompanied them on either side.

She began to walk alongside the furrows, following their route but keeping a weather eye on Harlow all the while. They traced the perimeter of the yard and led towards a rusted back gate. Past the gate was an alley broad enough to accommodate a land speeder. Here the furrows terminated.

Just then Shepherd Book connected on her comm link.

"Yes?" Zoë said in a low voice.

"Zoë, I'm at Guilder's," said Book. "The man who signed off on our repairs and paid for the shuttle was Mal Reynolds, but he was not the captain."

"I don't understand. Explain."

"He called himself Malcolm Reynolds but it wasn't our Mal. Sandy hair. Scarred face."

Same man Harlow met. Has to be.

This was not looking good. This was looking like a shuttle robbery—and possibly a kidnapping.

The "traitors" graffiti. Referring to Browncoats. Like Mal. And her.

Zoë aimed her Mare's Leg at Harlow and said loudly, "Don't leave," just to remind him, in case he got it into his head to try sneaking off.

"Sure thing, Hopalong."

Lowering her voice again, she said to Book, "Did the clerk tell you anything else? Was anyone with this guy?"

"Hold on," Book said. "Let me put him on."

"Hello?" It was a young-sounding man, voice quavering with uncertainty. "Um, we don't know how this happened. We asked for identification and the fella had it. It said 'Malcolm Reynolds' and there was a picture of the man who took possession of the shuttle. It's not the same man as the Shepherd is showing me now."

A fake ID, doctored especially for this occasion. So this whole thing had been planned. "Were there other people with him?"

"No, ma'am. Least, not as I saw. That ain't to say they weren't waiting outside. Of course, Guilder's can't be held liable if—"

"Did this Malcolm Reynolds file a flight plan?"

"No, but it ain't compulsory for spacecraft of a shuttle's tonnage, only for those that are category five weight-class or above. Now about our loaner—"

"We're keeping it as collateral until this is straightened out," Zoë said. "Book, can you handle that?"

"Oh, yes." The confidence in the Shepherd's voice gave her a little boost. Everything in her was shouting at her to find the captain immediately. Trouble was, she didn't know how.

"Let's talk later."

"I'll keep you posted," Book assured her.

She broke off the connection and turned to Harlow. "What else do you know about the man who hired you?"

He calmly shook his head. "What was his name again? Covington? I've told you everything. I swear I have. Would you like to hire me to see if I can trace your friend?" he asked without missing a beat.

"I want you to contact Covington," she told him, but he shook his head.

"He got ahold of me, like I said. I don't know nothing about him. I could put it around that I'm looking for him, see what shakes."

"Do that," she said. "But be discreet. I don't need the entire 'verse hearing about my situation."

"Agreed."

"Give me a way to contact you."

"Such as my wave address? Not a chance. Waves, trails, remember? You need me, try Taggart's. I'm not there, someone'll soon get word to me and I'll come."

"Okay. There'll be coin for you if anything comes of this."

"'Bout gorramn time. I was startin' to think you were taking the 'free' part of freelance much too seriously." Harlow grinned at her and gestured with his head to the Mare's Leg. "We finished?"

"We're finished," she said. "For now."

"Then may I have my iron back?"

She returned his six-gun to him.

"Be seeing you, Hopalong, maybe." He tipped his hat and disappeared off through the back door, back into the house.

Watching him go, Zoë reviewed the situation. It was obvious that the flophouse had been the site of a handover. Covington and accomplices had kidnapped Mal on behalf of a third party and passed him on like so much hundredweight of lumber. A business transaction, only the goods in question were human. This jibed with the possibility of Covington being bondholder to a bondswoman—the kind of guy who regarded people as little more than a commodity to be owned and exchanged.

Given that somebody posing as Malcolm Reynolds had lately retrieved *Serenity*'s shuttle from Guilder's, the odds were good that that was where the real Mal had wound up. The odds were good, too, that wherever the shuttle was now, Mal was on it. And, moreover, that whoever had him bore no great fondness for those who'd fought on the Independent side.

Zoë crossed the yard and headed back through the building, still favoring her bad leg.

Out front, she spotted Harlow. His flashlight beam was flickering ahead of him.

She had planned on following him at a distance anyway, simply so that she wouldn't get lost trying to find her way back to the comparatively more civilized parts of town. But she was curious to know where he was going now. It was possible he had been bluffing about Covington and knew the man more closely than he was letting on.

While Zoë kept to the shadows, guarded and cautious, Harlow ambled along as if he didn't have a care in world. She kept the Mare's Leg at the ready. This could be a trap set for her, after all. Maybe they'd taken the captain first, with the plan to lure her into their clutches next.

I want this to be a big misunderstanding. I want Mal to mosey up this very street right now, she thought.

Harlow took a different route from last time but ended up where they'd started, at Taggart's. As he entered through the double doors, Zoë holstered her gun and took up a position across the street, where she could watch the comings and goings of the bar's clientele without being seen.

While she waited, she connected with the ship.

"Hey, babe," Wash said. "How's it hanging?"

"Crooked," she replied. "This whole situation stinks, and the more I look into it, the stinkier it's getting. How are things at your end?"

"Been in touch with Book. He told me about the shuttle and asked me to find out from the port authorities about all recent shuttle takeoffs, but I haven't gotten anywhere with that. Shuttles aren't high on their list of priorities, being personnel-only with limited range, and they've got much bigger beasts to focus on, and lots of them, too. We could call the police, of course, but I don't think that's particularly wise, on account of the whole hate-hate relationship we have with law enforcement."

"You're right. I learned a little more about Hunter Covington, by the way, but not a lot. He has a woman." Zoë relayed the description Harlow had given. "Sounds like she's not a willing partner. Could be a bondswoman maybe. Don't know if it's any use, but I thought it worth a mention."

"Got it," said Wash. "Our resident fruitcake has calmed down a bit. You'll no doubt be glad to hear that, but not as glad as I am. Simon's managed to pry her out of her dining-table fort. Now she's playing her flute in the cargo bay.

Inara's keeping her company. You're missing all the fun."

"Why is River playing the flute?"

"To make Badger's crates go to sleep. They're restless and they need a lullaby, apparently. Tell you this, Zoë, my blood pressure'll be a whole lot lower once we get the band back together and are heading for our drop-off."

"I hear you, dear. And I agree."

"You keep safe, Zoë. Got that? Don't do anything crazy."

"Ditto, Wash."

They cut the link.

Just then, Harlow walked back out through the double doors. Zoë merged deeper into the shadows. He sauntered down the street in the opposite direction that he had taken her.

She swung in after him. As before, he seemed in no rush. His movements weren't cautious—just a guy in a giant, silly hat and an ankle-length yellow coat out for an evening stroll. He entered the main square of shops and administration buildings where Alliance Day crowds packed the sidewalks and spilled into the street, waving flags and beer bottles, and yelling at each other. Harlow made a few turns after he cleared the square. Nothing evasive; he didn't seem to be trying to shake pursuit. When he reached a warren of small, single-story buildings, he ducked down the walkway that ran between them. He stepped up to an innocuous-looking front door, opened it, and entered.

The glass in the building's peeling windows was painted opaque white so Zoë couldn't see inside. She crept up to the door and pressed her ear against it. She could hear nothing.

As she loitered in the lee of the building opposite, she tried to contact Jayne. Nothing, not even static. What if he had been kidnapped too? What if there was some conspiracy afoot to abduct every member of *Serenity*'s crew one by one?

Just bad comms. Has to be.

Then Harlow reappeared.

Zoë kept him in her sights and herself out of his as he continued his rambling, returning the way he'd come. It was difficult to limp stealthily but she did her best. The pain in her leg was more than a mite trialsome but she refused to let it distract her. She'd been injured worse during the war and still managed to acquit herself handily on the battlefield.

Once more she pondered all the bitterness that had been spewed at Taggart's that night, and that was embodied in the DEATH TO ALL TRAITORS graffiti. The history of the Unification War had been rewritten to benefit the victors, Zoë knew that. She wasn't naïve. But the Browncoats hadn't been the aggressors. They had mustered because the Alliance had posed a threat, not because they wanted territory or power or any other thing. They just wanted to be left in peace. Nor had they betrayed anyone, unless standing up for your right to live free was considered betrayal.

Was this what children were taught in school now? That the Browncoats as a group were just one step above Reavers? It sickened her soul.

Pay attention. You're on a mission, Zoë reminded herself.

Gradually, their surroundings became more and more familiar. She started to recognize the storefronts and bars of the neighborhood. And then it dawned on her where Harlow was headed. Under her breath, she unleashed a withering torrent of Mandarin curses.

Wincing from the pain in her leg, she closed distance as, some fifty feet ahead, Harlow calmly approached the headquarters of a certain not altogether reputable individual, who went by the name of Badger.

8

Allister seemed to be recovering some of his wits as he and Jayne walked to his apartment. To Jayne it was obvious the kid had never been in a fight before. It wasn't just that Allister hadn't managed to land a decent blow on his opponents. He had been shocked by the violence itself, as though he just hadn't been expecting it and didn't know how to cope with it. That, as much as the blows he'd received, was what had left him stunned and shaken, and only now, nigh on a half-hour after the event, was he starting to get over the experience.

Jayne, at Allister's age, had already known his fair share of scraps. But then he'd always been a rough-and-tumble youth who let his fists do most of the talking because his mouth wasn't so good at it.

"Maybe," Jayne said to him, "you can explain to me why someone as young as you was hanging out at a dive like Taggart's."

"Just wanted to celebrate Alliance Day, like everyone

else," Allister said. "Taggart's seemed as good a place as any. You never drank underage?"

At that, Jayne could only shake his head guiltily. "Got me there, kid. But you could've chosen any bar. There's plenty a whole lot nicer'n Taggart's, and plenty where you're less liable to get your head busted."

"Maybe I wanted to be where the action is."

"Or maybe you wanted to be nowhere near home."

Allister looked furtive. "Kinda."

"So's you're less likely to bump into someone who'd recognize you and could rat on you to your mom. She even know you're out?"

The kid shook his head. "She doesn't pay much attention to my comings and goings, on account of how sick she is. I look after her, do my best for her, but I need a life of my own. You understand? I need to get out now and then, have a little fun. Caring for a sick person ain't easy, 'specially one with Foster's Wheeze. Mom's coughin' all the time, sometimes like as though she's going to choke up a lung. I never know from one day to the next how bad she's gonna be, but I do know she's not likely to get better."

Jayne sympathized, perhaps more than Allister realized. His little brother Mattie suffered from an incurable respiratory disorder not unlike Foster's Wheeze: damplung, and it blighted his life and that of their mother too.

Eavesdown's riverside district might once have been pretty—desirable, even—but its heyday was long past. The river itself, which had never been graced with a name, was a slow, turgid waterway clogged with weed, junk and sewage, and the houses which clustered along its banks were low, mean edifices with tumbledown roofs and sagging walls.

Allister led Jayne up a precarious outdoor staircase to a fourth-floor apartment that was not what you might call spacious. Anyone who got it in mind to swing a cat in there could expect a lot of thumping and irate meowing.

On a cot in a corner of the main room lay an emaciated woman whose complexion was the color of cream gone sour. Blood-flecked tissues were scattered around her like gruesome confetti, and dried encrustations scabbed her nostrils and the corners of her mouth. The air smelled of stale sweat, human waste, and, beneath it all, the faint whiff of rotten flesh.

The woman managed, with some considerable effort, to raise herself as Allister and Jayne entered. Her hair hung lank about her face like damp seaweed, while her eyes were sunk so deep in their sockets, they were almost lost, like pebbles embedded in deep hollows. Jayne could tell she had been attractive once, before the sickness had ravaged her. She was still fairly young, although her haggardness made her look about a hundred years old.

"Allister?" she said in a frail voice. "That you?"

"It's me, Mom."

"Your face. Those bruises." Her brow furrowed. "What happened to you? What have you been doing?"

"Nothing, Momma. Just had a little... mishap, is all. Got jumped by a couple guys."

Not far from the truth, Jayne thought.

"They tried to take my money," Allister continued, "only I didn't have none, so that made 'em mad, and... Well, you can see the result. I'm fine," he added. "Really. Just a few lumps and bumps. This man saved me. His name's…"

Allister suddenly looked puzzled.

"Not sure I caught it, as a matter of fact," he said.

"Cobb," Jayne said. "Jayne Cobb. Pleased to meet you, ma'am." He removed his hat. Mama Cobb had raised him to be polite when the circumstances demanded.

Allister's mother eyed him up and down. "That was mighty kind of you, Jayne Cobb. I am much obliged. My name's Barbara, by the way. Barbara—"

Then a coughing fit overtook her. Her body heaved, wracked with spasms. She covered her mouth, but Jayne saw blood and sputum spatter against the palm of her hand.

Allister hurried to her side, handing her a tissue. Then he fetched her a glass of water, which she sipped gratefully.

"I thought I should return Allister home safe and sound," Jayne said. "He told me you might be able to fix him up. And now that I've done that…"

"Won't you stay?" Barbara said. "We've food in the house. Coffee too. Ain't much but we're willing to share, 'specially with someone who's helped us out."

It was tempting. Jayne was hungry, and he was never less than a slave to his appetites. However, there was Mal to think about. He couldn't hang around.

"Thanks, but I got some pressing matters need attendin' to."

"You mean partyin' with all the other fools."

"No. Yes. No." Jayne was not proficient at lying, so he changed the subject. "Fools, you say? I'm guessing you're no fan of Alliance Day, then."

"Ha!" Barbara swung her legs over the side of the cot.

The strain of moving herself even that much showed on her face. "Well, put it like this. There's some as reckon the war was the best thing that could ever have happened to the 'verse, and there's some, like me, as think it was the worst. Not to mention the pain and sufferin' it caused.

"I used to be a nurse. Worked for the military a whiles. The Independents, only I don't make a big noise about that owing to the fact that they were the losin' side and folks round here don't feel too kindly disposed towards them, as a rule. I was stationed at a number of forward operating bases—"

She broke off to cough again. It was painful just to watch her; Jayne could only imagine how painful it was to *be* her, undergoing this torture. He knew that Foster's Wheeze was invariably fatal; but the condition could be managed for years, its worst symptoms reduced almost to zero, if you had access to the right drugs and the wherewithal to pay for them. Barbara had neither, which meant she was sentenced to a purgatory of chest pain, restricted breathing and these brutal coughing fits. The disease would gradually run its course, killing her by degrees, but it might be as much as another three or four years before it finally polished her off.

"They were just tent hospitals," she continued. "Describing them as crude would be paying them a compliment. Sometimes it would come down to medical techniques like out of Earth-That-Was history. You know, sawing off ruined limbs without any anesthetic beyond a shot of bourbon, which we also used as disinfectant. That bad. But we made do, us doctors and nurses. Had to. It was an endless parade of misery, Mr. Cobb. Men, women—kids, even, scarcely older than my Allister—being brought in on stretchers, screaming, riddled with bullet wounds, guts mangled, maybe an arm hanging on by a shred of flesh, some of 'em pleading to be put out of their misery…" She shuddered at the recollection. "Alliance put those Browncoats through the mincing machine and didn't even think twice about it. That's what we were fighting against, that level of slaughter, that level of callousness. Shoulda won, deserved to, but I guess it was not to be."

"Kind of an unpopular opinion to hold," Jayne said, "place like this, on a day like this. I ain't heard nothing but abuse against the Browncoats all evening."

Barbara gave vent to a bitter laugh, which degenerated into yet another fit of coughing.

"Abuse?" she said. "That ain't all. There've been rumors…"

"Mom, I think maybe you've said enough already," said Allister. "You don't need to go bothering Mr. Cobb with any of that other stuff."

Jayne himself didn't much want to be bothered with any of that other stuff either. He was chafing to get going. But the woman was desperately sick. Least he could do was fake interest. "Rumors?" he said.

"You tell him, Allister," Barbara said. "You're the one that overheard it."

"Weren't nothing," Allister said after a moment's hesitation. "Just some guys talking. I was fetching some groceries, you see, and—"

"No, you weren't, Allister," his mother snorted. "Fetching groceries! I know what you were up to. You were picking pockets."

"Was not!" her son protested.

"Don't think I don't know how you help us make ends meet, boy. I see how you come home sometimes and you've got cash in your hand."

"Which I earned, doing odd jobs."

"For who?"

"For people. Just… people."

"Just because I'm sick doesn't mean I'm blind," Barbara said. "You're only telling me that to protect me. That cash is ill-gotten gains. I see it in your face every time, that little furtive look. A mother can tell these things. I don't condone it, but I don't disapprove neither. You're tryin' to do your best, seeing as I can't make a living outta nursing anymore."

"Say," said Jayne to Allister, "those two guys who attacked you at…" He almost said *at Taggart's.* "In the street," he amended. "Had you just tried to rob them?"

Allister looked sheepish.

"I knew it!" Barbara declared. "You weren't mugged at all, Allister. You were pickpocketin' and you got yourself caught."

Allister looked even more sheepish. "Well, this ain't relevant anyways," he said, deflecting. "Jayne wanted to hear about the rumors."

"This conversation is far from over, young man," his mother said. "If you're going to go around committing thievery, at least try not to get hurt doing it. Speaking of which… Mr. Cobb, there's some antiseptic cream over there, and some cotton swabs. While I'm up, I may as well set to fixing Allister's face."

Jayne brought over the materials, and Allister submitted

to his mother's ministrations, which she halted every so often in order to turn aside and cough. Jayne was keener than ever to leave, but he felt he had to stay at least until Allister told him what the rumors about Browncoats were. Politeness again, coupled with a glimmer of curiosity. Could it be the Independents weren't as noble-hearted and clean-handed as some folk, namely Mal and Zoë, liked to paint them? That'd be ammunition for Jayne, next time those two got on their high horses about the war.

What Allister said, however, was nothing like what Jayne had been anticipating.

"So this man I was shadowing…"

"With a mind to liftin' his wallet, no doubt," Barbara interjected.

"Shadowing," Allister continued, still vainly maintaining the pretense that he was as pure as the driven snow. "This was about a week ago. He met up with another man in the street, and they talked awhile and I just kinda hung back, biding my time. Wasn't eavesdropping, exactly, but I couldn't help hearing what they were saying. Conversation turned to Alliance Day, 'cause it was coming up, and the first man said something about how the Browncoats won't be celebrating, and the second man laughed and said the Browncoats have even less reason to celebrate this year because it seems there's a whole bunch of people on Persephone who think they're nothing better than war criminals and who are going around bringing them to justice. Kind of like a vigilante movement, or even a lynch mob. That's why you need to be extra careful these days what you say about the war, Mom, and what you did in it."

"When you're as sick as I am," Barbara said, "kinda doesn't matter so much what you say or don't say."

"Matters to me," said her son. "At any rate, those two guys seemed to think it wasn't just talk. Those vigilantes were real. Both of them thought it was pretty funny, too. Browncoats getting attacked for being Browncoats. Like it was no more'n they deserved."

"They say anything else?" said Jayne.

Allister shrugged. "That's as much of it as I recall. Conversation moved on to other things."

"Might be gossip," Jayne opined. "Might just be the one guy spinning the other a line of bullcrap."

"It wouldn't surprise me, though, if there are Persephonians out there who've got a mad-on for former Browncoats," said Barbara. "In case you haven't noticed, Mr. Cobb, the majority of folks on this planet are misguided souls who think the Alliance winning was a godsend. They're happy to grovel to the victors, and I guess you could say targetin' the losers for punishment is a form of groveling. Maybe the ultimate in groveling."

"Huh." Jayne processed what he'd just learned in the manner in which he always processed things, which is to say slowly and tentatively, like someone picking their way barefoot over wet, slippery rocks. There was, he reckoned, the possibility of a connection between Mal's mysterious disappearance and the existence of a group of anti-Browncoat vigilantes. Equally, there might easily be another explanation for where Mal had gotten to, and the vigilante rumors were just that, rumors. Second-hand rumors, indeed, given they were reaching him via someone else, namely Allister.

He shifted his feet. It was way past time he made tracks. "Well, been nice meetin' you an' all," he said, "but…"

"But you should be going," said Barbara.

"Yeah. I really do have business to attend to."

"Thank you again, Mr. Cobb, for lookin' after Allister and bringin' him back."

"Please," Jayne said, "call me Jayne."

"I think, Jayne, that you may be a good man," Barbara said. "I think, deep down, you have compassion. That's a rare thing."

"I think you may be confusin' me with someone else," Jayne replied gruffly, but as he left the apartment there was a quiet and rather sad smile on his lips, nestled amid the rough bristles of his goatee.

He clicked his comm link.

"Zoë?"

No reply.

He clapped the device against his palm, hoping he might joggle it back into life. Then he tried calling Zoë again, with the same lack of result.

Damn contraptions. What good was technology if it didn't work like it was supposed to?

Swiveling around to get his bearings, Jayne set off towards the dock where *Serenity* was berthed.

9

Cold. Cold, cold ground. And hard.

Mal's hips, shoulders, knees, and head bounced as tremendous explosions roared, shaking the earth under him. Out in the open, where there was no cover within reach, the falling firebombs burst in successive waves. They gouged out massive pits, sending tons of rock and debris into the air. The pressure of the detonations crushed the air from his chest. He wanted to run, but his legs would not support him, and there was nowhere to go anyway. Death fell randomly from the skies, and the flashes of the explosions flickered orange against the overhanging clouds.

Serenity Valley. Where the Browncoats lost sixteen brigades and twenty air-tank squads, near as. Where the two thousand warriors Mal was leading got whittled down to a hundred and fifty. Where the 57th Overlanders, his platoon, was all but wiped out. Where High Command obliged the troops on the ground to surrender when, given air support at the crucial time, they could maybe have won.

In the deepest recesses of his brain, Mal knew he was reliving a past moment. But it sure as hell felt real. Vividly, viscerally so, like he was experiencing it for the first time. Instant obliteration lay on all sides. The terror and paralysis he felt was genuine. As falling rocks pelted him, he curled into a fetal position with hands covering the back of his head.

Then, in the midst of the hellish bombardment, the flying dirt and the dark smoke, a white chicken appeared out of nowhere. Oblivious to the danger, it strutted up close to his face and, cocking its head to one side, said, "Evenin'."

At that shocking moment Mal concluded he had to be dreaming. In his experience, no chicken had a voice that deep. But he was sure someone had spoken because now that he was wide awake, heart hammering up under his chin, the sound of it was still ringing in his ears.

He couldn't see anything. Everything was so inky black, it made Mal wonder if he had somehow, someway, suddenly been struck blind. He couldn't tell if his eyes were open, nor move his hands to find out one way or another.

Then, as his brain stopped tumbling like a juggling ball inside his skull, the scratchiness at his ears and the end of his nose put the lie to that assumption. Well, damn it, there was a bag over his head. From the coarse feel of it, a burlap bag. No mistaking one thing: it smelled like… chickenfeed. He was lying on his side on a grated or ribbed surface, perhaps a metal deck.

Explosions weren't squashing his chest; it was the shifting g-force mashing him down. And the explosions weren't explosions at all, but the sustained din of rocket exhaust. For sure, he was on some kind of ship, maybe even his own boat, lying on the floor with his hands cinched up behind his back and his ankles tied too.

That would likely mean I'm in trouble.

Last thing he remembered, and that only foggily, was fighting Hunter Covington and his three goons outside Taggart's. And holding his own until Covington zapped him with some kind of knockout gas from his cobra-head cane—a dirty trick if ever there was one. Whatever happened to a good old-fashioned whack on the noggin with a gun butt?

His Liberty Hammer was gone, of course. He couldn't feel its familiar weight on his hip. Confiscated, no doubt. A sensible precaution on his captors' part. Not that he could have reached the weapon anyway, with his hands fastened as they were. He tested the bonds, feeling the roughness of rope around his wrists. Whoever had done the tying had done it right. The knots were so tight, his fingers were numb. Same went for the ropes around his ankles.

Over the sound of the engines, Mal heard the shuffle of boots on the metal deck.

"Evenin' to you, too," he said affably to whoever the heck it was had spoken to him a moment ago, although it most definitely was not poultry. "Could you please remind me what I did to piss someone off so much?"

The burlap sack was yanked off his head, and a gust of sour whiskey breath hit him square in the face. He blinked from the floor, staring up into a bright light, in the middle of which was the silhouette of a man's head with a feathery halo of sandy-colored hair. Mal squinted harder, trying to make out the man's features, but the contrast between the head and the bright light was too extreme.

"Evenin'," the man said again.

"Is it?" Mal said. "Hard to tell the time when you've got a sack over your head. Just sayin'."

The man bent over him. When he moved his face closer, the details of it became clearer. A set of heavy jowls formed the foundation for a block-shaped head. He wasn't Covington, or for that matter one of Covington's trio of thugs. Mal had never seen him before.

But he had seen the interior of this vessel before. It was *Serenity*'s shuttle, the one that had been sent to Guilder's Shipwright for repairs and that he, Jayne, and Zoë had been planning to pick up after the meet at Taggart's.

Gorramn. Don't this beat all.

"We going somewhere?" he inquired cheerily, like he was on some kind of excursion into the countryside, with maybe a picnic thrown in. "In my shuttle?" he added.

"We sure as hell are," the sandy-haired man said, squatting on his haunches, hairy hands dangling between his legs like a baboon.

Mal's vision finally adjusted to the light and he saw that his captor had bloodshot brown eyes. His face was scarred, with what looked like knife cuts or blast wounds on the right side from jawline to temple, although his right ear below the patchy, straw-like hair was still pretty much intact. He had perhaps half the regularly mandated quantity of teeth, and those he possessed were browned, thin as rice, and only just clinging on to their foundations in his gums. The well-worn gun belt around his waist held two pistols, and they were as roughened and ugly as his mug. A third gun—Mal's own Liberty Hammer, in a lot better condition than the others—protruded from the belt.

"Nice piece," Mal said, nodding to it. "I've got one just the same, only I appear to have mislaid it."

Scarface smirked. "I agree, it's a nice gun. Have me a mind to keep it, once all this is over."

"'All this?' Care to enlighten me about that?"

"You'll find out soon enough."

"Well then, I don't suppose you'd mind answering my earlier question. Where we headed? Not Pelorum, by any chance? Ain't so far from here, and I hear it's lovely whatever the season but especially at this time of year. Sun, sea, gambling, and so many folks lookin' for a casual hook-up, I reckon even someone as deficient in the looks department as you could get laid."

Anger flickered like lightning across Scarface's distorted features. "We're deliverin' you to justice," he grated.

That sounded ominous.

Mal tried to sit up, and failed. The man's upper lip curled in amusement as he savored the struggle and defeat.

"Hmm. Justice," Mal repeated. "Can you be a little more specific? I like justice, big fan, but I hadn't planned on any side trips today. Did you take back the loaner shuttle? And do you know Hunter Covington?"

"He was right about you. You *are* stupid," Scarface said.

"Covington insulted me? I'm crushed. I thought we were pals."

"No, not him. Someone else."

"Who?"

"You'll find out soon enough."

Mal was putting up a confident front, but he was right

uneasy. It was now pretty obvious to him that Covington had never planned for him to deliver anything to anybody. That talk of a lump of metallic ore and somebody called Professor Yakima Barnes had been just so much hogwash. Covington had lured Mal out of Taggart's for the sole purpose of shanghaiing him. And like a big dumbass, Mal had fallen for it.

"Maybe," he said, "if you could explain to me what your beef is, I'm sure I could clear things up."

"And maybe you could just shut up, traitor," Scarface snapped.

"Traitor?" Mal wrinkled his forehead. "Who's calling me that?"

"Donovan Philips," Scarface said, slapping his chest. "That's who's calling you a traitor."

"Glad to make your acquaintance, Donovan Philips."

"And I ain't alone in holdin' that opinion of you," Philips spat. "There's a whole passel of us that think scum like you are the lowest form of life and should be exterminated."

"Call me sensitive, but I'm picking up a distinctly hostile vibe here, Donnie ol' pal. I'm reckonin' you've got me confused with somebody else. There another Malcolm Reynolds in your address book? This could turn out to be one of those embarrassing mix-ups we all stand around and laugh about it afterwards over a beer or two."

"No misunderstanding," said Philips. "We got the right man."

"But I ain't no traitor. Never have been. A traitor to who? Or is it 'to whom?' Never could get that one straight."

"You're being called to account. And you'll pay for what you done."

"Been a lot of places, conducted a lot of business," Mal said. "Fairly or not, I suppose I riled some of the folks I dealt with. They were expectin' more, got less. But as to treason, maybe you could do me the kindness of dabbing a bit more paint on that canvas?"

"You ain't the first and you won't be the last to face the music for that particular crime."

"Now that's starting to sound a touch serious."

"You'd be right in thinking that and wise not to be so flippant about it."

Mal was still no nearer an understanding of what the *gū yáng zhōng de gū yáng* this was all about. What was clear was that there didn't seem to be any room for negotiation with his captor. Donovan Philips hadn't subtly floated the possibility of ransom, to be paid cash or barter. It was very much like the sentence of death had already been read and all that was left was the manner of execution.

Mal knew better than to show fear, even when helpless, with no cavalry in sight. "Where might this account-calling be located?" he said. "Can you at least tell me that? Is it far from Persephone? Am I going to be able to take my shuttle back? As I think I might have mentioned, I'm in the middle of a few important things—"

"Shut up."

"No, listen. I really think there's been a case of mistaken ident—"

"I said *shut up*!" Philips balanced himself on one hand and punched Mal square in the face with the other.

A searing flash of light filled Mal's skull, blinding him as completely as the chickenfeed sack so recently had. In a world of hurt, with the taste of blood in his mouth, his head dropped, slamming hard on the metal.

Back to the black, the drifting black, tumbling, tumbling, tumbling.

Explosions.

10

Zoë gave her comm link one last, futile try, then hustled over to Badger's hideout, into which Harlow had disappeared not half a minute earlier.

At the door, her way was blocked by a big man whose bloated belly strained against his sleeveless gray T-shirt. Blurred brown tattoos of Chinese characters ran up and down both arms from wrist to shoulder. He held up one hand in front of her face, and the other dropped to the grip of the machine pistol slung over his shoulder. Which reminded Zoë that even if Badger was smarmy and low-class, he and his minions were still capable of causing a great deal of trouble for them.

She said to the guard, "I'm here to see Badger. Tell him it's Zoë Washburne and that it's urgent."

"You want in, give me your weapons," he growled. "All of 'em."

"First go tell him I'm here," she said. She knew this was Badger's standard procedure for a private interview. And his excess of caution, which bordered on paranoia, was one of the reasons he was still sucking air. Zoë didn't like the idea of being outgunned when everything seemed to be going to hell, but under the circumstances she had no choice. She noted to herself that Harlow hadn't been forced to disarm when he'd gone in. She knew he was carrying that six-gun inside his duster. The lack of even a pat-down to check for weapons indicated that he was either a friend or a lackey of Badger's. Her money was on lackey.

The guard smirked and waved a finger under her nose. "No, first you give me your weapons."

With a shrug and a certain amount of chagrin, Zoë handed over her Mare's Leg. Then she unsheathed the eight-inch hunting knife that balanced out her holster rig.

The guard gathered the weapons like a haul from under the Christmas tree.

"Borosky!" he called through the door over his shoulder.

The door opened a crack and a second man stuck out his head. His doughy, pale face was blotched with red. To Zoë, it looked like an allergic reaction, maybe mild radiation poisoning.

"Tell Badger that Zoë… Washbasin, is it?"

"Washburne."

"Zoë Washburne is here to see him."

"And it's urgent," Zoë reminded him.

"And it's urgent," the guard relayed in a sarcastic drawl.

Borosky nodded and closed the door. Presently he returned, signaling for Zoë to follow him.

They strode through a dingy, poorly lit foyer cluttered by packing crates and metal drums. Borosky pushed open the Moroccan print curtains that passed for office doors. Badger's office was gritty, with obnoxious royal-blue walls, and decorated with rug-market odds and ends. The man himself sat in a shabby, overstuffed brown leather office chair, behind a desk covered in miscellaneous papers, soiled plates, unidentifiable gizmos, and an overloaded wire mesh in-and-out box. Badger looked her up and down, dark eyes glittering.

"Wotcher, Miss Washburne," he said.

"Mrs.," said Zoë crisply.

"Yep, sorry. *Mrs*. Washburne. It's just, you never seem like a married woman."

"And how should a married woman seem?"

"I dunno. A bit more… wifely?"

"Well, what a pity I don't live up to that high standard."

Badger shrugged, as if in agreement. "Can't 'elp notice you're looking a little lame in the leg there. Tsk, tsk. 'Urt ourselves, 'ave we?" Before she could answer, he picked up an apple and crunched into it appreciatively. "What I find most interesting about you and your mates," he went on, "is how predictable you are. Don't tell me. Let me guess. Dare I say, bar fight?"

Zoë canted her head to the side, the most reluctant of admissions that he was correct.

"And you've come to see me why?"

"First of all, where's Harlow?" she asked, scanning the room.

"You got business with 'im?" he asked, very interested. "Of what sort, may I ask?"

"That's none of your concern," she said. "He walked in here, but he didn't walk back out." She lifted her chin and raised her voice. "Harlow, if you're in the building—"

"'E's not," Badger said. "And shouting isn't going to bring the bloke back. 'E left by that door." He gestured with his head towards the back of the room. "You might be able to catch up with 'im if you break into a run." His wry smile told her that he didn't think that was too likely.

The two of them regarded each other, a momentary standoff. Badger could be lying about Harlow being gone, Zoë thought, but what did he have to gain from that? A more important question was, since Harlow and Badger seemed to be connected, could Badger be behind Mal's disappearance? Was he the one who had orchestrated the whole scheme? He could have hired Covington to abduct Mal, and Harlow had just now reported back to say "mission accomplished."

On its face that scenario seemed unlikely. Taking Mal out of the equation would impede delivery of the important cargo, and possibly stop the transfer of related bags of coin into Badger's coffers. Still, Zoë knew the shabby criminal thought himself capable of playing more than one level of simultaneous chess—despite all evidence to the contrary. Was that what he was doing?

"Harlow wasn't here long," Zoë observed, breaking the brief interlude of silence between them. "Couldn't have been but two minutes since he came in."

"I work fast," Badger said. "Time is money."

"What was he here for?"

"Well now, that's interesting. Dunno if it's coincidence or not, but 'e 'ad some info for me. About a certain woman who was looking for a certain missing friend who may or may not've been nabbed by someone—Hunter Covington, no less."

"You know Covington?"

"Can't work in Eavesdown and not know Hunter Covington."

"Harlow said he didn't."

"Harlow's a daft wanker. Anyway, apparently my name came up in the conversation, and Harlow thought I oughter know. Thought I might slip him a coin or two in return for telling me. You can imagine my views on that."

"Less than positive, I'd have said."

"Too right! Too bloody right! Sent 'im packing, with a flea in 'is ear. Not sure why anyone would reckon I care about being talked about behind my back. I mean, I'm a local celebrity. Goes with the territory. But that's the trouble with geezers like Harlow—bottom-feeding grifters who've somehow got it into their heads they're entrepreneurs. If there's even a chance they can turn a profit from something…"

Badger's expression, sly by default, turned slyer still.

"Funnily enough, it just so happens the woman he spoke about sounded an awful lot like you, Mrs. Washburne. 'Balls of brass,' he said, 'with a side order of gorgeous.' Which leads me to wonder whether I might be well acquainted with your friend what's gone missing."

Zoë decided she had no option but to come clean. There was a chance, however remote, that telling Badger the truth might help her. It might at least prompt Badger into initiating a search for Mal, because Badger had a dog in this fight. Without Mal, his cargo might not make it to its destination.

"I'm looking for Mal Reynolds," she said.

"Oh-ho!" Badger chortled, clapping his palms together.

He leaned back in his chair, planted his boot heels on his desk top, and laced his fingers behind his neck. "That's it, is it? Captain Malcolm Reynolds has taken a sudden, unexpected leave of absence. What a surprising development."

"I take it you didn't have anything to do with it."

"I'm shocked!" Badger declared, hand on heart. "Truly, deeply shocked. And not a little offended. Answer me this, Mrs. Washburne: Why the bleeding 'eck would I kidnap him? Captain who's transporting goods for me? That would run counter to my own immediate interests, wouldn't it? My suggestion is, since it's Alliance Day, you should inquire at the local lockup. Maybe Reynolds got loaded and a bit lairy. Wouldn't put it past 'im. The authorities don't hold much with drunk-and-disorderlies around here. They expect everyone to comport themselves in a genteel fashion, like what I do. Mind you, if Reynolds had got himself thrown in the detox tank, he'd surely have used his right to a single wave and contacted you or your ship. Assuming, of course, that the arresting officers had granted him that privilege on what would have to be one of their busiest nights of the year."

"Mal wasn't drunk this evening and never got the chance to be disorderly," Zoë said. "Something else has happened."

Badger took another big bite of apple and, eyes narrowed, methodically crushed it to mush between his back teeth. "Well now, ain't this a pretty predicament? Especially with my crates of HTX-20 in your hold."

"We're taking care of them."

"Time is of the essence," he said. "The very essential essence." He fished an apple seed out of his mouth. "In fact, all things considered, I find it a touch perturbing that you're still planetside."

"We'll be leaving shortly," Zoë bit off.

"That's good. And I'm sure once Captain Reynolds wakes up from his drunken stupor he'll give you a wave to tell you everything's hunky-dory."

She maintained her silence.

"Tick-tock-tick-tock," Badger sang out. "Clock's running."

"We can't lift off until Mal's aboard to give the signal," Zoë said resolutely. "If that's a problem for you, you can find someone else to transport the goods."

Badger's eyebrows shot up. "Surely you wouldn't renege on our deal. I'd hate for a lapse like that to become public knowledge. Remember what happened to Reynolds and your husband when you disappointed Adelai Niska."

"Remember what happened to Adelai Niska's henchmen," Zoë shot back.

"Oh, dear lady, I'm no one's henchman," Badger said. "I'm the big cheese. The kingpin. A force in the community. If I spread word that you lot can't be trusted—"

"I'm unloading the crates," she declared. "You can find someone else to transport your cargo."

Badger frowned. "It's too late for that. The HTX-20 is already breaking down. It's got a limited shelf life. And we have an agreement," he protested.

Just then Borosky gestured to his boss. He might have been the forklift operator who'd loaded the crates, Zoe thought, but Badger's men tended to look alike—solidly muscled and unkempt. The man was holding out a comm tablet.

Badger said, "Excuse me, missus. One moment." He hurried over to the man and took the tablet, his lips moving as he scrolled with a fingertip. He said something under his breath to Borosky and they both looked at her. Badger walked back to her with the tablet, which he waved in the air like a trophy.

"Well, seems you got no choice but to keep my goods in your hold and get the ruddy 'ell out of here." He tapped the tablet with his finger. "This is a bulletin, just got sent out all across the Cortex. Feds are hot on your tail. Seems you people have something they want. What is that, I wonder? What you got on board they're so flaming interested in?"

Zoë scanned the bulletin, suppressing a sigh of exasperation.

What are the Alliance so interested in? Only River and Simon Tam. Has to be.

The Alliance was desperate to get its hands on the Tams, especially River, whom it seemed to consider its property. That detail was absent from the wave, and just as well, or Badger would even now be trying to detain Zoë, rather than urging her to leave, so that he could garner a portion of the bounty on the Tams' heads.

If, however, another bulletin came through that mentioned the Tams explicitly or, even worse, if the Alliance caught up to *Serenity*, the siblings would be bound by law and River would be sent back to the place that her big brother had sacrificed everything to get her out of.

Qīng wā cāo de liú máng, Zoë thought. Badger was right. Mal or no Mal, she had to get *Serenity* off this world. ASAP.

"Well?" Badger prompted.

"Can't say," Zoë replied. "Could be any number of reasons. You know us. We sail close to the wind."

"Not too close, I hope. For my sake."

"Don't worry, we're going to finish the job," she told him.

He grinned at her. "You mean you'll skedaddle."

She gave Badger a hard look. "And let me get something straight. If you are entertaining any notions of double-crossing us, sending the Alliance our way—"

"Whoa, whoa, whoa." Badger held up his hands. "I'm crushed you think so little of me. I don't peach on my partners. I've got a reputation to protect. I've got roots in the alternative income community. I *live* 'ere."

"Still, if Alliance troops come, and I find out you sent them," she persisted, "you won't be living anywhere."

He chuckled. "Such loyalty to your captain. What do you see in that cranky old sergeant that makes you do-or-die for him? It can't be that he pays you well. As near as I can tell, he 'ardly ever pays you."

"I don't think you'd understand even if I had the time to explain it to you." Zoë said. "But please, if you do get any information about Mal…"

"No worries there, darlin'. I'll let you know, of course. And for a fair market price."

Disgusted, Zoë spun on her heel and left his den. Overhead, as she recovered her weapons from the tattooed sentry, the bunting and pennants of Alliance Day flapped as if waving her on: *Hurry, hurry.*

Limping away down the street, she contacted *Serenity*.

"Did you find him?" Wash asked her, first thing.

"No, I didn't find him," Zoë said in a rush. "Now listen up, lover. According to Badger, the Alliance is closing in on us."

"When are they ever not?"

"But I saw a bulletin, and this time it sounds like they mean business. I need a ride back to the ship, pronto. I'm moving slowly."

"My desert flower, are you hurt?"

"Just a bit banged up." It bugged her to confess it.

"I'm on my way in the Mule to get you myself," he said.

"No. You need to be ready to lift off in case the Alliance shows up."

"Zoë—"

"Is Book back?"

"Just got in."

"Send him to fetch me. If we get in a scrape at this end, he'll be able to help." More than once, Alliance military personnel had shown deference to Shepherd Book. No one aboard the ship knew why, and Book hadn't seen fit to elaborate, but she knew he would be her best bet.

"What if the feds board us before you two get back?" Wash said. "The preacher might do more good here. We can't risk Kaylee, either. Someone's got to hold *Serenity*'s engine together during the pre-flight warm-up. Inara's free. Well, not free, but you know what I mean."

"She's not regular crew."

"But she is a Registered Companion. She did great on Higgins' Moon. People always bow and scrape and do whatever she wants."

"I'm here," Inara said through the comm link. "Of course I'll come, Zoë."

"Thank you, Inara. I'll find Jayne, if I can, and we'll meet you by the store where the captain bought Kaylee her dress."

"All right," Inara said.

"Wash, after Inara leaves, you see them Alliance bastards coming for the ship, don't wait for control-tower clearance. Forget the gorramn blast zone safety recs. You light her up. Hear me?"

"Roger, baby," Wash said. "We'll be out of here like a cat with a firework tied to its tail. Not that I'd know what that's like, because I never tied a firework to a cat's tail as a kid, and anyone who says I did is a liar."

11

For several minutes Wash fidgeted with his collection of model dinosaurs, too distracted to stage exciting claw and fang fights. It was hard to keep a lid on his freak-out. Once upon a time at Li Shen's Space Bazaar he had cracked open a fortune cookie that read, "You will live in interesting times." Enough with the interesting. Bring on the boredom.

"They back yet?" Kaylee asked, poking her head through the hatchway. She was wearing overalls decorated with happy teddy bear patches and a pink T-shirt splotched with engine grease.

"No," Wash told her, depositing a T-Rex into the pocket of his vintage Hawaiian shirt for safekeeping.

"*Niú fèn*. And what's this I'm hearing about the Alliance maybe boarding us? Inara mentioned it as she was getting into the Flying Mule just now. She said there wasn't time to explain and I should ask you."

Wash pulled up the latest Cortex-wide Alliance bulletin onscreen, which was undoubtedly the one Zoë had been referring to. It advised security personnel to be on the lookout for a Firefly-class transport suspected of an illegal smuggling operation.

"Has to be us," he said.

"And has to be about River," said Kaylee. "How come it doesn't mention her by name, though? Or Simon?"

"Mal has a theory about Alliance bureaucracy. He reckons different departments create bulletins like this and fling them out at random like a drunk guy playing darts— one in the bullseye, one in the back of Joe Bob's head. Some of the agencies know about the existence of the Tams and some don't, and they don't always talk to each other, at least not in the same language. Not that I much care. To a snail, a duck is a vengeful god."

"What?"

"It's a saying."

"A saying said by who?"

"By, uh, me?" said Wash. "More and more, though, this situation with River and Simon is giving me the heebie-jeebies. It's like we're playing roulette every day, and every day there's another zero on the wheel. There are times when you have to ask yourself if we mightn't be better off ditching River—"

"Oh! Hey, sweetie," Kaylee said, pointedly cutting Wash off.

Wash looked over to see River standing on the threshold of the bridge. Her eyes were enormous and streaked with tears. She was shivering as if she were freezing. Simon rushed up behind her, his gaze connecting with Wash's.

"Let's get you to your bunk, River," Simon said, his

cheeks reddening with embarrassment or consternation, or some of both.

River held out her hands and started waving them around as if brushing away spider webs. "They're coming. They're coming…"

Wash recoiled at the sight of the waving hands. *Wǒ de tiān a*, talk about the heebie-jeebies. The crew had already had a run-in with two men wearing powder-blue gloves who were after River. Alliance officers who had gotten in the gloved men's way had wound up dead, blood gushing from all their orifices.

"River, do you think they're after us?" he asked carefully. "The men with the hands of blue?" River seemed to have a way of sensing things. Or maybe it was simply that because she rambled all over the place, on occasion she made sense. It was so hard to tell.

She looked at Wash, then saluted. "Avast ye, matey. Hit the turbos and set sail for the horizon."

"Yeah. Sure. I'll do that." He buzzed Zoë. "Honey?"

"I haven't located Jayne," Zoë reported. "But… Wait a moment. That's Inara in the Mule. She's just spotted me. Is something wrong, Wash?"

"River's singing about the blue hands," he said.

By way of replying, Zoë let loose a long and complicated curse.

Wash said, "Please hurry."

12

Inara hard-banked the bulldozer-yellow MF-813 Mule to avoid a mob of Alliance Day revelers who had staggered into the middle of the street. Dressed in a shimmering gown and her jeweled golden snood, she allowed everyone to see that a Companion moved among them. An armed Companion; in the folds of her gown, a gray buckskin shoulder holster cradled her Ruger Mark II, .22 caliber pistol, with flash suppressor. The hovercraft had no windscreen or overhead canopy for the pilot, just low tubular railings along the sides. Although it could carry four passengers—two seated, two standing—its primary function was cargo transport.

The street was packed with Alliance Day partygoers on their annual celebratory whoop-de-doop. With no way to avoid them, Inara advanced the hovercraft at a crawl. The crowd cheered and bowed, drunk yet impressed. Rug and jewelry stands lined both sides of the avenue. Hookah bars, outdoor grills, noodle shops spewed forth a riot of smoky and spicy aromas.

At the designated rendezvous point, she spied Zoë, who stepped out from the shadows, pushed through the crowd, and approached the Mule as it decelerated and touched down. To Inara she looked tired and frazzled. She grimaced in pain as she climbed on board and then dropped heavily into one of the passenger seats.

"Are you badly hurt?" Inara asked with concern.

"I'm fine," Zoë said.

"Where's Jayne?"

"Don't know. We split up."

"Hey!" a deep voice bellowed from close by.

The sound of heavy footfalls followed. On instinct, Zoë reached for her Mare's Leg, relaxing as she saw Jayne jogging over towards the Mule.

"Good thing I ran into you guys," he said. "I was gettin' tired of walking." He clambered aboard.

There was no room to turn the Mule around, what with all the pedestrians and the shopping stalls spilling over the curbs. Reversing course was out of the question because of the traffic that had backed up behind them. Inara steered the Mule forward and at the first available side street turned right, wending her way back to the docks by a circuitous route.

As they floated above the potholed roadway, Zoë's face took on a placid, masklike expression. Outwardly, she looked completely calm, but attuned to people's moods as Inara was from her years of Companion training, she knew that Zoë often affected this expression when the *gŏu shĭ* was flying in the direction of the fan and the ship and crew were in real trouble. She bit back her questions about what had happened, and where Mal was. She herself knew a thing or two about self-control, and about patience.

At the docks, Inara drove across the airfield along designated pathways fringed by painted hazard stripes. On all sides, lit by kliegs on widely spaced stanchions, rows of parked spacecraft sat. Clusters of transporters loaded and offloaded their cargos. Here and there was a crater in the ground where a vessel had crashed. The Mule passed a line of passengers in shiny silk print robes with belongings in hand and balanced on top of their heads, queueing for an incoming passenger liner. The docks never slept.

When they reached *Serenity*, Inara drove up the illuminated gangplank and into the hold. She parked gingerly, but with precision, beside the crates of HTX-20. Simon and Shepherd Book came down the stairway as she killed the engine. Jayne vaulted out of the Mule. With difficulty, Zoë climbed to the deck and took a hesitant, limping step. She stiffened and froze, in obvious pain.

Simon hurried over to her and, bending down on one knee, examined her ankle and shin.

"Mmmf," Zoë said, pulling away from his touch.

"We have to get you to the infirmary, see what's going on with your leg," Simon told her, straightening up and looking her in the eye. "Shepherd, we'll need the gurney and—"

"I can walk there," Zoë insisted. To Book she said, "Any news on the captain?"

Shepherd Book shook his head. "Not yet, I'm afraid. But since there's no Alliance in sight, perhaps we can afford to wait a few more minutes to see if he might arrive before Wash lifts us off."

"We don't have much more than that," Zoë said. "And I don't think he'll be arriving at all."

Briefly she outlined her theory that Mal had been abducted. She mentioned the stolen shuttle and expressed her hope that Mal was aboard it, if not of his own volition.

"Who?" Inara said. Her throat felt tight. "Who would do that?"

"Number of enemies Mal's made in his life, take your pick," said Jayne. "Could be he ain't just been kidnapped; he's dead already. What?" Dagger looks were coming at him from all directions. "I'm only saying what we're all thinking."

"None of us is thinking that, Jayne," said Inara.

"None of you's tryin' to, is what you mean," Jayne said.

"I hate to say it," said Zoë, "but we're going to have to take off without him."

"No!" Inara cried.

"You know it's the only way, Inara. We've got a time-sensitive cargo and we've got the feds snapping at our heels. The captain'd be the first to agree with me. We can't afford to hang around. It'll be all of our necks if we do."

"Yeah," said Jayne. "As a wise man once said, the needs of the many outweigh the needs of the few."

"That kind of logic doesn't apply here," Inara retorted. "It's Mal we're talking about. Our captain. Our friend. Our…"

She tried to think of a word to encapsulate how she personally felt about him. She didn't know if there was one. What was going on between her and Mal was too complicated for a single descriptor. It was a tangled knot of inhibitions and unspoken emotions which they themselves might never get around to unraveling.

"I know," said Zoë. "I've followed that man into hell. More than once. And I'd follow him again, he just gave the word. But this time hell's following us, and he wouldn't want us to get burned any more than we want to."

Inara recoiled at the idea of leaving Mal behind, and moreover of quitting the planet without even knowing where he'd gotten to. It wasn't the first time she had feared that she'd seen the last of him. Mal had come through every scrape, landing on his feet like a cat. But even cats eventually ran out of lives.

Zoë limped over to the shipwide intercom and clicked it on. Only Wash and Kaylee weren't with her in the cargo bay, but she made the announcement as if addressing everyone.

"This is Zoë. I'm the acting captain. Captain Reynolds is… not here, and the Alliance is bearing down on us. We have cargo aboard that can't wait, so we're taking off in two minutes."

Her shoulders slumped. Saying what she'd just said must have taken every ounce of her energy.

Inara offered Zoë an arm to help her up the short flight of stairs to the infirmary, but the acting captain, for all that she moved stiffly and in obvious pain, appeared determined to make the climb under her own steam.

Leaving Zoë in Simon's care, Inara headed for the bridge, accompanied by Book.

"We are one hundred percent hot and ready to trot," Wash said from the command chair, his hands on the yoke. "Time to go."

He tapped buttons, and *Serenity*'s engines roared, straining. The vessel shuddered as it broke gravity.

"*Wĕi!* Look out, *hún dàn*!" Wash shouted at the ass-end of the deep-space liner slowly descending above them.

The other craft's landing lights blazed in their faces, flooding the flight deck. Violent vibration from combined conflicting gale-force rocket exhausts rippled through the superstructure and the buffeting sent Wash's dinosaurs flying off the console.

"*Tā mā de*," he yelped, putting the ship into a sickening lurch and barely avoiding a midair collision.

The buffeting immediately ceased and *Serenity* continued to climb.

"Piece of cake," Wash said, staring down at his shaking hands in disbelief.

Inara watched the windshield as the curvature of Persephone shrank from view and they lifted into the Black. The preacher found her hand and held it.

"The captain is a very resourceful man," Book said.

She nodded.

"And we're resourceful, too," the Shepherd continued. "We'll find him. We just need to get organized. Let's all powwow with Zoë in the infirmary and discuss our next move."

"I should stay here, in case there's a need for evasive action," Wash said. "Autopilot won't cut it. Our alarm system will alert us to any vessel in our proximity, but this is the Alliance we're talking about. No do-overs."

"Agreed," Book said.

Wash got on the horn. "All crew who aren't me please convene in the infirmary," he said. "In the infirmary now, please."

Inara and the preacher left the flight deck and met up

with Kaylee, who was just leaving the engine room. She was not looking best pleased.

"We took off without Mal?" she said glumly.

"We had to, *mèi mèi*," Inara gentled her. "There's a bulletin out for Simon and River, and Badger told Zoë that the Alliance is coming after us. We can't stay."

"But where is he? Inara, he could be in trouble. I mean, he *is* in trouble. If he wasn't, he'd have let us know by now what's going on. He'd have found some way to."

Inara nodded. "What I'm hoping is we've misconstrued the situation and Mal has gone after whoever it was who stole the shuttle. That's why he's incommunicado. He can't break radio silence for fear of giving himself away."

Kaylee shook her head. "This is bad. Really, really bad. We don't leave our folk behind! That's not us."

"We'll find him, Kaylee." Inara wiped a blotch of engine oil off the end of the engineer's nose with a fingertip. "It's going to be all right, I promise."

Kaylee saw the oil on Inara's finger. She took out a handkerchief and started rubbing at her face. "He's just reckless sometimes. No, not reckless. More like daring."

Reckless is the better word, Inara thought.

She put her arm around Kaylee's shoulders and they headed for the infirmary.

Zoë sat on the examination table with one boot off and her pants leg rolled up. Spread across her shin was a bulbous fresh bruise, roughly crescent-shaped and purple as a plum. Kaylee made a face.

"No wonder you're limping," she said. She looked at Simon. "Is her leg broke?"

"Hairline fracture of the tibia." He said to Zoë, "It's minor, even though it might not feel that way, but you need to ice the affected area and stay off the leg for a couple of days."

Kaylee visibly drooped. Zoë ticked her gaze at the engineer and said, "It's nothing to worry about, Kaylee. I can still do what needs doing."

Kaylee nodded and managed a weak smile. She said, "I know." But she didn't look reassured. She was twisting her fingers together. "We're going to look for him soon as we can, right?"

"We need to have a plan," Shepherd Book said. He inclined his head in Zoë's direction. "If you're up to it."

"She's gotta be up to it." Kaylee frowned. "You are up to it, right, Zoë?"

Zoë nodded, wincing as Simon applied ointment to her scratches. "First, I'll tell you everything I know."

Inara listened intently as Zoë described in full the events of the evening, including the bar fight, her encounter with Harlow, and her trip to Badger's. While she was doing so, Jayne appeared in the doorway and listened in.

"Don't know what any of the stuff about 'betrayal' and an 'overdue price' Covington said might mean," she said, "but it's got to mean something. Same goes for the graffiti on the gate of the place where he handed Mal over to the kidnappers."

"Yeah, about that," said Jayne. "I've got wind of an interestin'—"

"And you're quite sure that Badger isn't involved with the captain's disappearance?" Book said. He either hadn't heard Jayne or felt that the big man didn't have anything of value to contribute to the discussion. The latter was more likely, since it was usually the case. "It wouldn't surprise me if he is."

"I doubt it," said Zoë. "Badger wants his cargo delivered, so why would he hold us up?"

"As I was saying, I heard something might be relevant," Jayne tried again. "Seems there's—"

"What if it's been Alliance all along?" Simon suggested. "What if Mal's disappearance and the Alliance bulletin are part and parcel of the same thing? This Hunter Covington fellow could be an Alliance informant, perhaps, or a stooge. Right now Mal could be a prisoner in a cell aboard a Tohoku-class cruiser, being pumped for information."

"Not a nice thought," said Kaylee. "Why would you say such a thing, Simon?"

He shrugged. "We're brainstorming. The idea just occurred to me. I felt it needed to be said. I'm sorry."

"You should be," Kaylee scolded.

"Vigilantes!" Jayne thundered.

Everyone turned and looked at him.

"What?" said Zoë.

"*Now* you're all listenin' to me," Jayne said. "I was wondering what a man had to do to get his voice heard around here."

"Vigilantes?" said Book.

"The kid," Jayne said, "the one Zoë and I rescued at Taggart's, Allister—he and his mom told me there's this group of vigilantes on Persephone who've taken a strong dislike to Browncoats."

"And you're telling us this only now?" said Zoë.

"I've been trying to get a word in edgeways. 'Sides, it ain't a dead cert. Could be it's got nothing to do with any of this whatsoever. But still, Allister overheard some guy claimin' there's folks eager to take revenge on Browncoats for all the wrong they done during the war."

"Browncoats did not do wrong," Kaylee cut in. "Did they, Zoë?"

"What was the name of the group?" Zoë asked Jayne. "Did he say?"

"No."

"Vigilantes," Book said. "Targeting Browncoats. You know, it wouldn't be the first time I've heard tell of such a thing."

"Care to elaborate, Shepherd?" Inara said.

"After the war," Book said, "there were a number of extremist Independent factions who felt that certain aspects of the peace were inadequate. Their thinking was that members of the Browncoat leadership had surrendered too easily and conceded too much to the Alliance, and that these people were in effect wrongdoers who had escaped punishment. Secret societies formed in order to mete out justice."

"Is this true?" said Kaylee.

"Even in the cloistered confines of Southdown Abbey, rumors to that effect reached us," Book replied. "The vigilantes were known to sneak into houses at night and kidnap people out of their beds while they slept. Their victims were never seen again. Anyone who got in their way was taken care of, too. Seems a gang of such ruthless individuals might well be operating on Persephone."

"So if someone is saying Mal is a traitor," Zoë said, "it isn't too much of a stretch to assume vigilantes—the kind you're talking about, the sour-grapes-about-the-war kind—have taken him."

"Oh, no!" Kaylee cried. "What would they want with the captain? He never did nothing wrong!"

"Maybe he did, and you just don't know it," Jayne said with a fierce grin.

The room went quiet again. Everyone stared at Jayne in disbelief. Even though they knew his loyalty was always in doubt, to accuse the captain of betraying the Browncoats seemed a step too far. As mysterious as Mal was, as protective of his past, Inara knew that he had given his all in the fight for independence, and that he would do it over again even if he knew the result would be the same.

Jayne was unrepentant, and defiant in the face of unified opposition. "Just sayin', people done all kinds of things in the war they ain't proud of."

"No," Kaylee said. "I know the captain. I mean, I don't know everything about him, but I know that isn't him."

"But you don't," Jayne argued. "You just know what you want to know."

"Mal laid his life on the line more than a hundred times during the fighting," Zoë said, her teeth clenching as she struggled to maintain her composure. "I saw it with my own two eyes. I was there."

"Maybe you saw what he let you see?" Jayne said smugly. He thought he was on a roll.

"Jayne, you don't want to be here right now," Zoë said, beginning to rise.

"Zoë, please, hold still," Simon said. "You're going to waste my doctoring efforts."

Kaylee said, "What if some vigilantes only *think* Mal did something wrong? What if they took him captive and…" Her eyes grew so huge Inara could see the whites all around her irises.

"That would be one *hóu zi de pì gǔ* of a mistake," Zoë said.

Shepherd nodded. "The sad truth is, there were plenty of Browncoats who were responsible for atrocities during the war. It wasn't just the Alliance who conducted massacres and refused to observe the conventions on the fair treatment of military prisoners. There were horrors on both sides. Sinners on both sides, too."

Jayne narrowed his eyes, maintaining a safe distance from Zoë. "How come you know so much about that, preacher?"

Inara wanted to know the answer, too. The Shepherd's past was cloaked in mystery, but on several occasions the Alliance had extended deferential treatment to him—life-saving medical assistance, for example—and he had proven a fierce fighter on many occasions, including the assault on Niska's space station to rescue Mal. Where did a man of God learn advanced martial arts techniques?

"Our abbey provided refuge for any and all affected by the war, no matter which side," Book said. "It's often said that confession is good for the soul. Many of those who came to us, Browncoat and Alliance soldier alike, unburdened themselves of their past sins. It was not our place to judge, but to listen. Everyone wants a chance to be heard." He paused to look at each person in the infirmary in turn. "At the abbey, we have sworn a vow to respect the privacy of those who have entrusted us with the secrets of their souls." Holding up a finger, he added, "Unless by not speaking up, we become complicit in wrongdoing."

Jayne said, "Huh?"

"Jayne, why are you still here?" Zoë demanded.

"Hey, I care about Mal," Jayne said. "*I* never said he was a traitor."

Inara realized that somewhere deep in his avaricious heart, all appearances to the contrary, Jayne actually believed that.

"Kinda did," Kaylee said. "What the Shepherd means is that if someone confessed that he was going to do something really bad, the monks would tell on him."

"Yes. We would tell on him," Book agreed. "Or her."

"Now at least we have another potential lead," Zoë said, "although I don't know how much good it does us."

"I'm prepared to volunteer to go back down to Persephone," Book said. "In light of what I've just learned, I can think of someone who may be of assistance."

At that moment, Wash's voice sounded over the intercom. "Guys? I just got a wave from Guilder's. They really want their loaner back and they're saying that if we haven't contacted the police about our shuttle, they're going to make us sign a statement saying that we release them from all liability."

Zoë looked even more tired.

Inara said, "We don't really need the other shuttle. I haven't scheduled any clients for the next couple of weeks. Book can use mine if he wants."

"Who is he?" Zoë asked him. "This 'someone?'"

"An old acquaintance," Book replied. "An Alliance officer by the name of Mika Wong, who headed up the team tasked with gathering intel on vigilante groups. He used to talk about retiring on Persephone, and I believe he now has."

"A retired purplebelly?" Kaylee said, aghast. "We don't have time for this. If a bunch of no-good *hún dàn* scumbags have kidnapped the captain, we gotta go after 'em."

"But if we don't know who they are, or where they're headed, we're just chasing our tails," Simon put in.

"There's gotta be *somebody* on Persephone who saw the whole thing or who knows about it," Kaylee persisted. "Zoë, we should put back down and—"

"We can't go back," Zoë reminded her. "We have unstable cargo and the Alliance is looking for us."

"Yes," Simon murmured, "there is that."

"And anyway, I've already tried beating the bushes looking for Mal," Zoë went on. "Didn't get hardly anywhere."

"We can't leave Mal behind like this and just go on with business as usual," Kaylee implored. "Especially if there's fanatics involved. We have to *do* something."

"So send this Wong guy a wave, Book," said Zoë.

"No," Book said. Everyone looked at him. "We didn't part on the best of terms, he and I, and I'm not positive we can trust him."

"But you just said—" Kaylee began.

"I said I'm willing to return to Persephone and stay planetside, making investigations of my own. Those may or may not feature Mika Wong, depending on how desperate I get. Either way, the rest of you can continue on to the delivery point, and somebody will still be doing something productive about Mal."

"Sounds shiny," Kaylee said. "Don't it?" She looked around at the group. "Don't it, Zoë?"

"Yes," Zoë said. To the group she said, "We can spare the Shepherd." To Book she said, "Make sure your comm link works."

"I most certainly will," Shepherd Book said. "I'll head back down immediately, and I'll take Guilder's shuttle rather than Inara's. I can return it to them and get them off our backs. Kill two birds with one stone."

"Maybe someone should go with you," Simon said. "As backup."

"Yeah," said Kaylee. "How about Jayne? He can watch your back."

Jayne huffed. "'Nother gorramn babysitting job," he grumbled.

"With all due respect to Jayne," said Book, "I think I'll manage better on my own. People tend to lower their guard when they're around a Shepherd, more so than they might if I'm in the company of a hulking great bruiser of a man with a scraggly, mean-looking beard. No offense, Jayne."

"None taken." Jayne seemed to think Book's description of him was more than fair.

"Then couldn't Zoë go?" Kaylee said. "I just don't like the idea of you down there alone, Shepherd. And two can cover more ground than one."

"Zoë's needed here," Book replied. "Wouldn't you agree, Zoë? This ship needs a captain, and in Mal's absence, that responsibility falls to you."

Zoë acknowledged it with a nod.

"Besides, that leg of yours will be a serious hindrance. You may not be letting on how much it hurts, but I can tell. It'd be better if you rest it up." Book smiled kindly at Kaylee. "I promise you, Kaylee, I will do everything in my power to track down Mal and bring him back safe and sound. Just remember, I may be just a man all on his lonesome, but"— he pointed a finger heavenward—"I have someone mighty riding shotgun with me at all times."

Inara linked arms with Kaylee. "If anyone can find him, dear, Book can."

Book nodded to her, appreciative of the vote of confidence.

"It—it can't be that somebody took Mal to punish him," Kaylee said, sniffling. "He never did anything wrong in the war."

"Except fight in it," Jayne said.

Zoë glowered at him, then hit the intercom. "Wash, slow us down for shuttle launch."

"I'll just go to my bunk and grab a couple things to throw in my satchel," Book said.

Inara wondered what he would take along. Coin? Weapons? Body armor? Secrets? Probably some of each.

As Book stepped out of the infirmary, *Serenity* began to slow, her engine note lessening in pitch and intensity.

"Oh God…" Kaylee said, a tremor in her voice.

"It's going to be all right," Inara said, but the comforting words rang hollow even to her.

"You don't know that," Kaylee shot back. She looked from face to face. "Everyone understands that this is a big deal, right? Just because Mal usually comes back okay from whatever tight corner he gets into, it don't mean he always will. This might be the one time he doesn't."

That was exactly what Inara thought, too. Her mind raced as she fought down panic. Though she was skilled in dozens of relaxation techniques, at that moment she couldn't remember any of them.

"Book will find him," Zoë vowed. "We can trust him to do his best, and his best is better than most people's."

"But will Mal be all right?" said Kaylee. "Will he even be alive?"

"He hasn't been gone that long," Zoë said. "And if you could have seen Mal in the war, you wouldn't ask that. I saw him get out of all manner of tough scrapes that would have done in anyone else. He'd dust himself off and live to fight another day, usually laughing about how close the call was."

Inara could tell Zoë believed that. Deep down, she herself believed it too.

"There, you see?" she said to Kaylee. "It's going to be okay. Why don't you come have tea with me in my shuttle? We can center ourselves and be prepared in case we're needed."

13

Serenity's close call with the liner had pushed Simon closer toward anxiety. *Serenity* and crew had had to leave their captain behind to an unknown fate, because unless they offloaded Badger's cargo, it could conceivably blow up and kill them all. And on top of that, it seemed the Alliance were narrowing in on him and River.

Kaylee was fond of calling things "shiny." This situation, to Simon, felt like the opposite of that. Gloomy. Dim. Leaden. Dismal. Pick your antonym.

Carefully he observed River at the dining table, which had been relieved of fort duty—River's blankets and pillows taken back to her bunk, and the table itself righted. Though the dismantling of her safe zone had clearly agitated her, his sister hadn't protested beyond a few barely audible and unintelligible complaints. But he could see it in her eyes: River was still terrified by the threat of what lay in *Serenity*'s cargo bay, the crates of precarious HTX-20 mining explosive.

Inara had taken it upon herself to braid sections of

River's hair and wind them across the crown of her head, allowing a few stray brown wavy locks to brush her shoulders. Then the elegant Companion had added little trinkety bits of shimmer, and made up River's eyes with black and turquoise, and dressed her in a brocade tunic and flowing black pants. The result Simon found both wonderful and painful to behold. It comforted him that River had allowed Inara to touch her face and head. He didn't know what the Alliance had done to her, but she usually panicked when someone besides him laid hands on her.

What was wonderful, above all, was how sophisticated and grown-up she looked, like the beautiful, responsible young woman his parents had assumed she would one day become. But hadn't.

After he had decoded the letters River sent from the Academy—the Alliance-run experimental center that had methodically driven her mad—Simon had spent countless sleepless nights wondering if she was dead.

In a way, she was.

The fantasy of her future had turned to dust.

Steam rose from the two clay cups of tea Inara had prepared for them. Simon had hoped that the soothing, warm beverage would ravel his sister back together, at least temporarily. His happy, smart, accomplished *mèi mèi*. Was she still in there somewhere, lost amid the swirling maelstrom of post-traumatic stress disorder and brain damage?

While he sipped and contemplated what to do next, River drained her cup. Then she sat ramrod straight in her chair beside his at the dining table, staring into the bottom of the cup as if she were a fortuneteller reading the tea leaves.

He heard her muttering and leaned forward to catch what she was saying. She was repeating the phrase "getting closer" over and over again, like a mantra or a witch's spell. Or a crazy-person recording loop. The Alliance was after them, no doubt. It was always after them, and getting closer and closer, just as River was saying. When would it end? Maybe never. Or at least not until it had River back in its pitiless clutches.

She glanced up at him. Suddenly clear-eyed and focused, she shook her head in the negative, and a frisson of apprehension skittered up Simon's spine. Had she actually just read his thoughts? Could she see into his mind?

"Shh," she said. She lowered her voice to just above a whisper. "You-know-who." She tipped the teacup left, then right. "There."

Simon's hair stood on end. A sudden, chilling thought had occurred to him. What if Mal being taken was a distraction, and the real scheme centered on seizing River and him? With the Alliance's near-infinite resources, faking some business contacts and ID papers was child's play. Removing Mal from the equation left the remaining crew weakened and rudderless. What if there was an Alliance vessel hailing *Serenity* right now, ready to exercise boarding rights and exploit Mal's absence? Had that been the plot all along, and the business about anti-Browncoat vigilantes nothing more than a red herring?

"Closer, closer," River murmured.

Jayne appeared in the corridor, ducking through the doorway into the dining area.

River rolled her eyes meaningfully.

Ah, thought Simon. *That's what she meant by you-know-who.*

Jayne strode past the table, directing a wary look at River and then a dismissive shrug at Simon. Simon and the big mercenary had arrived at an uneasy truce after Jayne sold out the Tams to the Alliance during a caper on Ariel. A remorseful Jayne had changed his mind at the last moment and saved them. His excuse for the lapse: the money had been too good. Since then, the bounty for River's capture had increased many times over, and Simon knew Jayne was a simple, reactive man. He liked to think Jayne wouldn't succumb to temptation a second time, but he wasn't convinced that someone with such a thirst for lucre would be able to hold out forever.

"So that was bracing, huh, Jayne?" he said. "The near-collision."

"Yeah, well, we were both in a hurry. Us and the liner." Jayne glared at him. "Guess why *we* were."

River stared intently at her tea leaves and whispered to herself, making a rhythmic *swish-swish-swish, swish-swish-swish* sound.

"If—*when*—the Alliance next comes after us," Jayne went on, "and believe me they will, we gotta figure out where to stash you two. Feds'll take the ship apart, bit by bit, looking. It might be best to have a couple of suits ready so's you can go outside again, like that one time."

Simon experienced a wave of vertigo as he recalled clinging to the hull of the ship, with no up or down, only the endless night. River had been enchanted by the vastness of space, the velvet black dotted with fields of stars. Simon had grappled with a low-grade panic that had threatened to paralyze him. Now, that same panic reared its head, building and nibbling at his carefully maintained composure.

Still, it was comforting to hear Jayne talking about helping them hide, as opposed to handing them over for the reward money. Unless, that was, Jayne was simply saying what he thought Simon wanted to hear. Lulling him into a false sense of security.

"It's an experience I'd wish not to repeat if at all possible," Simon said.

"Yeah, well, if wishes were horses, they'd ride beggars. No, wait, that ain't it. Beggars would ride unicorns? No, that ain't it either. Somethin' about beggars, anyways."

River looked up from her tea leaves again and gave Jayne a long, measured stare.

For a second Jayne squinted at her, a look you could interpret either as kindly or as hostile. With Jayne, the two things weren't that far removed from each other. Then he said, "Any more of that tea going, or did the pair of you hog it all?"

"Perish the thought," Simon said. "The teapot is on the stove."

"We used to put tamarind in it," River said to her brother.

Simon smiled at her. "Yes, at home. I remember."

"I miss home. Why did we leave?"

"Mother and Father thought it was best for us. You at the Academy, me at medical school. They... didn't realize the consequences."

"Yeah," Jayne muttered. "The consequences being one of you'd end up with a stick up his butt, the other as mad as a gopher in goggles."

"Jayne, that's not helpful," Simon said, which was

about as stern as reproof as he dared give the much bigger and burlier man.

River made circles of her thumbs and forefingers and placed them over her eyes, like goggles, then stuck out her front teeth goofily.

In spite of himself, Simon laughed. River laughed too, a sound he didn't hear often enough and yearned to hear more.

"Who made these cookies?" Jayne said as he rummaged in the galley's cabinets. His cheeks were bulging, and cookie crumbs sprayed as he talked. "They're powerful good."

Simon didn't reply. He didn't know or care about the authorship of baked goods. As he turned back to River, he saw that she had stood up and was now rotating in a circle, gracefully waving her hands, and tilting her head in what appeared to be ancient, courtly poses. She slid a glance towards him, her eyes glittering like polished topaz.

"They dance like this there," she said.

"Where?" Simon asked.

"In the crates. The busy crates."

"The crates in the cargo bay?"

Jayne was happily munching away on cookies while pouring himself some tea, seemingly oblivious.

"Yes. The crystals inside. They dance in their hearts, getting faster and faster."

River swayed back and forth, her arms swooping and diving as if she was holding two large folded fans. The she abruptly halted, holding a pose, her body still, only her head moving, winding sinuously from side to side like a snake's.

"When the music stops, they'll stop dancing," she said. "Everyone will stop dancing, and we'll all go into the light."

Then she melted back into her chair. "I'm so tired, Simon."

Simon watched as his sister picked up a drawing pad and a charcoal stick and began sketching. He soon saw that it was a picture of him. It was amazing how fast she worked and how well she captured his likeness. He smiled and she frowned back.

"Don't smile," she said. "You weren't smiling when I started."

Humoring her, Simon reassumed a serious face.

River erased the left half of his mouth with her thumb and redrew his lips on that side into a scowl. She added lines across half his forehead and a tear welling in his left eye. One half happy, one half sad.

"You're homesick, but you're getting used to being here," she announced.

"That's true," he said.

"You're angry with me but you love me."

"That's not so true."

"It is."

"I could never be angry with you."

"You saved me," River said, working again on her drawing. She shaded his cheekbone and began adding his hair. Then, looking puzzled, she said, "Something's missing. I know! Your mustache."

"I don't have a mustache," Simon pointed out.

She leaned across and scribbled one under his nose with the charcoal. She giggled and pulled back.

"You are such a brat," her brother chided, his voice breaking just a little. He ruffled her hair and she shook her head, pushing him away.

"You have no idea," she said. Then, putting aside the drawing pad, she stretched and yawned.

"Do you want to rest?"

"Rest in peace," she said. She closed her eyes and crossed her arms over her chest like a dead girl.

Unnerved, Simon rose. He looked down at her placid face and wished that for her—peace. For himself as well.

"Let's get you to your bunk," he said. "Okay?"

She nodded and he escorted her back to her quarters. River lay down on the bed in all her finery and closed her vividly painted eyelids.

"I'll come check on you later," Simon said. River did not answer. Maybe she was already asleep. In repose, she looked relaxed and tranquil. All the tension was drained from her face. She looked how a girl her age should look, unencumbered by cares. He kissed her lightly on the forehead and slipped out of her bunk.

As he climbed back up the ladder into the corridor Simon found himself nose to nose with Kaylee. She raised her brows and cocked her head appraisingly.

"Nice 'tache, Doc," she said. "Makes you look more distinguished. Like a proper gentleman."

Awkwardly, hurriedly, he rubbed away River's handiwork with the back of his hand.

"How's she doing?" Kaylee made as if to look around him so as to peer into his sister's bunk.

Simon put a finger to his lips. "Asleep." Gently he pulled the door closed and gestured for Kaylee to walk with him.

They headed back for the kitchen. Jayne was gone, and so were all the cookies. Simon glanced over his shoulder, assuring himself that there was no one within earshot, and said, "Kaylee, I know the Alliance is hounding us and all, but do you think there's a way I could contact my parents somehow? I mean, a way that's safe? Just to let them know River and I are alive and okay. I've been thinking about them, and I know I'm kind of estranged from them, but I miss them. River misses them. And maybe they miss us and are worried about us."

Kaylee sighed and shook her head. "It's just too risky, Simon," she said. "The Alliance is probably monitoring your parents' wave accounts real close in case you try to make contact. If you look into how they're doing, the Alliance finds out how *you're* doing. They'll know for sure that you're both still alive, and they'll be able to triangulate which sector you're in. Next we know, we'll have the I.A.V. *Magellan* or some such looming over us, sucking *Serenity* in like a bug into a vacuum cleaner." She pulled a sad face. "Sorry."

"No, it's fine. Just thought I'd ask. Should have known it wasn't possible."

"You just have to accept that you and River are your only family for now. Well," Kaylee added, "and us too. The crew, I mean. All of us. Not just me. I'm not saying *I'm* your family. Perish the thought. 'Cause that would sound like we're, y'know, related, and we're not related, and that's good, real good, since us not being related means…"

She was flustered. She seemed to have got herself all tangled up in her own words.

"I'll stop talking," she said.

Simon looked at her. Kaylee was the kindest, sweetest person he had ever met, and she, more than anyone else in the crew, was doing her darnedest to make him feel at home aboard *Serenity*. Not only that but sometimes, the way her eyes flashed when she looked at him, he got the sense that she was trying to tell him something about herself. She was sending him a coded message which he couldn't quite interpret correctly.

She reached over and touched his upper lip. "Missed a bit," she said. "Just there."

Self-consciously he wiped away the last smudge of charcoal.

"There," Kaylee said. "Now you look like the Simon we all know and… like."

And with that, she trotted off back to the engine room, leaving Simon nonplussed but the kind of nonplussed that felt good. He put a fingertip back to where she had touched him, and for a brief while he forgot about his parents, about River, about the Alliance, and was consumed instead with thoughts of this wonderful, baffling young woman with the thick chestnut hair and hazel eyes and quirky smile who loved his sister almost as unconditionally as he did and who enjoyed teasing him and who would let him kiss her, he was sure, if only he could summon up the nerve to do so.

It had been a long time since Book had piloted a shuttle, and it felt both odd and good to be in the driver's seat. On *Serenity* he often served in what some might consider a passive capacity—as an observer, counselor, and father confessor, roles he had embraced willingly at Southdown Abbey and fulfilled on the ship in a somewhat more secular manner. He also prayed for everyone aboard, something Inara, when she'd found out about it, had advised him to conceal from the captain.

To a true believer such as Book, prayer was as active a pursuit as shooting a gun or repairing an engine. But for Mal Reynolds it was a reminder that, to his way of thinking, God had deserted him and all the people he had fought for, and would have willingly died for, during the most crucial part of the war. Believers, in Mal's view, were deluded fools, and he made no secret of the fact.

It signified a profound loss of faith, and Book was very sorry for it. He was sorrier still that Mal was denied that source of strength and comfort in the trying times they lived in. The burdens the captain carried were heavy indeed.

As Book guided the shuttle into a slow, careful descent to Eavesdown Docks, he beseeched the Lord to protect the crew and the captain, and for a successful outcome to his mission. He added a sincere plea to soften Mal's heart and to help him find a way back to the comforts of belief.

At least part of his prayer was answered as he completed his landing maneuvers at Guilder's. The shipwrights seemed to buy his explanation that the missing shuttle was the result of a "family matter" and that that was why the authorities were not being called in. His clerical collar often eased his way, much as Inara's status as a Registered Companion did for her. He knew Inara had some history, as did he—and like him, she kept her past to herself. He had always wondered why, if she had loved her home planet so much, she had left it. Had she done so willingly or had she been pressured to leave? He pondered on occasion if anyone was actively searching for her in the way that the Alliance was looking for the Tams. He would never bring it up—everyone had enough to worry about, and he wouldn't want to put Inara on the spot—but he did cast a watchful eye on the waves and bulletins they received. When they spent time planetside, he stayed alert in case she might need assistance, but so far he hadn't detected anything that could validate his concern.

He left the shuttle with his satchel slung on his back. Inside were a few toiletries, some coin, and a high-tech stun gun and a charger for it. Some of the money came from Mal, a cut of the profits from previous jobs, which the captain distributed among the crew in accordance with the traditional pirate custom of sharing spoils, and Book had supplemented the sum with cash of his own. He might have taken a vow of poverty, but it was difficult to bribe people for information just by appealing to their better natures.

"Hey, Shepherd," Wash said through his comm link. "You down safe and sound?"

"That I am," Book replied.

"You're gonna find Mal, right?"

"If providence is on my side, yes."

"When would providence not be on a Shepherd's side?"

"Quite. Now you get that Firefly to Aberdeen in one piece, you hear me, Wash? And everyone on board, too. I'll be praying for you."

"Amen to that," said Wash. "Be careful, Shepherd."

"Never knowingly not."

Ending the call, Book walked along the perimeter of the bustling, chaotic docks. Overhead, one of Persephone's two moons, Renao, was riding high and bright. Its smaller counterpart, Hades, had yet to rise.

He found himself studying the sides of buildings and spacecraft wreckage for anything that might help him solve the mystery of their missing captain. Mika Wong would likelier than not prove useful in that regard, but Book was loath to call upon his old friend unless it was unavoidable. When mentioning Wong to the crew, he had shaded the true nature of their association. He knew his shipmates wondered about his past, but there was no benefit to be gained on either side by full disclosure, as yet. The time might come when Book could share his life story with them—a reverse confession, if you will; a preacher shriving himself of his sins to the members of the laity. Until then, his past and all its uncomfortable truths were better left buried.

A grizzled older man fell into step beside him. The newcomer walked using a steel crutch, dragging his left foot. His entire left leg seemed atrophied. A birth defect, if Book didn't miss his guess. The man was deft with the crutch and evidently accustomed to the disability, since it barely slowed his pace.

"Can I be of help, Shepherd?" he offered. "If you're looking to find the local abbey, be my pleasure to take you there."

"No, thank you, friend," Book said. He decided to chance his arm. Nothing ventured, nothing gained. "Although actually, you may be able to assist me in another regard. You strike me as a knowledgeable sort."

"Some'd say."

"I'm looking for somebody, name of Hunter Covington. Would you happen to know how I can contact him?"

The man's bushy brows shot upward. "Hunter Covington, you say? You, ah, sure that's who you want? The kinda line of work he's in…" He smiled uneasily. "It ain't what you might call holy."

"What line of work might that be?" Book asked neutrally, without slowing his pace to accommodate the hobbling man. He swept the surroundings with a sharp eye, alert to the possibility that this apparently harmless fellow had a confederate or two and that he was trying to waylay Book so that they could rob him. What was that old Earth-That-Was saying? *Trust Allah but tie up your camel.*

"Well, not to speak ill of a fellow man, especially in this

company, but some of what Covington gets up to is a little on the disreputable side."

People tended to edit themselves around a man of the cloth. "Care to elaborate?" Book asked.

"Not really."

"Well, how about the rest of his business? The more reputable side. What can you tell me about that?"

The man nodded, eager to ingratiate himself. "Whatever you need, I've heard Covington can get it for you. He's connected."

"Connected," Book said.

"Knows everybody."

"That's good. Then he may well be whom I need."

"May I be so bold as to inquire what you want Hunter Covington for?"

Sometimes you had to give a little to get a little. "As it happens, I'm trying to track down an old friend. I know he's on Persephone and I have it on good authority that he's somewhere in Eavesdown."

"Well, now..." The man with the crutch scratched one of his prodigious eyebrows, causing the clustered gray and white hairs to spring out in all directions. "If your friend's alive and in Eavesdown, Covington should know his whereabouts. And if he's dead, Covington may well be able to tell you where he's buried."

"Sounds like the ideal man for the job, then. Where might I find him?"

"He's got a few haunts, when he's in the city. At the docks, you can find him at the quartermaster's HQ, or in the Sea Wolf Tavern. Downtown, it's Taggart's Bar. I can take you there."

Book stopped and turned to face his newfound companion, who halted too. "No need," he said. "I'm not unfamiliar with Eavesdown. I know my way around. But I thank you for your time nonetheless." He reached in his pocket and pulled out a generous amount of platinum, which he held out to the man. "For your trouble."

"Mighty kind of you, sir," the man said, plucking the bounty out of Book's grasp as if he feared the Shepherd would suddenly change his mind. A wave of relief came over his dirty, weather-seamed face and Book gave a quick, silent prayer for him to find an easier path.

"Might I have your name and a way to contact you if I need further assistance?" Book said.

The man bobbed his head. "I'm Charlie Dunwoody, sir. I, uh, you can just ask anyone around here to get a message to me."

Book translated: Dunwoody had no comm link, nor any way to be waved.

The crippled man leaned forward in a conspiratorial manner, holding his hand to the side of his mouth to keep from being overheard. "I like to move around a lot, the state of my leg notwithstanding. I stay loose."

"Understood." Book smiled at him. "I'll be sure to get a message to you if the occasion should arise. And thanks again for your help." He adjusted his satchel and moved on. To his surprise, Dunwoody started walking again, too, right on his heels.

"Yes?" Book said pleasantly, but inwardly steeling himself for a second dunning.

The man chewed the inside of his lip for a second, then

appeared to come to a decision. "Ah, Shepherd, I feel it's only fair to tell you that around these here parts Hunter Covington is a bit… well, *feared*."

"As in violent?"

"Well, sir, since you put it that way, yes, violent is as good a word as any. Leastways, he employs people who'll do violence on his behalf. Just make sure what you're getting into, if you don't mind my advice."

The revelation was hardly a surprise, but Book affected apprehension. As far as Dunwoody was aware he was a mere Shepherd, with all the connotations of defenselessness and unworldliness that came with that.

"I appreciate your concern," he said. "Now I'll be on my way," he added pointedly.

"Yes, yes of course." On his open palm, Dunwoody mimicked running motions with two fingers. "You have things to do."

"Yes. I'm on a bit of a timetable."

"Yessir, of course, sir." Dunwoody took a few steps away from Book and made a formal little bow.

Book began to walk on, leaving Dunwoody in his wake. Then he turned back and said, "You say you know where an abbey is."

The man nodded. "All of 'em on-planet."

"If you're looking for work, you might go to Southdown. It's not far. Ask for the head abbot. Tell him Shepherd Book recommended you. The brethren are often in need of an extra set of hands."

"Oh." Dunwoody's face lit up. "Thank you. I will do that, Shepherd Book."

Book realized at once that it might have been a better idea to keep his identity concealed, but what was done was done, and if it benefited this poor man, then the risk was to a good purpose.

With that, Book moved on, increasing his speed in order to guarantee that he left Dunwoody behind this time. He melted into the haze of smoke and dust, into the boisterous crowd that packed the street alongside the landing field. The Alliance Day celebrations were still ongoing, although to Book's way of thinking they were starting to simmer down. The hour was approaching midnight, after all, and there was only so much roistering a body could handle before it began to flag.

Some folks tipped their hats or pulled their forelocks when they saw his collar; others glared; most simply ignored him. Book was just an ant in a swarm of ants, some dark-complexioned, some light, some practically naked, some decked out in smothering layers of silk brocade.

He made his first stop at the quartermaster's office, passing two armed guards to gain entry into the single-story aluminum-clad building. The office itself consisted of a large main room without any seating. It was busy at this late hour, even on Alliance Day. Everyone stood in line to reach windows protected by metal bars and transaction drawers. A stocky woman towards the front was bellowing about being charged twice for her docking fees.

All the clerks were occupied and the lines weren't moving, so Book passed some time scanning the various flyers, advertisements and notices tacked on a large bulletin board along the wall. There were a plethora of recruitment posters urging youth to join the Alliance galactic military force. PATRIOTISM! ADVENTURE! OPPORTUNITY! Words chosen carefully to stir young women and men to enlist, without spelling out the inherent risks, both to their own physical and psychological well-being and to those people whom the Alliance, in its infinite wisdom, turned them loose on. Nothing had changed in all these years.

Then, in their midst, Book spied a WANTED poster. It was several months old, to judge by the brittleness of the paper and how deep it was buried among the others. What stood out on it, what had caught his eye, was a name: Hunter Covington.

Book snatched the poster off its pins and studied it. The wanted person in question was not Covington himself, but a woman named Elmira Atadema. She was lovely, with coffee-colored skin, dark hair that curled around her shoulders, and striking gray-green eyes. The poster listed her vital statistics and last-seen location and date. She hadn't been missing long at the time the poster had been issued, but from the bounty being offered, someone was taking her absence very seriously. And that someone was named on the poster as Hunter Covington.

Book recalled Zoë's description of the woman who had accompanied Covington on his meeting with Harlow. Zoë had intuited that she might have been a bondswoman, and lo and behold, Elmira Atadema was indeed an escaped bondswoman, according to the poster. She had run away from Covington, her bondholder, six months ago. The reward for her return—"alive and unharmed"—was substantial. For a lot of folk it was equivalent to a year's wages.

Maybe someone had ratted on Elmira, or Covington had lived up to his given name and hunted her down. Either way, he must have got her back, if she was the one who had been with him for the meet at Taggart's two days ago.

There was a proud set to Elmira's posture that spoke of someone who had not been beaten down by her position in life. Being a bondsperson meant someone "owned" you for however long your contract stated, to do with as they pleased. Mal had masqueraded as Inara's bondsman on Regina, when they had stolen some cargo from a train for Adelai Niska. As soon as they had realized what they'd taken—all that stood between the folk of Regina and a slow, agonizing death— they had returned it, earning the wrath of Niska. That they had dealt with, but word got around that the crew of *Serenity* had somehow botched a job and they had yet to fully restore trust among some that hired ships for transport.

The line moved, and within a few more minutes Book was stepping up to one of the service windows. A pasty-faced man wearing metal-framed glasses was seated behind the barred opening. The clerk wore a white shirt, garters on the sleeves, and a plasma visor across which the docks' arrivals and departures scrolled.

"How may I help you, sir?" the man asked.

Book glanced down at his plastic name tag. "Hello, Mr. Smotrich," he said. "I'm looking for a man named Covington. Hunter Covington. A gentleman I just met at the docks suggested I look for him here."

Smotrich blinked, then his eyes narrowed. "Mr. Covington has not been in of late," he replied.

Book noted the sudden redness in his cheeks. Either

Smotrich was lying or the subject of Hunter Covington was upsetting in some way. It might well be both. He pressed the clerk further. "Do you happen to know where else I might begin to look for him?"

"No," Smotrich snapped back. He looked down at some papers and began shuffling them.

"I see." Book held up the WANTED poster. "Well, perhaps you could help me with another matter. I presume the lady in this poster is no longer at large."

"You know her?" the clerk said in a tone that bordered on accusatory. "Or are you chasing that reward? Didn't think Shepherds cared much about earning coin."

The question had clearly hit a nerve. Book knew he had to proceed carefully.

"As a Shepherd, I'm naturally concerned for her welfare," Book told him. "I'll pray for her safe recovery if she has not been found."

"Well, sir, can't say she has," he said. "Or leastwise, I haven't heard if she has. I don't know anything more about that." He nervously examined his paperwork for a second, then croaked out, "Sorry, sir, I have to close this window. It's past the end of my shift."

"Oh, of course. Thank you for your—"

Time, Book had planned to say, but Smotrich yanked down a hunter-green shade, effectively ending their conversation.

Book considered engaging another clerk with the same questions, but they were all occupied with customers and he would have had to start over at the back of the line. The stocky woman was demanding to speak to the quartermaster himself. Someone else was complaining that the utilities weren't functioning at their docking site. Business as usual—the clamor and struggle of everyday life, which Book had eschewed for the peace of the abbey. Sometimes he wondered why the still, small voice inside him had urged him to emerge from that place of serenity and board a ship of that name.

He turned and left the building. "Peace be with you," he said to the two guards outside. One of them nodded in acknowledgement; the other scowled.

From the quartermaster's office, Book plunged headlong into the seamier depths of the city, which bordered the space dock. Threading his way through the crowds in the street, he graciously declined the offers from the sidewalk hawkers of food, drink, jewelry, housewares, mood-altering substances, and temporary companionship.

The exterior of the Sea Wolf Tavern was as he had remembered it. A pseudo-antique mermaid masthead overhung the entrance, arms flung wide as if to take to her ample bosom all those seeking a certain kind of shelter. When he entered the crowded bar, he could barely hear himself think over the din of voices and music. The Sea Wolf fancied itself one of Eavesdown's classier joints, but there was still plenty of Alliance Day rambunctiousness in evidence, from boozy singalongs to raucous toasts where the clinking together of glasses was more like a contact sport.

He took an empty seat at a table near the bar. A Zulian spider monkey squatted on the bartender's bare shoulder. The furry little creature appeared to be drunk, eyes half closed, mouth hanging slack, nearly falling off its perch again and again, catching itself at the last possible instant by coiling its long tail around its master's neck, then promptly letting go as the bartender swatted at it.

Book's religious order forbade the drinking of alcohol so he asked a harried server for some water. Unfortunately, it tasted even rustier than what he made do with on *Serenity*. He had offered to do Kaylee's share of the dishwashing for a month if she could upgrade the filtration system, but even that had not helped. He thought wistfully of the fresh artesian spring at Southdown Abbey. He was slipping into nostalgia, probably because the abbey lay close by and civilization, such as it was, demanded different things from him than did a life of contemplation.

He sipped gingerly, getting the lay of the tavern as he sat alone at a dirty, rickety table. Orange lamps glared all around, catching dust motes and revealing long strands of cobwebs among the fishing floats and nets that adorned the low ceiling. He scanned around the room, on the off-chance Covington was here. He hadn't seen Covington's wave to *Serenity* but he had seen the screen-cap picture, so he had a fair idea of who he was looking for. No luck.

"Can I get you another drink, preacher?" a passing waitress asked. She was wearing as much makeup as a singer in the Chinese Opera and a highly abbreviated pirate costume including a low-cut, frill-edged blouse. Her figure was the right amount of voluptuous.

"Sorry for the mess," she said. "This should have been cleaned before you sat down. We're short-handed."

"Thanks, I'm still working on this drink. But I wonder if I might ask you a question. Is Hunter Covington in here tonight?"

Straightening and folding her dish rag, the waitress looked wary. "Not as I know of."

"Do you think he might be in later?"

She shrugged and gave Book a forced smile. "You never know with Mr. Covington. He comes and goes."

"Thank you. I'm wondering if you know where else I might look for him. I've tried the quartermaster's, and here."

"Taggart's," she said without hesitation.

That was the same thing Dunwoody had told him. It was also where Covington had arranged to meet with Mal. Probably it was going to have to be Book's next port of call. And if he struck out there, then—and only then—would he try Mika Wong.

"That's his home base," the waitress explained.

"Thank you," Book said again. Then he reached into his pocket, took out the folded paper, opened it, and showed it to her. "And by any chance, do you know anything about this woman, Elmira Atadema?"

The waitress drew back slightly, then shook her head and clicked her teeth. "Be careful, preacher," she said. "The wrong person overhears you asking them kind of questions and you could get yourself dispatched to meet your Maker afore your time, that there fancy dog collar notwithstanding."

Book raised an eyebrow, and the waitress glanced from side to side so as to make sure no one was listening. She leaned over the table again. He leaned to meet her halfway.

"I will tell you this," the waitress said. "People around here are saying that woman got herself mixed up in something way over her head. Not that she wasn't already mixed up with criminals, professionally speaking, being a bondswoman and all. But this time she got her own hands bloody. Her bondholder—Hunter Covington, no less, but you know that from the poster—dragged her into it. People are saying Mr. Covington might even have gotten her murdered."

Book cocked his head. "Murdered. Good heavens above. Why?" This situation was getting murkier by the second.

The waitress ran her fingertips along her white sash, not provocatively, but as a way to collect her thoughts. "I don't know why. Maybe because the others involved were afraid she was going to give them up?"

"What was the nature of this supposed crime?"

She lowered her voice. "Something they were planning. Kidnap with violence, that's what I've heard."

He kept his face neutral. "Whom were they supposed to be kidnapping?" Was it Mal? Almost certainly it was.

"I'm sorry, sir," she said. "It was an organized thing, that's all as I know."

"A gang of criminals, you mean?"

She nodded.

"Who are they?"

She shook her head and rolled her eyes. "I work three jobs and I still can't get all the bills paid. I don't have the energy to keep track of all the idle gossip that's swirling around, know what I'm saying?"

He decided to take a chance at revealing that he might know something himself. "Have you heard anything about people taking the law into their own hands because of things that happened during the war? People whose violent endeavors might be directed against—" he lowered his voice practically to a whisper "—Browncoats?"

"Some folks aren't willing to forget about the war," the waitress said. "They say wrongs were done, and they want to right them."

It sounded as if she might agree with that notion. "And can you provide me with any information on these folks?" Book said. "Or the nature of the wrongs they want to right?"

"I might be able to." She shrugged and toyed with the sash again.

Book pulled out a heavy coin and waved it at her. She took it from him, and after depositing it safely into her cleavage, she nodded. "Yeah, there's a group of guys around here who seem like they want to stir up trouble. Rake up the past. Can't tell you their names or where they hang out. Don't know. They keep themselves to themselves. But they're definitely active."

"Is that all you have on them?" He was exaggerating his disappointment, but not by much.

"I'd name names if I could, Shepherd, I swear to you, but I can't. Now can I ask you something?"

"Of course."

She raised one penciled brow. "Why is a man of the cloth so interested in Elmira Atadema? And in Hunter Covington for that matter."

"I'm asking about Elmira because one of the brethren is a relation of hers," he lied smoothly. "I promised him I'd look into her disappearance. So, I suppose you could say I'm interested for his sake."

She smirked. "Well, doesn't that just take the gorramn cake. Imagine two grown men both connected to Elmira, both asking me where she is on the same day."

Book was an expert on maintaining an empathetic but otherwise neutral expression, a requirement for someone whose life's calling entailed listening to the often-grisly confessions of others. But it was also a skill he had honed from his earlier, less honorable life. Though it was anything but the case, he appeared only moderately interested.

"May I ask what the other man looked like? Maybe you caught his name?"

All at once she looked stricken. "Oh," she said. "No. I, uh, I made a mistake." She was spooked, just like Smotrich. Clearly she had said more than she felt she ought to.

He said, "I won't tell anyone that you told me." When the silence dragged on with no end in sight, it became clear the pump required more priming. He fished out another coin and she, after a moment's hesitation, took it.

"Guess if you can't trust a man of the cloth…" she said. "He's retired Alliance. He comes in now and then, goes in the back room with the manager, comes out smug. I think…" She lowered her voice. "I think we're paying him protection money." She swallowed. "Maybe I shouldn't have said that."

"No, it's all right. It will go no further. I promise." Book waited a beat and then he asked again, "Can you tell me his name?"

She squeezed the coin in her fist, deliberating. "His name," she said eventually, "is Mika Wong."

Book managed to mask his astonishment, just about. *Wong? Protection money?*

"Do you know where I might find Mr. Wong?" He readied another coin. It was like feeding money into a slot machine. You pulled the lever, the reels turned, but you never knew what combo was going to result.

The waitress hesitated, and then she shook her head. "No, I can't shake you down for that," she said. "I really don't know where he is. But he was in here not two hours ago."

The facts were starting to dovetail and the trail was heating up. Book wondered if Mika Wong was somehow mixed up in Mal's disappearance. Might a ransom demand come in shortly?

"Thank you. You have been an invaluable help," he said.

Silently, she nodded. It was clear that she regretted confiding in him.

He gently pushed the water away and rose. "I should be going." He gave her the last coin, even though she had failed to fully earn it, and she deposited it with the rest. Her cleavage was nothing if not capacious.

"Bless you," he said, and the waitress nodded without looking at him. He patted her shoulder and took his leave.

He saw himself out, and once in the street, he scanned the sidewalks. His eye fell on the man Dunwoody, who was standing at the mouth of a narrow passageway to his left. The crippled fellow was holding himself up with one hand on the passageway wall and waving weakly at Book with the other. His mouth was bloodied and he looked dazed.

"Dear Lord," Book said, dashing over to him. He put his arm around Dunwoody's shoulder, peeling him away from the support of the rough brickwork. "What happened?"

"Oh, Shepherd Book," he moaned, "hide me. Hide me quick." He tugged at Book's arm, urging him back into the passageway, which was barely wide enough to walk down two abreast. "This man, he saw my money—like a fool I was counting it in plain sight—and he came at me."

"Robbed you?" Book asked, and Dunwoody nodded.

"Yes, but only after he sucker-punched me a good one. Then I got mad and I gave 'im a piece of my mind, and he's gone back to get some others, and he said they're going to beat the living tar out of me and make me lame in both legs."

"No, they won't," Book said. "There's two of us now, my friend."

Dunwoody grabbed onto Book's jacket and with a surprising turn of strength pulled him deeper into the shadows inside the mouth of the passageway. At their feet, a rat squeaked and darted away.

"Please, Shepherd, don't let them see us," he begged. "They'll beat me black and blue."

"They won't," Book promised. "I'll protect you."

Dunwoody glanced round into the street. Suddenly he jolted, his eyes widened, and he stuffed his fist in his mouth.

"They're coming, oh, they're coming," he whispered around his hand. "Oh, dear God, they're going to hurt me bad."

Book turned, hand digging into his bag for his weapon. As his fingers closed on it, something hard slammed down on his shoulder from behind and pain shot down his arm and back. He staggered in a half circle.

Dunwoody stood with his crutch aloft. He had just hit him with the implement.

Book raised á hand to defend himself, but not in time. The crutch came down again, hard. He managed to twist sideways, so that the blow was a glancing one. Nonetheless it caught him on the side of the head, staggering him. Sudden pain cast a veil over his vision. His ears rang.

Now there were three more men, rushing up along the passageway to join Dunwoody. Accomplices. This was all an artfully staged con. The blood on Dunwoody's mouth, his dazed look, his panic—all designed to get Book to lower his guard. And Book, like a perfect idiot, had allowed himself to fall for it.

"I'm sorry about this, Shepherd," Dunwoody said to the still dazed Book. "Truly I am. But I got me this bum leg, and Southdown Abbey is just too far a walk. I wish you hadn't flashed your coin so freely. It caused a mighty temptation in my heart, I'm sure you understand." He wiped his gory mouth with his hand, then licked at his fingers. "Yum," he said. "Plum sauce."

Then he turned to hail the three new arrivals.

"Coin bag's in his pants pocket," he said. "Plenty there."

"Let's soften him up a little first," said one of the others. He was carrying a baseball bat.

"Yeah," said another, this one armed with a cudgel. "I went to one of them schools run by priests. The strict kind. Don't got me no love for religious types."

Nor for grammar, Book thought. *Your education was clearly wasted on you.*

As one, the four men set about belaboring Book. They got in several good licks, until the apparently cowed Book surprised them by giving the cudgel wielder a solid punch to the gut. The man doubled over, winded, gasping for breath. Book managed to wrest the cudgel out of his hand and brandished it at the man with the baseball bat.

The man stepped back, out of Book's range, and whirled the bat. Whether by accident or by design, he clouted the cudgel out of Book's grasp, leaving him weaponless again.

"Put the guy out of action, somebody!" Dunwoody declared. "Come on, there's only one of him, and he's just a preacher."

Yet the ferocity with which Book fought back was anything but cleric-like, and in the close confines of the passageway there wasn't room for more than two of his assailants to attack him at once, which evened the odds somewhat. Grunting furiously, he dove at Dunwoody, head down like a linebacker. Dunwoody slammed into the passageway wall, his grip on his crutch loosening. Book snatched the walking aid from him and drove it ferrule-first into Dunwoody's groin like a lance. Crutch met crotch, and Dunwoody let out an agonized *whoof* of air, sinking to his knees with his hands clasped around his private parts. He looked about fit to vomit.

Then the baseball bat slammed into the backs of Book's legs, and all at once Book, too, was on the ground. From the thighs down he had lost all feeling and his legs were as supportive as two rubber bands.

The bat whirled at him a second time, on a collision course with his head. Book blocked the attack with the crutch but not as solidly as he would have liked. The bat transferred much of its momentum to the crutch, which then crashed into his temple with brain-jarring force. For a second time Book's vision became unfocused and his ears sang like a tabernacle choir.

The fourth attacker now lunged for Book's pants pocket, determined to get what they had arranged this elaborate setup for. Book was woozy, all but powerless to prevent him.

Then, abruptly, the man with the baseball bat was screaming. "Get off! Get your gorramn hands off of me!"

This was followed by a series of sickening pops and cracks, the sound of several small bones breaking in swift succession. The bat fell to the ground and bounced away, making a noise like a rapid tattoo of notes on a xylophone, while the man who had been holding it stared down at his right hand. The fingers were twisted every which way like a bunch of mangled bananas. He looked at the appendage as though unable to believe that it belonged to him. His face was riven with agony.

A figure slipped past him, a blur of motion, and all of a sudden the man who had been going for Book's money was flying backwards, propelled by a flat-palmed punch to the sternum. It was as though he had had a rope lashed around his waist, the other end tethered to a horse, and someone had whipped the steed into a gallop. He hurtled all the way out into the street, coming to land on his front in the gutter. He attempted to rise but fell back with a strangulated groan, his face plunging into what was either a puddle of spilled liquor or, more likely, the spot where a drunken reveler had recently relieved himself. Book, although the thought was uncharitable, rather hoped it was the latter.

The man whose hand had been injured was in too much pain to do anything but whimper and mewl. This left just Dunwoody and the cudgel man still standing. Thanks to Book, neither had much fight in him, but that didn't prevent the fast-moving figure—a savior, it seemed—dealing with them as decisively as he had their compadres. Dunwoody went down like a collapsing house of cards, victim of a savagely forthright closed-fist knockout punch. The cudgel man's turn was next. The figure shot out a leg, toes catching him under the chin. His head snapped back, his eyes rolled white, and he was out cold even before he hit the ground.

Gradually Book's head cleared. He looked up to see a hand reaching for him, not in aggression but with the obvious intent of helping him to his feet. Blindly, faithfully, he took it.

As his eyeline drew level with his savior's, a bemused smile spread across Book's face.

"As I live and breathe," he said huskily. "Can it really be?"

The man opposite reciprocated the smile. "Mika Wong, at your service. Long time no see, Derrial."

15

"Not the gorramn chickenfeed hood again," Mal slurred as Donovan Philips came towards him with the burlap sack in his hands.

Mal had come to just moments earlier, sitting propped up against a bulkhead. He had no idea how long he'd been out, or where he was, but he was thirsty and he had to pee. The shuttle was still spaceborne, that much he could tell from the rumble of its engines. Whatever its final destination was, it hadn't yet made planetfall or even entered atmo. The artificial gravity was still on, and artificial gravity felt different from real gravity. On-world, your weight distribution was more even and there wasn't that vague dizziness which dogged you all the time when you were shipboard and which you never quite got accustomed to, no matter how good your "space legs" were.

"It's so's you can't go sharing any information about us," Philips said.

"Furthest thing from my mind," Mal said "I swear by

your uniquely scarred face which would make it easy to describe you to the authorities and them to catch you that I will never breathe a word to anyone about you." He shut his eyes tightly and braced himself, anticipating that his witticism would annoy the irritable Philips, who was in a perfect position to kick him in the teeth.

"You really do love to hear yourself talk, don't you?" Philips said. "Bet you talk, talk, talk in front of a mirror and always crack yourself up. Got some news for you, traitor: being clever and using big words ain't going to save your backside this time."

"Please don't hate me for my vocabulary," Mal said.

"Shut up," the man snarled. Then he bent down and drew the bag over Mal's head, cinching the draw cord around his neck so he couldn't shake it off.

There was no escaping the hood's aroma. Or the fact that his captor was just inches away. For a split second, Mal debated whether to spring up and lunge for him in the hope of taking him down. But while he was effectively blind and his hands were tied, he knew it would be futile. He'd doubtless ended up getting hurt for his trouble.

Something scraped against the ropes that held his ankles pinned together and his legs were suddenly free.

Philips grabbed him under the arm and said, "Stand." He yanked hard, nearly dislocating Mal's shoulder but barely budging him from the deck.

"I would, except my feet are asleep," Mal said. It was the God's honest truth. Philips yanked him up anyway. Caterpillars by the billions skittered up his legs and his knees buckled. Philips grunted and pushed him forward.

Mal floated over the ground as Philips alternately shunted and guided him from behind.

"We're at the coaming," the man said. "Lift your feet up."

Mal couldn't feel a thing but did his best to comply, raising his leg to step over the lip in the floor that was part of the hatchway and bulkhead wall. On sea-going vessels, the coaming kept the ocean out if it had occasion to spill across the main deck and into the ship. On spaceships, it could halt the path of a fire or the vacuum of space by creating a seal with the hatch.

Again he contemplated, and discounted, some kind of escape attempt. What if he feigned falling over, dragging Philips to the floor with him? Then while Philips was sprawled off-balance, he could scissor his legs around the guy's neck and try to choke him out. As long as the sack was on his head and his hands remained tied behind his back, however, Mal stood about as much chance of pulling off this feat as a one-legged man stood of winning an ass-kicking contest.

"Where we goin'?" he asked.

"You'll find out soon enough," Philips said. "Now, stop here and hold still."

Mal heard footfalls thudding on the deck plates, faint at first, then growing gradually louder and louder. Sounded like four or five sets.

"*Lǎo tiān yé*, what in heck do you still have a hood on him for?" someone new demanded.

From the edge the voice carried, Mal figured this to be someone in charge. Philips's superior, at least.

"So's he can't tell no one anything 'bout us," Philips said.

Mal refrained from pointing out that he already knew

Phillip's name and could identify him. What Philips hadn't reasoned through couldn't hurt him.

"Don't concern yourself with that," Someone New snapped. "He won't be telling anyone about anything. Unless ghosts can gossip."

That does not sound hopeful, Mal thought. *No sir, not one bit hopeful.*

"Well, I'm leaving it on anyways," Philips shot back. "It makes him easier to handle."

"Actually, not as much as you might think," Mal ventured. "My feet are asleep and I'm swaying a bit. Difficult to keep my balance. Could go down in a heap any second."

"Yeah," Someone New said, "we were told you were tricky, Reynolds. The sort of guy you need to watch out for, in case of shenanigans."

"Shenanigans? Me?" Mal said. "What lyin' no-good polecat told you that?"

"I'm surprised you haven't pieced it together yet."

Mal thought for a second, then said, "Just for the sake of clarity, and of putting all cards on the table, let me ask: did I do something to piss off Hunter Covington? Because I've only met the fella the once, and all's I thought he wanted was to hire me for a job, and now I'm a missing person and a prisoner, and if this is some kind of test of loyalty or personal grit, I would like to think by now I've surely passed it."

"Just shut up," said Someone New. "You're right, Donovan. Keep the damned bag over his head. It muffles the sound of that voice."

Oh ha ha, Mal thought. Beads of sweat rolled down his forehead, stinging his eyes and the cuts and bruises he realized he had around his mouth. He ran his tongue over his teeth. All still there. Who *had* he pissed off this bad? His ex-wife and former partner in thievery, YoSaffBridge? Niska? Both were still at large as far as he knew, and either would have been capable of chicanery like this. But it didn't feel like their handiwork to him. What about that ornery old horse thief, Patience? No. She wouldn't bother with leaving Whitefall, the moon she was currently bullying, and anyway, by now she would have already shot him several times. She was tetchy that way.

Mal tried again. "If there's something I can do to put this right—"

His olive branch was rewarded with a punch on the jaw that sent him reeling. He would have collapsed except that one of his tormentors—he had no idea which—grabbed his shoulder, twisted him around, and slammed him head-first into a wall. For the briefest instant, Mal saw stars. Which, actually, was no improvement over seeing nothing.

"No more talking," Philips said, "or I'll cut out your tongue."

Mal wondered why a gag wouldn't be the rational first choice, but fell silent.

"That's better," Philips said. "See what I've been putting up with the whole way here?"

You have so not, Mal thought indignantly. *I've been unconscious most of the time.*

"Okay, enough of this," Someone New said. "Prepare for landing."

"Sit down," Philips said to Mal. "And keep your mouth shut."

Mal crossed his ankles and sank to the deck unsteadily. Though thick-headed, with his trapped hands now joining his feet in the Land of Numb, he began playing and replaying everything that had occurred since first contact with Hunter Covington.

Yesterday—if more time than that had not elapsed— had been Alliance Day, and judging by the ruckus that had come from Taggart's during his own confrontation with Covington, he was confident Jayne and Zoë had enjoyed a big juicy bar fight with a side order of fisticuffs. He hoped his two crewmates had left the bar safe and sound and were at that very moment zeroing in on where he was and figuring out how to retrieve him from whoever had captured him. But there was also the less delightful possibility that they'd followed him out of the bar and gotten themselves taken, too, or worse, left for dead in some Persephone back alley. If the crew of *Serenity* were coming to save him, that meant they'd put the delivery of the crates on the backburner, a decision that while good for him could very well undermine business deals for the foreseeable future. After Niska, they needed to cement their reputation for reliable and on-time service. Their new motto: Smuggling Be Us, or some such.

The roar of retro-thrusters shut off his line of thought. The shuttle was breaking atmo at a seriously flawed angle. The too-steep re-entry made Mal's cheeks go saggy and flutter wildly against his clenched teeth. Buffeting. Buffeting. He hoped to blue blazes someone had taken the time to check the heat shield before they started the descent. One crack could turn to two, and two to ten, and before you knew it you were a gorramn meteor. More buffeting. Harder. It was like being trapped inside a cocktail shaker without the booze.

Then the vibration stopped and the welcome pull of real gravity replaced the ship's artificial. Mal's ears popped. He still had to pee, and thanks to the sudden appearance of normal grav, with considerably more urgency. The vessel settled down on the ground with a resounding crunch, and the engines cut out.

Then he was pulled brusquely to his feet, maybe by Philips, maybe by Someone New. He flexed his hands over and over, trying without much luck to bring the feeling back into his fingers. There were other people around him, aside from Philips and Someone New. From the combined body warmth and parts per million of sweat odor, he knew he was well and completely surrounded, as though being escorted by an honor guard. As they dragged him off, he couldn't come up with a single stratagem that could turn the tables and save his life. He was plumb out of imaginary heroics.

After a heap of clanging boot soles on metal deck plates, the path they were taking angled downward. He felt a rush of cool air and realized he was being herded off a gangplank. Then the footing under him got soft. Sand or fine soil, maybe. Earthy odors penetrated the chickenfeed stink of the burlap sack—mud, dirt, rock.

Down they walked, or rather, his escorts walked and Mal stumbled. After a bit, their breathing and grunts of effort suddenly got louder and their footsteps began to echo. Mal's right shoulder scraped something hard and sharp, like chiseled rock. The air was noticeably damper and clammier and they were traveling on a shallow downward incline. He rationalized that they were taking him into a cavern or a tunnel. Something sizzled on the right side of his body, and he sensed a rush of heat, which quickly passed. He smelled burning rags and oil. A torch, most likely, stuck in the wall in a sconce.

The angle of their descent grew steeper, and it became even more of a challenge not to trip and fall. Mal didn't want to give these guys any excuse to hit him. They were already a bit too fond of the exercise and he figured he might need his every speck of brains later.

Without warning the group stopped.

"That him?" someone double-new asked. The question echoed into the distance. *That him… him… him…*

Who else might it be? Mal wondered. A feeble hope fluttered in his throat that the kidnappers had somehow grabbed the wrong person outside Taggart's, confused one Mal Reynolds with another of similar features and identical moniker. And then the hood was yanked off Mal's head. Moldy subterranean air hit his face. Torches, dozens of them, flickered against the gloom of dark rock walls and ceiling.

The man glaring at him from arm's length looked familiar to Mal. He had biggish ears, smallish eyes, and a decidedly crooked nose. It was the singular beak that tapped at Mal's memory. There was no forgetting that narrow blade with the sudden dogleg to the right. Or the downright marvel that the two holes at the drippy end hadn't by force of momentum ended up somewhere on his opposing cheek. That busted-to-hell nose had fought beside Mal's own nose in the war, Mal was sure of it. He and the other man had taken on the Alliance nose to nose, as it were.

The man said nothing, only watched him with a calculation in his eyes.

The rows of torches on the walls hissed and sputtered, and gave off ribbons of black smoke.

"Help me out here," Mal said. "I know you, right?"

"You'll get it," the man assured him. "Just take your time."

After a few seconds it all came rushing back.

"Deakins," Mal said, triumph and relief flooding his voice. It was Stuart Deakins, late of the so-called "Balls and Bayonets" Brigade. For two years that at the time seemed like a hundred and twelve, Stu Deakins had been a ground pounder under Sergeant Malcolm Reynolds' command. Mal had half-carried, half-dragged the wounded man to safety in a firefight during the New Kasimir offensive, running a gauntlet of Alliance gunfire. He was glad to find his soldier still alive and, hopefully, on-scene to set straight whatever terrible misunderstanding had arisen. "Deakins—Stu—it's me. Malcolm Reynolds. Sergeant Reynolds, as was."

"Yeah, Sarge, I know who you are," Stu Deakins said, "and who you were."

With that, he dipped a shoulder and swung hard for Mal's gut. The punch seemed to come at Mal in slow motion, and Mal tensed to absorb the blow. Surprise more than pain doubled him over. But the impact still knocked the wind out of him.

As he struggled to catch his breath, Mal looked up at Deakins in disbelief. Before he could speak, the men surrounding him caught him under the arms and steered him onward. Mal looked back to see Deakins spitting on the very ground where he had just stood. That utterly dumbfounded him.

I saved his life. That's not something normally makes a man hit you, then hawk and spit in the dirt. Not unless the etiquette for gratitude has changed some since the war.

His captors led him on down a tunnel hewn from virgin rock. There were cavities in the walls and ceiling that marked where timber braces had at once time provided support. An old mine of some sort, then.

The tunnel split in two after a ways and his escorts shoved him down the right-hand fork. After a bit more walking, the rock corridor ended, opening onto a cavern whose floor was twenty feet lower. When Mal and his captors stepped to the edge, they were met by a chorus of shouts from below. Lit by torches and oildrum fires, a group of forty or so people stared up at them. Even in the flickering light, he could see the men and women all wore the traditional Independent outerwear: a knee-length coat of brown suede. It made his heart swell to see folks thus decked out, honoring the side for which he'd fought and bled, and would do again if given the opportunity. It wasn't a costume party. They all looked to be roughly his age, certainly of a vintage that he could have served with—veterans of the war.

He thought he recognized a few of the faces. There was "Panda" Alcatraz with the wine-colored birthmarks around his eyes, and that guy Lucas, the sly bastard who had traded the now-deceased Tracey Smith a can of beans for what turned out to be the 'verse's bluntest bayonet. Mal wondered if this whole shindig was some kind of elaborate Alliance Day practical joke, starting with a hazing and ending in a reunion of old comrades-in-arms. If so, it had been a little on the sadistic side, but all was well that ended well, right?

"Hail, Browncoats," he called down happily.

As the echoes of his greeting faded away, the yelling stopped. Pins could have dropped in the cave and he would have heard them plink.

Mal then realized the people were all glaring up at him, not a smile or a friendly wink from the lot. Swallowing down any other felicitous words he might have spoken, he felt the force of gazes brimming over with anger and hatred and was baffled by it. What had he done to warrant such a reaction?

On the far side of the vault, he saw a raised wooden platform. Next to it stood what looked like the tower of an oil derrick, only about a tenth-scale version. It was, Mal thought, the remains of a drilling rig the miners would have used. It looked old. Somebody had prospected here once. Somebody had gone home empty-handed, doubtless having sunk some capital into the enterprise and bankrupted themselves. That would explain leaving equipment behind. No point throwing good money after bad.

The rig's uppermost deck was raised about six feet from the floor. The familiar green and yellow flag of the Independents hung from the guardrail. Normally the emblem would have been an encouraging, uplifting sight to Mal, telling him he was among friends. Now he wasn't so sure he was.

A chant began to rise from the crowd of people, low and scattered at first, then rapidly building so loud in the enclosed space that it hurt his ears—as well as his feelings.

"Trai-tor! Trai-tor!"

He blinked incredulously. Him. They were yelling it at *him*.

"Settle down!" a voice boomed over the crowd. "All of you, settle down!"

The Browncoat men and women immediately stopped yelling at Mal and turned to face the platform, where a man had just stepped into view. Mal's jaw dropped as he recognized the speaker.

"Hey, Mal. Welcome to the end of your life," said Toby Finn.

The planet Shadow, long ago

They were known as the Four Amigos. Their antics were legendary, at least amongst their peers, although amongst the inhabitants of their hometown, Seven Pines Pass, and most of the neighboring towns, they were considered tearaways and a liability. They drank. They got into and out of scrapes. They drank some more. They fell foul of the law from time to time. They drank even more. But they were essentially good-hearted, a bunch of kids on the cusp of adulthood who liked to mess around a bit and didn't much care about the consequences.

There was Tobias Finn, the youngest of the four, known to his friends as Toby. Toby was pliant, going along with pretty much whatever the rest of them did, just glad to be in their company. This meant the others sometimes took advantage of him, like that time they persuaded him to shave all his hair off because they said girls found bald men attractive, or that time they dared him to steal Sheriff Bundy's seven-point-star badge right off his lapel, which earned Toby a night in jail and a hefty fine.

There was Jamie Adare, the oldest of them, who considered himself their leader. Jamie was the one who usually came up with the harebrained schemes which the others would either agree to carry out or not, depending how much booze they'd imbibed and how reckless their collective mood was. He was a clever kid who could have done well at school if he'd made an effort but he preferred to dedicate his brainpower to having fun, and it could be argued that that was a better use for it than learning algebra and slogging through dull-as-ditchwater literary classics from Earth-That-Was.

Then there was Jamie's sister Jinny. Beautiful Jinny, she of the long, flowing ash-blonde hair and the cute uptilted nose with the smattering of freckles across the bridge like a map of some uncharted star system. Jinny, who was even cleverer than her brother, academically speaking, but possessed just as much of a wild streak. Jamie and Jinny were the despair of their parents, two unbroken colts that would not be tamed. Ma and Pa Adare longed for their offspring to make something of themselves, maybe leave Shadow, where your life options were frankly limited, and relocate to one of the Core planets. Out here on this mudball on the fringes of the Georgia system there was nothing but arable farms and cattle ranches, and that was fine but not necessarily suitable for anyone with smarts and a low boredom threshold. There were worlds where a young man or woman with the right grades and the right attitude could prosper—and maybe send a portion of that prosperity to the folks back home.

The fourth member of the Four Amigos was a handsome devil with too-long hair and a heck of a swagger for a kid scarcely out of his teens. The twinkle in his eye and the twist of his cocksure grin had won him the hearts of countless ladies in this county and the next, and gotten him into their beds too. More than once—many times more, in fact—this incorrigible Romeo had been turfed out of a young woman's room by an irate father wielding a twelve-gauge, and he had enough buckshot scars peppering his backside to prove it.

His name was Malcolm Reynolds, but he preferred just "Mal."

Mal's father was long gone, and his mother ran the family ranch, with forty hands answering to her. Mrs. Reynolds had the lined, pinched face of a woman who was, if not thriving, then at least surviving in a life that never made things easy. The skin around her eyes was heavily wrinkled, and she had a permanent squint from staring so long across Shadow's prairie vistas. From time to time she would call on her son to help out with work—shoeing, branding, rounding up, plowing, and so forth—and he would, but she knew she couldn't rely on him; and the older he got, the less reliable he became. Mal had too much else on his mind, namely chasing after girls and trouble. His personality seemed just too big for a small planet like this one to contain, and his feet were itchy. His destiny, Mrs. Reynolds couldn't help thinking, lay elsewhere, out there in the 'verse. She hated the thought that he would leave Shadow but knew the day would inevitably come. It was simply a question of how soon.

Meanwhile the Four Amigos' exploits just kept getting more and more outrageous. Perhaps the capstone of their careers in mischief came one especially hot and dusty summer when Mortimer Ponticelli rustled several head of cattle off the Hendricksons' land, rounding the cows up as though they belonged to him and spiriting them off to his corral. Ponticelli even went to the effort of erasing the Hendricksons' brand off the cattle's flanks using dermal menders and replacing it with his own.

It was out-and-out larceny, and everyone knew he was guilty as sin, but there was no proof, at least not as far as Sheriff Bundy was concerned, and anyway Mort Ponticelli and Sheriff Bundy were best buddies—Bundy was actually married to one of the old geezer's many daughters—so the idea of the theft being investigated, let alone a prosecution being brought, was laughable.

"I say we do something about it," Jamie Adare proposed one evening at the Silver Stirrup Saloon, the one and only drinking establishment in Seven Pines Pass. "Old Man Ponticelli's been pulling crap like this since as long as anyone can remember, and it's about time someone set him to rights."

"And that's us, huh?" said Mal.

"You bet your ass it is. Ain't nobody gonna lift a finger against him, not while Bundy's in his pocket."

"In his pocket?" said Jinny Adare. "Sherriff Bundy kisses Ponticelli's ass so hard, he's got permanent lip sores."

"But what?" Toby Finn asked. "What can we do?"

"We can get those cows back," Jamie said. "We can go there tonight and just take 'em."

Toby looked dubious. "Mort Ponticelli'll shoot you soon as look at you. Don't know about you guys, but I value my life. I got more left to live of it than you."

"He won't kill us," Jamie said. "Wouldn't dare. Stealing's one thing, but murder? Not even Bundy could get him off that rap. He'd hang for sure, and he knows it."

"I don't know…"

"Oh, come on, Toby," Jinny said, patting his cheek. "Don't be scared. I'll look after you."

Jinny was always affectionate towards him, and Toby preened at her touch. Though her junior by three years, anyone with eyes in their head could tell that he was madly in love with her. He had been since he was in fifth grade and she was in eighth. Now that he was at last old enough for the age difference not to seem such an unbridgeable gulf, it was only a matter of time before he declared his feelings towards her. He had confided as much to Mal, and Mal had encouraged him to wait at least a little while more. You didn't just go telling girls you loved them, he had counseled Toby. If, and only if, you were completely sure that she was the one for you, did you 'fess up that you liked her deeply, rather than just in the carnal fashion. In the meantime, Mal's recommendation to Toby was that he should play the field, just as he himself was. Get some notches on his belt and then go for the big prize. You had to have a few go-rounds on the carousel first before you reached for the brass ring, after all. Otherwise you'd grab for it and miss, and you'd have blown your shot, maybe for good.

Mal gave this advice for reasons that were not entirely honorable and disinterested. 'Cause while he was indeed playing the field, treating himself to many a go-round on that metaphorical carousel, there was one girl he had set his sights on above all the rest; one who captivated him and whose presence never failed to thrill him; one who in the fullness of time, when the moment was right, he would make his. And she was called Jinny Adare.

Now, as Jinny worked her wiles on Toby, all the kid could do was blush and nod.

"Since when has Jamie ever led us astray?" she added.

"I could count the times on my fingers, but I'd run out of hands," Toby replied. He scrubbed his head. "My hair ain't ever felt the same since it grew back."

Jamie chortled. "Fair comment. But this time it ain't just some prank, Toby old pal. This is serious. Nobody else is gonna hold Ponticelli to account. The old bastard's been riding roughshod over this town for years. We can show him what we think about that, and if we do it right, he won't even know it was us."

Several beers later, the plan—such as it was—had been finalized.

They rode to the Ponticelli ranch on horseback, leaving their mounts tethered to a tree a mile out and going the rest of the way on foot. Mal took point. He was generally agreed to be the best plainsman among them. He knew the lay of the land like nobody's business, having spent much of his childhood exploring and roaming the county. Growing up with no father at home to curb him and his mother too busy to tend to him, he had been more or less a free agent. His attendance record at school had been patchy verging on nonexistent. He had invariably found the lure of the wilderness far stronger than the lure of the classroom.

The night was moonless but the starlight bright enough to see by as Mal led the other Amigos along a back trail, down a narrow defile, and across a dry creek bed. They moved in a wide circle around Mort Ponticelli's homestead so that they approached it from the rear, coming at it from the cover of a thicket of tall scrub and knotty cactus. The longhorn cows in the corral lowed nervously as they tiptoed closer.

"Which ones are his and which the Hendricksons'?" Toby whispered.

"No way of telling," said Jamie. "But it makes no nevermind. He poached a dozen, so we take a dozen, any dozen. That's fair and square."

Mal, Jamie and Jinny slipped over the corral fence while Toby kept lookout. There were no lights on in any of the windows of the house, and just a single porch lamp winking on the veranda at the back.

They had brought rope, and carefully they fashioned halters and slipped them around the necks of a dozen cows, joining them together in pairs.

Then Jamie unlatched the corral gate and opened it, nice and slow, and the others began leading the tethered cattle out two by two, like latterday Noahs with a very singular notion of which species they were going to load aboard their Ark.

All was going smoothly until one of the final pair of cows got it into its head to complain. It began to make those anxious, hiccupping moos that signaled bovine distress, and Mal could only assume that it was one of Ponticelli's own livestock, rather than any of the Hendricksons'. It had been born and raised on this patch of land and didn't cotton to the idea of being removed.

Jinny laid a hand on the cow's nose and murmured in its ear in order to quieten it. She had a way with cattle. They seemed to succumb to her charms as readily as any human male. The steer bowed its head, almost as if in apology for having caused a fuss.

Mal cast an anxious eye towards the house. No lights coming on. No one shouting. They'd gotten away with it.

Then they hadn't.

The back door burst open, and there on the veranda was Mort Ponticelli himself. He powered up a thousand-lumen flashlight and swung the beam towards the corral. It was as bright as the sun, a ray of incandescent brilliance that dazzled all of the Four Amigos, freezing them in place.

"You lousy varmints!" Ponticelli yelled. "I see you. You stop right there. I got a rifle and I ain't afraid to use it."

To underscore his point, he loosed off a round. He aimed high deliberately, but not that high. The bullet zipped only a few feet above their heads, buzzing through the air like an angry and very lethal wasp.

"Warning shot," Ponticelli said. "Next one goes right through one of you."

They all looked at Jamie.

"What do we do?" Toby said.

Jamie's jaw was set firm. "What we came here to do."

So saying, he thwacked the hindquarters of the nearest cow, which was not one of the dozen tied in pairs. It let out a shrill objection and charged for the open gate. The other cattle in the corral saw this as an invitation to stampede. All at once, the whole herd, which numbered close on a hundred, were making a beeline for the gate. As they thundered through, the roped pairs which were already outside started running ahead of them. Freedom beckoned and they were all suddenly keen to seize the opportunity.

It was pandemonium, added to by Ponticelli, who began firing at the quartet of cattle thieves. Ducking low, Mal grabbed Jinny and hauled her towards the fence, using the fleeing cows as a shield. Jamie followed suit. They jumped the fence and kept running, joined now by Toby. Bullet after bullet zinged towards them, one coming so close to Mal that it struck the cow right next to him. The beast went cartwheeling over, 1,500 pounds of flailing legs and meaty body, and Mal had to fling himself to one side to avoid a collision. If the cow had rolled on him, he would have been flattened.

"Sonofabitch!" Ponticelli hollered from the house. He was clearly very upset to have killed one of his own cattle. "You'll pay for that, you scumbags."

Mal rose just in time to see another cow plunging towards him, head lowered. He was simply an obstacle in its way and it seemed to have no qualms about mowing him down.

Jinny saved him, yanking him by the scruff of the neck. Together they tumbled backwards onto the ground, and the cow lumbered past. They were back on their feet in no time, but Ponticelli had his range now. The next bullet he fired off came so close, Mal's hair was wafted by the pressure wave of its passing. He and Jinny sprinted after Jamie and Toby, trying to put distance between them and the house, but a further bullet made the ground directly in front of their feet erupt in a tiny plume of dust. Mal was certain that Ponticelli wasn't going to miss again.

Desperately he looked around for cover. There was nothing except the thicket, still fifty yards away. Then an idea occurred.

Yet another cow was trundling towards them. Mal grabbed it by the horns and hoisted himself onto its back. It was a feat of athleticism he would never have attempted under any other circumstances, and might never be able to repeat even if he wanted to.

"Jinny! Quick!"

He reached out to her. She accelerated to keep pace with the cow. Hands clasped forearms, and Mal swung her up behind him. The cow lolloped onward. Even burdened with two passengers, it was barely slowed. Better yet, just as Mal had hoped, Ponticelli was loath to take a shot at them and risk losing another head of prime beef. He obviously valued his livestock higher than his desire to see malefactors get their just desserts. His impotent shouts from the veranda trailed after them, dwindling in volume.

Mal and Jinny rode the cow for half a mile, by which time the stampede had begun to lose impetus. As they slowed, they looked around for Jamie and Toby, and discovered that the two of them had copied their example and were also mounted on cows. All four exchanged grins of exhilaration and relief.

"That was about the craziest thing ever, you bareback-riding a steer," Jamie said to Mal. "Hadn't seen it with my own eyes, I'd never have believed it. But I thought, 'You know, if Mal Reynolds can manage it, so can I.'"

"I fell off twice," said Toby. "Reckon my butt's gonna be black and blue for days. But it was worth it. We did it! We've gotten away with it!"

They dismounted and rounded up the roped-up cows, which they drove towards the spot where they'd left the horses. The remaining cows were at liberty to do as they wished, which probably meant traipsing back to the Ponticelli corral eventually. Cows were homebodies that way.

It was a short hop to the Hendrickson farm. Day was dawning as the Four Amigos led the cattle down the front drive, anticipating a heroes' welcome.

What they got was Anders Hendrickson emerging from the house in the company of Sheriff Bundy. Hendrickson looked perturbed, even frightened. Bundy had his thumbs hooked in his gun belt beneath his bulging gut.

"Get down off of them horses," he ordered.

The Four Amigos complied. None of them was armed, whereas Bundy had a pistol at his side and a hand hovering close to it.

"Shoulda known it'd be you four," he said, shaking his head ruefully. "You think Mort Ponticelli didn't call me soon as his cattle were taken? You think I wouldn't know where they might be coming? Paid Anders here a visit first thing, and he swore to me it weren't nothing to do with him."

"It ain't," Hendrickson said. "Honest to God."

"You didn't put these kids up to it, then?"

"No, Sheriff."

"Might be as I believe you," Bundy said, "seeing as how this is just the sorta stunt these four would pull without needing to be asked. It's you I particularly feel ashamed for, Jamie and Jinny Adare. You two could make something of yourselves, and you're just fritterin' it all away. Toby there is too young and callow to know better, while Mal Reynolds ain't been nothin' but a disruptive influence since the day he was born and will likely continue to be such till the day he dies, which the way he's going won't be that far in the future."

"I have a problem with authority," Mal said, "not least when said authority is a big, fat, corrupt lawman with poor personal hygiene and a face that'd give a moose nightmares."

Bundy strode down the front steps and sauntered over to Mal, thrusting his face up close.

"Say that again, boy," he growled.

"Did I mention bad breath too?" Mal said. "Because seriously, Sheriff, would it kill you to try a mint every once in a while?"

The backhand slap came out of nowhere, hard enough to send Mal reeling to the ground.

Clutching his face with one hand, the other clenched into a fist, Mal sprang up again. Bundy's gun, cocked and leveled with his face, halted him in his tracks.

"Just try, Reynolds," he said. "You just try, you insubordinate piece of *fèi wù*. I won't regret blowing your brains out the back of your head. I'll even take pleasure going and telling your momma what I did and why I did it. Wonder if she'll cry or she'll just shrug like she knew you had it comin'?"

Mal ground his teeth. Jinny, who could see he was getting ready to hit Bundy come what may, put a restraining arm across his chest.

"Don't," she said. "Don't give him the excuse."

Mal backed down reluctantly. If it had been anyone but Jinny, he might not have heeded the advice.

"We're sorry, Sheriff," said Jamie. "It was high spirits, is all. We didn't mean nothing by it. We'll return Old Man Ponticelli's cattle."

"You better. You're also gonna pay him reparations."

"For what?" Mal said.

"Because I damn well say so, that's for what!" Bundy snapped. He named a figure that was equivalent to a month's salary for the average working stiff. He knew it was far more than the Four Amigos could readily scrounge up between them. "And I want it in his hands by tomorrow sundown, or else the four of you are going to be spending time in the county lockup and I'm gonna see to it myself that you get half rations and the most lice-ridden bedrolls we got."

It was Toby who got them the money. The Finns were well off by Shadow standards, Liam Finn being a land surveyor and Marla Finn a practicing lawyer. Toby begged them for a handout, which they gave unwillingly. Every spare coin the four of them earned over the next few weeks went towards paying back the debt.

In hindsight, they'd had a heck of an escapade, but it was a couple of months before the Four Amigos could truly laugh about it, and it was another couple of months before they plucked up the nerve to try anything even near as audacious again. During that time, Toby seemed to stand a little taller and carry himself with a little more confidence. Since he was the one who'd bailed them out—with parental assistance, but even so—he seemed to feel he had attained an elevated status within the group. He was no longer just the kid who tagged along. He was the equal of any of them.

This clearly gave him the impression that he stood a better chance with Jinny now, and he stepped up his campaign to make her his girlfriend.

And, much to Mal's chagrin, it appeared to work. Jinny,

at least, ceased treating Toby like a little brother: she no longer patted him or smiled at him with the same hint of condescension, but had gained a newfound respect for him, mirroring the newfound respect he had gained for himself. Now she and he would share confidences. Mal would catch them, in unguarded moments, with their heads together, chatting, sometimes giggling.

It stuck in his craw. And yet he couldn't challenge Toby for Jinny's affections, not now. It wouldn't have been right. They were the Four Amigos. They were as tight as a knot, as thick as thieves, bonded together by a shared love of roguery, famous for it, notorious. Mal couldn't let his jealousy jeopardize that.

Could he?

17

"Toby," Mal said softly. "Toby Finn."

Toby, his one-time Amigo, his another-time brother-in-arms. The man he would have gladly given his life for both before and during the war.

Now, here he was, up on the platform, and from what Mal could make out of his appearance, Toby was much changed. He was thin, positively emaciated, and was stooped over like a crookbacked octogenarian. His face was gaunt, and the mop of unruly ginger ringlets that Mal remembered was now a wispy cap, the few strands remaining atop his head coarse and kinked like copper wire. Toby used to catch holy hell in Independent bootcamp over those carroty curls of his. The other recruits called him Rusty and Little Orange. Seemed the postwar years, as for so many others, Mal himself included, had not been kind to Toby.

But he was alive, and here, and Mal was overjoyed. He cupped his hands and shouted, "Tobias! Tobias Finn! Toby!"

His voice ricocheted off the surround of rock walls

and ceiling. From the cavern floor, heads twisted in his direction. On the dais, Toby Finn stared up, his expression blank, unreadable. Mal was taken aback. Did Toby not recognize him?

"Toby, it's me," he called. "Mal. You remember me, right?"

His words were met with boos and hisses. Shocked, as though the catcalling had a physical force, Mal took a step backwards. Someone, a hatchet-faced woman with a lazy eye, grabbed his arm and held him still. The chorus of ill will rose in volume, buffeting him like body blows.

This is insane, Mal thought. *It's like I'm public enemy number one. What in tarnation is going on?*

Then Toby raised his hands for silence. Gradually the din died down.

"Ladies, gentlemen, comrades one and all," he said to the crowd, "it's been a long time coming, but I have done what you asked and what I promised." He thrust out his arm, pointing at Mal. "I have brought to face justice the man who conspired with the Alliance and stole victory from our grasp. I have brought you the traitor Malcolm Reynolds."

At the word *traitor*, which rolled off Toby's tongue with great emphasis, a fresh barrage of boos and shouted curses flew in Mal's direction.

"String him up!" someone yelled over the din. "String him up!"

It quickly became a new chant, not "Trai-tor! Trai-tor!" now but "String him up! String him up! String him up!"

Mal's brain strove to process this turn of events. On either side of him, his captors grinned and nodded to each other, as if seeing him humiliated was a rare and memorable treat.

This can't be right, he thought. *It* ain't *right. I must be asleep on the floor of my shuttle, still dopey from that gas Covington spritzed me with.*

But he wasn't. And now that his eyes had completely adjusted to the dim and shifting light, he picked out a couple of other faces below that he recognized. Other Browncoats whom he had fought alongside in Serenity Valley. Sonya Zuburi, her raven hair prematurely streaked with white, looked like she wanted to take a bite out of him. Her husband David had his hand wrapped firmly around her arm and was holding her back. Mal had saved both of their lives at the risk of his own, advancing into the teeth of an enemy barrage, laying down covering fire so they could retreat from a burning barn. The expressions on their faces said his selfless act was long forgotten and had been replaced by something other than eternal gratitude.

Sonya raised her fist and shook it at him as she chanted along with the others.

David must have loosened his grip on her, because she suddenly broke free, pushing away, shouldering between two burly men, one of whom stood aside to let her pass. As Sonya rushed towards the foot of the wall below the ledge, she bent down and picked up something from the floor. In the process, she sideswiped a fellow veteran, knocking him onto his back in the dirt.

Her face contorted with rage, Sonya flung the rock at Mal. The men flanking him dodged the projectile, but Mal stood his ground, and he felt the breeze as it zinged past his left ear, missing him by millimeters.

"Enough of that," Toby Finn shouted at the backs of the

crowd. "Stand down, Sonya. We aren't a gorramn rabble. We're soldiers! We will be disciplined about this."

Mal turned to the man standing beside him and said, "What is it that you think I've done?"

A blank stare was his only response, as if Mal had spoken in a foreign language. For one weird second he wondered if the man was a robot with a malfunctioning neural cortex. The sense that this couldn't actually be happening, that this was all some feverish dream, welled up inside him again; yet he couldn't deny the reality of his predicament. Not ten minutes ago, his biggest problem was a full bladder. Death by lynch mob was looming larger as a source of concern.

A peal of hurrahs rose up as a bald man scrambled up the front of Toby's platform with a coil of rope. He stopped near the top and held out his arm, dangling a hangman's noose from his fist. To roars of approval, he tied the end of the rope to the handrail and let the noose drop free.

The crowd's frenzy bubbled up, soon on the verge of boiling over. And when it did, Mal was pretty sure they were going find the courage to stretch his neck.

Mob mentality. It could turn so quick. During the war, Mal had heard tales about noncombatant folks weeping at the sight of the Browncoats arriving in their town to help them, then dry those tears when it came clear that as hard as the Independents fought, the town was going to fall to the Alliance. Heard that they blamed the men and women who had taken up arms to keep them free and turned on the exhausted soldiers, offering them to the Alliance commanders, even begging for them to be killed, as tears streamed down Browncoats' war-worn faces. Sometimes folks went crazy with despair and did the killing themselves.

They blamed us because they believed in us and we failed, Mal thought. *Is that why I'm here?*

"String him up! String him up!" the crowd continued, surging to the foot of the wall.

Tightly spaced gunshots rang out, sharp and deafening in the enclosed space. Armed men stepped forward, moving in front of the dais, their weapons shouldered and aimed at the spectators.

"We will have order!" Toby bellowed at them. "We will follow the rule of law. The accused will get a fair trial and be judged by his peers. I know you're eager to see justice done, but we are not thugs. Malcolm Reynolds will get his day in court."

"And *then* we'll string him up!" shouted someone in the crowd.

"Due process," Toby Finn reminded them sternly. He gestured to Mal. "We are not criminals. We are not like him. A traitor is the worst kind of bad man there is. No allegiance to flag or brigade, no allegiance except to save his own stinking skin. Lock up the prisoner. Guard him well. We don't want nobody taking it on themselves to do anything unlawful. Do you all hear me?"

"Toby, just listen to me for one moment," Mal said. "Please."

Toby could scarcely hear him over the tumult. He beckoned for silence. "Fella wants to say something. You've got a moment, Mal. Speak."

"I don't know what's gotten into you, Toby," Mal said, "but I'm minded to think it's something we can work out.

Let's sit down together over a drink, you and me, just like we used to at the Silver Stirrup back in the day, and talk it over. We were friends. Still are, to the best of my knowledge. I realize things on Shadow didn't end as we'd have liked, 'specially where Jinny Adare's concerned. That... That is one of the real tragedies of my life. But I always thought we'd put it behind us. Leastways that's how you always acted during the war. What's changed since?"

"What has changed, Mal?" came the reply. "Why, only everything. I'm not the naïve kid you used to know. I'm older, wiser. I've learned things."

Mal sensed he wasn't going to get anywhere with Toby, not in the time available, so he addressed himself to the crowd in general.

"I don't understand what's happening. We're all Browncoats here, am I right? We all fought in the war, fought the Alliance. I'm one of you. You must appreciate that. I've never done *anything* could warrant such treatment. Whatever crime you think it is I committed—and I would surely love to someone to tell me—I am innocent."

"Fine words," Toby said, "from a lying *tā mā de hún dàn*." He jabbed a finger in Mal's direction. "You *know* what you did. And all this time you've gotten away with it, until now. Now, at last, your sins are catching up with you. How's it feel? Maybe it feels like all along you've known this day was coming, and now that it's arrived you're glad, almost relieved. Your life of skulking around, of passing for honorable, is at an end. You can finally face up to who you really are."

Baying cries rose up as Mal shouted, "That's bullcrap, Toby. If anyone's guilty of being dishonorable, it's you with this here three-ring circus of yours. You've got this bunch of morons all whipped up into a lather with your pandering and your speechifying, but you're the one who's lying, and they're gonna realize it sooner or later, and then where will you be? Huh?"

He realized he wasn't helping his case any, insulting Toby and the other Browncoat veterans, but he was darned if he was going to let them make him their patsy or scapegoat or whatever it was they wanted him to be. He wasn't going down without a fight, and for the time being at least, his best and only weapons were words.

Sure enough, the crowd went berserk, stomping and hollering. They were out for blood—his blood—and Toby didn't hesitate to egg them on.

"Listen to him," he said. "That's how little he thinks of you. That's the attitude of a man who'd sell out his brothers and sisters. Get him out of here! I want him out of my sight."

A barrage of hate crashed down on Mal as the guards formed a huddle around him and herded him back down the tunnel, led by the hatchet-faced woman with the lazy eye. His legs were wobbly. His wrists chafed in their bonds. Everything that didn't throb ached and everything that didn't ache throbbed. He felt about a hundred years old.

This time when they reached the fork in the tunnel, they took the other branch, away from the shouting and the fury. Away from Toby Finn, one of his best friends growing up on Shadow, who, by some inexplicable twist of fate, planned to be his executioner.

In the light of the torches, the hatchet-faced woman stopped. She turned towards the wall on the right, yanking open a rusted, wire-mesh door. The hinges squealed. Hatchet Face gestured impatiently at the opening. Mal's escorts bunched in tight around him like they expected him to make a run for it. Like they hoped he would, so they could beat him down. His lizard brain told him to do just that. *Make your gorramn play. See what it gets you.* He knew if he walked through that opening, he was never going to come out again. Might as well make a stand here and now, even if it only hastened the inevitable.

As the guards shuffled Mal forward, time seemed to slow. Details of his surroundings became magnified, larger than life. Water trickled down one of the tunnel walls, drop by drop, disappearing into a dark puddle of muck. A moth circled a burning torch, flirting with fiery death. Something made a little screechy noise farther down the tunnel in the darkness. A bat, maybe. Hanging upside down, trying to fall back to sleep.

Mal's heart pounded to a funereal cadence, the kind where widows in black veils walk lead-footed behind the caisson, the dead soldier's boots dangling backwards from the stirrups of his horse. Damn, he was in such strange ungodly trouble.

As they reached the doorway in the wall, he slid his glance into the dim hole where they planned to plant him. It must have been a storeroom of some kind. Nothing on the floor, no straw for a bed, nor a blanket to cover himself. Just dirt. And rock. Behind him he could sense the mass of the guards, blocking his way out. Once more his very soul protested, screaming at him to save himself. To do *something*.

No. It would make more sense to be compliant. Do what

they wanted him to. Bide his time. That would give him the leisure to think of a way out of this situation.

So a calmer portion of his mind advocated.

But then adrenaline took over, a surge of fight-or-flight, an impulse whose dictates were impossible to refuse. There was no decision to act. It just happened, of its own accord, like water flowing downhill. Mal spun on his heel, bent low and charged the nearest guard, shoulder-striking the man mid-chest and knocking him off-balance and backward. As hands reached for Mal, he used the space he'd created, lashing out with his right boot. Contact, as he kicked the man between the legs. Without his arms free to counterbalance him, the kick was a little off-center, a little too far back to cause maximum pain, but it was still enough to elicit a squeal and a gasp. Mal spun again, one complete turn, building momentum. The man was on his knees, mouth gaping, so Mal didn't have to kick high to hit him in the jaw. He felt the impact all the way to his hip joint. It felt good.

Someone in front of him grabbed his shoulders and Mal lunged forward, using his head as a battering ram, driving the crown of it into the other's midriff. The hands released him. Mal whirled around, then charged the person blocking the doorway, Hatchet Face herself. Before he could reach her, fists from all sides, all angles, rained down on him, slamming into his solar plexus, connecting with his jaw, his kidneys. Mal staggered forward under the onslaught, fell to his knees in the dirt, then toppled forward.

A crushing weight came down on his back, grinding his face deeper into the soft dirt. He couldn't breathe. He grunted. It was the only noise he could make as the fist-pounding continued. Black washes of pain filled his mouth as the weight suddenly came off and he was dragged backwards by his legs into the storeroom, which was clearly going to serve as a holding cell. Angry shouts played counterpoint to the toecaps battering his sides. Then hoarse laughter as the door clanged shut with the sudden force of a coffin lid. A bolt clanked as it was shot home.

Oh, God, that was dumb, Mal chastised himself. *Why'd I go and do that?*

The man he had so soundly dropkicked pressed his bruised mouth to the rusted mesh of the metal door. "You're gonna die," he said to Mal, his voice dripping with relish just as his split lips dripped with blood. "And it's gonna be slow. Reeeal slow."

"And don't get to thinkin' anyone's coming to rescue you, neither," Hatchet Face crowed. "Apparently you captain a Firefly these days and have a crew. Well, we took you in your own shuttle from Guilder's and made it look as though you were piloting it, and the reason for that is nobody'll suspect otherwise, not even your people. They'll just assume, being the yellow-belly turncoat you are, you lit out on 'em, and they won't be bothered none to go after you."

"If you believe that," Mal said, "then you have sorely underestimated my crew. They ain't easily fooled. They're coming for me. I know it in my bones. And woe betide you when they get here, darling, because they'll be pissed and they will seriously mess up your day."

"Sure, sure," said Hatchet Face. "Even if that's the case, they're bound to be too late. How long do you think you've got? We're just waiting on a couple more folks to show.

Soon as they arrive—and it'll be any moment now—the trial will begin. And rest assured, it won't be a long trial. Your life can be measured in hours, Reynolds. Savor what time you have left, because it ain't much at all."

18

The room was large, with an artificial rock waterfall that towered at least fifteen feet high. The water spilled into a tiled pond. Golden koi fish swam lazily beneath lily pads, now and then mouthing the surface.

Opposite lay a big, rectangular picture window bordered by gleaming swords and battleaxes. The view was of a particularly beautiful section of Persephone, where large swathes of cultivated gardens hung between the silvery sky-rises. A wealthy district. If the docks were hell, this was heaven.

Mika Wong, having ushered Book into the room and allowed him a moment or two to admire his surroundings, gestured for him to take a seat in an ornate overstuffed chair. He picked up a remote off a small table and clicked on a holographic fireplace next to the chair. Then he instructed a servant, a man dressed in a butler's brass-buttoned livery, to fetch drinks. The butler filled two gold-hued cups from a matching decanter and handed one to Book and the other to Wong before gliding back over to a corner and stationing himself there, fixing his gaze in a dispassionate middle-distance stare.

Book lowered himself into the chair and sniffed the liquid. He had anticipated wine, which he would have had to decline, but to his delight found that he was drinking clean, fresh water. Cooled to a perfect chilliness, it was nectar on his tongue and went a long way to dispelling the ache in his head from the blows he had received at the hands of Charlie Dunwoody and company.

Wong sat opposite. The years had been kind to the former commander of the Alliance Anti-Terrorism Division. Taller than Book, his spine was ramrod straight. He was tanned and fit, his once-black hair now a sleek silvery gray instead of plain white like Book's. He was wearing black trousers and a slate-colored shirt, appearing almost militaristic.

"So," he said, "Derrial Book got rolled. Who would have thought? You, of all people."

Book smiled sheepishly. "Maybe I'm losing my edge."

"I doubt it. What happened?"

"I offered charity to a man who decided I was being too stingy." Book shrugged. "As they say, no good deed goes unpunished."

"Well, you were certainly punished."

"I'd like to say I had the situation under control..."

"But clearly you did not."

"And you, equally clearly, have not lost *your* edge," Book said. "That was some fancy footwork, for an old man."

"I keep in shape," Wong said. "I have a dojo on the premises and spar practically every day with my trainer. Just because I'm retired doesn't mean I have to atrophy. Also, I had the element of surprise. Those fellows didn't see me coming until it was too late to do them any good."

"A dojo. A room like this. A house this size. Staff." Book motioned at the butler, who acted oblivious, as though he was not even present in the room. "You're doing pretty well for yourself, Mika." *Especially*, he didn't say, *for a man living on a military pension*. For sure, the commander of an entire department would receive a decent annuity and plenty of perks, but enough to afford this kind of lifestyle? Not likely.

"I get by," Wong said. "How about you? Still sequestered away at Southdown?"

"I left the abbey a few months back. Thought I'd walk in the world a while."

"Why?" Wong crossed his legs and sipped from his glass. "I avoid it as much as possible."

"I find I still have things to do. A life of contemplation and prayer provides one with a peace that passeth all understanding, but our universe is far from peaceful. It seems self-indulgent to live apart, when so many are in need of help."

"You always were a bit of a radical."

"Or a pragmatist. We raise ourselves up by lifting others."

"You're full of pithy quotes." Wong smiled, but his gaze was sharp, brittle. Assessing. "It's been a long time," he added. "You'll have to catch me up."

"Quid pro quo," Book returned. "I never dreamed you'd retire."

"Forced out." Wong's tone was rueful and not a little

resentful. "New guidelines for mandatory retirement. They thought I was past it."

"That's a shame," Book said. "Shepherds don't retire. We just… redefine our vocations."

As Book took another swallow of water, he studied Wong. When he had known him before, the commander had been all spit-and-polish, a minimalist who traveled light. The Mika Wong of the past would have scoffed at the luxury in which the two of them now sat, and would have questioned the method by which such obvious wealth had been acquired if he were investigating someone else. He might well have accused a retired Alliance officer who lived like this of illegal practices. And Book recalled the waitress in the Sea Wolf saying as much about him. Forcing businesses to pay for protection? Could such a thing be true?

"At any rate," he said, "I'm glad you happened along when you did. Otherwise I'd be a whole lot poorer than I already am, and a whole lot more damaged, too."

"Yes, how are you feeling? Recovering from your ordeal?"

"More or less. I'm going to have a few lumps and bumps to show for it, but that's nothing new. Not to look a gift horse in the mouth or anything, but was it sheer chance you showed up?"

"You ask the question in a manner which suggests you don't think it was."

"Let's just say I'm wary of sudden turns of good fortune."

"Even when they might all be part of God's divine plan?" Wong laughed teasingly. "It was sheer happenstance, Derrial, genuinely. I was in the area, just passing through. Although, that being said, I *was* keeping half an eye out for a preacher, because I'd lately got word that one such had been asking around about Hunter Covington and Elmira Atadema."

The remark was a probing stiletto. Book parried. "Was it by any chance a waitress at the Sea Wolf told you that?"

"Saskia?"

"If that's her name. A bountiful woman in every regard."

Wong shook his head. "No, not her, although she has been known to send the odd piece of useful information my way now and then."

"No, come to think of it, I was set upon almost as soon as I left the Sea Wolf. You must have heard about me earlier than that. I know. The clerk at the quartermaster's office. Smotrich."

Now Wong nodded. "Smotrich earns a very modest salary. If he spies an opportunity to supplement it with a little extra cash, he seizes it with both hands. He's aware that I have an interest in Covington and Elmira. The funny thing is, as soon as he mentioned a Shepherd, you were the person I immediately thought of. What does that say about me, I wonder?"

"Says to me you don't know that many Shepherds."

"You know, in some ways it came as a surprise when I learned that Derrial Book had gone into the church. Back in the day, when you and I were both in uniform, I'd never have pegged you as a candidate for the clergy."

"At the risk of you accusing me again of being full of pithy quotes, the Bible has something to say about there being more joy in heaven over one sinner that repents than over ninety-nine just persons who need no repentance."

"You were a sinner?"

"Aren't we all?"

"I suppose you might consider yourself that, in light of what you did—or rather what you were accused of doing. Me, I always considered you a just person. There was a fundamental integrity about you which, I can see now in retrospect, makes you well fitted for the religious life. Tell me, was it hard making the switch?"

"Exchanging one institution for another? The Alliance for the Order? Not really. It's all just structure and hierarchy, at least on the surface." Book was choosing his words with care. His past—before Southdown Abbey—was a minefield. He didn't much enjoy revisiting it, and he always trod warily when he did. There were so many things that could explode in his face, and Wong knew more than a few of them. "Listen, Mika, much as it's pleasant to catch up, and much as I appreciate you interceding when I needed it, I'm currently conducting some business that's, to put it mildly, urgent. I have some associates I'd like to check in with."

Wong made a be-my-guest gesture.

Book pulled out his comm link. "In private, if I may."

"As you wish." Wong turned to dismiss the butler.

"I mean complete privacy. Some other room, perhaps? Where I can be on my ownsome?"

"How about I show you to my office?

"Well, I wouldn't mind stretching my legs," Book said amiably, "and to be honest, I'd like to see the rest of your home."

"Not what you expected, eh?" Wong said with some pride. "I came into an inheritance shortly after I retired."

"What luck," Book said. He didn't believe a word of it.

Wong stood and Book followed him out of the room, moving a little stiffly from his injuries. They walked together down a corridor sided by rainbow-hued glass behind which exotic ferns and flowers bloomed. Insects fluttered and crawled among the brilliant foliage. Book had never seen anything so opulent in a private home. Members of domestic staff trotted silently by. It was gone midnight, but still they were on duty, ready to respond to Wong's every beck and call.

Withholding comment, Book followed Wong into an austere office consisting of a metal desk, several metal upright chairs, and dozens of framed commendations, medals, and pictures with various departments and divisions. This was more like the Mika Wong he had known before.

"Here you go," Wong said. "I'll leave you to it. I imagine you might be hungry; I'll have the cook prepare something to eat."

"Thank you," Book said, waiting until Wong left.

That, he thought, *could not have gone much better.* If Wong hadn't himself suggested going to his office, Book would have dropped hints to that effect; or else, as soon as he was alone, he would have snuck through the house looking for just such a room.

The truth was, he had very little that was new to report to Zoë and the others. What he did have was the near certainty that Mika Wong was dirty—running some sort of protection racket in Eavesdown, a gamekeeper turned poacher— and that Wong was connected with Elmira Atadema and therefore, by inference, Covington. It was strange that Wong had not inquired *why* Book was so interested in those two people, at least not yet. His lack of curiosity was in itself curious. Perhaps, over a meal, he might broach the topic. Well, Book would deal with that eventuality as and when it arose. Until then, he was going to make the most of the window of opportunity he had wangled for himself.

Wong must have information about Elmira and Covington, most likely in this very office. Book scanned the room for security cameras, to see if his search would be detected. Just because he saw none did not mean there were none, but it seemed unlikely that Wong would monitor his own workspace in the heart of his own home. Acting as fast as possible, Book opened and closed drawers and folders both in the man's actual desk and onscreen. Strange codes and addresses of businesses on Persephone—Wong's protection racket? He kept looking, freezing when he came upon a hard-copy folder in the lower desk drawer labeled ATADEMA, ELMIRA.

He opened the folder and began to skim an official-looking document.

SUBJECT: Missing; unable to locate.

So Wong had been keeping tabs on Elmira Atadema at the very least. The date the subject had gone missing was marked as the day before Alliance Day. Clearly "missing" meant something different to Wong than it did on her wanted poster. She had escaped from her bondholder months before and been recaptured, but Wong had lost track of her within the last twenty-four hours.

Book was so engrossed in the document that he lost situational awareness. He should have heard the footfalls in the corridor outside sooner, but by the time he did they had stopped at the door and the door itself was opening.

He froze, the document in his hands. If it was a member of Wong's staff, he would bluff his way out of trouble, playing the role of hapless, innocent Shepherd.

But it was Wong himself standing in the doorway.

"Derrial," he said, scowling unhappily. "What the hell?"

Book decided he had nothing to lose.

"You know that I'm looking for Elmira Atadema, Mika," he said. "I've been asking around on Persephone for information on her, and everything points to you having some kind of professional interest in her." He raised the folder. "I've just confirmed that for myself."

"Then why not just ask me outright what I know about the woman?" Wong said, grabbing the folder from him. "Why all the cloak and dagger?"

"We haven't seen each other in a long time," Book said. "I've only recently started looking for her and I'm learning the lay of the land." *And you're living rich, and a certain waitress accused you of some very nefarious dealings.*

Wong frowned. "But Book, it's *me*. We go back a ways. We were both officers. We served on the *Cortez* together. I was there when you got shafted over the *Alexander* disaster and took the fall."

Book bowed his head, acknowledging perhaps the darkest, most ignominious episode from his former life.

"I thought... I thought you were someone I could always trust," Wong went on. "I respected you. I was your superior officer but still I looked up to you. Why in hell else would I have helped you out with those muggers? Soon as I saw who it was they were beating up—Derrial Book!—I weighed in. Didn't think twice about it. And this is how you reward me?" He sounded genuinely upset. "So I suppose the only reason you agreed to accompany me back to my place was so that you could snoop around?"

"In part, yes."

"Huh. Guess you're not the 'just person' I thought you were after all."

"I don't pretend to be perfect, Mika," said Book. "I try my best to be virtuous, but oftentimes the circumstances demand a touch of deceit. For what it's worth, I'm sorry."

Wong seemed in two minds whether to accept the apology.

"You have every right to throw me out on my ear," Book continued. "Wouldn't blame you at all if you did. But I beg you, in the name of the respect you once had for me and indeed I once had for you, help me out here. I'm floundering, and there's a great deal riding on anything you can tell me about Elmira and Covington."

Wong deliberated, conflicting emotions chasing one another across his face.

Finally, with an audible sigh, he relented.

"What do you need to know?" he said, lowering his defenses but not putting the folder down.

Book used much the same story he had told Saskia the waitress. "One of my erstwhile brethren at the abbey is a cousin of Elmira's. He contacted me, worried about her. I came to Eavesdown, and what do I find but a missing person poster for her? The more I've learned, the more it seems she's gotten herself into a dire situation and may well be dead. As a matter of fact"—he nerved himself to deliver a deeper lie—"I was considering approaching you if I drew a blank everywhere else. You used to head up the Anti-Terrorism Division, and your remit included dealing with vigilantes." He paused, but Wong remained poker-faced. "And one of my respondents connected Elmira to a group of vigilantes."

"Who was it?" Wong pressed.

Book could have admitted that it was Saskia, but she had only verified what Jayne had discovered earlier. He didn't want Wong to think the waitress had given away too much. It might scupper any further dealings she had with him, and might even earn her a reprisal. "Somebody who prefers to remain anonymous."

"Okay, so what kind of connection did your anonymous source tell you there is between Elmira and these vigilantes?"

Book sat back in the chair and steepled his fingers under his chin. "It seems to me that it's your turn to share some information, Mika. I've been forthcoming, but I've gotten nothing in return."

"This isn't a trade," Wong said.

Book remained patient. "Most things are. Don't see why this should be any different."

Finally Wong said, "You're still a Shepherd, yes?"

Book nodded. "I am. I've left the abbey for the time being, but I haven't left the Order."

Wong tapped the folder again. "Then here's how we do this. What I'm about to tell you falls within the purview of benefit of clergy. In other words, if you tell anyone what I'm about to discuss, in my opinion you will be violating the holy orders you took."

Confession didn't exactly work that way, but Book wasn't about to raise any objections. "Yes. Provided, of course, that withholding such information wouldn't make me complicit in the commission of a crime. If that's the case, then I'm under an obligation to reveal it."

Wong thought a moment, as if mentally reviewing what he planned to say and checking it twice. Book refrained from adding that there was nothing in his vows that would prevent him from *acting* on the information, as long as he didn't disclose who had shared it with him.

"This goes against the grain," Wong said. "I've been conducting this operation on a strictly need-to-know, and so far I've been the only one who needed to know."

Book remained placid. Then Wong said, "But your inferences are on the money. There are vigilantes active on Persephone—Browncoat vigilantes—and they have been committing atrocities on this planet and others. The Alliance is unhappy about it. They want all citizens to be safe. So I've been reactivated by my old division to stop them."

"I see," Book said.

"A few days ago the vigilantes here stepped up their operations. They've some sort of new objective that's gotten them all very excited, and Elmira told me she had found out what it was. We had a rendezvous scheduled for the day before Alliance Day so that she could lay it out to me in person, but she didn't make it. I haven't heard from her since."

Could this "objective" have something to do with Mal's disappearance? "How is she in a position to know what they're doing? Is she an Alliance plant? A spy?"

"A spy, in a sense. She was my CI—my confidential informant."

Gradually the pieces of the puzzle were coming together.

"How did you find her in the first place?" Book asked.

"During the war, a battalion of Browncoats burned down the Atadema family homestead and razed the surrounding land. Elmira's parents starved to death. She herself was in dire straits, close to dying the same way, so she made a choice. She sold herself as a bondswoman. It was her only way out."

"Dear Lord. That's shocking."

Wong frowned. "Well, you know how the Browncoats were. Declared themselves the champions of the people and then stole or destroyed everything they could. Damn barbarians."

There was no sense arguing with him, and Book was not there to change his mind. As far as Wong knew, Book had no truck with the Independent cause. He maintained a neutral expression and waited for Wong to continue.

"Life as a bondswoman can be very unpleasant," he prompted.

Wong's lip curled. "Yes, not least when your bondholder is Hunter Covington. He is, his suave demeanor to the contrary, not what you would call a nice man. At any rate, I'd got wind that Covington was in league with the vigilantes. Maybe not a sympathizer, as such, but associating with them on a commercial basis. Covington's a mover and shaker round these parts—when it comes to shady dealings, that is. He trades in information, people, data, whatever. Makes a tidy living out of it, too. On Persephone, and in Eavesdown in particular, knowing who's coming and who's going and what business they're about can set you high on the totem pole."

"Covington tipped the vigilantes off to something. Something big."

"More than that. He helped facilitate it, from what I hear."

The something big being... Mal?

"This I got from Elmira," Wong said. "Not the specifics, which she didn't know, but an overall picture that the vigilantes had major plans."

"You still haven't told me how you recruited her to be your woman on the inside with Covington."

"It was when she ran away from him. It came to my attention that there was a bondswoman, a fugitive on the run from Hunter Covington. By then I'd already established Covington's links to the vigilantes, and I realized here was my chance. I had someone who was ripe for cultivating. Elmira was hiding out in one of the slums not far from the docks. I approached her and promised her I'd set her up in a new life if she became my CI for a while. I sweetened it by promising to pay the full amount of her bond, when the time came."

"But in order to do that, she had to go back to Covington first." In effect, Elmira had exchanged one kind of servitude for another. Book, however, refrained from voicing this observation aloud.

"Which she did, voluntarily, albeit reluctantly," Wong said. "That's why Covington didn't kill her, when he almost certainly would have if he had simply caught her himself. You don't cross a man like that, not if you know what's good for you. Elmira went crawling back to him on hands and knees, making out as though she was sorry, she bitterly regretted what she had done, she wouldn't run away again. She begged him to take her back, and you know from that poster that she's a fine-looking woman. Face like hers, gazing up at you full of pleading and contrition—well, you just couldn't say no to it, could you? Even if you're a cruel-hearted piece of *lè sè* like Hunter Covington."

"Still, it chills me to think how he might have dealt with her. You took a huge gamble with her life, Mika."

"Elmira knew what she was getting herself into, and she thought the risk worth the reward."

"It may yet be that the risk has proved too great. Elmira has disappeared. Rumor is she may be dead."

Wong's shoulders sagged. "You heard that too, huh?"

"What if Covington has discovered she's your informant?"

"I reckon she'll be okay. She's had a tough life, and it's made her crafty and strong. But I always told her, if she ever felt she's getting in over her head, she can contact me and I'll pull her out. I'm trusting that because I haven't heard from her yet, nothing untoward has happened."

"Or it has and she was unable to get word to you in time."

"There is that," Wong admitted.

"So you're just crossing your fingers and hoping Covington hasn't murdered Elmira, most likely in some dreadful way?"

"No. Well, yes, maybe a little. But I have a contingency plan."

"Namely?"

"In case of emergency, I can locate her. Before Elmira returned to Covington, I had her fitted with a subdermal tracking implant, networked via the Cortex with heavy encryption and shielded internally so that it can't be detected by any electronic scan. It registers her bio-signs as well, so if she's alive, or otherwise, I'll know. All I need to do is activate it and I can pinpoint where she is, anywhere in the 'verse, to within a half-mile radius."

"Then why haven't you done so?"

"Why do you think I was downtown earlier?" Wong said. "I was trying to gather some solid intel on her disappearance. There's a great deal of tittle-tattle goes around Eavesdown and it can be an effort sorting the wheat from the chaff. I didn't want to go after Elmira to pull her out without good reason."

"Wouldn't want to blow her cover unnecessarily," Book said with undisguised sarcasm. "Waste of a good asset."

"Don't take that high moral tone with me, Derrial. I'm not an inhuman monster. I'm concerned about Elmira and I'll do all I can to get her back safe and sound, on the proviso that it doesn't happen unless there's absolutely no alternative."

"I'd say you've reached that point, based on current evidence. You need to fire up that tracking implant, find out where the hell she is, and go fetch her. Whether she's alive or dead doesn't matter. You owe it to her to try."

Wong studied him, flinty-eyed. "Ever the man of principle, huh?"

"If you won't do it, I will."

"I don't doubt you would." He looked down at the folder, which he was still holding. His fingers had dug into the card cover hard enough to make dents. "And I might let you and all. I require a level of deniability here. If I go in to get Elmira myself, or even using any of my known associates, people are going to draw the conclusion that I've been reactivated by the Alliance."

"And that might compromise the sweet little protection racket you've got going here."

Wong blinked. "How did you—? Never mind. I guess people will tell a Shepherd anything and everything, feeling confident it'll go no further. Much like I've been doing."

"It's a gift," Book said, "and sometimes something of a curse. Besides, I only need to look around me at this extravagant lifestyle of yours to know you're doing far better for yourself than an ex-military officer has any right to. You must be working some sort of angle, and protection seems as likely an explanation as any." Again, he had the waitress Saskia to thank for this apparent deduction, and again, he wasn't going to credit her in Wong's presence.

"So, if I give you Elmira's whereabouts, you guarantee that you could rescue her?"

"I can be very resourceful, and I have some no less resourceful friends who, given the right motivation, will back me up. We'll get her." Book knew that Wong could probably steer him direct to Hunter Covington, cutting Elmira out of the equation. But Elmira seemed to know as much about Mal's situation as Covington did, and it was information Covington was unlikely to supply willingly, whereas she might be a different story. And then there was the secondary consideration—the woman was clearly in serious jeopardy, assuming she wasn't already dead. If the crew could pull her fat out of the fire as part of the process of doing the same for Mal, so much the better.

For a long time Wong said nothing, deep in thought.

"I wouldn't do this for just anyone," he said, and turned and went over to a framed oil painting, a genuine Earth-That-

Was artifact that must have set him back a small fortune. The picture was on a hinge, and he swung it out to reveal a wall safe beneath. A quick but thorough biometric scan—fingerprints, retinas, breath, voice recognition—unlocked the safe. The door eased smoothly outward and Wong rummaged inside for a few moments, producing a handheld unit equipped with a tiny screen and a digital readout.

"Well, here goes," he said, and pressed a button on the unit.

The screen lit up. A map of the 'verse and its plethora of suns, moons and planets appeared, all these elements linked by lines representing channels of communication, like a complex web. Bit by bit the image zeroed in on a single quadrant, a single solar system, a single planet, a single zone of that planet, a single subdivision within that zone, narrowing down the search for the tracking implant. As soon as it made contact, it gave a *ping*. The tracking implant responded to its prompting, offering as accurate a set of global positioning coordinates as it could manage.

"She's alive," he said. "That's something. And even better, she's still planetside."

"Where?"

"Not far. Looks like some kind of spread out in the boondocks, couple dozen miles from town. Covington has a place out yonder, kind of a country retreat. Pretty sure it's that."

He passed the tracker device to Book.

"This is a marker of my implicit faith in you, Derrial," Wong said. "I pray it's merited."

"Faith," Shepherd Book replied, "is sometimes all we have and all we need."

As Simon was making another pot of tea—purely for something to occupy his mind—Zoë appeared in the corridor from the direction of the flight deck. He had seen her looking happier and knew she was not the bearer of glad tidings.

"Alliance is tracking us," she informed him. "Wash just confirmed it. They're coming out of deep space and their course is straight for us. We're hanging a U-turn and looking for a rock to hide behind, but there aren't any big enough in these parts."

"Back towards Persephone?" Simon's stomach clenched. "But they're looking for us there."

Zoë smiled grimly. "Simon, they're looking for you everywhere," she said.

She could have thrown him out the airlock in a spacesuit and he might have been only slightly more afraid. Dread rendered him speechless. He was paralyzed, rooted to the spot.

River will know, he thought. *Get to River.*

His heart was pounding so hard he was afraid it would bruise his ribcage. He tried to swallow, to respond. Zoë narrowed her eyes at him.

"Simon," she said, "you're having an anxiety attack. Take a breath."

He finally managed to give his head a little shake. He made a rough cracking sound as he tried to clear his throat.

"*Breathe*," she said. "They haven't come for us yet. We have time to make you safe. But you have to snap out of it."

You can't *make us safe. Don't lie,* Simon thought. But the crew of *Serenity* had taken him and River in, had protected them before. On their own, they would have already been caught.

He finally took a deep breath. Zoë nodded approvingly and took his arm.

"You all right now?"

"It depends on your definition of 'all right,'" he said.

"Well, you're talking, so that's a start. Go find River."

"Has Shepherd Book checked in about the captain?" he asked.

"Haven't heard a word." Zoë's words were clipped, the way she sounded when she was very angry or tense. She tapped the bulkhead and said, "Stay on alert. We may need to get creative."

"I have no idea what that means," he said.

"Keep track of your sister."

He went to River's bunk, but she wasn't there, and a paroxysm of fear shot through him. He was hurrying back along the corridor when he ran into Kaylee and Zoë coming the other way. Kaylee's face was pale and her expression grim.

"It's no good," Zoë said. "They've caught up and they're demanding to come aboard. Wash estimates they'll make contact in about fifteen minutes." She looked hard at Simon. "We need to get you and River off the ship."

Creatively, he thought, and he guessed what she was driving at. "Right, like before," he said, as a wave of queasiness rolled over him at the mere thought. "Going outside and attaching to the hull."

"Can't," Zoë said. "We had the hull degaussed at the docks."

"*Zāo gāo,* that's right." Kaylee turned to Simon. "See, that means we neutralized the ship's magnetic field. We have to do that now and then to clean *Serenity* up. Like when ships sailed on the ancient sea and they scraped off all the barnacles."

"So?" Simon didn't follow.

"So there won't be any way for you to cling to the hull," Kaylee explained. "The magnets on your suit's boots and gloves will be useless."

"Well, you can tether us, or glue us, or we can just hang on," he said. He was new to spaceflight, so he knew his suggestions might be off base, but the point he was trying to make was that the crew was very good at coming up with alternative solutions.

"We don't have time for any fancy stuff," Zoë said. "You're both going to get in Inara's shuttle and leave, pronto. Wash can lay in a course for you to take so that your readouts will be shielded by *Serenity*'s mass until the Alliance vessel closes in on us for boarding."

Simon's lips parted. "But I can't even pilot a shuttle."

"I can," Kaylee said.

"Sorry, Kaylee, but we need you here," Zoë said brusquely. "Inara will go with you, Simon. Now go wake up your sister."

"She isn't in her bunk. I was going to look for her."

"Okay. Be quick about it, then get to the shuttle. Inara will meet you there."

"But what if they come after us?" Simon said.

"Try to stay calm," Kaylee urged, putting her hand on his forearm. "I know it's hard not to be real scared."

"I'm not afraid for myself. I'm afraid for River. What they'll do to her."

"We have to make sure they don't have a chance to," Zoë said. "Let's move it."

"Yes. Yes, all right." Simon faced Kaylee. She was gazing at him with wide eyes, as if she were memorizing him.

As if she thought she might never see him again.

"You're gonna be safe," she said, bobbing her head and smiling through what were clearly tears. "And we're gonna find the captain and… and…" She trailed off, struggling. She balled her fists and bit her lower lip, falling into silence.

"And it's going to be fine," Simon finished for her.

"Not unless you get in that shuttle *now*."

Simon leaned towards Kaylee with the intention of kissing her goodbye. But Zoë was there, and Kaylee was… He didn't know why his courage failed him. He rushed past her, into the dining room.

"*Mèi mèi?*" he called softly, as if the Alliance could hear him. "Where are you?"

She wasn't there, either, or in the galley. Cursing under

his breath, Simon hurried back down the hallway, checking the cabins on either side for River as he went. His sister had a habit of disappearing—or losing her tether—at the most inconvenient times. It came on like contrarian clockwork.

The voice coming from Jayne's cabin gave him a rush of hope. The way Jayne was holding court, Simon was sure there was someone else in the room. When he stuck his head through the open doorway, he realized that wasn't the case at all. Jayne had been talking to Vera as he cleaned her barrel with a flexible ramrod and a bit of oily rag, in a tender voice telling her what a good and proper girl she was. From his seat on the rumpled bunk, Jayne shot Simon a sour look.

And he thinks River's crazy.

Simon moved on without explaining the problem or attempting to enlist Jayne's aid. He had learned the hard way that Jayne Cobb needed a lot of explaining to in order to get the big picture—or any picture, even a sketch—and Simon didn't have time to spare for the snail-crawling Socratic dialogue, the circular questions and angry accusations that were the meat and potatoes of Jayne's conversational repertoire.

He found Zoë and Kaylee in the same spot he'd left them. Both looked surprised to see him.

"No idea where she's got to," he informed them, somewhat out of breath. "I looked in the other cabins on the way back here. She isn't on this deck. She's just gone!"

"Maybe she telepathed that you were going to leave in the shuttle?" Kaylee said, her expression dead serious. "You know, with her tested certified genius brain. Maybe she's up there now, waiting for you?"

Zoë gave her a disbelieving look. "Simon, use the ship's

intercom," she said. "Tell River to meet you at the shuttle. Hurry her up but don't scare her too much. You know how to do it. Kaylee, you go check the shuttle to see if she's already there. If she's not, stay there and wait for her. Simon and I will search down in the cargo area."

"River, this is your brother," Simon said into the intercom microphone. His voice boomed out of the speakers scattered throughout the ship. He tried to sound calm, reasoned, not frantic and about to blow a gasket. "If you can hear me, we have a situation right now. Nothing to worry about. Just get to Inara's shuttle. I'll meet you there. We've got to leave *Serenity*. We're going on a little trip, is all."

There were a thousand places to hide on the ship. Places that without an infrared scanner—something an Alliance boarding party would certainly have on hand—would be difficult and time-consuming to check. River might be anywhere: ceiling ducts, gear lockers, any number of crawlspaces. She even could've climbed into a space suit and slipped out into the Black, for all they knew.

Simon and Zoë headed aft, going through the storage area, bypassing the cargo bay. Their searches of the infirmary and the engine room turned up no trace of her. Simon hated the queasy fear churning in his stomach, the ever-tightening pursing of Zoë's lips as they came up empty everywhere they looked.

"Zoë, Alliance is nearly here," Wash reported. "Why hasn't the shuttle detached?"

Then Kaylee's voice shrilled through the comm unit. "I'm in the shuttle with Inara and River's still not here."

"Roger that," Zoë said. "Wash?"

He let forth with a string of epithets. "You need to hustle, my friends. Proximity scanner's lit up like Christmas, Hanukkah, Diwali, and Kwanzaa all rolled into one. Ship's ident is the I.A.V. *Stormfront*. Longbow-class mid-range patrol cruiser. More armament than a porcupine's got quills."

Simon blinked. "Zoë. The crates. She was playing the flute to the crates before. Maybe she's there again."

Zoë about-faced and began to run-limp in the direction of the cargo bay. She said through her comm link, "Inara, are you prepped for launch?"

"Yes. Standing by to uncouple," Inara said.

"We can't leave her here. We can't," Simon pleaded as he scooted around Zoë because he could move faster.

"Tell me something I don't know," she snapped.

Simon's mind was racing ahead, kaleidoscoping with unsettling what-ifs. What if they couldn't find River? What if the Alliance got there first? What if they found her hiding place but it was too late to escape into the Black without being noticed? There was no way a shuttle could outrun an Alliance cruiser or its ferocious armament. If they didn't get off *Serenity* in time, they would get off her in chains and at gunpoint. And so much for saving his beloved sister.

He and Zoë rushed out into the ship's dim, sprawling hold. Zoë hit the ceiling lights and the gray metal deck stretched out below them. The cargo bay seemed close to empty. Even so, there were lots of places to hide in and around the perimeter.

"There she is," Zoë said, pointing.

Simon didn't see her at first. He scanned each crate in turn. "Where? Where?"

Zoë pointed. River had prostrated herself on the lid of

one of the crates, her arms spread out, clutching it like a life raft on a storm-tossed sea. Simon could hear her babbling away softly to the contents.

"Let's go get her quick."

Simon hurried after her, catching up as she crossed the deck.

"Hush, little high-ex, don't say a word," River crooned to the crate's contents, her voice breaking with emotion. "Papa's gonna stop you and your crazy whirl."

"River?"

She looked up at him, wild-eyed and a little tearful, and said, "They're coming."

"Yes," Simon said. "So we have to go."

She sniffled. "If they open the crate, everyone will die."

"They will?" he said. Beside him, Zoë grunted.

She nodded. "It's all busy." She flicked her fingers, imitating fireworks.

"What are you talking about?" Zoë said.

"Getting hot," she said. "Getting busy."

Zoë and Simon shared a glance. "We'll look into it," she said.

"Die," River moaned.

"They won't open the crates," Zoë said.

"River, you and I have to leave now," Simon said. "You have to come with me." He took her hand and helped her off the crate. She didn't resist. She seemed drained; her eyes had lost their luster.

"We have to explain," she repeated. "They are dancing, Simon. Faster, faster." She tried to pirouette on one foot but he stopped her.

"Zoë will convince them."

"Simon, get her to the shuttle."

"I can make the *crates* listen," River said. "Tell them to stay calm. They have terrible tendencies. They must fight them."

Zoë swore under her breath and rolled her eyes. She took River under her arm. Simon did the same. They crossed the deck, then took the stairs two at a time, supporting River between them. Zoë was limping hard. Each movement cost her. Not only was she in pain but she was putting weight on bones and tendons that needed a chance to knit.

What are we doing? Simon thought. *We're abandoning the crew.*

He thought about offering to stay behind. If he turned himself in, surely the Alliance wouldn't bother with examining the cargo too closely. But then Wash, Zoë, Jayne, and Kaylee would be taken into custody for harboring a fugitive. And if the Alliance found Simon Tam aboard *Serenity*, it wouldn't be a stretch to assume River had left in one of the two missing shuttles. A shuttle couldn't hope to outrun an Alliance patrol cruiser hot on its trail.

"No, Simon, no," River said.

Zoë said into her comm unit, "Inara, we found her and we're coming in hot. Repeat, we're coming in hot."

"I copy, Zoë," Inara said.

As they reached the high gangway, Simon stole a quick glance at his pocket watch to see how much time was left, but in his brain's frazzled state found he couldn't do the math. "Can we still make it?" he asked Zoë.

"Shut up and move!" she bellowed at him.

She bodily lifted River into her arms and raced for the shuttle. Gone was her limp. She was operating on pure adrenaline. Simon puffed to keep up with her, seeing stars when he didn't round a corner as sharply as she and he slammed into the bulkhead.

Someone grabbed onto his shirt and dragged him along. It was Jayne.

"Tourists," Jayne groused.

The large man easily kept pace with Zoë. Footfalls clanged as Zoë shouted, "Go, go, go!" and ran ahead. She disappeared inside the shuttle and came back out, circling around Jayne, who was on his way in.

Before Simon knew was what happening, Jayne flung him into the shuttle and the door slammed shut. The engine roared and the shuttle detached. The beautiful silk brocade curtain that was usually drawn closed to conceal the navigation section from Inara's place of business was open and River was hunched in the seat beside Inara's, who was guiding the shuttle out of its resting place on *Serenity*'s flank. River was muttering to herself. Simon staggered toward her, expecting her to be whispering about the hands of blue.

"Don't blow, don't blow," she was chanting.

"River, *bǎo bèi*," Inara said, "please keep quiet."

"Where are we going?" Simon whispered.

"We're staying out of range by remaining in the same spatial plane as *Serenity*," Inara said. "We're on the side opposite their approach so we're out of their line of sight, shielding ourselves with the ship. We can't maintain the position for long, but hopefully it'll be long enough." Seeing that he wasn't following, she said, "Essentially, we're hiding behind *Serenity*. Wash is pinging me the latitude and longitude of the cruiser. Each time it moves, I'll correct my course to match it."

He nodded. "River's very worried about the crates."

"I'm sure she's not alone in that," Inara said. She added gently, "Perhaps River would be more comfortable in my private quarters."

Simon took the hint. Clasping River's hands, he eased her out of the chair and guided her to Inara's couch. He put his arms around her and rocked her.

"Kaboom," she whispered.

20

No sooner were Simon and River inside the shuttle than Zoë sealed and locked the hatch. Inara wasn't kidding about being ready to launch. Once the red light beside the hatch winked on, indicating a closed airlock, the shuttle uncoupled from *Serenity*'s power and sensory connections.

"Good riddance," Jayne grumbled.

Zoë, Jayne and Kaylee watched through the door's porthole as the shuttle undocked and the released umbilicals retracted. When the shuttle had drifted clear of the docking bay, its thrusters roared and flared. The blinding pulse of light grew rapidly smaller and fainter, until it winked out and vanished into the Black.

Jayne expelled air from his cheeks. "Do you think they'll be all right?"

"Sure do." Kaylee sounded forlorn.

Zoë knew Inara had shut down all the shuttle systems, including life support. They'd be breathing canned air for a little while, but it wasn't for long, so it should be okay.

They'd be coasting through null grav at high speed, putting distance between themselves and the cruiser. With no electromagnetic signature, nothing to draw the attention of the Alliance sensors, the shuttle would look like a small asteroid or a hunk of drifting space junk.

Zoë doubted Simon and River had even had time to buckle in before Inara lit 'em up. Now all they could do was hunker down and wait, hoping the initial blast had gone unnoticed.

"Where was River hiding?" Kaylee asked.

"She wasn't really hiding," Zoë said. "She was down in the cargo bay, in plain sight, talking to one of Badger's crates. She was really worried about them."

"I am too," Jayne said. "Worried we ain't never gonna get paid for all the trouble we're goin' through."

Engineer and first mate shared a look.

"Maybe I better check the cargo? No point in taking any chances," Kaylee ventured.

"Yeah, maybe you better," Zoë said with a sigh of resignation. "Everyone needs to stay calm. Alliance will be here soon."

Jayne grumbled something about feds and sticky fingers and that he was going to go back to his quarters to hide all his weapons. Zoë let him go. Kaylee headed for the cargo bay and Zoë hurried to the flight deck.

Her husband was hunched forward in the pilot's chair, his fingers flitting over the controls, eyes darting from viewing port array to console readouts and back. He was way in the zone.

"How far off is *Stormfront*?" she asked Wash as she stepped up behind him.

"Three hundred klicks out, and decelerating," he said over his shoulder. "Maybe an hour until they slide up alongside us. If Inara plays her cards right, if she can stay dark for a bit longer, she'll be okay. You know, the Alliance's line-of-sight blind spot gets bigger and bigger the nearer they come."

Yeah, she knew that. Everybody who wasn't a complete idiot knew that. Wash was being hyper and jangly, and he had good reason. The inbound Alliance cruiser had to have its missiles and cannons locked onto *Serenity*. The bastards didn't need much of an excuse to cut loose.

"We played it really close," Zoë said. "But they're gone."

"And it's not over," Wash said. "I could've made a break for it when we first saw the cruiser, maybe lost them with some *jīng cǎi* astrobatics, but now it's too late. We've got to stay here to run interference for Inara and the Tams. We better pray that Badger's paperwork is rock solid."

"And the feds don't mess with the crates."

"With all those warning decals all over them?"

"They might think we slapped those decals on just to dissuade them from looking too close," Zoë said.

What would Mal do if he were here? Give the Alliance officers a whole load of bluff, bluster and baloney. But amiably, with a winning smile on his face.

Push comes to shove, she thought, *that's what I'm going to have to do too.*

Her game wasn't nearly as good as Mal's. But as long as it was good enough…

The planet Shadow, long ago

The day Mal realized he truly loved Jinny was the day he caught her and Toby kissing.

He had been away from Seven Pines Pass awhile. His mother had sent him off to Da Cheng Shi—the largest city on Shadow, although not quite the major metropolis its name might suggest—to buy engine parts for a beat-up old combine harvester she had bought from a scrapyard and was hoping to sell to Bo Hopkirk on the next-door farm. She and Mal had been restoring the vehicle together for the past few weeks, and Bo Hopkirk's crops were just coming ready and his own combine was on its last legs, so she was expecting he would jump at what she was offering and give her a decent price for it, too.

The journey to and from Da Cheng Shi was forty-eight hours each way by train, and Mal came home travel-weary and sore to his bones from poorly upholstered bench seats. He hadn't been able to afford a berth in a sleeping car and had been forced to sleep sitting upright. Still, he had the parts they needed, and he'd haggled long and hard not to pay over the odds for them. He felt pleased with himself, and was looking forward to getting reacquainted with the gang.

Sure enough, the Four Amigos arranged a meet-up that evening at the Silver Stirrup Saloon. Toby even told Mal that he had an announcement to make. That ought to have been a clue as to what was coming, but Mal was too exhausted to see it. Mal himself, during the long, fitful nights on the train, had been coming to the conclusion that now was the time to make his move with Jinny Adare. He knew how much Toby liked her, and he knew that him horning in on Toby's plans was going to cause ructions, and no mistake. It might even mean the end of the Four Amigos.

But Jinny was so gorramn beautiful, so perfect. Her sense of humor was as dark and acerbic as Mal's own. He felt weirdly elated whenever she smiled his way. He couldn't help himself. He had to let her know what was in his heart.

In a cold, calculating corner of his mind, Mal was confident that Jinny would favor him over Toby. Carrot-topped Toby Finn, all earnestness and gawky immaturity, versus Mal Reynolds, the broad-shouldered, chisel-chinned swashbuckler who made girls go weak at the knees and warm in the nethers just looking at him. It was no contest. Jinny, given a choice, wouldn't even think twice.

Just to make sure, however, he had bought a gift for her at a pawnbrokers in Da Cheng Shi. It was a gold locket engraved with an ornate, curlicued "J" and suspended on a fine gold chain. It cost more than he could reasonably afford, but the moment he laid eyes on it, he'd known he had to buy it. The "J" was like an omen, something he just couldn't ignore.

Mal was taken aback, then, when he walked into the Silver Stirrup shortly after nightfall to find Jinny and Toby already there, at a table. That in itself wasn't so surprising. What was surprising was that they were engaged in a passionate embrace, lips locked.

Mal rocked back on his heels, as though swamped by an ocean wave. His head reeled. A herd of elephants could have thundered by and he wouldn't have noticed.

Toby and Jinny? Together? An item? How? Why? When? What?

Recovering some of his composure, he sashayed over to them. "Howdy all," he said, touching forefinger to forehead like some sort of cowpoke.

"Mal!" they both cried as one. Jinny leapt to her feet to hug him. Toby shook his hand, wringing it with all the strength in his body.

"Hey, hey, hey!" Mal said. "I've only been away four days. Ain't like I'm returning from a visit to the Core or nothin'."

"My round," said Toby, scampering over to the bar.

Mal sat down. "No Jamie?"

"On his way," said Jinny. "He said he'd be a little late. So, how was Da Cheng Shi?"

"Ah, you know. Dirty. Smelly. Full of folks looked like they wouldn't spit on you if you were on fire. Never mind that, though. I see what I thought I just saw?"

"What did you see?" Jinny asked coyly.

"You and Toby being a big old smoochy pair of lovebirds."

She looked at him sidelong. He'd tried to hide a note of jealousy in his voice but hadn't, he thought, done too good a job of it. "Wouldn't go so far as to say we're lovebirds, exactly, but yeah, we've kinda gotten together."

"Kinda?"

"Early days yet."

"How long's this been brewing?"

"A while now. Toby's been more and more attentive. You must have noticed."

"Can't say as I did." But perhaps he just hadn't been concentrating. Perhaps he'd been so wrapped up in his own growing feelings towards Jinny that he'd overlooked the way his rival for her affections was flourishing right under his nose.

"He's so sweet, Mal. Cute, too. He took me to a shindig over at Sageville the day before yesterday. We danced till sunup."

"A date?"

"I'd call it that. At the end, as we were leaving, he just up and kissed me. I wasn't expecting it, although I sorta sensed it might be coming. And it was a good kiss. I liked it. And it's just snowballed from there."

"So this is only two days old, this thing?" Mal said, reckoning the relationship was still young enough and tentative enough for him to nip it in the bud if he wanted.

"But it feels right," Jinny said. "Feels like it's been there much longer, bubbling under, only neither of us has realized it."

I think Toby realized it even if you didn't.

"What's Jamie think?" he said.

"Jamie doesn't know yet. You weren't supposed to know yet either. Toby wanted to tell the both of you tonight."

"Yeah, he mentioned a big announcement. I guessed he was maybe going to try and grow a beard, or dye his hair blond. That or something a mite more dramatic, like signing up with the Independents."

Jinny's expression turned sour. "Don't say that. Don't even mention the war."

"Ain't a war yet," Mal pointed out. "Right now it's just the Rim worlds making noises about secession and the Union of Allied Planets bragging and bullying and browbeating."

"Long may it stay that way."

"But it ain't gonna. Everyone knows that, and those who think otherwise are living in a fool's paradise. Sooner or later—and my money's on sooner—the outer planets are going to form an alliance of their own and mobilize, and the Union'll surely regard that as provocation, even justification for war. You can feel it coming. It's inevitable. Over in Da Cheng Shi, it's all anybody's talking about. There are even recruitment offices popping up. They've got all these slogans. 'Join the cause before it's too late.' 'A timely militia is a ready militia.' 'Don't get caught napping.' 'The outer planets need *you*.' You can pretend it's not going to happen, but that's not going to prevent it happening. Events have a way of developing, faster than you expect."

"You sound like you've half a mind to join up yourself."

"Half a mind is about half a mind more than most folk think I have," Mal said, "but yes, I'm givin' the idea headspace at least. For too long the Core's been exploiting the rest of the 'verse, strip-mining planets like ours for resources, sometimes literally, and leaving us with precious little for ourselves. It's way past time that ended, and if armed opposition's what it takes to make the Union sit up and take notice, so be it."

Just then, Toby returned to the table with their beers.

"Everyone looks very serious," he said. "What's up?"

"Nothing, Toby," Jinny said. "Nothing you need concern yourself about." To Mal, it sounded like something a parent might say to quell a fretful child's fears.

"Well, this here's a celebration," Toby said, raising his glass. "In case it escaped your attention, Mal, Jinny and I— we're boyfriend and girlfriend now. Ain't that great?"

"Just dandy," Mal said, clinking his glass listlessly against Toby's. "I'm happy for you both."

Toby might not have marked the stiffness with which he spoke, but Jinny certainly did.

"Mal's cool with it," she said. "I'm sure he is. He's taking a moment to adjust, is all."

When Jamie showed up, he, too, was taken aback when Toby told him he was now officially dating Jinny. He coped with the shock better than Mal had, though. "Of all the guys in this neck of the woods," he said, "she could do a lot worse than you, Toby. And, given her track record, has."

"Hey!" Jinny slapped him playfully.

"Some of the losers you've stepped out with in the past, sis," Jamie said. "It beggars belief. What was the name of that one, looked like a pig?"

"Marcus, and he did not look like a pig."

"If he didn't, how come you knew who I was talking about? And then there was the fella with the overbite. Chipmunk guy. Not forgetting the one whose nose squeaked when he breathed. Gary? Glen? Gil? Something with a 'G,' anyway."

"Greg couldn't help it with the nose thing."

"Like a gorramn pennywhistle it was," said Jamie. "You don't look like a pig, Toby, you don't have an overbite, and your nostrils don't make a noise, far as I'm aware. That puts you leagues ahead of the rest. Congratulations."

Later, Toby and Jinny danced together to the plinking honky-tonk of the player-piano while Jamie and Mal hatched plans.

"Sheriff Bundy made an ass of himself today, as usual," Jamie said. "Willard Krieger was saying stuff about the Union, badmouthing 'em. You know how that old coot is. Got an ornery streak in him a mile wide."

"Only reason Krieger moved to Shadow was to escape 'Union meddling,' as he calls it," said Mal.

"Right, and now he's incensed 'cause that meddling's spread as far out as here. He was saying his taxes have gone up threefold."

"Everyone's taxes have gone up." Hence Mal's mother's combine harvester restoration project. Anything to make a little extra cash on the side.

"But Krieger's now got to pay extra duties on the goods he imports for his hardware store. He's putting his prices up, of course, but he ain't best pleased, and neither are his customers. Anyways, he decided to go out into the town square and tub-thump for a spell. He stood on an actual soapbox and harangued passersby. Got himself a fair-sized audience, in fact. Then Bundy wanders along and arrests him on the spot."

"What for? Man has a right to free speech."

"Not if it's what Bundy considers 'seditious talk.'"

"There a law against that?"

"If there ain't, it doesn't bother Bundy none."

"So Krieger's in jail now."

"He is. And you know what, Mal? The Four Amigos are going to bust him out."

Mal was in such a cranky, belligerent frame of mind just then that Jamie's proposal didn't sound at all wrongheaded to him. It sounded, instead, like a very fine suggestion indeed. Not least because it would peeve Sheriff Bundy, and Mal was still smarting from the way the lawman had backhanded him at the Hendrickson place a few months back.

Jamie soon roped Jinny in on the jailbreak scheme, and naturally, where Jinny went, Toby was sure to follow.

"If Jinny's up for it," he said, "I don't need asking twice."

Jamie's plan involved a small amount of plastique, some detonation cord, a wheeled motor vehicle, a towrope, and a whole heaping of chutzpah. The barred windows of the cells in the town lockup were in back of the building. Jamie affixed a pencil-thick length of the putty-like explosive around the outside of the window frame, inserted the det cord, and attached one end of the towrope to the bars and the other to the rear fender of a quad bike. It all happened in an instant. Jamie lit the fuse. The plastique blew, loosening the brickwork around the window. Jinny gunned the quad bike's motor and torqued the throttle. The quad bike leapt away, hauling on the towrope and dragging the window-bar assembly loose. Before the dust even began to settle, Toby sprang into the hole, set to tell Willard Krieger he was free and should scramble out while he could.

Only problem was, they had got the wrong cell. Toby's face

said it all. "Krieger ain't here. No one's here. Cell's empty."

In that moment of frantic incredulity, as it dawned on the Four Amigos that all their efforts had been for naught, a familiar voice yelled at them.

"Hold it right there!"

Sheriff Bundy came huffing around the angle of the building, with his deputy, Orville Crump, close on his heels. Where Bundy was fat and aggressive, Crump was lanky and sly. They were the proverbial chalk and cheese, yet somehow they got along together and made a good team.

Both had their government-issue sidearms out and leveled at the miscreants.

"Oh, you've gone too far this time, my friends," Bundy said. "You've really screwed the pooch. Destruction of public property? Attempting to aid and abet the escape of a felon? Unauthorized use of explosive materials? You are going *down*!"

They didn't, in the event, go down. Marla Finn, Toby's lawyer mother, managed to get them off on a technicality. She and her husband, however, were furious with their boy and forbade him ever seeing the others again. Mal and Jamie, at least. They made an exception for Jinny, after Toby pleaded with them. He spoke about her so enthusiastically, with such evident ardor, that they couldn't bring themselves to keep her from him. They were, frankly, just glad that Toby had got himself a girl. They had begun to worry he might never find love. And Jinny was, all said and done, something of a catch.

It was, in effect, the end of the Four Amigos, although as far as Mal was concerned the end had already come, the moment he walked into the Silver Stirrup and the castle of hope he had been building for himself came crashing down around his ears. He consigned the gold locket with the fancy "J" on it to the back of a drawer and forgot about it—for a time, at least.

Seeing Toby Finn again after so long had brought back these memories of Mal's youth on Shadow. They played in his head like mind movies as he lay in that subterranean cell, cold, trussed up, miserable. They swirled like stirred-up sediment in the riverbed of the past, muddying his thoughts.

Toby. Jinny. Jamie. Himself. And how it had all ended in disaster and a fireball and a ton of recrimination.

Mal was only dimly aware of the clunk of a bolt being drawn back, door hinges creaking open. Footsteps shuffled towards him. He braced himself for another beating. There wasn't much he could do to prevent it, so he was better off just withstanding it, weathering it.

"Reynolds?" someone whispered.

Mal turned his head. He saw a vague silhouette in the semi-darkness of the cell, a man bending over him.

"Here," the visitor said. "Drink this."

Mal was being proffered an enamel mug. He struggled up to a sitting position.

"What's in there?" he said. "Poison? Piss?"

"Just water. Reckoned you'd be thirsty."

"You reckoned right." But Mal remained wary.

"Go on," the visitor urged, casting a look over his shoulder. "I ain't got long. Someone's bound to come by. Drink."

Mal put his lips to the mug. The visitor tipped it and he sipped the water. It was stale, brackish, but welcome nonetheless.

A glimpse of a busted-to-hell nose confirmed the man's identity.

"Stu?" he said.

Stuart Deakins nodded.

"Thought so. Why're you being nice all of a sudden? Couple of hours ago, you belted me in the gut, then spat at my feet."

"Yeah, about that… I kinda had to."

"I figure hitting someone's usually a matter of choice. As is spitting at them."

"But I had to show willing," Deakins said. "Had to show I'm part of the gang. Didn't want anyone to think I wasn't loyal."

"Well, my aching belly muscles would certainly seem proof of that," Mal said.

"And here's a protein block." Deakins unwrapped the foodstuff and held it up for Mal to munch on. Barbecue spare ribs flavor. Not Mal's favorite, but still he did his best not to guzzle the whole thing in one go. He was starving hungry. When had he last eaten? He could barely recall.

Meanwhile Deakins said, "Whatever else they're saying about you, Mal, I remember what you did for me on New Kasimir. If it weren't for you I wouldn't be here today and still sucking air. That earns you some latitude, far as I'm concerned."

"Enough latitude," Mal said around a mouthful of protein block, "that you'd untie these ropes and let me go?"

"Nuh-uh." Deakins shook his head regretfully. "Can't do that."

"Can't fault a man for askin'."

"They know I've come to see you. I asked for some time alone with you. They think I'm working you over. They find out I'd freed you, I'd be dead. That simple."

"Could always stage a fight. Maybe I freed myself, overpowered you, got away under my own steam."

"No, Mal. That ain't how this is gonna play out. I'm showing you some compassion, but it has its limits. You're still a traitor in these people's eyes. In mine too, if what I'm told is true."

"And what have you been told?" Mal said. "It's a mystery to me, that's for damn sure. What is this huge betrayal I'm being accused of committing? Been rackin' my brains and can't think of none."

Deakins studied him skeptically. "I can't tell if you're being straight or scamming. You can't surely be ignorant of your crime. I find that hard to believe."

"Trust me, if I knew what I'm supposed to be guilty of, I'd be the first to hold my hand up and admit to it."

"You really don't remember? Too bad. I'm sure it'll come back to you."

"You ain't even going to jog my memory a little?"

"Why? You'll find out when the time comes to face judgment for it—and it's coming soon. Might be best if you just acclimatize yourself to that reality."

Mal could see he wasn't going to get far with Deakins. The man had mercy in his soul, but a finite quantity of it. He felt he owed Mal something, even if it was just the kindness of a little food and water.

"Gotta go," Deakins said. "I was told I could only give you a few licks. I'm gonna refrain from doin' that, but if I stay any longer, people are bound to get suspicious."

"One thing," Mal said. "I'm bursting for a pee."

"Bucket over there."

"Sure, but my hands are tied behind my back. Kind of makes it difficult for a fella to get the old pecker out, know what I mean?"

"You want me to untie you? I ain't falling for that. You'd cold-cock me for sure."

"Okay, but I'm gonna piss my pants if I don't do something about it right soon. You want that on your conscience?"

Deakins was in two minds, Mal could see.

"Man to man," he pressed. "If the roles were reversed, I'd do the same for you. Swear."

"Tell you what," Deakins said. "I'll unbutton your fly. But that's as far as it goes. You'll have to manage the rest by your ownsome."

He fumbled gingerly with the front of Mal's pants, like someone fearful of touching a live wire. Mal then shuffled over to the bucket on his knees. He managed, through some awkward maneuvering and hip-gyrating, to liberate the part of him that needed liberating. What followed was a full minute of blessed, bladder-draining relief, after which, with a bit more wriggly dancing, he was able to stow everything away again back where it belonged.

"Thanks, Stu," he said, sincerely, as Deakins re-buttoned his fly.

"Don't mention it. Seriously. I mean it."

"I guess you couldn't see your way to slipping me a knife now? A gun, even?"

"Ha ha. No chance."

"Or you could just, you know, accidentally-on-purpose leave the door ajar."

"Not gonna happen."

"Stu, you do realize this is real bad company you're keeping, don't you? These people, these Browncoats in name only, they ain't playing fair. They're crazy. Toby Finn especially. I know Toby from way back when."

"Yeah, he said as much. Said he used to run with you when he was a kid. Trusted you. Loved you like a brother. And that's why you've been top of his list of turncoats for a long while. Backstabbing's all the more painful when it comes from someone you were once close to."

"Toby used to be a good kid. Don't know what turned him, but it's clear he's picked up some harum-scarum notions since then. That face of his? That's the face of a madman. Toby ain't someone I'd pledge my allegiance to, is what I'm saying. Someone as *fēng le* as that is liable to turn on the people around him at the drop of a hat. I don't reckon any of you's safe while you're around him. If he's calling me a traitor, I imagine he could do the same to anyone. All's it'd take is him getting some twisted fancy about you into his head, and that's it, you're next for the chop."

Deakins appeared to take this on board. "So you say."

"Think about it, at least," Mal said. "I mean, come on, you're so scared of these people you'd thump a defenseless man just to keep in with them? What does that say about them? Or you?"

Deakins did not reply. Instead, with a heavy tread, he left the cell, shutting and locking the door behind him.

Alone once more, Mal contemplated his situation. It looked bleak. Trying to turn Stuart Deakins against the rest of the vengeful Browncoats had been a long shot. Mal might have planted a few seeds of doubt in the man's mind but he doubted they would germinate into anything fruitful.

His main hope, slender though it was, was the crew of *Serenity*. Somehow, against all the odds, they would find him. He had to believe that. The only alternative was utter despair.

He sank back onto the floor and into reverie again.

22

After a sumptuous dinner of fresh vegetables and real chicken, Book took leave of Mika Wong. He hadn't wanted to stay for the meal. He had wanted to retrieve Elmira Atadema right away. But somehow it would have felt impolite to turn down Wong's hospitality, the more so since Wong had placed so much trust in him. And when might he next have the chance to eat such good, wholesome food? The soul got its sustenance from the Lord, but the body needed nourishment too. Book knew from experience that even a humble bowl of soup could make all the difference to a person.

He caught a rickshaw back from the town outskirts into Eavesdown proper. As the cart jolted along the neon-splashed streets, he fetched out his comm link and called *Serenity*.

"Shepherd," Wash said. "Where are you? Are you all right? Do you have Mal?"

"I'm on Persephone still," he said. "I have news. Nothing directly pertinent to Mal himself, but news that's nonetheless encouraging."

He filled Wash in on all he had learned from Wong about Elmira and Covington.

"That's good to hear," Wash said. "I can't escape the feeling that we're running short on time, though."

"Me either. How are things with you? Payload all safe?"

"Yeah, we've been making good headway. At least, we *were*, only now we're being overhauled by an Alliance patrol cruiser, the I.A.V. *Stormfront*."

"Not good."

"Definitely not. If it wasn't for bad luck, we wouldn't have any luck. They're hailing us and I've been stalling them with the old communications interference trick. You know, 'Oopsies, can't *skzzzz* make out *frzzzt* trying *skrrrtch* say.' That won't hold them for long, and just makes them more irate anyway."

"Are they after certain crewmembers?"

"Don't know, but we can't assume they're not, so we've taken appropriate action. I'm not going to say too much just in case *Stormfront*'s listening in. This channel's as secure as I can make it, but you never know. All I'll say is we've relieved ourselves of excess personnel for now and we're down to a shipboard complement of just four. Oh hey, Mrs. Washburne wants a word."

Zoë came on the line. "Shepherd? I caught what you told Wash. What are your plans?"

"Seems like I can't expect you to return to Persephone in order to assist me, not under current circumstances."

"No. If we were to make a run for it, the patrol cruiser would open up on us for sure, and we'd be just so much floating debris. Do you think you could go it alone?"

"I could," Book said with a trace of hesitancy. "I wouldn't like to, though. I have no idea what kind of reception I might receive. I anticipate that Covington would not leave Elmira unguarded or his property undefended. One man could, I suppose, infiltrate the premises fairly successfully, if he had the right skills, but it'd be better if there were more of us, in case of unforeseen problems."

"What if you had reinforcements? I'm thinking we could kill two birds with one stone here."

"Tell me more."

"I'll contact Inara on her shuttle first, bring her up to speed, then patch you through to her and you can take it from there. Wait one."

There was comms silence for two or three minutes. Book drummed his fingers agitatedly on the thin vinyl padding of the rickshaw seat. Patience was one of his strong suits, but even so, he had the unavoidable sense that every minute of delay was a minute Mal got further away and less easy to rescue. The fact that an Alliance patrol cruiser was even now bearing down on *Serenity* was yet another blow to his inner calm. Sometimes life seemed like just one setback after another.

"Shepherd Book," said Inara.

"Go ahead, Inara."

"As you know, I have the Tams on board."

"Shouldn't we be somewhat more circumspect in this conversation?"

"A Companion's shuttle has special multiphase communications enciphering programs that are impenetrable to practically every known decryption software. It enables me to conduct my business with absolute guaranteed discretion, a boon to my clientele."

"I didn't know that."

"I'd be surprised if a man of your calling did," Inara said. "Our status is this. We've managed to pull away from *Serenity* without *Stormfront* detecting us. I know that because it hasn't rerouted. It's still on an intercept course with *Serenity*, less than ten minutes away from docking distance. We started out by staying in *Serenity*'s shadow. Then, as chance would have it, we passed an asteroid field. We've diverted towards the edge of the field and are laying low here. The asteroids are providing enough scanner disruption that *Stormfront*'s instruments are unlikely to spot us. It should pass us right by."

"*Serenity*'s the bigger target anyway."

"And the bigger prize. They're likely to be focusing on her to the exclusion of all else. What this means is that, assuming our luck holds and we remain undetected, we'll be out of range of *Stormfront*'s scopes in about a half-hour."

"And you could then head down to Persephone."

"Correct."

"At full burn, that'd get you here by"—Book glanced at his watch, then performed a swift mental calculation—"oh-six-hundred hours local time."

"I know we're not the true cavalry," Inara said. "I know you'd be better off with Zoë and Jayne backing you up. But, in a pinch, we'll have to do."

Book had to admit to himself that he would have preferred it if the former Browncoat corporal and the gruff mercenary were joining him on the raid on Covington's house, rather than a Companion, a doctor and whatever River was. A very damaged girl? A human timebomb? An escaped lab rat? All of these and more.

Yes, he was looking at having three civilians backing him up when there was every likelihood he would need the two crewmembers with the most combat experience. On balance, that did not seem like a winning prospect. Instead of Serenity's big guns, he was making do with firecrackers.

Book knew, however, that God provided. It might not always seem as though He did. Indeed, to the untrained eye it sometimes looked as though the Lord's methods were just plain berserk. But in the end, all said and done, He always came through. It was a cornerstone of Book's belief, the rock he had rebuilt his life upon.

"You three will be more than enough," he told Inara. "I'm certain of it."

And he was.

Almost.

23

The main vid screen flickered, an Alliance logo appeared, and a faceless, nameless baritone voice told *Serenity* to prepare for immediate docking and boarding of an authorized government inspection crew.

Zoë could see Wash was not pleased at the prospect, but when he pushed his comm button to reply he sounded downright bubbly. "Great to see you guys. Sorry about all the trouble with transmissions earlier. We got circuits so old and cranky on this boat, they keep telling me to get off their lawn and turn my music down. But you're here now, and that's just super. Protecting our way of life. Go, Alliance!"

Serenity shuddered as the larger ship made contact. Once the airlocks had been lined up, the seals were secured.

Wash turned to his wife. "Okay, Zoë, it's your play. What do you have in mind?"

"Question. How sexy am I?"

Wash blinked. His eyes darted around apprehensively. "Is this a trick?"

"Just answer. Scale of one to ten, how sexy am I?"

"Twenty. Easy. Except when you're mad at someone. Then it's a fifteen. Mad at me, a twelve. But mostly twenty."

She leaned over and kissed him, a full-on smacker that, as soon as he had got over his bafflement, he reciprocated.

"Whoa," he said. "What was that all about?"

"A woman doesn't always need a reason to kiss her man." Zoë then undid a couple of buttons on her shirt and opened it out to expose more cleavage than normal.

"You're going to… seduce the feds?" Wash said.

"Not seduce, and not all of them. Just the senior officer. Bamboozle him. Throw him off his game if I can. Get him to drop his guard. That's assuming he's male and straight, which given the Alliance's gender equality policy is a fair assumption."

"Don't take this the wrong way, Zoë, but that doesn't really seem in your wheelhouse. Inara's, yes, but yours?"

"Don't take this the wrong way?" his wife said, stiffening. "How am I meant to take it? You're saying Inara is more attractive than I am?"

"No! I'm not saying anything of the sort, don't be mad, it came out wrong, I take it back." Wash's voice rose in pitch until it was virtually a bat squeak.

"I'm just messing with you."

"Phew."

"You're right, I don't have Inara's skills. But never underestimate the power of a hair toss, a pair of big eyes and showing off a little skin." Zoë pouted her lips and shimmied her shoulders. "Worked on you, after all, didn't it?"

"Yeah, but I'm easy."

"Oh, Wash." She stroked his cheek. "All men are."

As she exited the bridge, he called out after her, "Good luck! Or, er, not too much good luck. Maybe no luck. I don't know. Just don't do anything I wouldn't do, young lady. And be home by ten."

Zoë chuckled. "Okay, *Dad*."

Jayne joined her on the catwalk, descending into the cargo bay with her.

"You tidied up Simon's and River's bunks, like I asked?" Zoë said.

"Clean as a nun's panties. Bedding and personal effects all stowed away. You wouldn't know anyone'd been there."

"Good."

Kaylee met them at the foot of the stairs. "I just checked the crates," she said, talking in low, urgent tones. "Something River said got me rattled. Ran a full-spectrum diagnostic—temperature, vibration, electromagnetic frequency, radiation, seal integrity. River was right, Lord knows how. Something's changed in those boxes. The contents are heating up." She made a face. "Kaboom."

"What's our solution?" Zoë asked briskly.

Kaylee had a quick answer for that. "Maybe we can cool down the cargo to slow down the reaction. Make it as cold as we can."

"Seal off the hold and open the bay," Jayne said with a gleam in his eye. "Don't get much colder than space."

"Great idea," Zoë said.

"Yeah?" Jayne sounded a little surprised. Zoë could only assume this was because it wasn't often his ideas were classified as great. Or even listened to.

"Yes. But it's going to have to wait. We got company."

She hit the switch to operate the cargo-bay ramp. It had barely opened before a dozen-strong Alliance team, in full body armor and helmets, marched into the cargo bay in lockstep. They fanned out, most with weapons drawn and aimed towards Zoë, Jayne and Kaylee. A few carried compact, ruggedized flight cases.

Zoë, Kaylee, and most reluctantly Jayne raised their hands in surrender.

"Do not touch your weapons," the Alliance officer at the front of the pack said. "We will disarm you ourselves."

As the other Alliance officers were seeing to that, their leader asked, "Who's in charge here?"

"That'd be me," Zoë said. "Zoë Washburne, acting captain of this here vessel."

"And I'm Major Bernard of the I.A.V. *Stormfront*." He looked all three of them up and down, then said, "Is this your entire crew?"

"No, sir," Zoë said. "Our pilot is still up in the bridge."

"Get him or her down here on the double."

After Zoë relayed the order to Wash over the intercom, Major Bernard flashed his credentials at her so fast she couldn't read them. Not that she needed to. The patrol cruiser parked alongside *Serenity* was credentials aplenty.

"By authority of the Union of Allied Planets," Bernard said in a monotone, "I'll need access to all crew documentation and bills of lading on cargo presently carried aboard this ship. Also vessel registration forms and tax licenses. Any attempt to conceal information or cargo will be punished to the fullest extent of the law. Are you carrying any passengers who are not crew?"

"No, sir," Zoë said. "This is not a passenger ship."

He looked around at the largely bare cargo bay. "Did you just offload a consignment or is this the state of your business?"

"It comes and goes, sir," Zoë replied. *Usually goes*, she added inwardly.

"While I'm checking the paperwork, my team will run a routine search of the entire ship."

"A search for what?" Kaylee said, all wide-eyed innocence.

"Contraband or undocumented individuals," Bernard said. Then his eyes narrowed, and he addressed all three of them. "This can't be your first rodeo. You know exactly what we do."

"Don't want anyone touching Vera with their dirty paws," Jayne growled under his breath. "She don't like it."

"Vera?" said Bernard. "There's a fifth person on board?"

"Nope. She's a gun. Got the license for her and everything, before you ask."

Major Bernard did a double take. "You name your—? Never mind."

"All the paperwork you want is stowed in the galley," Zoë said. Then, flicking a lock of her hair behind her ear and lowering her voice suggestively, she said, "You'd be most comfortable working in there, Major. You can spread everything out on the dining table. I can even make you some tea if you'd like."

The change in her tone and attitude was not lost on Bernard. A small smile broke his blunt, coarse features. "That's most accommodating of you, Acting Captain Washburne," he said.

As he and Zoë made for the dining area, Bernard's subordinates began opening their flight cases and taking out multiple-reading scanners. Whose infrared setting, Zoë knew, could pick up the body heat of a fruit fly through ten feet of vanadium steel.

Bernard sat himself down at the dining table and Zoë spread out the documents in front of him.

"Hmmm," he said. "According to the registration this ship has two shuttles, but on approach we saw both bays are currently empty. Where are your shuttles, Acting Captain Washburne?"

"Please, call me Zoë."

"Very well." Again, that small smile, accompanied by a tiny, avid glint in the eye. Major Bernard was not a handsome man but he was, it seemed, vain enough to think that a woman like Zoë might be attracted to him. She noted the wedding band on his left hand. She noted, too, that he was making some effort to hide it from her. "I'll repeat the question, Zoë. Where are you shuttles?"

"We've had bad luck with shuttles lately," she told him. "Had to leave 'em both on Whitefall. They're awaiting spare parts for necessary refitting."

"Kind of risky going into the Black without one, don't you think?"

"Risk is built into the price for our services," she said.

Wash appeared in the dining-room doorway. His strawberry-blond hair was sticking up every which way like he had just rolled out of bed. But then it always looked like that. "I was told someone needed to see me," he said. "Went down to the cargo bay but got sent up here."

Major Bernard stared grimly at Wash's eye-searingly colorful Hawaiian shirt and the toy dinosaur poking a toothy head out of his breast pocket.

"Who might you be?" Bernard said.

"Hoban Washburne, pilot, husband." Then, remembering Zoë's plan, Wash said, "But not husband to this lady. No, sir."

Bernard frowned. "But you have the same surname."

"Brother and sister," Wash said.

Zoë shot him a scowl over Bernard's head.

"*Adopted* brother and sister," Wash amended. "It's funny, though. People often tell us how much we look alike."

"They do?" said Bernard, peering from Wash to Zoë and back again.

"Act alike, at any rate. Similar mannerisms. Similar gestures." Wash attempted to mimic a typical Zoë-esque posture, cocking a hip and resting his thumbs in his belt. He also widened his eyes in emulation of her naturally large eyes, although whereas on her it looked captivating, on him it looked just plain demented. "Like twins, some say."

"Hoban," said Zoë, deliberately using his given name rather than his nickname, as a sister might, "Major Bernard doesn't need to know any of that. Major Bernard is a busy man. Isn't that so, Major?"

"Aubrey," said Bernard.

"Huh?"

"I call you Zoë, you call me Aubrey."

"Sure thing, Aubrey." Zoë bit back a laugh. *Aubrey?* "So, Hoban, why don't you just hurry on back to the bridge?" She made a waggling wave with her fingers. "Assuming Aubrey doesn't need to discuss anything with you, that is."

"I have just one question," Bernard said to Wash. "What was your course prior to boarding?"

Wash told him the truth. He had no choice. It was all down in black and white on the manifest they got from Badger, which Bernard now held.

"That would be for delivery of five crates of mining chemicals?" Bernard scanned over the bill of lading. "On Aberdeen?"

Wash nodded.

"Very well," said Bernard. "That's all I need to know. You're dismissed, Mr. Washburne."

"Okay. Bye for now, uh, sis," Wash said to Zoë. "See you later."

He sauntered off, doing his best impersonation of Zoë's confident, take-no-prisoners gait.

"Strange fellow," Bernard remarked. "Hard to believe the two of you are related."

"Well, we're not, are we?" Zoë said. "Not by blood. My parents took him in after his own parents rejected him."

"I can see why they might have. His parents, I mean. Yours, not so much."

"Growing up, he was always a doofus. Hasn't changed a great deal. But never mind him, Aubrey. You keep examining that paperwork. I think you'll find it's all in order, but it never hurts to have someone cast an expert eye over it."

She braced both arms on the table, leaning close to the Alliance officer—so close that a stray strand of her hair brushed his cheek.

"Oh, I'm sorry," she said, in a not-sorry voice.

"No problem, Zoë." Bernard gave every appearance of

concentrating on the documents but she could tell his mind wasn't fully on the task. Every once in a while he darted a quick sideways glance at her, taking in her arm, the curve of her bosom, the profile of her face. Finally, he pronounced himself satisfied. "Registration code numbers on the engine manifolds are correct. Documentation all checks out. Guess I'd better have a look at the labels and seals on those crates of chemicals, just to be completely sure."

They left the dining room, Zoë leading the way. She was conscious of Bernard's gaze on her backside and walked with a little extra wiggle for his benefit. Her injured leg accentuated the motion.

Jayne and Kaylee were still where she had left them, down in the cargo bay. Wash was there too. Jayne looked ill-tempered as always but was trying to rein in his disgruntlement. Kaylee, by contrast, was an open book. She wrung her hands and gnawed her lower lip. As for Wash, he could put on a poker face when he needed to.

"HTX-20," Major Bernard said, walking around the crates but giving them a wide berth. "Satan's Snowflakes, they call it. That's some seriously hazardous cargo you've got there."

"It's what we do, Aubrey," Zoë said. "There's a premium on hazardous."

Bernard waved his subordinates over. "See if you can't shift them out of the way," he said. "I want to know what's under them."

Zoë and Kaylee traded glances. Kaylee said, "Sir, these crates should not be moved. The contents are highly volatile."

Bernard wheeled around, one eyebrow raised. "If

they're that dangerous, then why are they sitting in your hold without proper protection?"

"They didn't used to be so volatile."

"Move them," Bernard ordered.

The Alliance officers tried, but they couldn't lift the crates and they couldn't slide them across the deck, either. They were just too heavy to budge. With every grunting abortive attempt, the four crewmembers flinched.

Bernard turned to Zoë. He pointed at a forklift parked along the wall. "Does that thing work?"

Kaylee made a little involuntary squeak.

"What do you think's under there?" Jayne said, clearly on the verge of losing his couth and his cool. "How dumb do you think we are?"

"I don't know how dumb you, personally, are," Bernard said. "By the looks of it, pretty dumb."

Jayne's lips curled back from his teeth.

"Zoë, on the other hand," Bernard continued, "strikes me as an intelligent and discerning woman, which is why I'm asking myself how she could just let these crates sit here if their contents are really so unstable. Which in turn leads me to wonder whether they mightn't be hiding something, and someone's hoping we won't dare move them."

"I'll move them," Wash said agreeably.

Zoë watched as Wash climbed onto the repaired forklift, started it up, and with a grinding crunch, jammed it in reverse. Showing off his exceptional driving skills, he nearly backed over Bernard's foot. Would have done, if Zoë hadn't nudged the Alliance officer out of the path of the rear wheel.

"Aargh. Sorry about that," Wash said sheepishly as he

squealed the brakes. "Accelerator sticks a bit."

He surged forward, dropping the fork so low, it sent sparks flying off the deck. With a reckless nonchalance, he scraped under and scooped up the nearest crate. Zoë was holding her breath. Jayne turned away, a scowl on his face. Kaylee looked plain desperate.

"Where do you want it?" Wash asked as he raised the huge box, teetering, to eye level.

"Anywhere," Bernard said.

As Wash reversed away with the crate, Major Bernard seemed disappointed to find no trap door hidden underneath. There was nothing but solid, bolted-down deck plate.

"Move the others," he told Wash.

But it was the same story there. Bernard watched as his men tested the deck plates with their scanner wands, looking for voids that could hold contraband and stowaways. When they were done, they shook their heads.

"Ship is clean, sir," one of them reported. Then he added, hopefully, "A bit too clean maybe?"

Zoë chortled merrily. "Oh, hush! Don't you listen to him, Aubrey," she said, resting a hand on Bernard's forearm. "How can a ship be too clean? It's ridiculous!"

Her hand lingered. Major Bernard made no effort to dislodge it. Weighing up the evidence of his own eyes, and factoring in the obvious allure he held for Zoë, he came a decision. He scribbled something on the bottom of the manifest, then stamped it with his official stamp.

"We appreciate your compliance and courtesy," he said to Zoë. "You are good to go. We'll be out of your way shortly."

"Excellent work," Wash said, beaming at Bernard.

"Very efficient. Very thorough. A credit to the Alliance."

"Pleasure to make your acquaintance, Zoë," Bernard said, giving her a particularly snappy salute.

"Likewise, I'm sure, Aubrey."

The boarding team left the crew's weapons piled on the dining table and made a dignified, single-file exit.

As the ramp closed behind them, Wash sidled over to Zoë. "I've got to say, Zoë, seeing that performance of yours just now, I don't know whether I'm turned on or should start filing for divorce. Did 'Aubrey' give you his wave address? You two planning on seeing each other again, or was this a one-time thing?"

"You know I only have eyes for you, husband."

"I was thinking, maybe we could play at being brother and sister again sometime. To, y'know, spice things up in the bedroom."

"Don't push it, buster," Zoë said, giving him a whack on the arm that left him wincing and rubbing the affected area for a minute afterwards.

It took ten minutes for I.A.V. *Stormfront* to undock. By then, Wash was back up in the bridge. When *Serenity* was clear of the cruiser's exhaust, he fired a single pulse of the engines and gentled her away, in the opposite direction Inara had flown.

"We've got to do something about those crates," Kaylee said to Zoë. "It can't wait."

"If they're overheating, there's only one solution I can see. Jayne's idea. We strap them down and blow the atmo. Hard vacuum will bring down their temperature in no time."

"What if that doesn't work?"

"We jettison them out into space," Zoë said. She hated even thinking it, let alone voicing it. The crew were already so broke. But better broke than incinerated.

"If we lose our cargo," Jayne said, "we might as well quit flying."

Zoë rounded on him. "You care to rephrase that?"

He shrugged. "Choice mightn't be ours, anyway. We won't have the coin we need to keep this boat in the sky."

She kept glaring at him, but he was only saying what she was thinking. She said, "Strap down the crates. Fast. And keep your mouth shut."

"This is not our best day," Jayne muttered under his breath.

Zoë thought of Mal. Wherever he had gotten to, she reckoned he was having an even worse day.

24

Inara had seen larger, grander houses in her time, but Hunter
Covington's mansion was impressive nonetheless. It was
wedding-cake white and sprawled over two stories, with
Doric columns rising to the roof all along its front elevation,
creating a broad, shaded porch area. Twenty rooms in the
main building at least, she thought, along with a barn-like
stable block to one side and a wing adjoining the rear which,
to judge by the comparative plainness of its exterior, most
likely housed the servants' quarters.

The grounds were impressive too, if for no other
reason than the greenness of the neatly trimmed lawns and
shrubbery. The surrounding landscape was arid and harshly
brown, dotted here and there with vegetation but more or
less desert. To use so much water in such a parched region
to irrigate a garden was costly and profligate.

It was early, but in the cool of the morning a gardener
was already outdoors, clipping a hedge. He paused from his
labors to watch Inara go past. Not five minutes earlier her

shuttle had put down in front of the property. The gardener had been curious about that, but not as curious as he was to see a woman who was clearly a Companion sashaying forth. He touched a finger to the brim of his sunhat. Inara rewarded him with one her best and brightest smiles.

She walked up a short flight of steps to the front door, which opened before she had even got a hand to the bellpush.

The person on the other side was not some valet or butler, she knew that at a glance. He was a slab-faced bodyguard type, with a gun on his hip and an insolent, seen-it-all look about him.

"Who are you?" he demanded.

"Inara Serra. I'm expected."

"You sure as hell ain't. Nobody's expected."

Her forehead puckered into the slightest of frowns. "To whom am I speaking?"

"Who I am ain't none of your business, lady," said the bodyguard.

"Well, is Mr. Covington home?"

"Mr. Covington ain't home."

She looked flustered. "There must be some misunderstanding. I have an appointment with him this morning. Eight a.m. sharp. My credentials."

She showed him her Companion license and registration, etched with the insignia of House Madrassa.

The bodyguard had already figured out her occupation for himself and gave the documents only a cursory glance.

"He's really not in?" she said.

"Off-planet on business. You sure you have an appointment? Only Mr. Covington, he don't consort with

Companions, best I know. He has himself... alternative outlets for his needs, if you get what I'm saying. Must be there's been some kinda mix-up."

Inara was now doing an impersonation of someone very confused and not a little indignant. "Mistakes like this simply don't happen. I had a firm engagement with Mr. Covington at this hour. It was made over a month ago, and I've travelled a long way to be here. If he was going to cancel, he ought to have let me know in advance. I've a good mind to report him to the Guild over this. Wasting my time. He'll be fined at the very least, and if I have my way he'll be blackballed as well."

"Yeah, well, sorry about that," said the bodyguard unapologetically.

Inara insinuated herself into the doorway, so that he could not easily close the door on her. "May I make a small request?" He didn't say no, so she continued, "I've been in my shuttle nearly three days straight. The water tanks are running low and, frankly, I could do with freshening up. Is there a bathroom nearby I could use? I promise I won't be more than five minutes. You'd be doing me such a favor."

No one was impervious to Inara Serra's charm when she turned it on full blast. Age, gender, sexual inclination, professional obligation, none of it made any difference. A person's inner barriers simply melted like ice under a blowtorch.

The bodyguard could have no more refused her request than he could have forbidden the tide from turning or the sun from setting.

"I dunno..."

"Please?"

Whatever last few misgivings he had evaporated. "Okay. It's down this way. Follow me."

"You're too kind… Do you have a name?"

"Walter."

"Walter, you're too kind."

Walter couldn't help himself. A smile of appreciation plucked at the corners of his meaty mouth.

Inara entered a huge hallway with a curved, sweeping staircase and teak floorboards polished to such a gleam they dazzled the eyes. The downstairs bathroom had gold and marble fittings. Inara ran the faucets a while and made some minor adjustments to her elaborate, kabuki-inflected makeup in the mirror. She was steeling herself for what she had to do next.

Walter the bodyguard was waiting right outside as she re-emerged.

"I'll be leaving now," she said. "Do tell Mr. Covington that I was disappointed to have missed him. I'm still unhappy about the unannounced cancellation, but your courtesy, Walter, has gone a long way to allaying my feelings of offense. Oh. You appear to have something on your neck. A speck of lint, it looks like. May I?"

Not allowing him to grant permission, or even to try to remove the lint himself, Inara reached up and brushed the side of his thick neck.

Walter touched the spot where her fingers had just been. A small knot formed between his eyebrows.

"Feels odd," he said. "Like my skin's gone numb."

"A Companion's touch has been known to have all sorts of effects," Inara said.

"Yeah, but this ain't…" His eyes swam in their sockets. His body swayed. "What the hell'd you just do to me, you witch?" he said slurringly.

"It's a fast-acting, skin-contact sedative, Walter. An hour from now you'll wake up with a raging headache and a powerful thirst, but otherwise unharmed."

He made to grab for her but the action was feeble and uncoordinated. His legs were buckling under him. He could barely stay standing.

"Companions have these little tricks," Inara continued, "in case a client gets aggressive or otherwise fails to observe the rules. Now why don't you just sit down over there?" She guided him towards a gilt chair. "More comfortable than simply collapsing to the floor."

Walter sat heavily. His eyelids drooped. His head sagged.

"Shou' ne'er ha' trust… a whorrr…"

The words trailed off, to be replaced by deep snoring.

"And because you called me that," Inara said to his unconscious form, "I have even fewer qualms about doing what I just did."

She peeled off the oval-shaped transparent patch on the tip of her index finger. It was an impermeable membrane coated on one side with a dose of the sedative. All of the drug should have transferred itself to Walter but she was careful nonetheless as she rolled up the membrane and slipped it into a pocket.

At that moment, a maid entered the hallway carrying a stack of folded towels. She took one look at Inara, and at the slumped, snoozing Walter, and her face fell in astonishment. She seemed on the brink of yelling.

Inara hurried towards her, adopting a mask of anxiety. "Help me," she said. "This man just collapsed. I don't know what's happened. I think he's unwell."

The maid was unconvinced. "I don't know who you are, lady, or what you're doing here, but we're told to be wary of all strangers, even fancily dressed ones."

"I imagine so. For what it's worth, I mean you no harm. That said, I can't have you screaming the house down either."

She was now only arm's distance from the maid. There was no time for finesse or subtlety. She struck her a blow to the carotid with the edge of her hand like a sideways ax chop. The blow briefly interrupted the blood supply to the maid's brain and stunned her temporarily, long enough for Inara to deliver a second deftly aimed jab to the vagus nerve in her neck. Instant insensibility ensued. Inara caught the maid as she fell, then dragged her to the doorway through which she had entered.

In a laundry room, amid shelves piled high with clothes and fresh linen, she laid the maid out on the floor, then went back into the hallway to fetch the towels the woman had dropped. She rolled up one of them and placed it beneath the maid's head. Like Walter, the maid would wake up with a headache but at least a stiff neck wouldn't be a problem.

Compassion was one of a Companion's strongest suits, even when it came to visiting violence on others.

25

While Inara infiltrated the mansion itself, Shepherd Book was moving stealthily round the perimeter of the grounds. He had no idea where Elmira Atadema was being kept on the premises, so his only option was reconnaissance. With Inara busy indoors distracting and neutralizing whatever security personnel Hunter Covington employed, Book crept along, keeping low behind the three-bar fence that encircled the property and studying the building from all angles. He reasoned that Covington would have Elmira under lock and key in an upstairs room, in order to make it that much harder for her to escape. To that end, he surveilled the house's upper story, looking for a window that was shuttered or barred or both.

The sound of a twig snapping behind him brought him whirling around. His stun gun was in his hand, fully charged and primed. Book almost pulled the trigger to unleash the electrified dart that would deliver a 50,000-volt shock.

"River?"

River Tam stood there, swinging her arms from side to side.

"I thought we told you to stay in the shuttle with Simon."

"Simon wasn't looking, so I came out," River said. "To help you."

"You're no help to me here," Book said gently but with a forceful undertone. "This is something Inara and I have to do. You're best off keeping out of sight with your brother."

"I know where she is."

"What?"

"The woman. Elmira. She's in there." River pointed, straight-armed, towards the stable block.

Just as Book was asking himself how River could know this—and be so certain about it, too—Simon came scurrying up.

"River!" he hissed. "You shouldn't have run away. I've been looking all over for you."

"Here I am," she said simply. "You found me."

"Sorry, Shepherd. I'll take her back to the shuttle. No harm done, I hope."

"Wait just a moment, son," Book said. "River, are you sure that's where Elmira is?"

River nodded. "Uh-huh. I can see her. She's sad. She's chained up. Straw in her hair. She knows she's going to die. Hunter's mad at her. She sold him out, he says. 'I'm going to fix you, woman.'" River's voice had suddenly taken on a gravel-roughness and a masculine note. "'See if I don't. When I come back, I'm going to show you what happens to bitches that snitch to the authorities. They get cut. All over.

Every part of their body. *Every* part. Cut till they bleed to death, but slow. Days-long slow.' And she knows he's going to do it, too." Her voice had reverted to normal. "He's not a man to lie about such things."

"Where precisely in the stable block is she?" River, if she was correct about Elmira's location, had just saved Book a considerable amount of time and effort. The stable block would have been the last place he looked.

"Easier if I show you."

Book looked at Simon, then at his sister, then back to Simon.

"Are you asking my permission?" Simon said.

"Preferably, but even if I don't, River's coming with me."

Simon debated inwardly. "Then I'm coming too. I already let her out of my sight once. I'm not doing it a second time. Who knows what we could be walking into?"

Book did not like having two people tagging along with him. One was bad enough. But he respected Simon's decision and his concern for his sister's welfare.

"All right. Just please stay out of the way. Leave the rough stuff to me."

"Here we go." River was already striding off towards the stable block. Book hurried to catch up, Simon at his heels. "Off to see the horsies."

They were halfway there when River said to Book, "By the way, there's a man just inside the doorway. He hasn't seen us yet. You have ten seconds before he does."

Again, Book wondered how the girl could have such knowledge. Those Dr. Frankensteins at the Academy had bestowed talents on her that were preternatural, that were even—although it seemed a mildly blasphemous thought—godlike.

But he didn't have time to dwell on it. He broke into a sprint, running towards the stable block as fast as his aged limbs would let him. Book was, in fact, in phenomenally good shape for a man of his advanced years, keeping himself that way through a routine of isometric strengthening exercises and abstinence from alcohol and narcotics. Within five seconds he had covered the thirty yards between him and the stable-block door. Two seconds later, he was inside the building and confronting the man stationed on guard duty, who was in the process of rising from the chair he'd been sitting on and raising the rifle that had been lying across his knees. The stun gun crackled in Book's hand. The guard tumbled to the ground, juddering, like he was doing some kind of wild horizontal dance routine. His teeth were bared. An eerie, strangulated ululation escaped his throat. A wet patch spread across the crotch of his jeans.

"There's another one," River said from the doorway.

Book wheeled to see a second guard appear from the shadows of one of the looseboxes. He was drawing his pistol. Book hit the switch on the stun gun to detach the wire linking it to the dart hooked in the first guard's chest. The gun was a two-shot deal, but it required closer range than he currently had. The second guard was a good five yards too far away. Book had no choice but to duck down and charge towards him, hoping he could bridge the gap in time. The guard was cocking his gun, however, and drawing a bead on Book. Book knew, with a dreadful certainty, that he was going to be too slow. The guard was going to shoot him before he could get him with the stun gun.

A horseshoe whirled like a discus over Book's head. It clouted the guard in the face, just above one eyebrow, with an audible *crunch*. The man dropped as though he had walked slap bang into an invisible wall.

Book glanced round to see River looking very pleased with herself, clapping her hands in glee.

"Nice shot," he said.

"I love playing horseshoes," River said. "I was always good at it. Better than Simon." She picked up another horseshoe from the dust at her feet. It and the one she had thrown must have been just lying around spare. "If he gets up again, I'll just hit him again."

"You do that. Where's Elmira?"

"Who? Oh, her. Yes." The girl tapped her lips, pondering. "Up there." She gestured towards a hayloft. "Straw in her hair."

Book shinned up a stepladder that led to the hayloft. The horses were stamping softly and whinnying in their looseboxes below, disturbed by the uncustomary activities of the humans in the stables. If luck was on Book's side— or some higher power—the beasts would not become so agitated as to draw the attention of people in the house.

As his head rose above the level of the hayloft floor, he peered cautiously around. There might well be a third guard on duty.

But there was nobody in the hayloft save for a young woman chained to a support post, with a piece of cloth tied tight around her mouth to form a gag. Her clothing was ripped and torn. Her hair was disheveled, and yes, as River had said, there were bits of straw in it, sticking out at all angles like pins from a pincushion. She had bruises and grazes all over, and she looked terrified.

As Book appeared, Elmira Atadema began to writhe and scream, despite the gag. He put a finger to lips and smiled reassuringly.

"I'm not here to hurt you, Elmira," he said. "I'm here to help."

Her expression was distrustful but she did calm down somewhat.

"Mika Wong sent me." Only the slightest distortion of the truth. "My friends and I are going to get you out of here."

Mention of Wong's name appeared to settle the matter as far as Elmira was concerned.

Book undid the gag. Elmira worked her jaw to ease the kinks out. The gag had been on so long it had left red welts.

"Who are you?" she croaked.

"All in good time," Book said. "First order of business: getting these chains off you."

The chains were secured with a padlock. Book studied it for a moment, then shrugged. It had the simplest kind of lever-and-ward mechanism. He could have opened it in thirty seconds with a paperclip or a hairgrip, but luckily he could do better than that. From his satchel he took out a compact, leather-bound Bible. Concealed within the binding, in a recess beneath a marbled endpaper that could be detached, was a comprehensive set of lockpicks. He selected one that in his judgment matched this brand of padlock and corresponded to the genuine key in length. He inserted it into the slot, feeling its teeth fit snugly against the actuators. He'd gauged right. A single clockwise twist of the wrist, and the padlock's shackle fell open.

"A Shepherd," said Elmira, "who can pick a lock?"

"'And I will give unto thee the keys of the kingdom of heaven,'" Book said, stowing the lockpick back inside the Bible and the book itself back in his satchel, "'and whatsoever thou shalt bind on earth shall be bound in heaven, and whatsoever thou shalt loose on earth shall be loosed in heaven.' Matthew chapter sixteen, verse nineteen."

He unwrapped the chains from around her wrists and helped her to her feet.

"Can you walk?" he asked.

"I think so," said Elmira.

"Then let's go. Time is of the essence."

26

Outside the stable block, Simon Tam was keeping watch. His specialty was medicine, however, not sentry duty. He didn't see the armed man stealing up on him from around the corner of the stable block. He wasn't even aware of his presence until the man pounced on him from behind, snaking an arm around his throat. The barrel of a gun dug into Simon's temple.

"Don't move," the man growled, "'less you want your brains spattered all over that there fancy vest of your'n."

"P–Please don't shoot," Simon stammered.

"Don't give me no excuse to. State your business. Quick about it."

"I'm—I'm a guest of Hunter Collington's. Good friend of his. Arrived just this morning. I'm only taking a stroll around, admiring the spread."

"Hunter who?"

"Your boss. Hunter Collington."

The man chuckled gratingly. "I have a boss, but his

name ain't *Collington*. You maybe wanna try that again?"

"Covington!" Simon exclaimed. He could have kicked himself. What a rookie mistake, getting the surname wrong. He just wasn't cut out for this sort of clandestine stuff. Nothing in his upbringing or education had prepared him for a life of skullduggery and violence. "Slip of the tongue. I meant Covington."

"A so-called good friend of Mr. Covington's wouldn't have gotten his name wrong, pal. I don't reckon you know him at all. I reckon you're some kinda spy or somethin'. We're under orders to be on the lookout for intruders, anyone sneakin' around looking suspicious. I'd say you fit the bill. Now tell me the truth. You got until the count of three, and then it's brain surgery by bullet. One. Two…"

River drifted out of the stable block, hands behind her back. "Hey, Simon. Who's your friend?"

Simon felt the man holding him stiffen in surprise. "Where'd you come from, girl?"

"In there," River said. "I was just stroking the horses. They have such soft noses, did you know that? Apart from the bristles. And their breath, when they snort, it's warm on your hand. I like it. It smells of friendliness."

She took a step towards the man and Simon.

The gun moved from Simon's head, swiveling towards River. "Best you stay where you are," the man said to her. "I got plenty of rounds in this thing, and I only need one for the each of you."

Simon's breath caught in his throat. With the tiniest twitch of his head, he tried to indicate to River that she should stop moving.

Whether she saw the instruction or not, River halted. She twirled one foot, drawing circles in the dust with the toecap of her boot. The man with the gun looked down at what she was doing. When he looked up again, River had brought both hands out in front of her. The right held a horseshoe. In one blindingly swift action she flung it at the man. It connected with his gun hand, knocking the weapon out of his grasp. Before he was able to collect his wits, River sprang. Simon stumbled aside as River and the man went crashing to the ground. Straddling her opponent's torso, she rained punches on his face and ribcage in such a rapid flurry that her arms were twin blurs, like the pistons on a locomotive pumping at full speed. The man was utterly unable to defend or deflect. Within seconds River had rendered him unconscious. Still she kept up the barrage of blows, until Simon laid a hand on her shoulder.

"River? You've done it. He's out cold. Keep that up and you might kill him."

"He was going to kill you," she said. "And me. Fair's fair. An eye for an eye, a tooth for a tooth, a candy for a candy, a penny for your thoughts."

"Still and all. We don't kill unless we have to."

River reflected on this, then smiled brightly. "Okay! That's a good rule."

"I like to think so."

She picked herself up and dusted herself off. "Oh, hi, Shepherd. And straw-in-hair lady."

Book had just come out of the stable block, one arm around Elmira Atadema to support her. He cast a glance at the man on the ground.

"No problems here, I take it."

"None that couldn't be dealt with," Simon said.

"Then let's make haste. Covington seems to have an endless supply of thugs and I've no idea if we've met them all yet."

27

Inara saw them from a window: River, Simon, and Book, with Elmira, hurrying across the front lawn. She herself had been conducting a painstaking search of the first-floor rooms, ever keeping an ear out for bodyguards or servants, to avoid any further run-ins.

It seemed she had been looking in vain. Elmira had been elsewhere.

Inara made her way back to the front door and out into the daylight. She greeted the others with a wave, joining them on the driveway that led towards her shuttle.

"A Companion too?" Elmira said. "Who *are* you people?"

"Right now," Book said, "your liberators. And hopefully, in a few minutes, once we've made good our escape, we're going to be the recipients of some crucial intelligence from you. Namely the whereabouts of your bondholder."

"I can tell you that right now," Elmira said. "Hunter isn't on Persephone anymore. He departed last night on his private yacht, after doing some business over in Eavesdown."

"Do you know where he's gone?"

"Yes. He was boasting to me about it only yesterday, up there in the hayloft. He'd just been… been using me." Her mouth downturned in a grimace of disgust.

"You mean abusing," said Inara.

"Yes, well, same difference. And then he told me he was going away but when he came back he'd…"

"Cut you," said River. "Cut you till you bled to death, but slow. Days-long slow."

"Yes," said Elmira, startled. "His exact words. How do you know he said that? Have you been speaking to him?"

"Never mind how we know," said Book. "Where is he?"

"He was off to meet up with some associates. Bunch of renegades, I think. One-time Browncoats, now working some new angle. Hunter's been dealing with them quite some while, providing them with intel and such. It's what Wong wanted me to find out about, why he had me come back and infiltrate Hunter's operation."

"Vigilantes?"

"Yeah, I guess you could call them that."

By now the group had reached the shuttle. Inara looked back towards the house, half expecting to see pursuers emerging. It seemed that the alarm had yet to be raised.

River climbed aboard first, followed by Simon. Inara went next, extending a helping hand to Elmira. Book was last, and as soon as they were all safely ensconced in the shuttle, Inara darted over to the controls and started the engine cycling.

"So he met the vigilantes in Eavesdown, and then what?" Book said to Elmira, raising his voice above the steadily mounting whine of power coming from the thrusters.

"Then he was going to follow them to their destination. Seems as though they had plans to take some guy captive in Eavesdown, subject him to a trial, and then hang him. They paid Hunter to help them nab the man. That's what they've been doing for quite a while, all across the 'verse. They track down people they believe betrayed the Independent cause in some way or other, run them through a kangaroo court, then execute them."

Inara's stomach knotted. *Mal…*

Over her shoulder she said, "Did you just say 'execute?'"

"I'm afraid so," said Elmira. "Hunter's gone to watch. They invited him along and he accepted. It doesn't pay to turn down a client's request, not if you want to work with them again in future. Plus, I imagine he's curious to see the end result. In case you hadn't appreciated, he ain't a nice man. Got a cruel streak in him a mile wide."

"You sound as though you speak from experience," said Simon.

She gave him a hard, steady look. "I most certainly do. I can show you the scars, if you like. I'll say this for Hunter. He's a sadist but a careful one. Never leaves marks where people'll see them. But that still means there are plenty of places where he can leave them."

She began unbuttoning her blouse, until Simon stopped her. Mumbling an apology, he turned away. Point made, she did the buttons back up.

"Now, Elmira," said Book, "I know you've been through a lot, but I want you to be very clear about this. That man you're talking about, the one the vigilantes are going to kill, is a friend of ours."

"Oh my God, I'm so very sorry."

"It's okay. All I want from you now is where they've taken him; wherever Covington is headed. You have to understand how important this is to us."

The shuttle rose from the ground with a lurch, pitching forward until its nose was almost scraping the dirt. Inara corrected, too preoccupied to worry if their ascent was perfectly smooth or not.

A ricocheting bullet snapped off the shuttle's hull with a *spanggg!* To the people inside, it sounded like a mallet blow. Two men were running out of the mansion, toting rifles. The alarm had been raised at last, it would appear. They were both firing at a run, which meant their shooting was far from accurate. Not only that but they must know their rounds would not penetrate the skin of a spacecraft designed with sufficient armoring to protect it from micrometeors and other small colliding objects. Presumably they thought it was better to waste the bullets than have to admit to Covington later that they had done nothing whatsoever to prevent the shuttle taking off.

Inara poured on speed. The shuttle veered away from the mansion in a wide, yawing arc.

"Hades," Elmira said. "They're on Hades."

28

Kaylee looked for work to occupy her mind. There was no end of that to be found aboard *Serenity*, but the distraction of a simple, involving task wasn't always sufficient. As she started lubricating a flanged coupler gasket on the transverse manipulator hose, digging her fingers into a bucket of grease, the cogs in her head resumed their unhappy, circular turning.

After *Serenity* had been flying for an hour with the cargo-bay door wide open, Kaylee and Jayne had donned spacesuits and gone down to check on the condition of the payload. Exposed to the -270 °C chill of the deep Black, ambient condensation now coated everything in the cargo bay—every surface, every deck plate, bulkhead and piece of machinery—with a shimmering, onionskin-thin layer of frost. It was like being inside a twinkling, multifaceted jewel.

The only objects in the entire place that were clear of ice were the crates of HTX-20 themselves. Their warmth had prevented the frost from forming on them. But a quick scan had shown Kaylee that the explosives within had cooled considerably, almost back to the temperature they'd originally been at when they'd come aboard. It had worked! And that was all the more remarkable an achievement because it was an idea suggested by Jayne Cobb.

Kaylee had closed the cargo-bay door, and atmo had slowly begun hissing back into the ship's bowels.

Now she wiped the sweat from her brow with the back of her hand, smearing a band of grease across it. She was worried sick about Mal, and would start to sniffle quietly every time she thought about what he might be suffering— the more so when she allowed herself to entertain the notion that he might already be dead and lost to them forever. There was still no word from Book or Inara. Still no update on Mal's likely whereabouts. And on top of that, Kaylee was afraid that the crew wouldn't be able to survive this dangerous mission without Mal's guidance. He had a way of seeing past trouble and finding a path to safety, even in the direst of situations.

Zoë's voice crackled through the comm. "Kaylee, we need you to recheck the cargo, make sure it's stopped simmering."

Kaylee cleaned her hands on a rag and tossed it in the general direction of the trash can. She didn't really want to go back near the explosives, but at least it was something to do.

29

After Stuart Deakins left, Mal examined every inch of his cell, searching for a way to escape. If he could find a weakness in a wall or a soft spot in the floor, maybe he could burrow his way out with his heels. He found nothing, just solid, bare rock. Then he tested the mesh door, applying pressure first with his shoulder, then with his feet from a seated position, legs straight out in front of him. He could budge it some, but not nearly as much as he would have liked. Not enough to give him hope that he could force the door out of its frame with brute strength or even bend it slightly out of true so as to create a gap he might wriggle through.

Accepting the futility of escape, he propped himself in the corner with his elbows bent, his fastened hands in the small of his back, his knees nestled against his chest. He dozed off a few times in this awkward position—he was exhausted—but kept snapping awake. Cramping in his shoulders wouldn't let him rest for long. He eased out the discomfort as best he could but invariably it returned.

Approaching footfalls echoed down the tunnel. They sounded purposeful. Mal hoped it was Deakins again. Perhaps something of what Mal had said to him had filtered through to the reservoir of good which he was sure still resided in the man. Perhaps Deakins's conscience had been fully awakened and he was even now coming to set Mal free.

No such luck. The new arrivals were David Zuburi, David's wife Sonya, and the hatchet-faced woman from before.

"Howdy, David," Mal said. "Sonya. And you…" He looked at Hatchet Face. "Well, I know you and I have met, but we haven't been formally introduced."

"This ain't no social gathering," she retorted. "But, for your information, my name's Harriet Kyle."

"Miss or Mrs.?"

She kicked him in the ribs. Her boots must have had steel toecaps because it hurt unreasonably.

In strained tones, Mal said, "I'll take that as a check in the 'neither of the above' box."

"Your trial's starting," David said. "Up on your feet."

Mal struggled upright. "I thought we were waiting on some latecomers."

"We still are," Sonya said. "They're en route and should be here soon, but Toby couldn't hang on any longer. Nor could anyone else."

The low tunnel ceiling seemed to press down on Mal's sore shoulders as he walked between his guards back to the cavern. There, a banjo was playing and people were belting out the Independents' battle hymn with all the zeal of a platoon of Browncoats after a victory.

"Browncoats, look up to the skies!
Browncoats, hail the dawn!
Today will see tyranny
Dying with the morn.

"Browncoats, are you weary?
Browncoats, rise and sing!
Your time has come, your war is won.
Victory takes wing."

The battle hymn had heartened Mal on many a hopeless-seeming night. On this occasion, his spirits were not lifted. The song seemed more like an accusation than a rallying cry.

David, Sonya, and Harriet escorted him through the crowd to the old, disused drilling rig and shoved him up the stairs. On the platform beside it, Toby Finn stood with his arms outstretched, almost as though he was conducting the music. Mal kept his face impassive, wondering all the while just how short and one-sided this "trial" was going to be.

"All right, Browncoats, simmer down," Toby said, spying Mal and his escort. "The moment we've been waiting for is here."

The group burst into cheers, raising their hands above their heads, high-fiving each other, applauding.

Mal looked for Stuart Deakins. Their gazes met. Deakins looked away.

Toby gestured for the Browncoats to be quiet, and eventually they wore themselves out. Then Mal's former friend said, "I declare this trial open."

A few stray hurrahs were quickly quashed. Aware that

eyes were on him, Mal maintained his neutral expression, fixing it on like an iron mask.

"Here's how this will work," Toby said. "I will call witnesses and present evidence against the accused. And the accused will defend himself." He slid a glance towards Mal. "Since no one volunteered to defend you."

"What are the charges?" Mal asked.

"You are out of turn," Toby snapped. "You will speak when you are invited to. Do you understand?"

Mal said nothing.

"I said, do you understand?"

"Oh hey, were you inviting me to speak?" said Mal. "I'm really not clear on the protocols. This is all new to me. Never had to defend myself in a trial before."

That drew a few chuckles, most of them derisive but one or two amused. Toby narrowed his eyes and wagged a finger. Mal got the message: no playing to the gallery. Although if that would save his life, he'd do it, of course.

Toby cleared his throat. "Malcolm Reynolds, formerly of the 57th Overlanders, you come before this court facing four major charges. One: high treason against the Independent Planets. Two: murder. Three: sabotage during wartime. And four: collaboration with the enemy." He counted off the alleged crimes on his fingers. "Three of the charges carry with them the penalty of death. The charge of sabotage carries with it the sentence of life imprisonment without possibility of parole." He stared intently at Mal. "Do you understand these charges?"

Since arriving in the mine Mal had not been this physically close to Toby before, and as he held Toby's gaze, he realized that his former friend was not simply much thinner than he remembered—he was sick. His eyes were bloodshot and his skin was sallow, his cheeks tinted gray. His brown coat hung loose on him. During those years that they had lost touch, what had happened to the strong, fearless fighter Mal had known? Or, for that matter, the puppy-eager youngster?

Mal realized that this was not the time for flippancy, not now. He needed to step up and tackle Toby head-on, meeting fire with fire, else he was doomed—doomed as a rat in a nest of rattlesnakes.

"I mean no disrespect, but I do not understand the charges at all," he said. "This ain't a true trial. Where's the jury of my peers? Where's the judge in robes? Don't see none of those, just some jumped-up veteran spouting trumped-up charges and a roomful of folks who oughta know better lapping up his words like it's mother's milk. Listen to me, Tobias Finn, and listen good. We have history, you and I. We both know it. We both know we did things back on Shadow that neither of us is best proud of. I'm not referring to how we misbehaved and got up the noses of Sheriff Bundy, Deputy Crump and all those other stick-up-their-ass types in Seven Pines Pass. I don't recollect any of that with anything but fondness; they were good times. It's Jinny Adare I'm referring to specifically."

Something sparked in Toby's eyes, briefly there, then gone.

"And if it's any consolation," Mal said, "I'm sorry. Truly I am. It was never my intention for anyone to get hurt. Least of all you."

Grimness tightened Toby's face. "The charges have been read," he said.

"Toby…"

"Shut up. I know, Mal. *I know*."

"What do you know?"

"That you're guilty. Guilty as sin."

"That's it? You know?"

"That's all I need. It's all any of us here needs."

"Is it? 'Cause I look out over this gathering and I don't see the same certainty on all of the faces."

He could tell that Stu Deakins was harboring doubts, if the way Deakins couldn't meet his eye was anything to go by, not to mention the benevolence he had shown back in the cell. And David Zuburi, who had earlier tried to restrain his wife from hurting Mal, was shuffling his feet. A couple of others seemed less firm in their resolve than the rest. It appeared that there were vigilantes here thinking for themselves and that not everyone was one hundred percent convinced of Mal's guilt. This could yet evolve into a real trial, despite the presence of a hanging judge.

"Maybe if we just, y'know, hash this out," Mal went on, "we might come to some resolution about how things happened from your point of view and from mine. I can't help but think there has been a massive misunderstanding—"

"That is not how we are doing this," Toby shouted, overriding him.

"Just kill him now!" shouted one of the onlookers. "We *know*—"

"You don't know anything," Mal shot back, "or I would not be standing here falsely accused. I would have given my life to our cause and there's people here who can be in no doubt about that." He found Deakins again and focused in on him. "And I don't know what has happened in your life since to make you this hard-hearted and bitter, but I guarantee you killing me ain't going to make you feel better."

"You shut the hell up!" Sonya Zuburi shrieked at him. "Do not try to confuse us, Malcolm Reynolds. We have searched the 'verse for you and you will not escape justice."

"Justice has not shaken hands with any of us," Mal said. "In a just 'verse, we would have won."

"You saw the Browncoats were going down at Serenity Valley, and you cut your losses and ran, Mal," Toby said, seizing the reins of the conversation. "Like a rat off a sinking ship."

"Huh? I never did anything of the kind."

"You did!" Sonya shouted.

"I challenge you to prove even one iota of that statement to be true," Mal said, and Toby smiled a sickly, sinister smile—the smile of a fanatic so convinced of his own righteousness that no power in the 'verse would dissuade him from it.

"Oh, I shall, I shall." Toby waved a hand out at the crowd. "And you will understand, my fellow Browncoats, beyond a shadow of a doubt, that we've got the right man and we will be doing the right thing."

30

The planet Shadow, long ago

"Mal! Mal! They have Jamie!"

Jinny Adare came galloping on horseback across the field where Mal was working, breaking up the rocky, hard-packed soil for planting. Mal cut the motor on the rotavator and mopped sweat from his brow with his sleeve.

"Who has Jamie?" he said.

Jinny reined in. "Bundy. Crump. They cornered him outside Camacho's Grain and Feed. Said they'd had a call about someone shoplifting. Jamie was coming out lugging a sack of cobnuts. He said to Bundy he'd paid for them fair and square and if he was a shoplifter he'd steal something way less bulky than a forty-pound bag of horse feed. Bundy and Crump took him away at gunpoint anyway."

"Who told you this?"

"Cat Camacho herself. She saw it all, and called me straight away. Bundy's had a mad-on for Jamie ever since we tried busting Willard Krieger out of jail."

"Had a mad-on for all of us," Mal said, recalling the

number of times either Bundy or Crump or both of them had hassled him in the street, at the Silver Stirrup, lots of other places, while he was innocently going about his business. Several times Bundy had baldly stated his desire to run Mal and the other Amigos out of town, or worse. He was itching for some payback after the humiliation of the jailbreak incident and Marla Finn's thwarting his attempted prosecution of the culprits.

This campaign of harassment had been going on for months, and all of the Four Amigos had done their best to ride it out, hoping the sheriff and his sidekick would tire of it eventually; but now Bundy seemed to have ratcheted things up a gear.

"They taken him to the jail?" he said.

"I don't know. That'd be the first place to look, I guess."

"Okay. Let me get a horse and saddle up…"

"No time. You can ride with me."

Mal heaved himself up behind Jinny, and she spun her horse round and spurred it into motion.

It was no hardship sitting with his arms around Jinny's trim waist, her back against his chest, smelling her lavender-scented perfume at close range and a slight but heady tinge of sweat beneath it. Despite the circumstances Mal wished the ride could have lasted longer. He'd had only sporadic contact with the Adares since the jailbreak and practically none at all with Toby. As far as he knew, Jinny and Toby were still an item. But in that moment, feeling this strong, beautiful woman in front of him, so capable, so determined, Mal's passion for her was rekindled. There was nothing he wanted more in the world—in the 'verse—than Jinny Adare.

The town jail was locked up. Empty. The sheriff's office was shut too. Mal and Jinny made inquiries all over town, and eventually they learned that Bundy and Crump had driven out of Seven Pines Pass in their official police hover cruiser, headed towards Sageville on Arroyo Road.

Mal and Jinny raced in pursuit. They had no idea what the police officers' plans were for Jamie, but they were sure Bundy and Crump intended no good.

Four miles out of town they came across the hover cruiser parked by the roadside. Three sets of footprints led away from the vehicle, out into the wilderness.

"We walk from here," Mal said, dismounting.

"Why? Riding'd be faster."

"Noisier too. My hunch is it's better if they don't hear us coming. We can get the drop on them then."

Jinny dismounted too and tethered her horse, then accompanied Mal as he began following the trail of footprints. Sheriff Bundy's heavier, deeper tread was discernible on the right of the three—the man could do with losing several pounds—and Mal could only assume the trudging set of footprints in the middle were Jamie's. The two police officers were manhandling Jamie along between them. This had all the hallmarks of a prisoner being walked towards the gallows.

Suddenly Mal gestured at Jinny to hunker down. He had heard voices up ahead.

They crept forward on all fours through the sagebrush until they caught sight of Bundy and Crump standing beside a tall mesquite tree. Jamie was with them…

And he had a noose around his neck.

Jinny bit back a gasp of horror. "They wouldn't…"

Mal hushed her. "They won't," he whispered, "not if I have anything to do with it."

As they watched, Bundy was jeering at Jamie, whose hands were cuffed behind his back. "This has been a long time coming, kid. Ever since the Finn woman got you off the hook, you and your deadbeat pals have been asking for it. Now the chickens are coming home to roost."

"You're not going to do this, Sheriff," Jamie said. It wasn't clear if he was making a prediction or a wish. "You wouldn't dare. You're just trying to scare me."

"Am I?"

"Yeah, and just so's you know, it's working. I'm scared. Okay? So can we call it off now? You've accomplished what you set out to."

Crump tugged on the rope, cinching the noose that little bit tighter around Jamie's neck. The rope was slung over a bough of the mesquite, tied off around the tree's trunk.

"Have you got a gun?" Jinny asked Mal.

"Nope, only a knife. You?"

"No. Didn't think to bring one. I was too panicked."

"It's probably for the best. Don't want to give Bundy and Crump cause to shoot us in 'self-defense.' Not that they'd need much excuse, by the looks of things."

"What are you going to do? Do you have a plan?"

"Definitely."

"Is it a good one?"

"Definitely not. Just stay low. When I give the signal, move."

"Move where?"

"I don't know. Just do something."

"Mal?"

"Yeah?"

She kissed him. Just once. Lightly, an inch to the side of his lips.

It made him feel ten feet tall.

Mal rose from the sagebrush, waving his arms over his head. "Oh, hi there, Sheriff. Deputy," he said at the top of his voice. "Fancy bumping into you guys out here in the middle of nowhere."

As one, Bundy and Crump turned and drew on him.

"Whoa," Mal said, striding out towards them. "Easy, fellas. I'm not packing, as you can see. I'm here to parley. I see that we have what some'd call a good old-fashioned lynching."

"What you see," said Bundy, not lowering his gun, "is the due process of the law. We caught Jamie Adare red-handed, in the commission of an act of thievery. We are well within our rights to sentence and punish him in the manner of our choosing."

"Not sure I recall there being a trial."

"Not sure I care what you think, Reynolds. You could say my deputy and I are teaching you owlhoots a lesson. We're fed up to the back teeth with your games and your tomfoolery. I run an orderly town, and I won't stand for any sort of misbehavior."

"And you know what?" Deputy Crump chimed in. "When the Alliance comes and incorporates Shadow into the Union—and it's gonna happen any day now—you'll find there'll be even stricter law enforcement. Those Alliance folks don't tolerate troublemakers. We've seen it on some of the Red Sun planets already, Alliance troops cracking down on anyone as gets too uppity. They call 'em insurgents but we all know they're just crooks and criminals."

"And what do they call that cracking down?" said Bundy. "They call it a 'police action.' So we, as police ourselves, are only emulating their example. Starting with you miscreants."

Mal shrugged. "I tell you, Sheriff, I'd already been giving thought to joining up with the Independents. Seems as though you've just pushed me a few steps further in that direction. But let's not bring politics into this. Let's keep things strictly personal. How's about this? You take that there noose off of Jamie, then we all shake hands and walk away, no harm, no foul."

"Or how's about I just plant a bullet in you right now?" said Bundy. "On account of you're committing an obstruction of justice. What do you say, Orville? Reckon that'd fly?"

"Reckon it'd fly right nicely," said Crump.

"Better still, you can halt there, Reynolds, exactly where you are. Don't come a step nearer."

Mal did as bidden, in the full knowledge that either Bundy or Crump would drill a hole in him if he disobeyed. He was now within ten paces of the mesquite tree, and somewhat closer to Crump than to Bundy.

"Good boy," said Bundy. "Stay put, and you can watch your pal Jamie dangle, knowing there ain't a thing you can do about it. Knowing, too, that it'll be your turn next."

Jamie cast Mal a frantic look. Both of them had come to the same realization: Bundy and Crump were not kidding around; this was not all just some piece of theater. They were going to go through with the hanging. Because they could.

Because they were the law. Because the prospect of war in the 'verse, which over the past few weeks had become less of a possibility and more of a cast-iron certainty, seemed to have given them the courage to act as intemperately and self-indulgently as they liked. Because when chaos loomed, reason and accountability went out of the window.

Behind his back, Mal flapped his hand at Jinny. He trusted she would interpret the gesture correctly. He was telling her to get out of there. Nothing was to be gained by her remaining. He and Jamie were as good as dead. No point her making it three for three.

In the event, the vagueness of his plan—the nonexistence of it, really—worked against him. Jinny, instead of fleeing, stood up out of the sagebrush.

"Well, well, well," said Bundy, pushing his wide-brimmed hat back on his head with the barrel of his pistol. "Lookee here. Got the whole gang, just about, apart from the Finn brat. Now we got us a proper audience. Ain't no one going to be more upset about Jamie Adare's neck getting stretched than his kid sister."

"Please, Sheriff Bundy, I'm begging you," Jinny said. "Let him go."

"You got something you wanna bargain with, girl?" Bundy's leer made it patently obvious what he was hinting at. "'Cause tempting though that'd be, I think I'd much rather watch you watch your brother die. Talk about satisfying. Orville? I'll keep my gun trained on these two. You set about doing what needs to be done."

Deputy Crump holstered his sidearm and unlashed the rope from the tree trunk. Then he took the strain and started to pull, using the trunk like a pulley to mitigate the weight on the other end of the rope. Jamie's feet left the ground. His legs kicked. The noose tightened and he began making horrendous choking, gargling noises. His face rapidly purpled.

Mal knew he had one shot at this. He might die as a consequence. He might die even before he was able to achieve what he was setting out to do. But either of those fates was better than allowing Bundy and Crump to get away, unopposed, with what was unarguably cold-blooded murder.

He whisked his knife from its sheath and slung it through the air.

The blade cleaved clean through the rope, inches above Jamie's head.

Sheriff Bundy's attention had been divided between Mal and Jinny. Hence he was slow getting off a shot at Mal, so slow that Mal had time to duck out of the way, even as Jamie tumbled to the ground.

Deputy Crump also fell as the rope was cut and went slack in his hands. Suddenly, with nothing to counterbalance him, his strenuous pulling was converted into strenuous falling backwards. He sprawled in the dust. Mal pounced, planting a knee on Crump's chest to pin him down, then slid the deputy's gun out of its holster. He drew a bead on Bundy, cocking the hammer.

Standoff.

Jinny ran to Jamie's side and released the noose. Jamie rolled over, retching and wheezing.

Bundy eyed Mal beadily. "You won't, boy. You don't have the stones. You ain't never shot no one in your life, and the last person you're going to start with is a lawman."

"Or maybe," said Mal, "the first."

And he fired.

Neither Jinny nor Jamie could believe it. Same went for Crump, who stared up at Mal aghast.

Even Mal himself was a little surprised. It was as though some part of him had known he had no choice, while another part reeled in astonishment.

Bundy went down like a sack of coal. For several long moments Mal was convinced the sheriff was dead. He hadn't known he had it in him to kill someone. Now he understood what it took: the right motivation, the right mix of necessity and desire. This was it. He had crossed a bridge he could not cross back. His life from now on would never be the same.

Then Bundy hauled himself up into a sitting position. "Gorramn owwww!" he cried, clutching his shoulder. "That hurts like a *tā mā de hún dàn*!"

Not dead. Just wounded.

Mal didn't know how he felt about that. Relieved, yes, but not entirely.

"You moron, Reynolds!" Crump exclaimed, still pinned under Mal's knee. "We weren't really going to hang him!"

"Huh? You expect me to believe you?"

"Believe what you want. It's true."

"Sure is," said Bundy. "You think we'd be able to get away with something like that? 'Specially not with that fancy-talking lawyer-bitch Finn woman around. Nope, all's we were doing was giving Adare a scare. I've heard tell it can take a man up to six minutes to pass out during a short drop hanging, twenty minutes till he's actually dead. We weren't going to let him dangle more than a minute or so."

"Making a point," said Crump. "Teaching him a lesson. Teaching all of you lot."

"Some gorramn lesson," Jamie croaked.

"Sure looked to me like you were going to go through with it," Mal said.

"And to me," said Jinny.

"Wouldn't have been effective if it hadn't been convincing," said Bundy.

"And that stuff about hanging me as well?" said Mal. "That just big talk too?"

"Damn straight," said Bundy.

Mal rose to his feet. "Okay," he said. "Fact remains, you crossed a line, both of you."

"As did you, Reynolds," said Crump. "Shooting an officer of the law."

Mal turned the gun on him. "I can always make it two officers of the law. Want that?"

Crump gulped and shook his head.

"Then shut up and listen. I reckon we all need to come to some sort of accommodation here. This is my proposal. Events went as follows. You, Sheriff Bundy, and you, Deputy Crump, came out into the wilds in order to carry out some target practice. There was an accident. Crump discharged his gun—this very one in my hand—and wounded his superior officer. That's it. No attempted hanging, bogus hanging, whatever it was. Jamie, Jinny and I weren't even here. What do you say? Sound reasonable?"

Bundy's expression was steely. Blood oozed out over the fingers of the hand he was pressing against the bullet hole. Finally he said, "Seems as though I don't have a choice."

"You do. You can choose not to go along with what I'm suggestin', and both you and your buddy Orville will find yourselves in shallow graves in the shade of this very tree. You think I'm not serious? I wasn't aiming to wound you just now, Bundy, I was aiming to kill. And now that I've started down that road, don't see as how I'm liable to stop. There won't be any witnesses to your deaths, at least none that'll testify against me. Ain't that right, Jinny? Jamie?"

Sister and brother both nodded resolutely.

"There we go," said Mal. "But just to make sure the three of us walk away unharmed and you don't get it into your heads to shoot us in the back, we're going to empty your gun of its shells, Sheriff, and this one as well, and take your ammo belts."

When that was done, and Mal had unlocked the handcuffs on Jamie using the key from Crump's belt, he and the Adare siblings took their leave of the lawmen, heading back to the road. While Jinny got back on her horse, Mal hotwired the police cruiser and drove it off with Jamie in the passenger seat. There seemed nothing to be gained by making it easy for Bundy and Crump to get back to town.

"Mal," Jamie said, "how can I ever thank you?"

"You don't need to. You'd have done the same for me."

"I would've at that." He fingered the line of rope burn on his neck. "I knew Bundy'd been getting more and more out of control lately. Just never realized he might take it as far as he did. Think he's gone a little crazy."

"Think the whole 'verse is going a little crazy. Bundy's craziness just a by-product of that."

"Yeah. I wouldn't have put it past him to kill me, though.

Wasn't any doubt in my mind but that I was a goner. And now you've interfered, he's only going to hate us all the more. That was some fancy knife-throwing, by the way."

"I was aiming for Crump," Mal said.

"Really?"

"Yeah, and I'd've got him too, if that damn rope hadn't gotten in the way."

They both laughed.

"Listen, were you being serious back there?" Jamie said. "About signing up with the Independents?"

"I'm giving it some proper thought. Crump wasn't wrong about how the Alliance is behaving on the Red Sun worlds, and elsewhere. As you can see from what I did to him, I would seem to have a problem with authority riding roughshod over people. Guess that sentiment extends way beyond Seven Pines Pass, Shadow, the Georgia system, all the way out into the wider 'verse. Besides, ain't as if there's much going on for me here. Just farm work, ranching, the day-to-day grind…"

"The call of adventure, huh?"

"Something like that."

"Got me a feeling that I'm hearing it too," Jamie said. "Maybe it takes a brush with death to put things into perspective. If you threw in with the Independents, I might just too. There's a recruiting office opened up in Da Cheng Shi, I heard."

"I heard that too."

"Not sure how I'd break it to my parents."

"Same with me and my mother. Might be best if we just didn't, simply hopped the train to Da Cheng Shi without telling 'em. You think Jinny would join us?"

"Not sure how she feels about the whole situation. She doesn't much like the Alliance, that's for sure, but I reckon it'd be better if she stays at home anyway, for our parents' sake. One child running off, like as to get himself killed, is bad enough—but both of them?"

"Yeah, I see your point." But Mal might quite have liked it, were Jinny to have come along with them to Da Cheng Shi. Might have quite liked to spend some time in close proximity to her, without Toby around. See what developed.

"You don't think we'd be running away, do you?" Jamie said.

"What do you mean?"

"From Bundy. Because if I know that man, he's going to be sticking to our agreement for a while, but when his shoulder's better, when he's back on his feet, he'll be fuming. He won't let it rest. He'll come after us again."

"You think? I think he's licked and he knows it."

"Maybe you're right. You've always been the confident one, Mal."

Or, Mal thought, *the one who doesn't think things through or care about the repercussions.*

They abandoned the police cruiser on the outskirts of Seven Pines Pass and walked the rest of the way in. Jamie announced that the drinks were on him, and they headed straight for the Silver Stirrup, where Jinny caught up with them later. It turned into one of the epic drinking sessions of Mal's life, five straight hours of necking beers and whisky chasers and laughing uproariously with the Adare siblings. And when it was over, Jamie staggered homeward in the dark while Jinny accompanied Mal to the Reynolds ranch, leading her horse because she was far too inebriated to ride.

What happened next was as inevitable as it was, in hindsight, regrettable. They got as far as the bluff overlooking town. Next thing they knew, they were kissing. Next thing they knew after that, Jinny had laid out her horse's saddle blanket on the ground. Beneath the stars, on a hot night, with all three of Shadow's moons on the rise and a slight cooling breeze, they made love. It was sweet and fierce, tender and spectacular. Unforgettable.

Afterwards, as they lay together with Jinny's head cradled in Mal's arm, she said, "We shouldn't have done that."

"What, taken the Lord's name in vain as much as we just did?"

"No, I mean it." Her face was serious. "Toby and I... We're still together. As far as he's concerned, we're a couple. I think he's going to ask me to marry him. He keeps mentioning engagement rings and stuff, and looking at houses for sale."

"That does surely seem like the talk of someone with marriage on their mind. What do you think about it?"

"I think I love Toby but I don't *love* love him, if you see the difference."

"The difference being two loves instead of one."

"Can you ever not be facetious?"

"If I knew the meaning of the word, I'd know what I wasn't supposed to be. So if Toby proposes..."

"I'll say no."

"And crush him forever."

"Don't say that!" Jinny snapped. "Please, don't."

"You know it's true. Guy like Toby, when he gets wrapped up in a girl, there ain't nothing going to untangle him easily, not without it hurtin' him plenty. 'Specially a girl like you."

"But I can't say yes if he isn't the man I want to be with for the rest of my life."

Mal wondered if *he* might be the man Jinny would want to be with for the rest of her life. He didn't dare voice the thought, for fear that he would be as crushed as Toby was going to be when Jinny rejected his proposal.

"Whatever happens," Jinny said firmly, "this thing tonight, you and me, it was a one-off. You hear me, Mal? It was terrific, it was lovely, but it's not going to be repeated."

"So, what, this was just my reward for saving your brother?"

"No. No! I need to figure out where I stand with Toby, apart from anything else."

Mal was crestfallen. He was also quite sure, within himself, that despite what she said, it was not going to be a one-off.

And he was right. He and Jinny kept contriving to be in the same place at the same time, their paths crossing seemingly by accident but not really. These random encounters all had the same outcome. And there would be guilt afterwards, and a vow not to see each other again, invariably broken.

Naturally Toby was appalled when he learned about what Bundy had done, or tried to do, and said he would inform his mother. She would have Bundy out of a job within a week, and sue him for damages, too. Mal and Jamie, however, persuaded him not to tell her. They reckoned Bundy was neutralized, Crump as well. Both lawmen were so far sticking to the story Mal had concocted about a firearms accident. Both were getting ribbed for it by the locals and were taking the mockery stoically. Their feigned chagrin suggested to Mal that they wanted to put the truth of the incident behind them, and involving Marla Finn might just stir up something that appeared settled. If Bundy were plotting any kind of revenge, he was hiding it well. Maybe, for all his pigheadedness, even he realized he had overstepped the mark and needed to pull back.

Then war broke out on Shadow. The Alliance had been pushing its influence further and further out from the Core, sweeping up more and more planets in its barbed-wire embrace. All across the 'verse there had been skirmishes between Alliance troops and opposition forces, ragtag militias that were poorly armed but made up for it with guts and determination. It was war in all but name, until finally the Alliance declared that a state of hostility existed between it and all worlds that resisted its influence. This was simply formalizing what had hitherto been implicit.

By then, Jinny had broken it off with Toby. She had also broken it off with Mal. Toby did not know that they had been seeing each other behind his back, but Jinny felt she could not simply take up with Mal, not so soon after ending things with Toby. She said she needed time out to think about their relationship and figure out what she herself wanted, promising it was just temporary. She was still bruised and fragile from having to jilt Toby. It had not been an easy decision.

Toby came to Mal for consolation, and one of the hardest

feats Mal had ever pulled off was offering the kid a shoulder to cry on. He ached to tell Toby about himself and Jinny but knew he never could. He couldn't shake off the feeling that he had lost her. Instead, he comforted Toby, got him drunk, was every inch the good friend.

Next day, he found himself on that train to Da Cheng Shi. Jamie was with him. So was Toby.

Once again, as before during the heyday of the Four Amigos, Toby was tagging along. His motives were straightforward. He couldn't bear to remain in Seven Pines Pass. He couldn't stay as long as Jinny was there, a constant reminder of what he had once had and could never have again. He hated the Alliance, that was for sure. He detested what they were doing. He wanted to stand up and be counted, to give those bullies a bloody nose, to draw a line in the sand. But whereas for Mal and Jamie that was reason enough to do what they were doing, Toby was driven by a still darker imperative. Misery.

Once more Toby addressed the crowd of Browncoats in the mining cavern.

"Here is how it went down," he said. "Less than a year after Mal and I enlisted, along with our friend Jamie Adare, the Alliance bombed the hell out of our home planet, Shadow. By then we'd all been through basic training. You all know how that was. Sometimes brutal, sometimes boring, sometimes downright amateurish. But we were all pulling together, all on the same side. It felt good even when we were slogging along knee-deep in mud, trying to keep formation, pretending to fire these broom handles they'd given us instead of guns because they didn't have any real guns to spare, aiming 'em at an enemy that wasn't there. Yet. Then came a lull. Our drill sergeants, some of whom seemed to be just making it up as they went, told us to go home. They'd taught us all they could. They would summon us when we were needed.

"The war was drawing closer to Shadow every day, like this big thundercloud on the horizon steadily growing bigger and bigger, more and more ominous. We were told to go be with our loved ones for a spell, and wait for the call. It'd be coming soon enough.

"Mal, Jamie, and I returned to Seven Pines Pass, our hometown. Jamie's sister Jinny was waiting to meet us off the train, and she wasn't happy with any of us, no sir, on account of we'd up and left her behind without telling her where we were going and she'd had to find out about it the hard way, through a wave from Jamie. Each of us had our reasons for keeping her in the dark, the details of which needn't detain us here. However, Jinny and a few of the locals were keen to do their bit, and so they'd begun stockpiling arms, against the likelihood of the Alliance occupying Shadow. They'd put together a sizeable cache—enough to equip a platoon or maybe more—and had stashed it out back of a meadow on the Adare property, in a cowshed."

Mal remembered that cowshed for various reasons. One was that he and Jinny had met there for a tryst on several occasions. The smell of mingled cow musk and hay never failed to evoke strong feelings in him, even to this day. Sometimes it was almost, in a bizarre way, an aphrodisiac. Other times, it could reduce him to tears.

He also remembered the cowshed for the smoking ruin it had become, all twisted spars of charred wood sticking upwards, with a halo of scorched earth around it.

And for the burned, mutilated corpse lying close by.

"Jinny's and Jamie's parents knew what was being kept there," Toby continued, "but turned a blind eye. Jinny took it upon herself to guard the arms cache round the clock. It was her way of showing support for the Independent cause. And here's the kicker. She was guarding it that night when the Alliance called in a Zeus missile strike to destroy it. She was there when a space-to-ground projectile fitted with a thousand pounds of explosive sailed in from heaven and obliterated that cowshed and everything in it and everything within a hundred-yard radius around it. Including Jinny."

Faces stared up at the platform, and Mal stared at nothing. All he saw was Jinny's dead body, burned into a contorted, skeletal parody of its living version. The face like a blackened skull, jaws opened in a soundless scream. The cindered remains that were barely recognizable as those of the first woman he'd ever truly loved.

All these years, Mal had assumed that rage had burned away the last of his deep grief, but now his heart sank down into another icy pit brimming with sorrow so thick he began to drown. Couldn't breathe, couldn't think.

The crowd had fallen silent, as if in respect for the dead. Exhausted, out of gas, Mal hung his head and mourned everything that had happened between Jinny and him, and everything that had not happened.

After a long moment, Toby stretched out a hand and

pointed at Mal. "When they told him that she'd died, the first words out of the mouth of Malcolm Reynolds were, 'She was supposed to be safe.'"

Mal recalled the moment. Those were his exact words, spoken to Jamie and Toby. Someone—he forgot who—came running into the Silver Stirrup to announce the missile strike. They'd all heard the detonation not ten minutes earlier, and seen the accompanying far-off flash in the sky; and they all had speculated what it signified, whether it was simply the onset of a thunderstorm or something more sinister. The moment they learned it was a missile aimed at the Adare ranch, they sprinted out that way. The farmhouse itself was intact, save for the fact that every single windowpane in it had been blown out and the roof was missing several shingles. Mr. and Mrs. Adare were likewise shaken but unhurt.

However, no sooner did Mal see the impact site, and Jinny's body, than he fell to his knees and uttered the sentence Toby had just quoted.

What he didn't grasp was why it mattered. What significance "She was supposed to be safe" carried for Toby.

That was when Toby slid a hand into his pocket and retrieved a small, rounded lump of metal that had been distorted out of its original shape by intensely high temperatures. It was roughly the size and shape of a fob watch, and for a moment Mal could not fathom what it was or why Toby had produced it.

Then it dawned on him.

It was the locket. The gold locket with the ornate "J." The one he hadn't given to Jinny, and then, later, much later, had.

Toby levered open the lid, with some difficulty. The hinge barely worked.

Inside was a mass of circuitry, fused into so much silvery goo.

"See that, everyone?" He displayed the locket to the crowd. "See that, Mal? A homing beacon. The homing beacon that you put there. The homing beacon which gave the Alliance the exact coordinates for the arms cache. Thanks to you, they couldn't miss. Thanks to you, Jinny Adare died."

31

"Hades?" said Zoë, leaning over the comms panel on *Serenity*'s bridge. "You sure that's right, Book?"

"That's what Elmira says," Book replied. His voice crackled, distance distorting the signal.

"As in the lesser of Persephone's two moons," said Wash. "Sibling to the larger, brighter Renao, and usually part-eclipsed by it."

"Sure," said Zoë, "but what in hell are they doing on Hades? There's nothing there."

"I think that's kind of the point," said Book. "If you take someone prisoner and have malicious designs on them, the best place to spirit them off to is somewhere remote and undesirable, somewhere no one goes."

"And the intel's sound?"

"Elmira has nothing to gain by lying. Put it this way. Hunter Covington enslaved her, abused her, threatened to kill her—it isn't in her interests to cover for him. In fact, her exact words were, 'If your friends catch up with him and manage to put a bullet in him, I'm not going to shed a single tear.'"

"Well, you can tell her from me," Zoë said, "if I see him, I'll do just that. Him and anyone else involved in Mal's kidnapping."

"I'm already plotting a course towards Hades, Shepherd," Wash said, stabbing buttons on the control console. "Just one question. Where precisely on Hades? Any idea? Because it's not the biggest rock in the 'verse but it's not the smallest either, and if we don't have any clear idea where to put down, we could be searching a long time."

"I asked Elmira that myself. She doesn't know. But you'll find the location, Wash. I'm sure of it."

"If I do, it'll be some kind of miracle."

"Miracles happen," said Book.

"Not in my experience," Wash muttered as Zoë cut the connection. He hit the ship's intercom. "Kaylee?"

"Yeah?"

"How are the engines doing?"

"Shiny… ish."

"Good enough, 'cause I'm about to go for maximum burn. We think we know where Mal is."

"Oh my God! For real?"

"Yup. You just make sure *Serenity* keeps spaceborne."

"On it!"

"Buckle up, honey," Wash said to Zoë. "I'm going to give you the ride of a lifetime."

"Promises, promises," Zoë said, strapping herself into a seat.

Wash thrust the yoke forward, and *Serenity*'s tail end

lit up like a Chinese lantern, coruscatingly bright. The ship diverted sleekly round onto her new course, Wash pouring on speed, extracting every ounce of thrust her engines could provide.

"Shouldn't take us more than an hour," he said to his wife. "Assuming nothing breaks or blows up."

Zoë laid a hand on his arm. "Just shut up and fly, Wash. This is what you do, so do it."

32

The planet Shadow, long ago

A week before Jinny died, Mal came over to her house and gave her the locket.

"What's this?" she said, staring at the trinket. "A love token?"

"Yes. I mean, no. No. Nothing like that. I saw it in a shop in Da Cheng Shi." He didn't say when he'd seen it. "Saw the 'J' on it and thought of you."

"Well, that's, er… mighty nice of you."

"Weren't it just. I want you to have it, not to remember me by or any of that stuff. That's not what this is about at all. Look inside. I've added a little something."

Jinny pressed the tiny catch which opened the locket. Inside lay a gleaming knot of technology.

"It's… a hearing aid?" she said, frowning at him, half smiling.

"A homing beacon," Mal said.

"And why do I need a homing beacon?"

"'Cause when the war hits Shadow, who knows where

I'm going to end up? I may not even be planetside. And you may get called away too. I don't believe for one moment that you're going to stay put and tend to this arms cache of yours indefinitely. Those weapons'll be gone soon enough, and the Jinny Adare I know isn't going to be content living at the old homestead splitting logs and shoveling cow dung."

"You got that right."

"No, she's going to become a… what are they calling us? A Browncoat."

"Ain't such a pretty name, is it?" Jinny said.

"No. And that reminds me—I need to buy myself a brown suede coat, otherwise I'm not going to fit in. But to my point. When you're a Browncoat and I'm a Browncoat, we could be light years apart, at opposite ends of the 'verse. But that there homing beacon is linked to a matching homing beacon which I have in my safekeeping, and if ever we want to find each other, or simply know where each other is, those two little doohickeys will be able to tell us. They're powered by thermoelectric energy, using the differential between body heat and the ambient temperature to keep them charged. As long as we're wearing them, they'll have juice. And if one of them stops working… Well, then the next time the other person activates their beacon, they'll know the worst has happened."

"Oh Mal."

He couldn't tell if she was touched or perplexed. Then he saw tears falling from her eyes, splashing onto the locket.

He took the trinket from her hands and draped it around her neck.

"Just wear it," he said. "For me. Doesn't mean we're

engaged to be wed or anything. Ain't that at all." *No way, definitely nothing of the sort.* "But know that I will always have my own beacon with me at all times, whether or not you have yours. If I want to check if you're safe, or you me, this is how."

They kissed, and it was long, lingering, and over too soon.

Then Jinny turned away from him and walked off, her head a little bowed, her step a little faltering, as though it was taking everything she had not to turn around and run back to his arms.

"May I speak?" Mal said. "I think it's my turn now. I'm owed the right of response."

"Hear, hear," said someone in the crowd. Mal wasn't sure but it sounded a lot like Stuart Deakins.

"Very well," said Toby, with a great show of magnanimousness.

"That homing beacon wasn't anything to do with the Alliance," Mal said. "Don't even know how you could think it might have been."

"I had a tech expert look over it. No question, it was designed to send out a location signal. You knew Jinny was guarding the arms cache twenty-four seven. You gave her the beacon to lead the Alliance right to it. You might as well have painted crosshairs on her back."

"And why in hell would I do that, Toby? What would I get out of it? Jinny was my friend. My good friend. You saw me after we found the body. You saw how I was a gorramn mess. For about a week after, I could barely speak. Came close to blowin' my own brains out several times. That's how bad her death screwed me up."

"Oh, it was a fine display of grief you put on, that's for sure," Toby said. "The rest of us were feeling it genuinely and showed it in our different ways, but no one could rival Mal Reynolds when it came to the histrionics."

"I ain't that good an actor."

"I'm not saying you were acting, Mal. I'm saying you just went over the top with it. You were torn up about Jinny, no question, but maybe you were so torn up because you knew you were the one responsible."

"Well, how am I supposed to argue against that kinda logic?" Mal said, exasperated. "Can't win either way. If I hadn't been upset, you'd be accusing me of not caring because I was her killer. Since I *was* upset, you're sayin' it's because I had a guilty conscience. Anyways, it was Sheriff Bundy who told the Alliance about the arms cache. Everybody thought so."

"It was a rumor," said Toby. "A rumor you yourself, Mal, did a great deal to spread about."

"Bundy hated us: you, me, Jamie, and Jinny. We'd pissed him off dozens of times, and I'd maybe pushed it too far by wounding him with a bullet that time he tried to hang Jamie, not that he didn't have it coming. He was looking at ways to hit back at us, and he knew what'd hurt me, you, and Jamie more than anything would be killing Jinny. She was the glue that held the four of us together. If he wanted to destroy us, her death'd do it. But he wasn't going to carry out the deed himself. Man was too cunning for that. If he could get the Alliance to do his dirty work for him, though, then his hands would be clean. Plus he'd be ingratiating himself with Shadow's soon-to-be overlords. And it worked, didn't it? Soon as Alliance troops stepped foot on Shadow, some of 'em came down Seven Pines Pass way, and next thing, the county governor had been damn executed on some spurious pretext and Sheriff Bundy was appointed in his stead. It was almost like his fee. For services rendered."

"Circumstantial. A theory," Toby said. "You didn't have any proof that that was what happened. All it was, was what you wanted everyone to believe was the case. If it was true, why didn't you go after Bundy?"

"Believe me, I was tempted. If I'd had hard evidence he was to blame, instead of just a strong suspicion, I'd have blown the bastard clean out of his socks. Before I could go about accumulating that evidence, however, High Command gave us our marching orders. And you know what? I was right glad to get the hell off of Shadow. Stayin' there a moment longer might've killed me. I've got a question for you, Toby Finn. How come you have that beacon at all? Wasn't it buried with Jinny?"

"I found it when I helped ferry her to the town morgue," Toby replied. "You weren't much use in that regard. You were too busy wailing and tearing your hair out and drenching yourself in misery so's everyone could see. Me and Jamie, we got on with the business of making sure Jinny got a decent burial. Once the ground around the cowshed had cooled enough for us to pick up the body, that's what we did. And while we were moving her, I spied that locket and I got curious about it. Wasn't something I'd given her, her parents neither. I asked 'em later, and even they didn't know how she'd come by it. So I took it off her body when no one was looking. Opened it up when I got home. Saw what was inside. I didn't know she'd got it from you, not then. All's I knew was that someone had planted a beacon on Jinny without her knowing and had used her as a living target, and I vowed that when I found out who it was, nothing'd stop me from exacting vengeance upon that individual. And at last, the day has come. A day I've been waiting for, looking forward to, dreaming of, for more years than I care to think."

"And how can you be so sure it was me that did it?" Mal said. "I didn't have evidence pointing the finger at Sheriff Bundy, and you don't have none pointing it at me."

"Are you so sure, Mal?" Toby sneered. "I think you'll find I have plenty of evidence."

"But that beacon isn't what you think it was. Like I said, it wasn't anything to do with the Alliance. It was—"

Before Mal could finish the sentence, there was a sudden ripple of activity amongst the assembled Browncoats. Heads were turning. People were murmuring to one another.

Somebody had just entered the cavern.

Not just anyone, either, but Hunter Covington, complete with cobra-head cane. Accompanying him was a person Mal also recognized, the man from Taggart's, the guy in the mustard-yellow duster who'd sent him outside to get bushwhacked by Covington and his goons.

"A very good evening to you all," said Covington. "Actually, that should be 'morning.' Day's dawning out there, in case you hadn't realized. Sky was brightening just as we came in to land. Looking like a peach of a day. And there is Mr. Malcolm Reynolds, all trussed up and set to swing.

Seems we arrived just in time, wouldn't you say, Harlow?"

Yellow Duster—Harlow—nodded agreement.

"You are indeed just in time, gentlemen," Toby said. "Just in time to watch one of the vilest men in Browncoat history get his comeuppance."

33

Serenity swung into orbit around Hades. It was a smooth ball of rock a couple of hundred thousand miles from Persephone, rolling in a slow, lazy ellipse around its mother planet. There were a few mountain ranges, a few craters, but apart from those it was featureless.

Terraforming had been attempted, but all Hades had to show for it was atmosphere. Vegetation had failed. There had been no release of water from its frozen poles. Colonization had therefore been impossible, and the moon had been abandoned as a failed project, left to carry on along its way more or less unmolested.

Since then, prospectors had sniffed around, digging down in the search for valuable minerals such as iridium, palladium, manganese and molybdenum, not to mention platinum and gold. Yet again, however, Hades had proved disappointing, yielding nothing more valuable than iolite and ametrine, semi-precious gemstones whose retail price was not high enough to justify the cost of their extraction.

"Nothing," Zoë said, surveying the moon's surface on the scanning screen. "Nothing but wasteland." There was a note of despair in her voice.

"If there was maybe a building of some sort," Wash said, "some sign of civilization, then we might have something to aim at. But there ain't. It's just a ghost world."

"Can you run a sweep?"

"Already doing that. Thermal scan in a grid pattern, with the gain turned way up high. If there's any kind of heat signature beyond natural background, it'll register. So far, nada."

Jayne entered the bridge, ducking under the lintel of the low doorway. "That it, huh?" he said, looking out at Hades through the viewing-port array. "Not much to write home about."

"If you don't have anything useful to contribute…" Zoë said.

"Just sayin'. Seen more life in a three-days-dead dog. Mal's somewhere down there?"

"Supposedly."

"Then we got no chance of finding him. Not unless we had a week to look, and I don't reckon we got nearly that long. Vigilantes'll probably have plugged him already."

"Really, Jayne, if you don't shut up…"

"Hey, Zoë, don't blame me if I'm the realist round here. Somebody has to be."

"Here's an idea. Let's just assume we are going to find Mal. We ought to make preparations. So why don't you go to your bunk, fetch out Vera, give her a good clean, and then she'll be all ready for if she's ever needed."

Jayne nodded. "That ain't a half bad idea." He retreated out of the bridge.

Wash said, "Did you really just tell Jayne to go to his bunk and polish his rifle?"

"Uh-huh."

"You know he'll never realize that was a thinly veiled insult, right?"

"Uh-huh."

"My God, woman, I so want to ravish you right now."

"Focus on the matter at hand, Wash."

"Too late. My mind has already gone down the dirty path. I'm thinking, when this is over, you and me, we— Oh wait. Wait just one *xī niú* second."

Something had flared on the thermal scan screen. Amidst the neutral grays and blues of Hades's surface, there was a tiny blob of glowing orange.

Wash tapped instructions into a keyboard to enhance the image and zero in.

"Ohhh yeah. Attaboy."

"What is it?" Zoë asked.

"Looks like the exhaust profile of a private yacht. Just landed. Engine's cycling down and the thrusters are cooling but still radiating residual heat."

"Enough to get a fix on?"

"Done. Coordinates logged in."

"Whose craft?"

"My guess is Covington's. According to Elmira, Covington headed out to join the vigilantes in a yacht, didn't he? That's him down there, parked wherever they are."

"Book said miracles happen," Zoë murmured.

"And so does amazing piloting," said Wash. "I'm calculating re-entry. Every moment counts. No time for slick and smooth. We're going in fast and we're going in hard."

Zoë smirked. "Is your mind still on the dirty path?"

Wash grinned. "Little bit," he said, and yanked on the yoke.

34

"Why're you even here?" Mal called across the cavern to Hunter Covington. "Don't reckon as you were ever a Browncoat."

"How can you tell?" Covington replied.

"On account of Browncoats have integrity, and you don't."

"For what it's worth, I did my best to stay neutral during the war."

"Yeah, like most gutless, profiteerin' streaks of *xióng māo niào* did."

"I was open to opportunities wherever they arose," Covington said. "Still am. To nail your colors to a single mast is so limiting. Except, you didn't nail your colors to a single mast after all, did you, Mal? In fact, you have no right to lecture me about integrity. Not if what Mr. Finn says about your past behavior is true, and I have no reason to believe it isn't. You have earned yourself a reputation around Eavesdown, and elsewhere, as someone with a very elastic approach to ethics. 'Give Malcolm Reynolds a job, chances are he'll let you down or wind up screwing you over,' that's what they say. 'Trust him no further than you could throw him.'"

"Couple of bad reviews, they stay with you forever," Mal said. "Everyone ignores the many satisfied customers I've had."

"And to answer your question, I'm here because I was invited. I've been in cahoots with these here Browncoat fellas for a while now, and I still haven't yet seen first-hand how they operate. As they were going to be on Hades, practically in my backyard, I thought I'd take up Mr. Finn's invitation and fly on over. It's always a good idea to learn as much as you can about a business partner's practices."

"And I guess maybe you got an appetite for summary executions as well, huh?" Mal said. "You get off on it."

Covington shook his head firmly but not that firmly. "I'm not that barbaric. I can't deny, however, a certain curiosity. How will a man like you face up to death, Reynolds? With a wink and a quip, or blubbering in abject terror?"

"I'd be curious myself to see how you manage it, Covington. Because, I get the chance, you're the one who'll be facin' up to death."

"Brave talk, considering how this trial appears to be almost at an end. Didn't I hear Mr. Finn just say you were about to get your comeuppance? Seems to me that sentence is shortly to be pronounced. Isn't that so, Mr. Finn?"

Toby Finn nodded. "You're quite right, Hunter. In fact, as I told you, you couldn't have timed your arrival better. All that remains is for me to furnish the clinching proof that Mal killed Jinny Adare, and then we can get down to the punishment. I have that proof right here. But a little background first. Mal was just saying that we were called up to fight shortly after the Alliance attack on Shadow. It wasn't even a week, was it? Jinny only just planted in the ground, and troop carriers arrived to ship us out. Only when we were aboard did we learn which regiments we'd be joining. We'd had our skills assessed at bootcamp and were assigned accordingly. Mal went to the 57th Overlanders, Jamie and I to the 19th Sunbeamers. Mal became a ground pounder, Jamie and I space commandos."

"The Sunbeamers acquitted themselves honorably in many a battle, so I hear," said Covington.

"I myself participated in dozens of ship-to-ship actions. I took my fair share of Alliance scalps. But Jamie? Jamie was in a league of his own. That man fought with a righteous fury that burned hotter than a sun. Alliance had just killed his sister. He wasn't going to let them forget that. Jamie Adare never took a single prisoner. You were an Alliance trooper and got in his way, woe betide you. He was single-minded, laser-focused, deadly as hell. I overheard a major once say that if he had a hundred soldiers like Jamie, the war would be over within a week. But he was reckless, too. Jamie, see, didn't care if he lived or died. He was just this big, seething ball of hate. Nothing mattered to him except taking out as many of the enemy as he could. He died at Sturges."

The Battle of Sturges was one of the bloodiest of the war, rivaled in ferocity and numbers of casualties only by Serenity Valley, and was fought over money—a hoard of victory spoils being carried by a freighter, the *Sublime*, back to the Core from the Rim. The Browncoats were keen to get their hands on this loot in order to help fund their war effort. Just off the planet Sturges, Independent ships attacked the freighter's armed escort, at considerable cost to their own forces. Space commandos then boarded the *Sublime* herself, only to discover that she had been booby-trapped, rigged to explode if a failsafe mechanism was triggered by the captain. Rather than let the loot fall into Independent hands, the captain sacrificed himself and everyone else aboard.

"Jamie was one of the first onto the *Sublime*," Toby said. "I didn't reach it. My spacesuit developed a radiation-shielding malfunction and I had to return to my ship. If not for that, I'd have gone up with *Sublime*, like Jamie and most of the rest of the regiment. That was the end of the 19th Sunbeamers. After that, the regiment was disbanded I got transferred to an infantry unit, the 31st Raiders."

"A heck of a squad," said Mal with sincerity.

"Damn straight we were. Not for nothing were we known as the Angel Makers. Wherever there was trouble, wherever the battle was at its thickest, that was where the 31st were sent."

A couple of people in the crowd yelled "Hoo-rah!" in support. Veterans of the same regiment, Mal presumed. There was no question the 31st Raiders had been one of the scrappiest units the Browncoats could boast. Their attrition rate was terrible. Life expectancy was around three weeks, a month if you were lucky. The fact that Toby had survived as long as he had was testament to his combat skill and tenacity. The little redheaded guy had been, it seemed, capable of meeting everything the Alliance could throw at him.

"I first fought alongside Malcolm Reynolds at the Battle

of Du-Khang," Toby said. "The Raiders had taken some heavy hits lately and we were merged into the whole Balls and Bayonets Brigade along with several other regiments, the 57th Overlanders included. Mal and I eventually got to meet up. That was some kinda reunion."

"Sure was," Mal said. "I was right glad to see you. Friendly face from home. Felt kind of impossible that we'd both come through all we had, and now here we were, fightin' alongside each other. Felt like it was meant to be."

"It did," Toby said, almost wistfully. "Even after all that happened on Shadow, I still thought of you as my friend. That was before."

"Before what?"

"Before we were dispatched to Hera. Before we made camp in Serenity Valley. Before the day I dropped by your tent to say hi. The fighting hadn't started yet. We were digging in on our side, Alliance was digging in on the other, both of us waiting on the attack command. Lull before the storm. I had a spare hour so I made my way along the lines, found where the Overlanders were, looked for you. Someone directed me to your tent, but you weren't there. I decided to wait. That was when I saw your kitbag. It was open. I saw something inside, glinting. I couldn't help it. Had to check. I just got curious. And it was this…"

Toby delved into his pocket again, as he had when producing Jinny's homing beacon. This time he took out a silver crucifix pendant, roughly three inches long and two across, its arms as thick as a baby's finger.

"*Tā mā de hún dàn!*" Mal exclaimed. "That's where that went! All this time, I thought I'd lost it. I ransacked my tent. Went through my belongings a hundred times. Looked everywhere." He had even accused his corporal of stealing it. Given that she was Zoë Alleyne, *that* had not gone down well. Mal was still amazed she had ever forgiven him.

Toby pressed a recessed catch, and the front of the crucifix sprang open. Inside lay circuitry.

"This," Toby said, holding up the device for all to see, "is another homing beacon. Its circuitry is the exact double of the circuitry in the beacon on Jinny Adare's body, just in a different configuration. The two units were linked reciprocally, each keyed to the other's unique signature. I didn't know that when I first saw it. Some instinct told me there was a connection between this beacon and Jinny's, but I had no way of establishing that for sure. Not then. Not yet. But I took it."

"Yeah, you thieving rat-bastard, you did," Mal snarled.

"I took it because suddenly things were starting to make sense. Things like how the Alliance knew exactly where the arms cache was at the Adares'. How they'd been able to precision-target the cowshed. Why Mal had said, 'She was supposed to be safe.' Jinny was supposed to be safe because Mal had come to an arrangement with the Alliance, and the Alliance had—surprise, surprise—reneged on it."

"That just ain't it!" Mal cried. "Those beacons were just so that Jinny and I would know each other was okay, is all. They were a way of us keeping tabs. The plan was she'd wear hers and I'd wear mine, and that way we'd each know the other was okay. Only, that never happened because… Well, we all know why. But I still kept that crucifix with me as a souvenir, to remind me of her."

Never once had he actually draped the pendant around his neck, however. Not only had the beacon become redundant and meaningless through the destruction of its counterpart and its counterpart's wearer, but the crucifix itself had started to seem that way too. Mal could pretty much date the loss of whatever religious faith he'd had to the day he lost Jinny Adare.

"You're reading this all wrong, Toby," he went on. "You're making out as if there was this whole terrible conspiracy, and it's all just in your head. Come on, think about it. Why would I have one of those homing beacons too if they were for giving away our location to the Alliance?"

"To keep yourself safe," Toby said. "Alliance wouldn't touch you as long as they knew where you were. That second beacon is as incriminating as the first, if not more so."

"Didn't make much difference at Serenity Valley, for example. I damn near died there."

"But you didn't before then!" Toby declared. "That's just it. You, Sergeant Malcolm Reynolds, the Alliance's mole within the Browncoat ranks, made it through a couple dozen previous hell-storms unscathed. All because you had that beacon."

"If you think that, then you—"

"I *think*," Toby said with a sudden snap of authority, "that we have heard quite enough from you, Mal. You can protest till you're blue in the face. The evidence is all here. These two beacons are all the verification anyone needs. You are a traitor, a saboteur, and a collaborator. Right from the very start of the war, you were disloyal to the Independent cause. Whether you intended it or not, Jinny Adare became a victim of your treachery, and in return you got a free pass from the Alliance. I have stated my case. The arguments are more than persuasive. I shall now put it to the good people before us to tell us if they agree or disagree. A show of hands, if you please."

Hands shot up in the air. There were growls of "Yeah!" and "Yee-hah!"

"One or two abstainers, I see," said Toby. "Stu Deakins. David Zuburi. You've yet to be convinced? Well, it doesn't have to be unanimous for the motion to be carried. The yeas far outnumber the nays."

Now the crowd swarmed forwards. The bald man who had brandished a noose earlier was once again ready with the length of rope. He and another Browncoat slung the loose end over a cross-brace of the drilling rig. Meanwhile, Donovan Philips motioned Mal to walk backwards, using Mal's own Liberty Hammer as a threat.

"Stop there," Philips said when Mal was next to the rig and right under the dangling noose. "Do anything dumb like try to resist, and I'll put a bullet in you. Won't kill you. Gut shot. It'll hurt like hell and you'll hang anyway. You want that?"

"Don't much want either," Mal said. "Everybody, listen up! I am innocent. There is no way I would have endangered Jinny's life and no way I'd have helped out the Alliance. I am one of you. Always have been, always will be."

But he could scarcely make himself heard above the baying of the slavering, eager mob. Their eyes were bright with bloodlust. They had come for a hanging and—by thunder!—they were going to get a hanging. This was the vigilantes' primary purpose in life, a fire they had kept stoked in their bellies since the war ended. Someone had to pay for their defeat, and if that someone was another Browncoat, why not? There'd been bad apples on both sides, and since they couldn't easily root out the ones on the Alliance's, they were rooting out the ones on their own.

The noose was looped around Mal's neck, the roughness rope scratching his skin.

"Remember Jamie, Mal?" Toby said. "Remember what Bundy and Crump tried to do to him, and would have if you hadn't come along? Same again, only this time it's you who's getting strung up, and you know what? Nobody's coming. There ain't no cavalry, no last-minute reprieve. This is your time, Mal Reynolds. Make your peace, if you can, but believe me when I say that hellfire awaits you. You're gonna burn for all eternity with all them other sinners, and you deserve every second of it, just for what you did to her."

Before Mal could reply, hands tightened the noose so that the knot was hard against the back of his head and the loop constricted his throat. His airway wasn't quite cut off, but he could only just breathe and certainly could not speak.

Mindful of the gun in Donovan Philips's hand, he didn't squirm or fight. He had no doubt that Philips would gut shoot him if provoked. Even if he did get out of the noose somehow, a wound like that would kill him regardless, and slow. He was alive and well right up until the noose strangled him and his legs stopped kicking. Between now and then, there was always a chance, however slim, that he might still escape. These were the mad calculations rushing through his head: how to prolong the little life remaining to him, how to postpone death until the last possible moment.

The bald man and his accomplice looked to Toby for final confirmation. Toby raised a hand and slashed it down through the air. Mal felt a tugging on the rope. All at once he was rising into the air. It was only a few inches. His feet were still in contact with the cavern floor, but just barely. He teetered on his tiptoes, the noose biting into the underside of his jaw. His vision began to blur. He felt vertebrae in his neck creaking. Breaths came in short, gasping sips of air. This wasn't going to be a simple lynching, then. It was going to be torture. The vigilantes were going to draw out his death as long as they could.

Their faces floated before him like lurid, gloating balloons. Their cries echoed thickly in his ears, seeming to come from underwater. Mal's toecaps scrabbled for purchase on the ground. Already his legs were starting to ache from the effort of keeping him standing. Then, all at once, one foot slipped out from under him. The clench of the noose increased. Mal felt his heartbeat pounding in his head as he struggled to regain his balance. Like some ungainly ballerina, he managed to get back up onto the points of both feet. He remained suspended just above the cavern floor, swaying ever so slightly, twisting clockwise and anticlockwise.

He heard some distant, piglike grunting noise and realized it was coming from his own throat.

So this was how it was going to be. This was how it ended. The long, wayward, wild voyage of Malcolm Reynolds, from rumbustious kid to combat-hardened warrior to ship's captain. Along the way there'd been triumphs, tragedies, and all points in between, but only in the recent-most portion had he found something like contentment. He owed that, he knew, to his crew, that mixed company of lost souls, misfits and renegades. They were a family, of sorts, the kind you made rather than were born into, the kind that came to surround you through twists of fate and a modicum of choice. They drove him mad sometimes but he wouldn't have had them any different. While he'd held them together as their captain and guided them safely through the 'verse, he'd been doing something right, he decided. Something good. That, set in the plus column of his life, surely balanced out everything—and there was a lot of it—in the minus column.

I've heard tell it can take a man up to six minutes to pass out during a short drop hanging, twenty minutes till he's actually dead.

Sheriff Bundy's words came to him, unbidden. How many minutes had it been so far? Mal couldn't even begin to tell. It might only have been two or three, and the rope wasn't even strangling him fully yet.

He felt the strength in his legs ebbing. He didn't know how much longer he could hold out. A haze was descending. Any moment now, he was going to sag in the noose, becoming so much dead weight. He hoped he would lose consciousness swiftly, sooner than Bundy's promised six minutes.

There was a gunshot. From a million miles away. Mal felt himself jerk. He didn't know what it meant.

It was time to die.

35

Zoë and Jayne hurtled along the tunnel, following the far-off roar of voices. The anger in that sound was palpable. She prayed she and Jayne weren't too late. No mistake, they were getting closer to where they needed to be, but she couldn't help thinking there had been too many delays along the way. A delay in *Serenity* departing from Eavesdown Docks. A delay when the feds boarded. A delay in finding a reliable source of intelligence about Mal's whereabouts.

That she and Jayne were in the right place was no longer in doubt. Zoë, in fact, had been certain of it as soon as Wash set *Serenity* down at the mine entrance. Three spacecraft had been sitting there, one of them *Serenity*'s own shuttle. Another was a yacht, which must have been Covington's, while the third was a Komodo-class resupply vessel, a war relic with the rust stains and impact pepperings all over the hull to prove it. Parts of it were salvaged from other ships, welded clumsily into place, giving it a patchwork appearance. She guessed it was the vigilantes' mode of conveyance and felt an odd tug of admiration. Anyone who traveled the 'verse in a flying death trap like that deserved respect. Or locking up in a lunatic asylum.

She and Jayne hastened out of *Serenity*. Jayne was more mobile than her and moved faster, loping along in limber fashion. Hampered by her bad leg, she struggled to keep up but was determined not to lose ground to the big man. She had her Mare's Leg; Jayne had Vera and Boo. They were both anticipating a gun battle and, each in their own way, looking forward to it. Zoë was also carrying something else: a remote detonator switch.

While she ran, she pictured Wash and Kaylee in the cargo bay, firing up the forklift. They had their roles to fulfill, and if all went according to plan, there wouldn't be the need for anything except threats. Not even gunplay.

Yeah, since when did anything *ever go according to plan?*

She and Jayne burst out of the tunnel into a cavern. Zoë took stock of the situation at a glance. The crowd. The platform. The drilling rig. Mal suspended from a noose, his eyes bulging, his face magenta.

Everyone was too preoccupied to notice her and Jayne's arrival.

"Jayne?"

"Yeah."

"Shoot the rope."

"Why not cut it?"

"There's a crowd of people between us and Mal. They'll stop us before we even get close. There's no time. No other option. Shoot the rope."

"That's a hell of a tall order. Fifty yards. Dim light. Rope's shiftin' about."

"Just gorramn do it!"

Jayne braced his legs apart and raised Vera to his shoulder, squinting as he peered down the rifle's sights. He switched from heavy-caliber cartridge to light, for greater accuracy. He took a breath and let it out slowly, forefinger tightening on the trigger.

If anyone could make the shot, Zoë said to herself, it was Jayne Cobb.

BLAM!!!

Vera roared.

The bullet struck the rope about ten inches above Mal's head.

"Damn!" Jayne growled.

He had nicked the rope rather than severed it. He readjusted his aim.

In the meantime, a couple of dozen faces had turned his and Zoë's way. The rifle report had startled the crowd. Among them Zoë saw Harlow in his familiar—and still fashion-disastrous—yellow duster. Harlow here? And he was with Hunter Covington.

Bastard. He'd lied to her through his teeth. All along, he'd known exactly who Covington was. Her hand gripped her Mare's Leg hard. There was going to be a reckoning between him and her.

Jayne was lining up a second shot. Mal looked as though he was just about ready to expire. He was going limp. If Jayne didn't cut the rope this time, Mal was dead.

"Don't let me down, girl," Jayne muttered to his gun.

Vera roared again.

The rope snapped and Mal collapsed to the ground.

A gaunt little man up on the platform yelled "No!"

The crowd were also aghast, and now, as one, they surged towards Zoë and Jayne, the interlopers who had deprived them of their fun.

Zoë held the remote detonator switch aloft, while Jayne swiveled Vera to and fro in front of the Browncoats menacingly.

"Everybody," she said, "stop. Know what this is in my hand? Remote detonator. Know what it's connected up to? A crate of HTX-20. A crate that has been offloaded from my ship into the entrance to this mine. It's sitting there right now, and all I have to do is let go of this here button, and *boom*! Cave-in. We performed a ground radar survey as we came in, mapping the mine layout. There's only one way in or out, and that's through that tunnel. The HTX-20 brings the roof down, and we're all stuck here from now till doomsday. I am not kidding."

The Browncoat vigilantes paused, studying her face. To them, she really didn't look as though she was kidding.

"Shoot her!" the man on the platform cried. "One of you, shoot the bitch!"

Guns were drawn.

"Yeah, about that," Zoë said unflappably. "If you look closely, you'll see it's a dead man's switch. I told you already, all I have to do is let go of the button. Anybody shoots me, guess what? I'll be letting go for damn sure."

"She will," Jayne said. "And in case you were wondering, this here's a Callahan full-bore auto-lock. A heavy-caliber round from this bad boy hits you anywhere, even if it misses vital organs the shock of the impact'll still kill you. So you've got to ask yourself one question: 'Am I gonna be stupid enough to take the risk?'"

"Now," said Zoë, "somebody—I don't much care who—is going to walk over to my friend there and loosen that rope off of him."

She waited for a volunteer.

"Someone's got to do it," she said. "Mood I'm in right now, I'm more than happy just to blow that high-explosive and have done with it. You people call yourselves Browncoats? This isn't how Browncoats act. I was one, and I'm ashamed even to be around you. Trapping you all in this mine, that'd be worthwhile even if I'm stuck along with you."

A man raised a hand. "I'll do it."

Zoë frowned. "Deakins? That you?"

"Sure is, Miz Alleyne."

"Been a while. You're with these people? I'd have thought better of you."

"To be honest, Corp, I'd have thought better of myself. I'll free him."

"Don't you do it, Stuart Deakins," the man on the platform yelled. "Don't you dare."

"Oh, hush your squawking, Toby Finn," Deakins said. "We've heard enough from you. If Zoë Alleyne thinks Mal Reynolds is worth rescuing—and worth putting her own ass on the line for, what's more—then that settles it as far as I'm concerned. Mal ain't guilty of what you're accusing him of. The man deserves to go free."

Toby Finn yanked a gun from his holster. "Not another step, Deakins. I'm telling you."

Jayne swung Vera so that the gaunt little guy, evidently the ringleader of the vigilantes, was lined up in the reticle of his gunsight. "Want I should take him out, Zoë?"

"Not if you don't have to," Zoë replied. "But he so much as twitches his trigger finger…"

"Gotcha."

Stuart Deakins shoulder-barged his way through the sullen crowd and knelt beside Mal. Mal lay so still that Zoë thought he must be dead. After all this, had everything been in vain? She choked back the fear. Mal was okay. Surely he was okay.

Deakins untied the noose, then rolled Mal over onto his back. Someone else Zoë recognized, David Zuburi, joined him. Together the two men conferred, then Deakins began to administer CPR to Mal, alternately pumping his chest and blowing into his mouth.

Zoë watched, her grip on the detonator switch growing slick.

O utside the mine entrance, Wash drove the forklift back towards *Serenity*. He had just deposited—*verrry* carefully—a single crate of HTX-20 roughly ten yards inside.

Kaylee was standing on the cargo-bay ramp. She looked jumpy, on edge, more so than previously.

"Why the face?" Wash asked as he braked to a halt.

"We need to offload the other four crates."

"What?"

Kaylee held up a scanner. "Just taken some fresh readings. The explosives are heating up faster than ever. They're going critical, and there ain't nothing I can think of to do to retard or reverse the process. I'd say we have maybe ten, fifteen minutes before they blow."

"*Fèi fèi de pì yǎn.* You've got to be kidding me."

"Wish I were. Badger sure handed us a *zhēng qì de gōu shī duī*. Wouldn't surprise me if he did it on purpose."

"What for? To piss us off? If so, mission accomplished. I'm pissed off. But I'm not sure even Badger would be that much of a crap-heel, not when there's money involved. Okay now, let's see what our options are."

Wash surveyed the area. The mine entrance had been dug into a mountainside. *Serenity* and the other three ships were positioned on the only level space available, a broad, windswept ledge with a sheer crag towering above and a steep-sided base descending to a barren plain below. There wasn't room to deposit the crates on the ledge a safe distance away. If they went off there, all four ships would be damaged, probably destroyed, and everyone would be stranded on Hades. But if he tipped them over the edge, chances were they would explode when they hit the bottom; HTX-20 did not like nasty surprises, after all. That, in turn, might trigger a rockslide, then there'd be a tangled mess of rubble and no-longer-spaceworthy ship at the foot of the mountain.

"No alternative," he said. "The other four crates have to go inside the mine entrance alongside the fifth."

"That's insane."

"It's that or we lose *Serenity*, the shuttle, the yacht, and that Komodo heap of junk."

"We only put the one crate there in the first place in case somebody calls Zoë's bluff and goes to check that she can seal them inside if she wants to, like she's threatening," Kaylee said. "It's all a ruse, right? That's the plan. She's got the detonator switch only as a prop. In fact, thinking about it, we should get that crate out of the mine right now, in case it blows up of its own accord. We shouldn't be putting another four of the gorramn things in there."

"If we don't, we all die," said Wash. "If we do, there's

a chance Zoë and Jayne can still get back out, ideally with Mal, before all the crates go up. I don't like it any more than you do, Kaylee, but I don't see any other option."

Kaylee gnawed her lower lip, then slowly, reluctantly nodded. "They won't have long. They don't hurry, they're dead."

"And so are we," said Wash, gunning the forklift's motor.

37

Everything was dark where Mal was. And warm. And weirdly cozy. A nice place. He wanted to stay there.

Then there was a stab of pain. Light flooded in. He heaved for breath.

There were a man's lips on his.

"Wait, wait, wait!" Mal yelped, sitting bolt upright. "Stu? What the hell, pardner?"

Stuart Deakins sat back on his haunches. "You're back, Mal. Thank God. Thought for a moment there we'd lost you."

Mal's throat felt as though it was lined with sandpaper. To speak, even just to breathe, hurt. His head seemed to be attached to the rest of him by a slender thread. Yet he was alive. Sweet Mary Mother of Jesus, he was alive!

He blinked around. There was David Zuburi. There was Hunter Covington. There was Yellow Duster. There were all the Browncoats, looking somewhat disgruntled. No sign of Toby Finn, though.

And Zoë. Jayne. They were there too?

"Sir," Zoë said across the cavern. "Glad to have you back."

"Me too. What kept you guys?"

"Oh, you know. This and that."

"Stu, you just resuscitate me?"

"I did."

"That would explain the kissing. Leastways, I hope it does."

"I owed you one for you saving my ass at New Kasimir," Deakins said. "It was the least I could do."

"Next time, maybe you can show your gratitude in a less intimate manner."

Deakins smiled. "Sure will. Weren't no picnic for me either. You ain't shaved lately and you're kinda bristly."

"Snake!" someone yelled. "Defector! Gorramn Judas!"

Next thing Mal knew, Donovan Philips was rushing towards them. He had Mal's Liberty Hammer out, leveled it at Stuart Deakins, and fired.

The top of Deakins's head vanished in a crimson mist. Deakins slumped sideways, nothing on his face but a look of utter incomprehension.

Mal moved faster than a man just brought back from the brink of death might reasonably be expected to. He sprang at Philips, grabbing his gun hand. The pair of them grappled, each trying to gain mastery of the weapon. Philips was at that moment the stronger of the two. He hadn't just been hanged. Mal, however, had blinding, all-consuming fury on his side. Stuart Deakins had proved himself to be a decent human being after all, and this scum-sucking son of a bitch had shot him from behind like the coward he was.

All at once the Liberty Hammer was in Mal's hand.

He didn't hesitate. Philips's scar-ridden face collapsed into terror. He held up his hands in surrender, but Mal was not in a merciful mood. He shot point-blank at the heart, and Donovan Philips was dead before he hit the ground.

After that, consternation reigned. The Browncoat vigilantes bellowed in shock and disapproval. They seemed to have forgotten all about Zoë and the detonator, until she reminded them by firing her Mare's Leg twice at the ceiling. That brought a measure of calm to the proceedings.

"Just a little reminder there," she said. "Now you are going to let the three of us leave. You are not going to get in our way. To reiterate: I am quite prepared to let go of this switch at any time. Don't anyone give me a reason to— Sir?"

Mal was on his feet and moving away from the drilling rig, but not towards Zoë and Jayne.

Toby Finn was gone. He had lit out while Mal was unconscious. There was a second tunnel leading out from the cavern, not towards the entrance but in the opposite direction, presumably deeper underground. Toby could only have disappeared down there.

Mal was determined to catch up to him. He and Toby needed to have words.

"Sir!" Zoë hollered behind him, but Mal paid her no heed. He headed off down the tunnel, stumbling on its rugged, uneven rock floor.

"Toby!" he called out. "Toby, I just want to talk."

Illumination from the cavern diminished the further he ventured in. Soon he was walking more or less blind, groping his way with one hand held out in front of him, the Liberty Hammer in his other hand.

"Toby? Hey, pal, stop runnin'. We can sort things out. We were two of the Four Amigos once. Don't see why we can't be that way again." The gun Mal was carrying somewhat gave the lie to what he was saying. Truth was, he would just as happily shoot Toby dead as reconcile with him. Much depended on how Toby acted now. If he showed even the tiniest amount of remorse or contrition, Mal might—just might, mind—be able to find it in his heart to forgive him. "Come on, ol' buddy. Why don't you—?"

If his brain hadn't still been fogged from the near-hanging, he might have seen the blow coming; might have been able to duck out of the way. As it was, something came out of nowhere and slammed into his face, knocking him flat. The Liberty Hammer flew from his grasp, skidding across the tunnel floor. His head reeled. He had been slugged with the butt of a pistol. He gasped for air.

"No, Mal," said Toby, a black silhouette in the dimness. "We can't be friends again. There can't be any Four Amigos again because you ruined it."

A gun barrel loomed in Mal's vision. His own gun lay several yards away, well out of easy reach.

"By killing Jinny?" Mal said hoarsely. "But it wasn't anything to do with me. You must know that. Those homing beacons were for me and her alone."

"Yes! And I know why!" Toby was all but screaming. "I know about you and Jinny. I knew just what you were doing behind my back."

Mal fumbled for words. "But… What? You knew? But why didn't you…?"

"Say anything at the time? How could I, Mal? It was

almost over between Jinny and me. I could feel it, but I didn't want it to end. Dammit, I was going to marry that woman. I had it all planned out. But I was losing her, and I began to notice little things, little clues that suggested maybe her heart belonged to someone else. You. Like, she would pause whenever your name came up in conversation. Sometimes she would avoid talking about you, steerin' around the subject like it was a boulder in the road. Before then, her face used to light up when you were mentioned, and suddenly it started darkening instead. I wasn't sure about it. I couldn't be certain she was cheating on me with you. But then, why wouldn't she be? You were the dashing Mal Reynolds, and me? I was just lowly little Toby Finn, not fit to tie the bootlaces of a girl like Jinny Adare. I'd lucked into becoming her boyfriend, but it was clear you and she were a better fit."

"Toby, I'm sorry," Mal said. "Truly I am."

"You can spare me the apologies. They don't mean squat."

"Maybe you could have said something at the time. Maybe we could have figured it out."

"I didn't know for certain," Toby said, "and I was scared to raise the topic in case I was wrong. It wasn't until Jinny died and I saw how you were about that, how cut up, that I realized I'd been right. Even then, I'd have forgiven you, in time. But the war came and we went our separate ways, until Hera, until that day I went to your tent and found the second beacon. That's when everything clicked into place."

"All of this," Mal said, piecing things together, "kidnapping me, trying me, hanging me—this isn't about me betraying the Independent cause. It never was. You *know* I didn't. That stuff about the beacons, that was just for the Browncoats. A smokescreen. This is all about revenge, isn't it?"

Toby seemed as though he was going to deny it, then shook his head ruefully. "Yeah. Not that I don't believe in what me and these other Browncoats have been doing. Rounding up true traitors and bringing them to justice. It's been a necessary evil. But you and me, Mal, this one's personal. I've been waitin' for this a long time. Only now did the stars align and everything come together."

"You got the rest of them to go along with it, even though you know the case against me was as flimsy as rice paper."

"Wasn't difficult. They're disgruntled, easily led. They've been at this so long, they've begun to lose sight of why. They just love the blaming and the accusing and the executing. Makes them feel good about themselves, and you've seen them. Do those look to you like people who've many reasons to feel good about themselves? Some of 'em needed more talking round than others, but we got there in the end. We paid Hunter Covington just about every piece of platinum we could scrape together in order to get a lead on you. Seemed a fair price. I even plundered my own savings, such as they were. Don't have a single coin left to my name."

"Yeah, but wasn't what you were doing dangerous to you? Mightn't it have backfired if the others had realized this thing was just a whole dog-and-pony show?"

"If so, what do I care?" Toby said with a hapless shrug. "My time's running out anyway."

Mal's eyesight was adjusting to the gloom. Toby's face looked pallid and haggard, a wreck of its old self.

"You ain't well, are you?" Mal said. "You're seriously sick. What is it? Damplung? Wilson's palsy?"

"Cancer. The terminal kind. All over. The whole meal, soup to nuts."

"Toby…"

"Got it 'cause of my spacesuit's shielding failing at Sturges, most likely. Docs reckon I must've received a dose of cosmic radiation, not enough to fry me on the spot but enough to send a few internal organs gradually haywire. The war's finally catching up with me, after all these years. I'm a dead man walking, but at least I finally got to see you paying the penalty for what you did to me."

"Toby, maybe there's a cure," Mal said. "I have a doctor on board my ship, a really good one. He can try and fix you."

"He can't, Mal. Nobody can. You know what, though? I thought I'd be happier to see you on the end of the rope, I really did. But somehow it just made me sad." Toby's voice was thick, husky. He sounded close to crying. "Sad that it's come to this, and sad for all that we lost. Not just Jamie and Jinny. Not the millions of men and women the war killed. The… innocence. The fun we used to have on Shadow. Foolin' around. Getting chased by Bundy. They were good times, weren't they, Mal?"

"The best, Toby. The best."

Now Toby really was crying, deep sobs wracking his body. "Oh God, Mal. I'm sorry. I'm so, so sorry. I shouldn't have… I should never…"

Toby's gun had begun to droop in his grasp. Mal cast a quick, sidelong glance towards his own gun. If he could just keep this conversation going a few seconds longer, keep

Toby distracted and off-beam, he might be able to make a bid for the Liberty Hammer.

He tensed, ready to bat Toby's gun aside and lunge for his own weapon. "It's okay, Toby. We're good. Come on, help me up and let's go see if we can't—"

A shot rang out.

Toby's body jolted. He fell against the tunnel wall, then slid down to the floor.

Mal, ears ringing from the detonation, turned to see Jayne standing some twenty feet away. Vera was in his hands, smoke coiling up from her muzzle.

"Got him," Jayne said with cold satisfaction. "You okay, Mal?"

Mal looked back at Toby Finn, now just an inert heap, chin on sternum, blood on his breastbone glistening in the faint light. In a way he was glad Jayne had shot Toby. Even after everything, he mightn't have been able to do it himself.

In fact, he reckoned Jayne had done Toby a favor. Toby had been dying anyway. Jayne had only hastened what was inevitable, ending his life quickly, unexpectedly, rather than leaving him to be eaten away, an inch at a time, by the slow horror of cancer.

"Come on," Jayne said. "We gotta go. Don't know how much longer Zoë's going to be able to keep the vigilantes at bay with that detonator-switch con. They're gettin' all kinds of antsy."

"Con?"

Jayne brought Mal up to speed on the plan involving the crate and the detonator.

"Not bad," Mal said. "Kind of sneakiness I might have come up with."

Wearily he got to his feet and retrieved his gun. He couldn't remember when he had ever felt quite so tired, or so old. Jayne turned back down the tunnel, and Mal staggered after.

38

Back in the cavern, Zoë was indeed finding it increasingly hard to keep the Browncoats restrained. Sonya Zuburi was giving her all manner of grief, calling her names and making feints towards her, trying to grab the detonator switch. Even back during the war there had never been much love lost between Zoë and Sonya. She'd been a good soldier but Zoë, even on her worst day, was ten times better, and whereas Zoë had been fast-tracked to corporal, Sonya had remained a humble private to the bitter end. That had been a source of great anguish and frustration to Sonya and she had tried to undermine Zoë every chance she got.

"You won't do it, bitch," Sonya goaded. "You don't have the balls."

"At least I don't keep my husband's in a purse," Zoë retorted.

Someone sniggered, and Sonya shot them a filthy look. David Zuburi himself seemed unamused, but appeared to acknowledge that there was some truth in Zoë's taunt.

Out of the corner of her eye Zoë saw Hunter Covington and Harlow sneaking towards the exit tunnel. She would have to deal with them later. Right now what mattered was the angry Browncoats. Where the hell was Jayne? She had sent him off in pursuit of Mal. He surely should have found him by now.

There was a gunshot from the tunnel Jayne had followed Mal into. Zoë recognized the deep, bassy boom of Vera. Moments later, Jayne emerged from the tunnel with Mal in tow. The already irate Browncoats became more irate still.

"Where's Toby Finn?" someone demanded to know. "What have you done with him?"

Zoë could tell the situation was about to spiral into chaos. Not even the threat of blowing up the mine entrance was going to keep a lid on it much longer. She began backing towards the tunnel, the barrel of her Mare's Leg tracking this way and that, pausing at random Browncoats and curbing their aggression, if only temporarily.

"I will shoot," Zoë warned, backing towards the exit. "I don't want to but I will if I have to, and anyone who knows me knows I am not the type to make idle threats."

Nonetheless the crowed kept edging closer, inciting one another forwards. An array of guns bristled around Zoë.

"Let's rush her," Sonya said. "Somebody grabs her hand, clamps it tight around that switch, there'll be nothing she can do."

Then Jayne and Mal were at Zoë's side. That gave her a little more leverage, and the Browncoats knew it. They weren't up against a lone gunwoman any more but a trio.

"We're outta here," Jayne said to the crowd, "and I'd

advise anyone who's thinking about getting in our way to not to. Get in our way, that is. Or even think about it."

As they retreated towards the entrance, Zoë kept an eye out for Covington and Harlow, who might be lying in wait somewhere along the tunnel. In her judgment, however, the two men wouldn't be hanging around. Instead, they'd be making for Covington's yacht and hightailing it off Hades as fast as they could. Neither was any slouch when it came to self-preservation, she thought, and they must have realized that if it came to a shootout between the Browncoats and Zoë, Jayne, and Mal, there was a good chance of getting caught in the crossfire.

She was mistaken about that, and nearly got a bullet through the head for her pains.

Where the tunnel jinked round a corner, Harlow was lurking. If Zoë hadn't caught a glimpse of the tail of his absurd yellow duster, she might not have been able to dodge in time. Her Mare's Leg thundered a riposte, blasting away a section of rock just inches from Harlow's hiding place.

"Mr. Covington told me to delay you people," Harlow called out. "Offered me damn good money for it, too. So that's what I'm going to do."

Zoë looked at Jayne, put a finger to her lips, and gestured at him to pass Boo over to her. Jayne duly unholstered the wheelgun, giving her a mildly quizzical frown. Zoë responded with a "trust me" look.

For what she had in mind, her Mare's Leg wouldn't do. She needed a solid round, not buckshot.

"Harlow," she said, softly cocking Boo's hammer, "listen. Let us past and we won't kill you."

"Nah. Figure I'll just pin you three down where you are. Those Browncoats are coming. I can hear 'em. They're following you up the tunnel. If I keep you there till they catch up, you'll have plenty on your plate, and Mr. Covington and me, we can just mosey on home at our leisure."

"I wish you'd said you knew all along who Covington was and what this was all about." Zoë began inching towards him, covering the sound of her advance by talking. "Would have made a difference."

"Fooled you, huh, Hopalong? And I led you a merry dance through Eavesdown as well, didn't I? After we parted company, I knew you'd follow me, so I gave you the runaround. I thought winding up at Badger's was a stroke of genius. Figured he'd tangle you up if nothing else did."

Closer she crept, ever closer, the wheelgun at the ready. "Yeah, you're a smart operator all right, Harlow." She studied the formation of the tunnel wall. The angles were just about right. It all depended on how good her eye was. "A real cool customer. You'd have to be to pull off that ten-gallon hat and puke-yellow duster combo."

"Aw, don't be like that. I thought we'd reached a kinda understanding, you and me."

"Oh, we have," Zoë said, lining up her shot. "I understand that you're a gasbag idiot who loves the sound of his own voice, and me, I'm the one who's about to deflate you."

"Now what in the hell do you mean by—"

Zoë fired. The round ricocheted once, twice, and then Harlow gave a kind of "ugh" sound and toppled forward into view, thudding to the tunnel floor.

"Ohhh," he groaned, blood leaking from the corner

of his mouth. "That was some nice shooting, Hopalong. Damn nice. And to think… you and me… we coulda had somethin' special…"

His eyes rolled white, his mouth slackened, his eyelids closed, and he was gone.

Zoë tossed Boo back to Jayne, who caught and holstered the wheelgun in a single, smooth action.

From behind, the clamor of the approaching Browncoats grew louder.

"Come on," she said to Mal and Jayne.

Nearing the tunnel entrance, the three *Serenity* crewmembers were greeted by Wash. He was just depositing the last of the five crates inside the tunnel.

"Wash? What the hell's this?" said Zoë. "We only needed one crate, not the whole gorramn lot."

"Yeah, well, about that," said Wash. "Turns out we're going to have to dump all of them here."

"Our entire cargo?" said Mal. "You better have a good reason."

"Great to see you too, Captain. Glad you're well."

"Never mind that. Get these damn crates back on my ship."

"Uh, no can do. Kaylee says the HTX-20 is about to go off, and when that happens, it's best we're not around."

"She sure about that?"

"I don't think she's just saying it for comedic effect."

"Gorramn it!" Mal said. "We never catch a break, do we?"

From outside came a high-pitched whine of a ship's

engine powering up, resounding down the tunnel.

"Oh yeah, that'll be Covington's yacht," Wash said. "He ran past me a couple of minutes ago. Didn't even stop to say hi. Guess he was in too much of a hurry. Pity, though."

"Why?"

"I had Kaylee sneak aboard his ship. She's disabled it. Listen to that?"

The engine noise stuttered, then became a horrendous metallic gurgle. Zoë pictured the yacht shuddering from stem to stern like a vomiting cat.

"Covington's going nowhere in a hurry. Kaylee's detached his pulse alternator and left it hanging off by its wires. It's an easy fix, assuming he figures out that's what the problem is."

Jayne and Mal hurried onward to the entrance. Zoë clambered onto the side of the forklift next to her husband.

"My leg's playing merry hell," she said. "Mind giving a girl a lift?"

"Don't normally pick up hitchhikers, but for you, pretty lady, I'll make an exception."

Wash deftly spun the vehicle around on its axis and drove it out into daylight. Just as they neared *Serenity*, shots crackled from the tunnel entrance. Rounds whanged and whined off the forklift's bodywork. Wash ducked and swore, while Zoë leaned round and returned fire, her Mare's Leg booming. Mal and Jayne, from the cargo-bay ramp, added their own salvoes to hers.

The vigilantes were positioned just inside the tunnel mouth, some distance past the five crates of explosive. It seemed they were keen that the people who had disrupted their lynching should not get away scot-free.

Sonya Zuburi was the one egging them on. "We can still take 'em down!" she yelled. Her husband David, at her side, looked less convinced.

"Hold your fire!" Zoë called out to them. "All of you, listen."

She was shouting at the top of her voice, but above the sound of gunfire she was inaudible to the Browncoats. Still she persevered. "Those crates are about to blow, and when they do, they'll bring this entire mountain down around our heads."

The vigilantes carried on with their broadside. Only David Zuburi seemed to have heard what Zoë had said. He was gesticulating and calling for a ceasefire, but he might as well have been dancing a jig for all the difference it made.

Serenity's shuttle abruptly burst into life. Zoë glimpsed Kaylee at the controls. Kaylee offered her a brief wave before goosing the engines to the very limits of their tolerance and launching. Wash scooted the forklift up the cargo-bay ramp and was off and running for the bridge before the vehicle had even come to a full stop.

"What about Covington?" Zoë asked Mal. "We can't just leave him there, can we?"

"Don't see why not. Guy's a bondholder and an all-round shark. He's got a chance to get away if he can mend what Kaylee did to his boat. If he can't, that's his tough *dà tiáo*."

Serenity began rumbling around them. Over the intercom Wash said, "Know those wonderfully genteel, laidback takeoffs I'm so famous for? This ain't going to be one of them. Hang on tight, everyone."

The ship lurched skyward with enough force to throw Mal, Jayne, and Zoë off-kilter. Zoë felt the downward press of g-force, like a giant invisible hand trying to squash her flat, and bent her knees to absorb it as best she could. *Serenity* seemed to be fighting for every inch of altitude she gained. Zoë had no idea when the HTX-20 was going to explode but she knew she didn't want to be anywhere near when it happened.

Then it came: a percussive blast like every thunderclap there had ever been, all rolled into one. It was followed by the tumult of the overpressure wave seizing *Serenity* and shaking the ship about like an infant with a toy rattle. Zoë, Mal, and Jayne grabbed whatever they could for support. There was a series of sickening swoops and soars, pitches and yaws, like riding the worst rollercoaster ever. In her mind's eye Zoë saw Wash up on the bridge battling to maintain control of the spacecraft and keep her on an even keel.

No one could fly like Hoban Washburne. It was one of the articles of faith in Zoë's life. If anybody could get them through this safely, it was him.

Some time later—seconds of juddering upheaval that felt like hours—*Serenity* righted and leveled out. Zoë staggered over to the nearest rearward viewing port. Below, a mountain was dying. Its slopes were sinking inward on themselves, sending up a mighty pillar of dust and debris like smoke from the cauldron of a volcano. Huge chunks of rock had sheared away and were slithering down towards the plain some quarter-mile below. Amidst the tumbling avalanche she glimpsed Covington's yacht and the vigilantes' Komodo-class vessel. Both were rolling end over end, losing sections of hull plate and chunks of airframe along the way. They crashed to the bottom and were engulfed by rubble.

Of the Browncoats themselves there was no sign, but then Zoë wasn't expecting any. They would have been vaporized when the HTX-20 went up. She wished she felt sorrier for them than she did.

Mal appeared beside her and looked on as the mountain continued to implode, shelving down into itself, becoming a crater. Gradually the turmoil receded into the distance as *Serenity* gained more height.

"Care to tell me what this was all about, sir?" she asked as the pale blue of Hades's atmosphere started shading into the inky blue of low-orbit space.

"Long story, Zoë," Mal said forlornly. "Long story from long, long ago. Another time, maybe. Right now, my throat's as parched as a sidewinder's belly and I believe there may be a bottle of sorghum wine somewhere in the galley. Care to join me?"

"You have some *baijiu*?" Jayne said. "That rotgut? I'm in."

"If it's not considered insubordination, sir," Zoë said, "I would rather go up to the bridge and smooch with my husband. I reckon he's earned it."

"Know what?" said Mal, with just a hint of the old familiar twinkle returning to his eyes. "I reckon he has and all."

So we're all back on one boat again, the nine of us. Serenity has both her shuttles nestled on her wings, the chicks back with mama bird, and we're heading off once more into the Black to see what we can find, work-wise. The usual deal: whatever's going, if it pays, we'll take it. Sorry state of affairs, but that's how it is. Ain't a kind or just 'verse, and nobody's owed a living.

Simon says my neck's healing nicely. Rope burns won't even leave a scar, thanks to his doctoring. Talking still hurts some, but on this boat, with Wash and Kaylee, to name but two, it ain't as if there's a scarcity of chitter-chatter.

Badger was rightly mad about his explosives. I pointed out that at least they'd blown up somewhere off my ship, 'cause if they'd destroyed Serenity and I hadn't been on board, right now I'd be introducing him to the business end of a gun, shooting off little bits of him one after another; and if I had been on board, my ghost'd be haunting him till the day he died. Guess he feels I owe him one. Guess I feel we're quits. Besides, Badger'll get over it. He's what you'd call the resilient type, too plain opportunistic or optimistic or whatever to burn a bridge permanently.

Elmira Atadema is a free woman now. Book's pal Mika Wong didn't even need to pay off her debt, what with Hunter Covington being buried under a mountain and no longer in a fit state to collect and all, so he was pleased about that. I met Elmira for all of five minutes, after we'd rendezvoused on Persephone with Book, Inara, and the Tams. Even in that brief span of time she made an impression. Despite all she'd been through as a bondswoman and a confidential informer, all that suffering and peril, she seemed as if she was coping and would be able to move on with her life. Like Badger, resilient. Also, unlike Badger, not a pain in the ass.

And now that we're flying free, I've got time to think. About the past. About lost loves, damaged friendships and heart-wrenching regrets. I won't ever be free of Jamie and Toby, I reckon. Wasn't free of Jinny before. But it does seem as though some things that needed fixing have been fixed and some loose ends squared away. Maybe if Jinny and me had been honest with Toby from the start, none of this would have happened. It was Jinny's call, though, and I went along with it because I respected her decision and I loved her. You can't change the past and you can't do aught but rue the way you sometimes acted back when you were young and stupid and thought you were immortal. Doesn't prevent you from wishing you could.

I've been thinking about stopping by Shadow, although not sure I'm up for that. I hear there's plants pushing up through the cinders now around the spot where the Adares' *cowshed stood. I might like to see that for myself, but then I mightn't want to reopen those old wounds either. Might also pay a call on Sheriff Bundy, Governor Bundy, whatever his title is these days. Assuming the overweight bastard's still alive and some clogged artery of his hasn't popped. Maybe he and I can have words, get to the bottom of what happened... and if he did what I think he did, I'll teach him the error of his ways.*

Maybe some other time.

For now, we'll do what we do.

Find a job. Keep flying.

Captain Malcolm Reynolds

ACKNOWLEDGEMENTS

I'd like to thank Nancy Holder for letting me pick up her ball and run with it; Miranda Jewess for remembering me when *Firefly* came to call; and Cat Camacho and Sam Matthews, each of whom was *zhēn de shì tiān cái* during the editing process.

ABOUT THE AUTHORS

New York Times bestselling author **Nancy Holder** has written numerous *Buffy the Vampire Slayer* and *Angel* tie-in novels, as well as co-authoring the first two Buffy Watcher's Guides. A four-time winner of the Bram Stoker Award, she is the author of dozens of novels, short stories, and essays on writing and popular culture.

ABOUT THE AUTHORS

James Lovegrove is the *New York Times* bestselling author of *The Age of Odin*. He was shortlisted for the Arthur C. Clarke Award in 1998 and for the John W. Campbell Memorial Award in 2004, and also reviews fiction for the *Financial Times*. He is the author of the Dragon-Award winning *Firefly: The Ghost Machine*, *Firefly: The Magnificent Nine*, and *Firefly: Big Damn Hero* with Nancy Holder, along with several Sherlock Holmes novels for Titan Books.

firefly

THE MAGNIFICENT NINE
James Lovegrove

Captain Mal Reynolds is in a fix. He'd like nothing
more than to find honest smuggling work that stays
under the Alliance's radar and keeps the good ship
Serenity in the sky. But when Temperance McCloud,
an old flame of Jayne Cobb, sends a desperate plea
across the galaxy, his crew has other ideas. On the arid,
far-flung world of Thetis, the terrifying Elias Vandal is
threatening to overrun Temperance's hometown and
seize control of its water supply. But when the crew
land at the hardscrabble desert outpost, they discover
more than a savage gang of outlaws: Temperance is
singlehandedly raising a teenage daughter, born less
than a year after she and Jayne parted ways. A daughter
by the name of Jane McCloud…

firefly

THE GHOST MACHINE
James Lovegrove

Mal and the crew take receipt of a sealed crate which
they are being paid to transport to Badger, no questions
asked. Yet once their cargo is safely stowed aboard,
River insists Mal should "space" it out of the airlock,
for it contains, she insists, ghosts. With supplies
running low, the crew desperately need another pay
day, but soon find themselves paralyzed by
hallucinations of their deepest hopes and desires,
so vivid they cannot be distinguished from reality.
River is the only one unaffected, and desperately tries
to awaken her crew mates, while the fantasies turn sour
and the ship begins to spin out of control…

firefly

GENERATIONS
Tim Lebbon

Captain Malcolm Reynolds ends a game of cards on
one of the Outer Rim moons as the lucky winner of an
old map. Ancient and written in impenetrable symbols,
the former owner insists it's worthless. Yet back on
Serenity, River Tam is able to read it, and says that it
points the way to one of the Arks, legendary generation
ships that brought humans from Earth-that-was to the
'verse. The salvage potential alone is staggering.
But the crew approach the aged floating ship, they find
it isn't quite as dead as it first seems, and the closer
they get, the more agitated River becomes. She claims
something is waiting on that ship, something powerful,
and very angry…

For more fantastic fiction, author events, competitions,
limited editions and more

VISIT OUR WEBSITE
titanbooks.com

LIKE US ON FACEBOOK
facebook.com/titanbooks

FOLLOW US ON TWITTER
@TitanBooks

EMAIL US
readerfeedback@titanemail.com